FLOOD

FLOOD

Richard Martin Stern

Doubleday & Company, Inc.
Garden City, New York
1979

All of the characters in this book are fictitious,
and any resemblance to actual persons, living or dead,
is purely coincidental.

ISBN: 0-385-14367-2
Library of Congress Catalog Card Number 79-7456

FLOOD

1

Jay vaguely supposed that the urge to visit the place of your origins was buried deep in everybody, but, being by nature a self-contained man, he had never bothered to ask how others felt about it, nor would he have cared what their answers might be.

For him there had always been great-grandmother Julia's journals and their descriptions of this place and of the old man buried here, the first Jedediah Harper, whose name Jay bore. And that was enough. Jay was here to see for himself, and he was some ten years too late. Guilty thought, and he had only his own procrastination to blame.

Sitting relaxed but anticipatory now on the stern seat of the rented boat, the outboard switched off, he waited while the ripples on the water died and the peaceful mountain stillness returned. And then he could look down and see clearly on the bottom of the lake the stone buildings.

Once they had been a village. Now, drowned by the water backed up by the dam, they were as dead as Pompeii or the huge breathtaking remnants of the Mesa Verde cliff dwellings. But at least they were still intact. With water movement, however slight, with inevitable erosion and silting, they would not last forever. He would see them now, or never.

"They was still there last time I looked," the man who rented boats said. "But why anybody'd want to go out on the lake this time of year just to look at them is more than I can see. Lot of stone ruins down in the mud." He waited, the implied question hanging. .

Jay ignored it, as he tended to ignore all questions that verged on the personal. In silence he took out his wallet.

"Folks," the man said, watching the wallet closely, "most generally use credit cards. That way I don't ask a deposit." His eyes widened at the sight of the hundred-dollar bill that emerged. He took it quickly. "But I guess this'll do fine."

Clutching the bill, he watched Jay cast off the painter, step into the boat, start the outboard with ease, and without a word or a backward glance head for the center of the lake.

A loner, the man thought; one of those who kept everything inside himself. It was an accurate enough assessment.

• • •

Looking down through the clear, cold water, it was here, one hundred and fifty years ago, Jay was thinking, that old Jed, his great-great-great grandfather, one of the fabled mountain men in real life, had made his solitary way through the towering mountains; wintered with a broken leg beside the mountain stream in the now flooded valley; and, remembering, returned one day to build a cabin by the stream and settle down. The village which grew up around Jed's cabin was called Harper's Park.

By old Jed's own accounts recorded in his very old age in great-grandmother Julia's journal, which as a boy Jay had almost memorized, in the young days in springtime deer and elk, unafraid, came morning and evening through flowered meadows to water at the stream. Trout were Jed's for the mere dropping of a baited hook into the pure, rushing water. Migrating waterfowl covered the surfaces of the small lakes and quiet backwaters.

Otters built their mud slides, and parents and pups alike cavorted endlessly out of sheer ebullience while solemn beavers toiled.

Bears searched out berry patches and occasionally fished the stream themselves. Jed had watched them as they stood belly deep in the cold water, unmoving in the strong current until a fish ventured near. Then, with unbelievable swiftness, a flashing forepaw would shower the bank with a spray of water and a flapping fish, a shining morsel for dinner.

Sometimes in the stillness, old Jed recalled, he might catch a glimpse of a fox or a hunting marten, graceful shadows quickly gone.

Beyond the meadows in those early days the forests began, evergreen and aspen, and in their depths uncatalogued woodpeckers and jays, flickers, chickadees, juncos, magpies, hawks, and even occasional haughty eagles went about their business as if man had never arrived.

At night the great owls hunted, each surrounded by his private zone of silence, his soft broad wings absorbing more sound than their movements produced.

Above timberline—at this latitude 11,000 feet—the mountains rose clear and almost bare against the cloudless skies. Here and there in sheltered hollows, breaking the harshness of solid rock and talus, small patches of alpine tundra, tiny, hardy plants defying wind and day-to-night temperature extremes— dwarf blue forget-me-nots, greenish-to-crimson mountain sorrel, white pussytoes, yellow meadow cinquefoil—clung valiantly to what soil there was in this high, harsh land.

So it had been, and the village itself had done little to change it. But two thousand feet below on the plain, wagons rolling west had reached the welcome mountain-born stream, paused beside it, and stayed. Cattle came, and the railroad, and more and more people. Mining and scattered industry centered on the growing city's strategic location. A highway came through, linking East and West. The mountain village withered, and when the dam was built to provide the growing city with water and hydroelectric power, the village was put to death by drowning.

· · ·

There was a man waiting on the dock when Jay swung the boat alongside, a large man, in uniform, with a holstered handgun and a western hat. He wore the severe expression cops around the world seemed to cultivate. Jay supposed they practiced in front of mirrors.

"John Boggs," the man said. "I don't think I've seen you here before." His voice was neither friendly nor truculent, merely official.

Jay got out of the boat and secured the painter to a cleat. "Should I have registered? Or maybe applied for a visa?"

"You don't seem to be a fisherman."

"True."

"And no camera."

"Also true."

"On the motel register," Boggs said, "you put your address—" He frowned. "Al Hoofoof. What is that, some kind of joke?"

"Al Hufūf. My last address. It's in Saudi Arabia. I don't happen to have a next address yet."

"Look," Boggs said. "We get all kinds of characters here. Mostly earlier, summers, but they can come any time. We had one said he wanted to try dynamiting fish."

Jay's expression did not change as he spread his arms as if for a body search. "No dynamite, gelignite, or other conventional explosives. No small atomic bombs."

Boggs took his time for a long, careful, appraising look.

The man wore a heavy, hand-knitted Norwegian crew-neck sweater, jeans, and sneakers—which, Boggs thought, could mean anything or nothing at all the way people dressed these days. Middle-sized fellow, late twenties or early thirties, compact, moves well and carries himself with assurance. Chip on his shoulder, but every cop is used to that. And the car by the motel wears rental plates.

"It's too late for the summer season," Boggs said, "too early for hunting, and you don't fish. You went over and poked around the dam after you sat for a long time looking down at the buildings on the bottom of the lake."

"And so I am a suspicious character?" Jay nodded. "Yes, figures. Tomorrow I'm going swimming—unless there is a law against it."

John Boggs's expression changed swiftly and his voice took on an edge. "What are you, some kind of smart-ass? Swimming in mountain water in late September?"

"I'll wear a wet suit and scuba gear. I want to see the village up close. Any objections?"

"What do you want to see those old buildings for?" And then, face clearing with vague comprehension, "The register says your name is Harper," Boggs said. "Any kin?" He waved his hand at the lake and the buildings of Harper's Park beneath the waters.

"Yes."

Boggs waited, but there was no more. "Oh, hell," he said at last, "I guess it's all right." And he added, "You sure don't talk much." He watched Jay start up the hill toward the motel and called after him. "What were you doing in Al—whatever it is, in Saudi Arabia?"

Jay stopped and turned. "Working."

There was resignation now in Boggs's face. You wanted answers from this one, he thought, you sure as hell had to ask the right questions. "Okay. What do you do when you work?"

"I'm a geophysicist."

Jay turned away then and walked on. The feeling of depression from the actual sight of that drowned village was still with him.

.   .   .

New places, and he had seen many of them, maybe too many, yielded first an impression, Jay had always found, then a few facts, and lastly, if you spent the time and the trouble, understanding. And knowledge, all knowledge, sooner or later had a way of turning out to be useful. The trick, which few people seemed to understand, was simply to ask a few questions and then really listen to the answers.

To the counterman-short-order-chef in the motel coffee shop, Jay said, "Have you been here long?" He was the image of a prototypical Mexican bandit, sweeping black moustache and all.

Information flowed as from a tap. The chef's name was Pancho and he had come from the city down on the plain. "Me, I was born there. Nice little place, nice little plaza, nice river, highway, railroad, that was all she was. I'm talking about right after the big war, what they call WW II, you know?"

Jay nodded, sipped his coffee, and listened.

"People going through," Pancho said. "To Los Angeles, Chicago, in cars, in those big Pullman trains air-conditioned and shiny. Nice place."

"But you left."

"Too goddamn many people now. Where the hell do they come from? Why don't they stay home? Up here I can fish, hunt, there are still deer if you know where to look, and ducks, geese in season, trout in the river. Trouble is, it's been damn dry, lake's way down. Dry. You've seen? More coffee?"

Jay pushed his cup forward. "Like California," he said. "They're dry too. The whole West. Long drought."

Pancho poured Jay's cup, and for himself a companionable inch of hot coffee in a heavy mug. "Yeah. I read." His face brightened and a smile appeared beneath the sweeping *bandito* moustache, white teeth flashing. "And they're gonna get that big earthquake too, no?" His pleasure at the prospect was palpable. Jay wondered what Pancho had against California.

"One day, probably," Jay said. Almost certainly, he thought. You didn't have to be a geophysicist to know that. The San Andreas fault was a lengthy pressure line that sooner or later would succumb to the enormous forces working upon it.

Pancho's smile had lost its happiness. "Maybe we get it here too, huh? Even this far away?"

"What makes you say that?"

Pancho shrugged. "We already had one, a little one. I seen worse, lots worse in Mexico."

Interesting. As far as Jay had known, this had been a fairly stable area. On the other hand, diastrophism, like gold and trouble, could be where you found it. Certainly there had been a lot of earth movement when the mountains were being formed. "Here?" he said. "Right here?"

Pancho shrugged again. "Who knows where the middle of the quake was?"

Jay said automatically, "Epicenter." The seismographs would have pinpointed it.

"That's the word they used in the paper," Pancho said. "But one of my *primos* said they didn't hardly feel it down in the city. Here—" Pancho paused and searched for explanation. "You know how coffee sloshes when you carry a full cup on a saucer. That's how the lake was. I watched it. Like somebody shaking the whole valley."

A seiche, Jay thought. It would be, if the local disturbance amounted to much; the entire body of water set to oscillating at its own rhythm by the seismic disturbance. The maximum movement, and force, would have been at the edges of the lake. The center node would have remained almost motionless.

Modern theory considered tides to be seiches induced not by seismic disturbance but primarily by the forces caused by the sun and the moon. And up in the Great Lakes any sudden rise in the water of a harbor or a lake was considered a seiche, whether the water was set to oscillating or not.

Calculating the force of a seiche was tricky business, but if you needed some indication of the enormous power which could be generated by it, you had only to consider the strength of the tidal forces at Fundy, Passamaquoddy Bay, or Lynmouth at the mouth of the Bristol Channel. Fluid in motion was something to be reckoned with.

"When was this earthquake?" he asked.

Pancho's shrug reappeared. "Couple weeks ago. You think we get more?"

Usually, but not always, earthquakes came in clusters. It was a matter of establishing equilibrium until forces again built to the point where further earth movement became inevitable. Earthquakes were not his specialty, but Jay was familiar enough with the basics. "Hard to tell," he said, "but this isn't considered a particularly active earthquake area, like some."

"California?" Again that expression almost of glee.

Well, Jay thought, California, like Texas, was big and brash and disliked by people in many areas. "And lots of other places," he said. The world around, as far as that went.

People tended to think of the earth as set like something poured in concrete. Wrong, dead wrong. The earth's crust was constantly in motion, fracturing here, creeping there, rising, sinking, contorting.

The continental masses, huge as they were, were now considered to be resting on larger masses called lithospheric plates, which in a sense floated on weaker underlying material and moved about upon it in response to forces so vast the mind could not grasp them, let alone exert over them any kind of control. Distortion of the earth's crust was the inevitable, incessant result.

Pancho had finished with earthquakes for the present. Pancho's attention span, Jay thought, was probably usually brief once the subject got away from fishing, hunting, or sports.

"Your first time here?" Pancho asked. He watched Jay's nod. "You got time, there's a nice walk up along the river above the lake. Take a rod—"

"I'm not a fisherman."

"So okay, just walk. You like walking?"

"That, yes."

And it was a pretty walk, through aspens and evergreens, the aspens just beginning to turn, but in some spots already brilliant yellow. The lake left behind and only the stream and the forest around him. It was, Jay thought, almost as it must have been in old Jed's day. He felt refreshed, relaxed, and at home, some but not all of the depression gone.

He saw squirrels who chattered, scolding him. A mountain chickadee spoke his unmistakable phrase in the privacy of the woods and, when Jay came into view, swung around on a small branch and hung upside down for a different view of the intruder. A Steller's jay followed him, shrieking the news that a human was coming; and then suddenly lost interest and flew off, banking, turning, and swooping among the trees as if he enjoyed the obstacle course.

Somewhere in the forest a woodpecker gave his drumbeat roll, pause, another flourish. A nuthatch marched headfirst down a tree trunk without even a glance at the man nearby. From a clearing Jay saw against the limitless sky a single turkey vulture soaring on dihedral wings, rocking gently in the updrafts.

What was the old saying? If a pine needle falls in a forest, the eagle or the vulture will see it, the deer will hear it land, and the bear will smell it. .

Man's senses were feeble things indeed. But man's capacity to alter what was, and sometimes, too often, to destroy it, was almost limitless. Another of those bitter thoughts flowing from his sight of the drowned village.

The trouble was, of course, that as the modern witch doctors would say, he, Jay Harper, "identified" with that village and had from his first reading of his great-grandmother Julia's journals.

He knew, actually, too little about Julia, and wished he knew more. Maybe one day, probably starting in Boston, whence she had come, or possibly in the massive genealogical records in Salt Lake City, he would try to learn something about her background, family, education, and the reasons which had brought her West and finally to Harper's Park, to marry and to realize that old Jed's tales were the stuff of history and legend and should be preserved.

Julia had been an educated woman; her journals demonstrated that. And her interests were catholic, ranging, among many other subjects, from thoughts on Reconstruction and the coming of the railroad, through the Franco-Prussian War, the Custer massacre, the flora and fauna of the Harper's Park area, the discovery of the tuberculosis bacillus by a man named Koch, the poetry of an Englishman named Kipling and some of Robert Browning's work, to the institution of marriage, homeopathic remedies, and the care, education, and raising of children, all, including tales garnered from old Jed, expressed in a small, precise hand and unambiguous language. Impressive to a young boy, and beckoning him forever to a village now sitting at the bottom of a lake.

•   •   •

It was near dusk when he came back to the motel. It was not much of a place, rusting, metal-framed windows, a garish green roof, and wall-to-wall carpeting badly scarred by cigarette burns. But his bed had felt comfortable enough to his probing touch, the plumbing worked and gave off no stench, and the bedding was clean. Jay had stayed in far worse places and he tended to take small notice of minor annoyances. Some places where he had worked you lived well—Prudhoe Bay came to mind, and that oil rig in the North Sea, or the air-conditioned luxury in Saudi Arabia.

But some places you slept in a bedroll or aboard a crowded ship jammed with electronic gear, maybe in a stifling tent as a defense against mosquitoes, or in a shack at night huddled as close to the stove as you could manage.

Cooley Parks had said it once, Jay remembered: "You want

to come home to the same house every night, you better go into another line of work." True. And Cooley had added, "Lots of people do. Poor bastards."

The motel desk clerk was talking to John Boggs when Jay walked into the lobby. The clerk stopped talking and waved a paper. "Phone call for you."

Think of the devil, Jay told himself, reading the message, because the paper bore a name, Parks, and a ten-digit number beginning with 403, which, Jay pondered and finally recalled, was the area code for Alberta, Canada. And what was Cooley Parks doing up there? Jay had seen him last when they parted in Rome after leaving Al Hufūf.

"I'll call it for you," the desk clerk said.

Boggs leaned against the counter, listening and pretending not to.

"In my room," Jay said, and walked out, automatic reaction. Maybe this passion for privacy was a flaw in himself; he had never decided. But it was there, and that was that. His thoughts were his own.

The phone was already ringing when he let himself in, and when he picked it up and spoke his name, the familiar voice roared, "Jay, baby! How they hanging?"

"Reasonably loose." It was impossible not to smile; Cooley's broad, solid presence seemed almost here in the room, filling it. "What are you doing up there?"

"Busting my ass trying to find you. I've run up a bill Ma Bell isn't going to believe. Jesus, you leave faint tracks! Look, boy, get on up here! *Pronto!* We've got oil! Jesus, how we've got oil!" There was a pause.

"But, what?" Jay said.

"Yeah." Cooley's voice dropped a full octave. "We got problems too." He sighed. "I know rocks." True; there was no one better. "But this is one of those fancy ones. And I've told them we could ruin the whole goddamned field just spudding in the way we used to without having a good look first. What we need is your fancy instrument-computer technology to see that we get everything there is and not waste a drop. There isn't that much any more."

Through the window Jay looked out at the lake, the dam, and the towering mountains. He glanced at the bag in the corner which contained his scuba gear, tank, weighted belt, mask, fins, and wet suit. He had not really bothered to think about it yet, but Pancho's description of the seiche caused by the recent tremor had started flags of caution flying.

When you were immersed in a fluid, as he would be down there having his close look at the Harper's Park village, you were at the fluid's mercy. If it began to move, you moved with it, and there would not be all that much room for maneuvering among the buildings if another tremor hit and the lake began to oscillate again. A man could take an awful beating against those stone walls.

But he was here, right on the scene after all this time, and those submerged buildings would not last forever. And once he had set his hand to something he had always hated to turn away. He smiled at himself now, as he often had, thinking that maybe old Jed's stubborn genes had something to do with that.

"I won't be here long," he said. "Day or two. Then I'll come up." A currently bulging bank account too, so there was not even that reason for hurry.

"This is a big one, baby, no chickenshit deal. And they want you. Bad."

"Just a day or two."

There was a long pause. Cooley's sigh was audible. "Okay. I've learned not to argue with you. Just tell me one thing. What in hell are you doing there, anyway? You're no fisherman."

Jay could smile again. "Hunting for ghosts," he said. "I'll be in touch." He hung up.

2

In his young days Bill Williams had tended to move in a series of straight lines, usually head down, hard fists punching, if necessary, as confident of his strength as a fighting bull, impatient of all obstacles.

The tendency remained, but he had tempered it, harnessed the inner drive, in a measure learned to contain the impatience. "You broke me to the plow," he had told Martha—how many times? "And I'll have to admit that it's a hell of a lot easier going around stone walls than going through them."

Martha had always smiled in her quiet way, shaken her head and denied either responsibility or credit. "You are your own man. You always have been. That was why I married you. One of the reasons."

Martha was dead now, and at times the world was an empty place, but Martha's influence remained. Call it habit. Subtlety was not his style, but he could be persuasive rather than demanding. As with his good friend the governor—how many months ago was it now? Damned near two years. Time seemed to go by faster and faster as you grew older.

They had sat that day in the governor's big office in the State Building, coats off for ease, and Clara in the outside office warned not to put through any calls.

"You've got the facts and figures right there, Harry," Bill Williams had said. "They don't lie. Oh, I know, there are liars, damned liars and statisticians. But what we're talking about is water and electric power, and there's a fancy lawyer's Latin phrase that means without them you don't have a goddamned thing."

The governor smiled faintly. "*Sine qua non,*" he said.

"That's it. That's what the figures from your own State Engineer *and* the Public Service people show. Without more power, *and* a larger assured water supply, we can't continue to grow, we're just as limited as a spadefoot toad in the little rain puddle he's come to the surface to sit in. When it dries up, he digs back down into the ground again. That's all he can do. We've got to enlarge the Harper's Park dam. We don't have any choice."

The governor got out of his chair, walked to the windows that faced the great mountains, and stood there with his back to the room. He was a slender, elegant man, always neat, well groomed, well dressed. It had always been so. "Another big fight, Bill," he said. He turned and smiled faintly again. "You love a fight."

Once, maybe, when his life capital was unlimited and he could afford to squander it, but not any longer, not for a long time. "I don't pick them any more, Harry—unless there's a damned good reason. I'm like the street fighter who finds out he can make money at it in the ring. No more saloon brawling just for fun. But this time there's a reason."

"Money, Bill?" In the silence the governor walked back to his desk chair and dropped into it. "Suppose we do push the project, get the funding, win the fight with the penny pinchers and the environmentalists, the property owners who don't want to move, the tax cutters quoting California's Proposition 13, the doom criers and everybody else—suppose we do go through all that and win. Then you'll stand to make a lot of money, won't you, Bill?"

"Probably. I'll get at least a piece of the job and maybe the whole thing. Do you think that's the only reason I'm pushing?"

Again that faint smile. "You lay it right on the line, don't you, Bill?" the governor said, and nodded. "It's always been your way. No, I don't think money is your sole reason. If I did, I wouldn't even listen." He sat up, glanced at the papers on his desk, and then looked at Williams again. "You are convinced that this is in the city's and the state's best interest, aren't you?"

"I am."

"I believe you. A number of people call you a number of things. That is not news to you. I think I know you better than they do, and I believe you." The governor sighed. "All right, Bill. You win. We'll set the wheels in motion. Do you plan to take an active part?"

"No. For the reasons you just said, Harry. To a lot of people, if I'm for something, they're automatically against it. But I'll be around if you need me."

"'Know thyself,'" the governor said. "I think you are one of the few who do, Bill."

That was two years ago. Tonight he sat over after-dinner caffeine-free coffee with Kate, his daughter, in whom there was much of Martha, and something of himself too, no denying that. "You ask why I have stayed out of this whole dam enlargement question, honey? Well, not entirely, but pretty much? Because I'm clumsy, like a bull in a china shop. I could lose my temper with some pipsqueak bureaucrat and louse the whole thing up."

"You're a fraud," Kate said. Her smile was fond, Martha-like. "Mother told me that when I was twelve, but I knew it already. You'll get the contract for the job. And the old Harrison land you bought a while ago will be very valuable waterfront property when the lake expands and reaches it. So you didn't want to be too much out in front. I understand."

There was even more of Martha in Kate than her looks and manner, Williams told himself. It was something to remember. "What do you know about George Harrison's land?"

"That you bought it. Before the question of the dam enlargement even came up."

He took his time, already on the defensive. "You think that's wrong?"

"Other people will."

"Screw other people. What do you think?"

"You're my father."

"That's no answer."

"Yes," Kate said slowly, "it is. It means I give you the benefit of the doubt. Every doubt."

"Explain that."

Even as a little girl Kate had a way of frowning when she was intent. A tiny crease appeared now between her eyes. "You say a larger dam is needed, more hydroelectric power for the city—"

"Right."

"And a more assured water supply. When this current drought ends and the expanded lake is filled—"

"Our water worries are over," Williams said. At least for the time being. Then, Jesus, he thought, what kind of talk is this with your own daughter? Why should she be even vaguely interested in a dam, water, electric power? The answer appeared automatically: Martha would have been, wouldn't she? Okay; remember that. "So?" he said.

"That's one side," Kate said. The small frown held. "The other side is that you stand to make a great deal of money too."

"And that's bad?"

"I don't know." Kate studied her hands briefly. She looked up again. "Do we need it? Don't we have enough?"

This at least he could meet head on. "There's such a thing as too little money," Williams said. "And there's such a thing as a hell of a lot of money." He shook his head. "But there's no such thing as enough money."

He sat there, a bear at the baiting. Ridiculous, a man having to justify himself to his own daughter. But there was this core of honesty in him which would not be ignored, and he could not leave the matter there. "But that isn't what you're saying, honey," he said in a softer voice. "You're asking if your old man is being honest, or if he's rigged the deck by buying

George Harrison's land and then pushing for the dam change. Isn't that it?"

Her eyes were clear, and the tiny frown had disappeared as she faced him. "That," she said, "is where I have to give you the benefit of the doubt."

There was a long silence. Through the glass wall of the big living room Williams could look out and up at the towering mountains now bathed in moonlight, their peaks almost bare after the long drought. Union Peak, Taylor, Washington, Baldy. He knew them all; he had climbed them all. This land was, and had always been, his home. "Honey," he said, "I built this city. Oh, not alone, I don't mean that." He was looking now at the girl, and his voice was gentle, even sad. "But there's a piece of me in everything this city's done—the Harper's Valley dam, the transit system, the convention hall, the stockyards, you name it, your old man was a part of it, a big part."

"I know, Daddy."

"And," Williams said, "in doing it, I made money, a lot of money. Is that what sticks in your craw? I made money and a lot of others didn't, is that it?" He was being unfair, and he knew it, using his weight, his force. "Does a man have to be poor to be honest?"

In her own way she was as strong as he, as strong even as Martha had been. "I told you," she said, "that I have to give you the benefit of the doubt. I am. I do. I always have."

And that, Williams told himself, was as much answer as he was going to get. The old fierce impatience stirred briefly. He forced it back. "Okay, honey. We'll leave it like that. You're going out tonight?"

Kate shook her head, smiling slowly as at an old, familiar joke.

Martha would have known what to say. Williams did not, and was conscious of his own shortcoming. "I always thought that girls—young women—wanted dates, good times, maybe a husband."

"Are you trying to get rid of me?" Kate's smile was gentle, but amused.

"You know better than that." He could remember all too vividly the time after Martha had gone and Kate still away, college, the East. "Big house," he said. "I'd rattle around." And then, realizing how the words sounded, "But, goddamnit, honey, that doesn't mean you have to stick around looking after me. What I mean is—"

"I know what you mean, Daddy." The amusement was gone. "Now you give *me* the benefit of the doubt." Smiling again. "And don't you stay up half the night talking business with the governor. You don't have to do everything yourself."

The hell he didn't, he thought as he walked out to his car. There were things even women as smart as Martha, yes, and Kate, just didn't understand. Somebody had said once that genius was an infinite capacity for taking pains, which was pretty close to the heart of the matter.

Oh, he was no genius. But he had in a sense begun this dam enlargement project, and although these last two years he had kept pretty well out of sight, he had been on top of every step of the negotiations because somebody had to unless you wanted to see it mired down in details, pure nit-picking.

It was as simple as that. Because between the Statehouse and Washington and the assorted pipsqueaks inevitably crawling out of the woodwork in both places, the Ten Commandments themselves would get so garbled, without somebody like Moses to keep them straight, that they'd read like a crossword puzzle—or one of those edicts forever coming out of some alphabet agency. They—

"Simmer down." He said it softly to himself there in the privacy of his car. What was that fancy medical term Jim Stark called those things that happened without warning, the fluttery feeling in his chest and the shortness of breath, yes, and, admit it, the nameless *fear* that went with them, certain knowledge that you were no longer indestructible as you had always thought yourself? Atrial fibrillations. Silly goddamn name. Arrhythmia, the basic term, which wasn't any better. But what it all meant was that the old pump, his heart which he had never even thought about, wasn't running too smoothly any longer. Letting himself get upset over things was just what he was supposed to avoid. Fat chance.

At the first traffic light on Baseline Avenue he took out the silver pillbox, opened it, and popped a small yellow pill into his mouth. Valium, what they called a tranquilizer. Jesus, Mary, and Joseph, how far he had come downhill from the old carefree brawling days!

. . .

The Governor's Mansion sat by itself on a ridge with a commanding front view of the city and the almost endless plain. The rear *portal* faced the mountains that surrounded Harper's Park Valley and reached northward into Canada, and on moonlit evenings such as this, it was there that the governor preferred to relax after dinner. With coffee and cognac, he listened while chamber music played on the record player, the *portal* speakers turned low. Mozart, Schubert, Mendelssohn, and Haydn were his favorites, tastes unknown to his constituents, who by a wide margin preferred country and western music with a sprinkling of hard rock. It was the governor's unpublicized view that his personal tastes, as well as some of his private activities, were none of the public's damn business.

He answered the door himself to Bill Williams's ring, shook hands briefly, and led the way straight to the portable bar in his study, where he poured a double jigger of bonded Bourbon over ice and put it in his guest's hand. In silence they walked out to the *portal* and sank into deep chairs.

"I didn't want to tell you over the phone," the governor said.

"These days God only knows who might be listening, and above all we want to avoid land speculation if we can. But the word from Washington is that we'll get the appropriation and the Army Corps of Engineers will take over and the enlargement of the dam will go ahead just as you laid it out."

Williams tasted his drink. It was good sipping whiskey, smooth as wine. It went well with the good news.

"I don't expect you'll have any trouble getting the contract," the governor said.

"We're the only ones in the state equipped to do the work. You know that, Harry."

The governor sniffed his cognac, then set the bubble glass down. "A lot of money. Are we spending it wisely, Bill?" The Mozart played softly and expertly, the Guarneri Quartet, according to the *New York Times* the best quartet around. (The governor concurred.) "Don't give me all the arguments again," he said. "I'm sick of them. You know what I think of, Bill? I think of that aqueduct Los Angeles built back in the twenties up into Owens Valley to supply the city with ample water for all time. Instead, they just sucked Owens Valley dry and had to reach out to the Colorado for more water. Are we making the same—mistake?"

Williams snorted. They were longtime friends, but the differences between them were vast, sometimes almost unbridgeable. "You're a goddamned intellectual, Harry. You see both sides of every question, and that isn't always good."

True enough. Once upon a time the governor had set his sights on the White House. He knew now that he lacked the ruthless decisiveness. He said nothing.

"There'll be a stink," Williams said. "We knew that two years ago when we made the decision to go. We've already fought the penny pinchers in the Legislature and the goddamned bureaucrats in Washington and the knuckleheaded Army Corps of Engineers. Now when the final word comes out, we fight the rest, the environmentalists and the ecologists and all the other -ists, as well as the Harper's Park property owners who'll start thinking their land is pure gold and want a million dollars an acre for it. And there'll be those who say the dam isn't safe—" He stopped for breath. "But the bottom line, Harry, is that we need it. We have to have it to grow, period."

"Unless we get rain," the governor said, "and a good snow-pack in the mountains, the whole question is going to be moot."

"It'll come."

"I wish," the governor said, "that I had your sublime faith that everything is for the best." He was smiling. "Although I never saw that faith tempt you into backing two pair very far in a tight game." His voice turned nostalgic. "You know, Bill, when we were kids growing up I only thought of you as a pair of fists and a hard head in hand-me-down jeans. Now you wear tailored four-hundred-dollar suits and maneuver behind the scenes—"

"And you're governor of the state," Williams said. "Okay. We've come a long way, like they say in the ads. You aren't thinking of changing your mind about the dam project, are you, Harry?"

Was there hesitation? "Just thinking, that's all. Don't worry about it. How's that stunning daughter of yours?"

Williams tasted his whiskey again. He would much prefer to toss it down and have another, maybe a few more, but Jim Stark had issued a warning about that too, along with real coffee and getting upset, tension. He felt hedged around with restrictions, a man in manacles. "She's sitting home alone," he said. "God only knows why." He looked sharply at the governor. "You're the man with all the education. You tell me what's wrong."

The Mozart quartet ended, and the governor listened to the last echoes from the *portal* speakers. "Try to explain what's in a girl's mind?" he said at last, and shook his head. "No way, Bill. Why don't you ask her?"

Williams could be brutally frank, to others, and to himself as well. It was one of his strengths. "Because I'm afraid of the real answer—which she wouldn't give me."

The governor's eyebrows rose. He said nothing as he waited.

"Martha's dead," Williams said bluntly, "and Kate's all I've got left. That's what I'm afraid she's thinking about. Christ almighty, Harry, we can't help getting old, slowing down, but why in hell does it have to rest on the young ones to feel responsible for us? Answer me that."

The governor swirled his bubble glass, sniffed appreciatively, and drank with an expression of finality. "I'm going to have another touch," he said. "Drink up, Bill. I don't want to have to make two trips to the bar."

Williams hesitated and then finished the whiskey at a gulp. It burned pleasantly in his throat. "Screw Jim Stark," he said, and held out his glass. "A long time since we just sat and talked, Harry. Too long."

3

Geologically speaking, the great mountains surrounding the Harper's Park dam lake were young, their jagged peaks and sheer cliffs not yet eroded into the softer contours of old age.

The mountains had been upthrust, not all at once, but over the millennia, bit by massive bit. As the earth's crust fractured and the rock was forced upward to form the mountain chain, the moisture which fell as rain or as snow upon the steep slopes began first to find, and then to gather in, natural channels leading down to the plains.

Running water exploits weaknesses, and through patient, constant erosion, these natural channels were carved into stream beds, deepening as the mountain mass continued to tilt and rise.

Where the gradient was relatively shallow, the downflowing water could afford to spread, eroding a broader channel, and in time in these places mountain meadows were formed, called locally *ciénagas*, flanking the stream.

But where the gradient was steep and the water was forced by gravity to hurry, the stream concentrated its cutting power in zones of relative weakness, producing narrow, steep-sided gorges and plunging cataracts.

It was across one of these steep-sided gorges immediately below Harper's Park village that the dam had been built and anchored solidly in the rock of the gorge sides.

Below the dam, where the stream continued after passing through the spinning turbines of the power plant, were more gorges—although none as high and as narrow as the dam gorge —and in places also *ciénagas* where cabins and, later, year-round houses had been built.

The State Game and Fish Department maintained a hatch-ery in one of these meadows and both the stream itself and the lake above the dam were well stocked with game fish—striped bass, rainbow and brown trout as well as the red-marked cutthroat trout known locally as "natives." Some fishing areas had been kept open for the public, but much of the river was now private water.

Where the river emerged from the mountains and made its final descent to the high sloping plain, it swung in a great curve called simply The Bend, where the city's wealthier resi-dents, Bill Williams among them, had taken advantage of the magnificent views, the high, clean air, and the proximity to the mountain parks and pleasures to build their homes and estab-lish the inevitable Country Club. A concrete wall and storm drain protected The Bend area from the annoyance of possible spring flooding.

The city itself had grown largely without plan, beginning as a mere settlement below The Bend on the banks of the river. Here, in what was to become the *barrio*, the original church had been built and still remained. But with thoughts of mias-mic fevers from the low land, and the spectacular, almost limit-less views as one moved to higher ground, the inevitable Town Square, or Plaza, some distance from the river and well above it had gradually become the center.

The old Governor's Palace, now a museum, filled one side of the Plaza. The Palace was a one-story adobe structure, fronted by a rudely columned overhang, called a *portal*, be-neath which blanketed Indians peddled their silver and tur-quoise wares and their pottery to tourists.

The other three sides of the Plaza were now filled with com-mercial buildings, most dating from late Territorial times at the turn of the century, and, by recent agreement, all now con-forming to the columned *portal* façade of the old Governor's Palace.

The center of the Plaza was planted with trees, cottonwoods

mostly, which in spring and early summer filled the air with their fluffy seed containers which give the tree its name, and its reputation for messiness. Concrete walks crisscrossed the area, dotted here and there with benches where old folks could sit in the sun and feed the pigeons or in season ogle the female tourists in their tight shorts and halter tops.

Bridges spanned the river, some of them, like the Central Avenue Bridge, old and suitable only for light automobile traffic; some of them new like the East-West Interstate and capable of carrying big commercial tractor-trailer rigs, eighteen-wheelers rolling day and night in a rumbling cacophony of traffic sounds that never ceased.

There were those who claimed that the city's population had reached the half-million count, but the last official census was eight years past, and no one knew the figure for sure. But that there had been growth (some said too much growth) no one could dispute.

Still, in many respects the city retained its recent small-town characteristics, among them the ease with which news circulated in knowledgeable circles.

•　•　•

George Harrison was possibly the first in the city to hear definitive word of government approval in Washington of the Harper's Park dam enlargement project.

George's family had lived in the area since early territorial times. In the city there was Harrison Park, Harrison Street, and overlooking the old Plaza the now aged but still desirable Harrison Building with its turn-of-the-century bow windows, high ceilings, and suites of law offices which had passed from father to son and now to grandson. In the Plaza there was also the statue of the first George Harrison, last of the territorial governors, which George tried not to admire too openly as he walked by.

George himself was unathletic, plump, pink, and in an area of the country where informality was the rule rather than the exception, inevitably well and carefully dressed in tailored suits and Brooks Brothers' shirts. No bolo ties for George.

George was also a scholarly man (and this alone would have tended to set him apart), widely read in the history of the region. His collection of American Southwesterniana, his pride and joy, was known to booksellers across the country.

There being two hours' time difference between the city and Washington, it was already late morning on the Potomac when George came into his office punctually at nine. The call was awaiting him from Bruce Haggard of the Library of Congress, who moonlighted in various directions and always kept an alert ear to the ground for all kinds of information.

"What I called about, George, is a little out of your line, I know, but you came to mind this morning and I thought you might be interested anyway. We have been offered, and we have turned down, a copy of Bernal Díaz's *The True History of the Conquest of New Spain*, the 1632 edition. You are familiar with it, I know."

George was indeed. Bernal Díaz del Castillo had accompanied Cortez in his 1519 campaign which had conquered Mexico City and its vast treasures, and years later in Guatemala Díaz had written his personal account, first published in Madrid in 1632, which in later editions remains the primary historical source.

George blinked. A copy would indeed be a treasure for his library even if it did not, strictly speaking, fit into his collection.

"It's an estate settlement thing," Bruce said, "and the Díaz is the only book of real value, so I doubt if they'll go to the trouble of one of the big auctions. Here's the executor's name and address."

George wrote them down carefully, but what Bruce had to

say next drove all thoughts of Bernal Díaz from his mind, and the note was forgotten.

"What made me think of you," Bruce said, "was at a cocktail party last night your part of the world was mentioned. You have a dam at a place called Harper's Park?"

"We do."

"Well, apparently they're going to enlarge it, one of those making-the-desert-to-bloom-like-a-rose things."

The ignorant insularity of the East was always annoying, and George's rejoinder was automatic, even while his mind was already elsewhere. "Harper's Park," he said with determined mildness, "is hardly desert. Its elevation is eight thousand feet, which puts it eighteen hundred feet above the top of New Hampshire's Mount Washington, which you consider high country for skiing. But thanks for the information. I'll try to repay in kind one day."

He hung up and leaned back, stunned. The Harper's Park dam was only ten years old, and although George had applauded its original construction, and had even exerted his not inconsiderable influence in its favor, he could not now understand the necessity for its enlargement. Nor had he thought that approval for it would ever be obtained. Had he even dreamed that it would, he would never have sold that property to Bill Williams. Never. He was, he thought, understandably upset.

Step one, of course, was to verify or disprove Bruce's information, and the place to start was, as George's father had always said, at the top. He instructed his secretary to put through a call to the governor.

It was, of course, one of the advantages of being named Harrison, although George rarely thought about it in just this way, that local doors which opened only slowly if at all to most people, opened quickly to him. George's secretary buzzed, George picked up the telephone, and over in the governor's office Clara's pleasant voice said, "I have the governor for you, Mr. Harrison. A moment, please."

"Yes, George?" the governor said.

"I have heard that the Harper's Park dam enlargement has been approved."

"Mind telling me where you heard that?"

"I think my source is not important. The question is, is it true?"

So the word was out already, the governor thought, and sighed. Leaks in Washington were publicized, but Washington had no monopoly on leaks; by their very nature all democratic levels of government were veritable sieves for information. "It *is* true, George."

"Bill Williams's doing." Statement, no question; George's tone held conviction.

"Not entirely."

"He bought property from me knowing that the enlargement would be approved, Harry. There is no other explanation. He is unscrupulous—"

"And not someone to treat lightly, George. You might remember that. I am not taking sides. My concern is for the welfare of this state, not for the squabbles of its residents. I assume that was all you had in mind?"

"It was. Thank you, Harry, for the information."

The governor hung up slowly and sat for a short time staring at nothing. Then he picked up the phone again and buzzed Clara. "I want to speak to Bill Williams, please," he said, and while he waited he thought, as he had before, about parents who inflicted names on their children which made life difficult either for the children or for others. How could you ask to speak to William Williams? He picked up the phone again when it buzzed. "Bill? George Harrison just telephoned. Word of the dam approval is out. I thought you ought to know."

"There was no way to keep it a secret, Harry. People talk.

It's a fact of life. Did George mention the property he sold me?"

"He did. With considerable vehemence."

"Okay, thanks. And that's good Bourbon you have. No hangover. See you."

. . .

Williams hung up and leaned back in his chair to look out at his office view of the mountains. He was thinking of his conversation last night with Kate. And, with that core of honesty in him which could not be ignored, he was wondering just how pure his motives *had* been for buying the Harrison land.

Had he, as he had told himself, merely been making a long-term investment when the opportunity presented itself, or had he already known that the dam enlargement would be his next project, and that with his push, his force behind it, the project would probably succeed?

The telephone on his desk buzzed and he picked it up automatically. "A John Boggs from the Harper's dam is on line one, Mr. Williams."

Williams pushed the appropriate button. "Yes?"

"I just thought you'd like to know, Mr. Williams," John Boggs said, "that there's a guy diving in the lake with that underwater gear you see on TV. I talked with him yesterday and he says he's a—geophysicist." The words flowed as if they had been carefully rehearsed. "I think he's harmless, but, well, there are a couple of things about him, and you being interested in the dam and all, you know, you've been up here quite a bit—well, I thought you might like to know. You asked me, maybe you remember, if people had been up here after those crazy threats we had—"

"Right," Williams said. "John Boggs, is it?" He wrote the name on his desk pad. "What are the things about him?"

"Well, his name is Harper and he says old Jed was his kin."

"Could be."

"He put his last address as Al—something, a place in Saudi Arabia. Yesterday he was looking at the dam. And there was a phone call for him from Alberta, Canada, somebody wants him up there and he wouldn't tell them what he was doing here. I don't know, Mr. Williams. It just *sounds* kind of funny."

"He's staying at the motel?" Williams nodded and wrote that down too. "Right," he said. "I'll take it from here. Thanks for the call."

Williams hung up and leaned back again, staring out at the mountains. Now why am I even interested in a man named Harper? Because the dam is on my mind? Or is there something else? That part of his mind he had always thought of as being like an ant's antennae, constantly searching, testing, absorbing messages from invisible sources, was now alert and almost quivering.

God, how he missed Martha! He could see her now, wearing that quiet smile while she listened, and he could almost hear her saying, "Follow your hunches. You always have. And your dreams too." He found himself wondering if Kate would understand.

Strange. Until Martha's death he, Bill Williams, had always thought of himself as, not self-sufficient in all things, but well accustomed to making his business decisions without benefit of advice. He had come to realize now that the advice had always been there even if it was rarely spoken aloud, and that he had relied heavily upon it.

The telephone buzzed again, and he picked it up.

"Mr. George Harrison is here, Mr. Williams."

Sooner or later, Bill thought, and it might as well be right now. "Send him in." He did not get out of his chair when the door opened.

"Come in, George. Sit down."

What was between them, Bill thought, was not open, active hatred, because it had never come to that and probably never would, but mutual dislike that went back to the schoolyard and beyond. George had been the plump boy from the big house on the hill, and Bill had been the scrappy kid from Avenue A. It was, Bill had heard some shrink say once, the classic situation which produced envy and even jealousy on both sides.

Because George, for all that he had behind him, had been physically afraid of Bill, envious of his strength and his instant willingness to shoot the works, go for the bundle, stand right up and spit in anybody's eye. And Bill, as Harry had said last night, in hand-me-down jeans, conscious of the world of difference between his background and George's, had always been ill at ease, uncertain how to behave in the plump boy's presence, constantly waiting to break into violent action if anything he did or said produced a laugh, or even a superior smile.

The funny thing was, even after all this time the feelings were still with them. "What can I do for you, George?"

"The dam enlargement has been approved."

"Has it?"

"You know it has. I have verified it with Harry. You are responsible for that approval. Don't deny it, Bill. I am not blind, I have watched you pull the strings, apply the pressure. Frankly, I didn't think you would succeed. I saw no reason why you should. But you did. You have. I suppose you have every reason to feel proud of yourself."

"You didn't come here to pat me on the back."

"Quite right. I came here with a business proposition. You have a quarter section of my land, one hundred and sixty acres."

"Not your land, George. Mine. I bought it over two years ago."

"I am quite aware of it. Having held it for that length of time, any profit will be subject to capital-gains tax, which is less than that on ordinary income and may be lowered even more if this Congress has its way."

"*If* I sell, George. And I'm not thinking of selling. Not yet."

"You paid five hundred dollars an acre, eighty thousand dollars, Bill."

"A fair price. You set it."

"I will give you a twenty percent profit, ninety-six thousand dollars."

"Thanks, George. But I don't think so."

"I will raise it to thirty percent, a hundred and four thousand dollars. And that is my final offer."

"No dice, George. Sorry."

"I dislike being bilked."

"If that means what I think it means," Bill said, "nobody bilked you. You put the land on the market. I bought it."

"With certain foreknowledge that it would become waterfront property when the dam is enlarged."

"I had no certain foreknowledge, as you call it, George. But even if I had been reasonably sure what was going to happen, I would have gone right ahead. It's how business is done."

"In some circles."

He could take just so much of George Harrison, Williams told himself, and the limit had been reached. "For Christ's sake, George, do you expect me to be conscience-stricken because I got the best of a business deal?"

"No. Your kind doesn't know the meaning of the word 'conscience.'"

Williams took a deep breath, held it, and let it out slowly. "Okay, George. You've said what you came to say. Now haul your ass out of here before I kick it out."

．　．　．

In his office at the First National Bank, Tom Gentry heard the news too, an hour later by telephone from Los Angeles from a friend in the holding company which owned Tom's bank, a large organization with widespread interests which prudently maintained private contacts in all major centers across the country.

"It's from the horse's mouth, Tom. Our New York guy got it straight from Washington. Approval was finalized this morning. Maybe you can put the knowledge to use."

It was widely rumored that Tom Gentry was distantly related to John Wesley Hardin, the gunfighter. Tom's expressionless face and cold gray eyes gave the rumor credence. His calm was unshakable. "Maybe I can at that," he said. He was already thinking hard. "Thanks for the call, Joe."

"If there's a piece of action lying around, don't forget where you got the word."

"I always remember favors."

Gentry hung up and went on with his thinking. It was an article of faith with him, as it was with many whom he considered smart businessmen who stayed on their toes, that once information was known to the general public it was usually worthless; but that before it was widely known, important information such as this could usually be made to turn a profit. The only problem was finding the right handle. Quickly.

He sat motionless for a little time and then leaned forward to flip the switch of the intercom. "Ask Jack Marble to step in, please." Okay, he thought he had the handle, but it would be wise to check it.

Jack Marble was in his late thirties, trim and fit, a jogger and a tennis player. He was on his way to the top, and eager to get there. His current position in the bank was loan officer. He was aware of the rumors concerning Tom Gentry's relationship with John Wesley Hardin, and he believed them. Tom Gentry, as everybody knew, was a tough cookie. Jack sat down and waited for Gentry to speak.

"Brooks Thompson," Tom Gentry said. "We turned down an extension of his loan."

"Yes, sir. I didn't want to. He's such a nice guy, but—" Jack spread his hands. "He isn't going to make that landscape business go. That's the bottom line. Without more capital to buy equipment, it just won't work, and even then it would be a gamble."

"He offered us some property as further collateral."

"Yes, sir. Property way up in the boonies above Harper's Park lake. Fifty acres, worth maybe four hundred, five hundred dollars an acre—if you could find a buyer for it."

"He's keeping up his loan payments?"

"Yes, sir. It's strapping them, but he's hanging on."

"Okay, Jack, thanks. Like you said, he's a nice guy. I'd like to see him make it."

Sympathy was not what you expected to hear from Tom Gentry, Jack thought, but there it was. It just went to show, he supposed, that you couldn't really tell what somebody was like way down inside. Something to remember. "Yes, sir," he said. "I'd like that too. He and Mary have worked like dogs."

Tom Gentry waited until the door was closed again before he took the heavy telephone book out of his desk drawer and hunted in the Yellow Pages under "Landscaping." He put the book away, asked the switchboard for and got an outside line, and dialed the call himself. A young woman's voice answered.

"Mrs. Thompson?"

"Speaking."

"This is Tom Gentry at the bank, Mrs. Thompson. I called—"

"If it's about this month's loan payment, Mr. Gentry, Brooks will be taking care of it this week for sure." Her voice sounded hopeful rather than assured. "We have until the fifteenth before we're actually delinquent, don't we?"

Gentry's voice was as soothing as he could make it. "It isn't about that at all, Mrs. Thompson. I just wanted to talk to your husband about your general situation. We had to turn down your application for a loan extension—"

"I know."

"But," Gentry said, "I've been thinking about that, and I'm sure we can work something out."

"You mean you could reconsider our application?"

"I'm not sure exactly what. But we like to help local businesses whenever we can, and I'm sure we can work something out. Do you suppose your husband could have lunch with me?"

"Why, why, I'm sure he could. When?"

"Today. The Hilton. Twelve o'clock. Do you think he can make that?"

"Mr. Gentry, he will make it. I'll see that he does. Oh, thank you!"

"Not at all." Gentry was tempted to add, "my dear," but restrained himself. He was, after all, hardly the avuncular type. To his secretary over the intercom: "Book a table for two at the Hilton for noon," he said, and leaned back to consider exactly how he was going to go about turning the handle.

4

Eighty feet down, the water of the lake was still clear and visibility reasonably good. Jay was glad he had not brought the underwater light, just one more thing to carry on this first dive.

It was cold, no argument there. He had studied the 7½′ 1:24000 USGS topographical maps of the area, and automatically noted that the stream which flowed into the lake rose in a hundred upland valleys, ravines, and *ciénagas*, steep-sided canyons and mere draws, some tributaries marked as intermittent and now with the drought presumably dry, others draining directly from hanging valleys and even small natural lakes, all of them snow- or glacier-fed. And the warmth of even the midday sun penetrated only a few feet beneath the lake's surface. So even with the wet suit he wore, the cold was something he had to accept.

And now that he was actually here among the buildings of the drowned village, what Pancho had told him of the seiche caused by the recent tremor was very much in his mind. Close up, some of the stones of the walls looked sharp, menacing. But this too was something he had to accept. So be it.

He had adjusted his belt weights to fresh water instead of the more buoyant ocean water he was accustomed to, and now, balanced easily a few feet above the bottom of the lake, using swim fins only, he glided along what had been the main street of the village.

Here was the mill. Reaching down into the clear depression that had been the bed of the stream, the waterwheel remained, an unmoving relic. How many hundreds, even thousands of bushels of grain had been ground to flour by this sturdy, simple, and efficient mechanism erected in what had been wilderness? How many tens of thousands of loaves of good nutritious bread had that flour produced in primitive ovens here in the village and in outlying farmhouses? Before "progress" arrived.

Those were futile, even poisonous thoughts, and he put them aside with effort as he glided on.

He paused suddenly in his swimming, and for a moment, evenly balanced in the water by his air tank and weighted belt, held his breath, all senses alert. Was that a current he had felt, the beginning of a surge? If so, the surface was the place for him. Fast.

But the moment passed and he remained motionless in relation to the stone building of the mill. He forced his teeth to unclench, let his breath out in a burst of bubbles, and drew another long breath from the demand valve. Sheer imagination, he told himself; nerves. He swam on.

Here was the smithy, the hand-built forge where the great leather bellows would have been worked, blowing the coals to white heat. And that solid stump must have been the mount for the smith's big anvil where the ringing metallic strokes would have sounded throughout the building and along the village street, and the sparks would have showered with each blow, reducing small boys to awe as bit by bit the iron was shaped. Silent now, lifeless, an underwater museum for fish.

Here was the first house, built by old Jed Harper. No, Jed's first house had been of logs. Jay remembered mention of that now in Julia's journal. This stone house had come later, so positioned, he noticed, as to afford a fine view up the valley to the mountains through which a younger Jed Harper had made his solitary way.

On another dive, Jay told himself, he would have a better look at Jed's house. Now he clung to his original plan of a general survey of the entire village, and then examination of specifics, standard procedure for him in new surroundings.

The church was next, even its modest steeple intact except for its bell, which had been carefully removed. Bells were expensive. Jay wondered where it rang now; there seemed to be no record, and he remembered that he had been struck by this evidence of—applying a term from geology—*discontinuity*.

Through the study of history, it had occurred to him, we attempt to tie together large movements, events, trends. Through genealogy, we sometimes trace families, and individuals. But *things*, even important things like church bells, special chairs, writing desks, beds, except in rare instances these disappear without a trace, fall into unknowing hands, are traded, sold, or scrapped, and are lost forever. Pity.

And behind the church was the graveyard, uneven row upon uneven row of headstones, none of them grand or fancy, and some quite crude. He would need a light to read them, he decided, and the underwater camera if he found anything of great interest; even on a clear day such as this, not enough sunlight reached the lake bottom to make out some of the weathered inscriptions.

But the headstones were there; that was the important thing, maybe old Jed's among them. No current had uprooted them, or buried them yet in silt.

Walking, strolling along the village street and through the graveyard really would have been preferable, he thought; smelling the air, absorbing the atmosphere that seemed always to cling to old places, perhaps, as he had once in a mother-lode ghost town, finding a fragment of broken glass turned violet by long exposure to the sun, or maybe a hand-forged nail, actual relics of what had been, tangible remains.

And yet, in another sense, floating among the buildings like a disembodied spirit gave him a feeling of observing from *within*, seeing, himself unseen, through windows, open doorways, even through walls themselves, a ghost among ghosts fraternizing with echoes of the past. And as yesterday in the boat looking down on the village for the first time, he had now that strange illusion of being at home.

He glided on the length of the village main street. Some of the houses and buildings he could identify from his research; some were relatively new and unknown; and here and there only outlines of foundations remained of buildings which had been. And the illusion of home remained.

So there it was, he thought at last as ahead the dam wall rose sheer, journey's end. He swung around and headed on a long slant upward toward the light. Pilgrimage to Mecca, he told himself, a silly business really, but unaccountably he felt better for having made the visit.

It was not until he had pulled himself into the boat and, mouthpiece hanging loose and faceplate pushed up, sat relaxed on the stern seat, that he realized how tense he had been underwater. His muscles ached, and despite the cold he was sweating. He started the outboard motor with its raucous clatter, more annoying after the silence of the village, and headed for shore. John Boggs was waiting on the dock.

"You look ready for a hot shower," Boggs said. "But this won't take long. There's a man wants to talk to you. I gave him your name and where you're staying. He'll be in touch. His name is Williams, Bill Williams, and he's something of a big wheel in these parts. He's interested in the dam."

"He wants me to dive for buried treasure? Or find him a mermaid?"

"That's between he and you." Boggs turned away.

There was a telephone message beneath the motel room door. It was from Bill Williams, with a local telephone number. Ahead of the name in a different handwriting, the title "Mr." had been added. Jay smiled at this indication of local deference as he went in to that hot shower.

Showered, dressed, and with most of the chill from the lake water worn off, he had the desk clerk place the telephone call.

He was put through at once. Williams had a no-nonsense approach, blunt and to the point.

"Bill Williams, Harper. I haven't any real reason, but I'm curious to meet you. You seem to be interested in the dam. I know all about it. Okay, I'll tell you what. There's no decent food up there unless you cook it yourself. Come down to my place for dinner and we'll both satisfy our curiosities."

Williams was not unlike Cooley Parks, Jay thought, the same kind of directness and lack of pretense. Warm thought. And Pancho's cooking *did* leave a lot to be desired. "Accepted with pleasure," he said. "Tell me where and when."

• • •

The old Plaza was still the heart and center of the city, its territorial architecture unchanged; but within a few blocks from it in all directions the changes began.

To the north and east, on ground rising toward the great mountains, the new high-rise office buildings dominated the scene, the banks, the insurance companies, the larger and more expensive retail stores, surrounding high-rent apartments, some houses, hotels, and off-the-street parking.

To the west, also on higher ground, were the state buildings, the federal courthouse and main post office, law and medical offices, and, once well out of town, but now an enclave, the general hospital.

To the south, crowding down to the river, and across, was the *barrio*, bilingual, a conglomeration of small houses, adobe, frame, cinder-block; mobile homes; shabby old small hotels; tenements; mom-and-pop *tiendas* and bars and liquor stores; the old grammar school where once Bill Williams had been cock of the walk; a single adobe church, the spiritual center of this almost separate community.

Before the building of the Harper's Park dam two thousand feet above, in springtime the river had regularly flooded over its banks as the winter's snowpack melted, and in some years the lowest streets of the *barrio* had been awash. When the waters receded those streets it had covered emerged cleaner than before, but they rapidly accumulated their usual litter of discarded paper and broken bottles and empty beer cans, and life went back to normal.

The city's mayor, José-María Lopez y Baca, had been born and raised in the *barrio*. He lived now in an alien, Anglo world, and resented it bitterly, a feeling which fueled his determination to beat the odds against the chances of his or any Chicano's success. And in a city in which there were two governmental chief executives, himself and the governor, clashes of authority were inevitable.

On the telephone to the governor: "You're going ahead with that Harper's Park dam enlargement, right?" the mayor said.

The governor would dearly have loved to know how the mayor had come by his information so soon, but refrained from asking. He would probably not get an answer, he thought, and if he did he was not sure he could believe it. "I haven't had official word yet," the governor said, "but that seems to be it."

"For once," the mayor said, "you and I are on the same side of the fence. We need it."

"I am happy to hear it."

"But water rates will go up. The job's going to cost money and somebody has to pay for it."

"Inevitably."

"Okay. I'm thinking about the little guy. Water rates are already high."

"Agreed." The governor wondered where the mayor was heading.

"A few bucks a month doesn't mean anything to a rich Anglo," the mayor said. "And it doesn't mean a damn thing to a big company. But to a poor Chicano family, a few more bucks a month means fewer beans in the pot. The trouble is, the rate structure's upside down, strictly ass-backward."

The governor thought about it. "Meaning?"

"There's a minimum charge," the mayor said. "Then as you use more water, the price per unit goes down, right? And yet we're trying to conserve water, right? So why not raise the rates on the big users, make them pay the premium—the more they use, the more they pay, instead of less. Give the little guy a break, *and* help conserve water. How about that?"

The governor thought about it. "You may have a point."

"So how about twisting the Public Service Commission's arm?"

He should have seen it coming, of course, the governor thought. His mind must have been elsewhere. "The Public Service Commission is autonomous," he said. "You know that, José-María."

"Shee-it!" the mayor said. "You can make them jump through a hoop any time you want to. You're a nice polite fellow, Harry, but there are a lot of characters walking around carrying their heads in baskets because they didn't do what you wanted them to do. And the politicians around here know it."

"You overestimate me," the governor said. "But I will give this some thought when the matter of funding and amortizing the dam enlargement gets to contract time."

. . .

Carlos García taught the seventh grade at the *barrio* grammar school and also provided what coaching the school had in basketball, baseball, football, track, and wrestling. Like the mayor, he was a product of the *barrio*. Carlos had once blacked the mayor's eye, and as happens not infrequently between males who have fought and then discovered that their differences are not irreconcilable after all, the incident remained as a kind of bond between them.

Carlos's English was not as good as the mayor's; he had

never lost the Spanish lilt. He said now in the mayor's office, "That drought over in Texas."

"What about it?"

"It's on TV, the drought is over. One place they got twenty-two inches of rain in twenty-four hours. That what they call tropical storm moving north and west."

"I heard. What about it?"

"We got a drought too."

"Carlito. What's your point?"

"They got bad floods. What if we get floods too? Remember how it used to be when the snows melted? Only with rain like that this could be worse, much worse."

"We've got the dam. That's why we've got it. One reason."

"Yeah." Carlos's tone lacked conviction.

"And they're going to enlarge it."

"I didn't know that." Carlos was silent for a few moments, thinking about it. "Okay," he said at last, "you probably know best. But just in case, you know, something goes wrong and we do get a flood. All those people in the *barrio*, low ground and lots more people than there were when we were kids, suppose, just suppose?"

"Okay," the mayor said. "Suppose. Then what?"

"Have we got a plan? I mean, have we got some idea what to do to get people out safe—just in case?"

The mayor leaned back in his chair. He said in a slow voice filled with sudden wonder, "Jesus Christ! I don't think anybody ever even thought about it. How about that?"

•   •   •

Brooks Thompson came back from lunch in a thoughtful mood. He was tall and lean, in his late twenties, with longish brown hair, plastic-frame glasses, and an eastern preparatory school accent. After college, Princeton, he had worked for three years with a firm of investment bankers in New York, decided he had had more than enough of the rat race, and with Mary headed West. The landscaping venture had been Mary's idea. She had always liked flowers, and knew quite a bit about them. They had discovered that that was not quite enough.

"What happened?" Mary said. "Sit down. Tell me. Everything!" She was a tall girl with long blond hair, dressed now in her everyday work clothes of short-sleeved shirt, faded jeans, and sneakers. "Well?"

Brooks sat down and stretched out his legs. He wore still the thoughtful expression. "I don't know," he said. "If this were still New York, I'd guess that somebody was trying to pull a fast one."

"Mr. Gentry?" Mary shook her head.

"He's what Wall Street calls a gunslinger. Or that's how I'd size him up if he came around hustling a bond issue, or was selling short in a bull market. Here—" Brooks shook his head slowly. "I just don't know."

"But he's president of the bank!"

"There are bank presidents and bank presidents. This one is all of a sudden just a little too friendly. He wants to give us a hand until we really get started."

"That's wrong?" Mary shook her head again. "Sometimes I wish you'd never worked in New York. You were getting so you didn't trust anybody."

Brooks's grin took ten years off his age. "That's what it does to you."

"All right. What does Mr. Gentry want to do?"

"Buy that property up above the lake. Where we're planning to build the cabin."

Mary was silent for a time. All those plans they had made, she thought, dreams really, but all the more precious for that. She said at last, "When we can afford it, I guess we can find other property. Did he mention price?"

"Four hundred fifty dollars an acre."

"How much is that?"

"Twenty-two thousand five hundred. A fair price. More than we paid."

Mary brushed her hair back with both hands, automatic gesture. "We could use it. We certainly could."

"No argument."

"But you don't want to sell. Tell me why."

"Why does he want it?"

"Honestly, Brooks! How do I know why he wants it? What difference does it make?"

"I don't know." Brooks spread his hands and smiled helplessly.

"We could pay off that loan."

Brooks nodded.

"And have plenty left for the things we need, that small tractor, the sprayer, maybe that used backhoe, all the things we've talked about."

"True."

"But you don't think we should."

"It's just a feeling. I don't have anything else."

Mary leaned her hip against the cluttered desk. "We could ask Daddy for a loan."

"No. We agreed on that. He doesn't think we can hack it out here, and maybe he's right, but we'll give it a damned good try —on our own." He studied her face. "Agreed?"

Mary's smile was less than convincing. "That was the bargain. I won't back out."

There was a long silence before Brooks heaved himself out of his chair. He took a deep breath. "Okay," he said, "I guess that settles it, doesn't it? I'll call Gentry and tell him he has a deal."

"You still don't want to."

"No, I don't want to. But I don't have any real reason against, and there are real reasons for, so it only adds up one way."

Mary closed her eyes. Tears stung their lids.

5

The Williams house was impressive, Jay thought as he drove in, large, adobe-colored, fitting into the brown earth and the scattered piñon and juniper trees as if it had grown there. As far as he could see, a low adobe wall completely surrounded the considerable property. A graveled drive led through an archway supported by carved and weathered wooden corbels into a courtyard where a three-car garage, also adobe, was connected to the main house by a covered walk.

The entire place reeked of money, and Jay was not at all sure he was glad he had come. He was not awed in the presence of wealth. It was rather that he resented the arrogant assumption of infallibility that tended to go with it.

Two German shepherd dogs appeared when he got out of his car. They inspected him gravely and, one on each side, walked with him to the carved front door, which opened before he could lift the heavy wrought-iron knocker. A girl smiled at him and held out a cool, firm hand. "Kate Williams, Mr. Harper," she said. And, to the dogs in a reassuring voice: "It's all right. A guest."

Jay watched the dogs walk away, no longer interested. "Bodyguards?" he said.

"In a sense." More trappings of wealth.

Inside, the house was pleasantly cool, with brick floors polished by age and care, whitewashed walls, weathered wooden ceiling beams; and at the rear, with a stunning view of the mountains, sliding glass doors opened on a flagstoned and sheltered *portal* where two men sat, drinks at hand.

There were brightly patterned rugs on the floor, Indian rugs,

Jay thought, although he knew little about such things. Here in this setting they seemed appropriate. He was aware that the girl was watching him, smiling.

"Do you approve of what you see, Mr. Harper?"

Money, of course, was his first thought. But admit it, he told himself, there is taste as well. "Very nice," he said, and followed Kate to the *portal* in silence.

A somewhat surly young man, Kate thought. Ill at ease? Hard to tell. She told herself sternly to reserve judgment. "Mr. Harper, Daddy," she said.

Williams heaved himself out of his chair. He was a big man, Jay thought, not overly tall, but broad and solid—and again the vague similarity to Cooley Parks came to mind. Even Williams's handshake, gently powerful, was somehow familiar.

"Glad you could come," Williams said. He nodded toward the other, younger, larger man. "Sam Martin. Sam's my chief engineer. Kate, put a drink in the man's hand and sit down with us."

When he thought about the evening later, Jay dwelt more on impressions than actual facts, although pieces of conversations remained clear, forming a pattern on which opinions, if not supporting evidence, could be set.

He liked Williams, as he liked Cooley Parks, but that arrogance of wealth was in the man, in no way concealed, along with a tendency to set a goal and head straight toward it at full throttle, and in Jay's judgment, these were flaws, sometimes dangerous.

He found that he disliked Sam Martin. He seemed reasonably knowledgeable as an engineer. He could, and did, listen when another talked. He smiled easily and there was no reason to think that the smiles were insincere. So what was there in the man to object to except that he was a lightweight? But the world was filled with lightweights.

About Kate he was not sure. She was decorative—medium height, slim, pleasingly rounded, moving with easy grace. She spoke little, although she did seem to listen, and she wore almost continually a small assured smile that could have been infuriating, and somehow was not. There was about her an air of directness that matched her father's, a quiet forcefulness that was yet wholly feminine and not unattractive. Jay could not decide whether he liked Kate or not. It didn't matter either way. He wasn't going to be around long enough for like or dislike to make a difference.

He, of course, was the stranger and quite naturally at first the center of attention. He had expected that. As long as the questions weren't too private.

Bill Williams, drink in hand, said in his blunt way, "You're old Jed Harper's kin, John Boggs tells me. There weren't any Harpers left when we built the dam ten years ago. As a matter of fact, even when I was a kid, I don't remember any Harpers up in the valley."

"They moved West. California."

"Gold Rush?" This was Sam Martin.

Jay shook his head. "Later, much later. Around nineteen hundred, I think." Julia's journal mentioned the breakup of the family only briefly. Julia had stayed behind. At least that was the implication.

"About the time," Williams said, "that my family came here. What there was of it." A raggedy-assed lot they must have been too, he thought; and saw Kate watching him as if she could see right into his mind. He grinned at her. "I won't say a word about them, honey," he said. "Let's just say they didn't like Kansas. For reasons." He looked at Jay again. "It was a pretty little place, Harper's Park," he said. "That's what you wanted to know, wasn't it? But then of course, you've seen it. How does it look when you're down there?"

"Empty. A ghost town. Just buildings."

"A movie set?" This was Martin again.

Jay looked at the man, but could find nothing in the question beyond simple curiosity. He shook his head. "Movie sets aren't real. This is. Was." Something not susceptible of explanation, he thought, at least not by a trained scientist.

"A sense of—having been lived in?" Kate said unexpectedly.

Jay thought about it. Slowly he nodded. "It's there. You expect to find wash hanging on a line. Even underwater."

"I've never really looked at it," Kate said. She looked at her father. "When you build the dam higher, the lake will be deeper, won't it? Will you be able to see the buildings then?"

Jay looked from one to the other. "Are you enlarging the dam?"

"It's being talked about," Williams said, but the impatience was strong in his mind, and he was, he told himself, sick and tired of pussyfooting anyway. If George Harrison knew all about it, then others knew too. And there was really no secret, as far as that went. "Talked about, hell," he said. "It's going to happen. Sam here has had plans for eighteen months. The Army Corps of Engineers has gone all over them, up, down, and sideways. We need more generating capacity for the city, and we need a secure water supply." He was talking straight to Jay now. "You're a geophysicist, Boggs tells me."

"Oil is my bag," Jay said. Cooley's telephone call. A new field? It sounded like it. Big country, Canada. Lots of virgin territory. There could be almost anything lying beneath it. And Cooley did know his rocks.

"I looked it up," Williams said. "Geophysics covers just about anything you can name."

True. Jay sipped his drink and said nothing.

"Suppose," Williams said, "we need some kind of expert testimony. You're here, and you've been down on the bottom where nobody else has been. Would you be available?"

There was no need even to think about it; he was committed. "I'm off for Canada in two, three days." And then, merely out of vague curiosity: "Why a geophysicist, anyway?"

"I learned a long time ago," Williams said, "that when it comes to open hearings, God and public opinion are all on the side of the fellow with the most experts, especially experts who can talk about things nobody else understands. Sam here thinks I'm kidding. I'm not. Fact of life, and if you can't change it, learn to live with it. An engineer on the other side wouldn't stand a chance against a geophysicist on ours. If it comes to opposition, that is, which I hope to hell it won't."

Jay grinned and sipped his drink.

"I won a hearing on water once," Williams said. "The other side had a hydrologist. I had *two* hydrologists *and* a water witch. It was no contest." And then that core of honesty that would not be denied. "As it turned out," he added, "their hydrologist was right, there wasn't enough water, but that's the way it goes sometimes. How about another drink, honey?"

Sam Martin said, "The engineering's all done, Bill, and nobody's going to argue with it."

Williams shook his head. "I count my winnings, Sam, after everybody else has thrown in his hand. Not before." His eyes on Jay were appraising. "You ever make mistakes, Harper?"

"I try not to be wrong too often."

"My feelings too." Williams held out his glass. "How about that drink, honey?"

Kate said quietly, "Dr. Stark—"

"If Jim Stark has been talking to you behind my back," Williams said, "I'll skin him alive and nail his hide to the barn door."

"You'll do no such thing," Kate said, but she stood up smiling and took the glass. "A half drink," she said, "and don't argue."

Dinner was superb, a standing rib roast of well-hung beef, baked potatoes with sour cream and chives, a crisp mixed green salad, California Zinfandel wine, cheese, crackers, coffee, port or cognac—scarcely what he would have anticipated, Jay thought. He wondered if Kate was responsible for the menu.

Williams explained the quality of the beef. "I have a small herd of Angus," Williams said. "The Pueblo handles it for me. We sell enough to break even. Almost. But the Pueblo gets employment and I get the kind of beef we like to eat, and I call it a fair trade." As host he dominated the conversation and sent it off on odd tangents without warning. "Canada in a few days," he said now, looking again at Jay. "You get around quite a bit, do you?"

"Here and there."

"Such as?" Martin said. The question held a challenge.

No, Jay thought, he did not like the man. "The last stop was Saudi," he said, his voice without special inflection. "Before that Iran, and before that a job in the North Sea on an anchored rig off Norway. Indonesia, Alaska's north slope, Lake Pontchartrain in Louisiana—" He shrugged. "I go where there's work for me."

"Like Red Adair," Martin said, and this time there was something else behind the words, resentment, perhaps, envy, whatever.

Jay ignored the overtones. He shook his head. "Red goes where there's trouble. My job is to try to prevent it, trouble or waste. They go hand in hand." And, because he could not resist: "If there are no emergencies, no heroics, then I've done my job. I like the quiet life."

Kate, watching, listening, allowed herself to wonder. Was it a quiet life on a drill rig in the North Sea, or in scuba gear on the bottom of a near-freezing lake? I am unable to judge, she told herself, and wondered what her father would say. Williams was a shrewd judge of men. She would ask him.

They sat on the *portal* again after dinner. In the high clear air the warmth of the day disappeared quickly. A maid appeared without summons, and lighted a fire in the corner fireplace, piñon logs standing on end, their burning fragrance filling the air. The warmth was welcome; and the only lighting, from candles in hurricane lamps on the table, cast a pleasant, unobtrusive glow. Stars were plain, the Dipper, Polaris, Cassiopeia, the Pleiades, Orion's belt, Rigel, Betelgeuse, these prominent, all close enough to touch.

Here, now, Jay thought, you can almost recapture the atmosphere old Jed knew, the sense of loneliness and yet belonging; like an owl he had heard last night, in tune with the environment, rather than against it, an invader.

Kate broke into his thoughts. "You will dive again tomorrow?"

"If it's clear, and it looks as if it will be."

Williams said, "God, how we need rain. But it will come."

Martin said, "To look some more at your ghost town?"

"That's right." Today the general, overall look; tomorrow a closer look at some of the details, the graveyard in particular. It would be nice to see old Jed's grave marker, and maybe Julia's too.

Kate said on impulse, "If I came up, might I go out with you? I've never really looked at the village since the lake covered it."

She was, after all, his hostess, Jay told himself, and the good dinner did carry a certain amount of obligation. "It'll be cold just sitting in the boat," he said. "But if you'd like to come, yes, of course." Something less than enthusiasm, but the best he could manage.

Yes, there was quite a bit of the evening to sort out before sleep came that night.

He was awakened by what he first thought was the sound of distant heavy explosions, but he lay quiet, listening, and realized that it was thunder echoing and reverberating among the high peaks of the watershed.

A break in the drought? Maybe yes; maybe no. In mountainous regions like this, dead accurate forecasting was next to impossible, and a heavy thunderstorm could be either a more or less isolated phenomenon, or a signal that a front was moving in. Whichever it was, Jay was glad he was snug in bed inside a sheltering building rather than camped out in a high valley where the storm was.

Thunderstorms in the high mountains were awesome displays of almost incalculable power, releasing energy in the nuclear-explosion range. And if you were close, there was about them a personal quality, inescapable, as if every sudden flash and every simultaneous crackling explosion were seeking you out, you alone, for who could tell what transgressions against what supernatural forces. The lightning flashes blinded you; the thunder deafened you; and on open, rocky slopes and in shallow hanging valleys there was no defense and no place to take refuge.

And the rain, which frequently turned to hail, was unrelenting and unbelievable in its ferocity. Rivulets turned in an instant to streams which became torrents, rushing steeply downhill unimpeded, catching up loose rocks, scree, even boulders, and flinging this detritus with shrapnel effect down upon lower elevations, where, when the storm at last subsided, it would lie alien and scattered to testify to the fury that had been above.

Caught among the high peaks in such a storm, man became rapidly aware of his puny mortality, which was perhaps a good thing, Jay had often thought, if it didn't happen too often.

Now, the bedclothes tucked snugly around him, he closed his eyes and with the ease of long practice in strange places went almost immediately off to sleep again. In the morning out of sheer curiosity he would see what effects of the storm he could find.

Before breakfast at Pancho's counter he went for a walk along the shore of the lake. About a mile upstream he found what he was looking for, a brownish stain in the lake's clear water, growing stronger as he walked on, silt carried by the multitude of tributaries down to the main stream, proof of the force and cutting power of the down-rushing water which the thunderstorm had loosed. Where the silt-laden stream met the still waters of the lake, its motion slowed and then stopped altogether and there it would precipitate the material it had carried in suspension down from the mountain flanks.

He met John Boggs as he walked back to the motel. "I had

dinner at Williams's house last night," Jay said. "In case you were wondering, there was no bloodshed. And his daughter is coming up to go out in the boat with me this morning, so nobody objects to my diving in the lake."

Boggs only nodded, but some of the official wariness he had previously shown had already disappeared. The mere mention of Williams produced change.

"That storm last night," Jay said. "Have you heard any weather reports? Is there a front moving in?"

"There's rain to the west. Whether we'll get it—" Boggs shrugged. His expression changed. "I hear tell you'll be leaving us soon. Calgary, is it?"

So the motel clerk both listened and talked, Jay thought, not that it mattered much. "You keep up on things," he said.

"It's my job to know what's going on."

Jay looked at the curving face of the dam and thought of last night's talk. "You know they're going to enlarge the dam?" he said.

"Where did you hear that?"

"Last night."

Boggs turned to look at the dam's concrete face, at the normal watermark twenty feet above the lake's present level. "It's too big now." The words were not so much protest as expression of surprise. He looked again at Jay's face, seemed to search it for verification. "That'll make the lake bigger, won't it?"

"And deeper. A lot of water for a thirsty city. More electricity to run more hair dryers." Jay was aware that the bitterness he felt came through.

"You're against it?" Boggs said.

"It's none of my business."

And yet, Jay thought as he went in to breakfast, there remained that feeling of kinship with the valley and with the drowned village, a feeling he found impossible to shake.

6

Father Rodriguez was the priest of the *barrio* Church of the Holy Faith, a small man in his late sixties, customarily dressed in rusty black, and usually, because he was weak enough to suffer from the human frailty called vanity, in a black beret as well to hide his baldness.

He had spent forty-five years in the *barrio*, and was content with his lot. His parishioners brought their problems to him as a matter of course.

Angelita Leyba, fat and fiftyish, mother of eleven, a widow, dressed as always in unrelieved black, had her problem on this day. It concerned Juan Cisneros.

"He says he can afford to go fishing now," Angelita said, "and with his big car and his store and all, I suppose he can."

Father Rodriguez was sure of it. The only thing was that he had never known Juan Cisneros to display the slightest interest in fishing before.

"You know that when he came back from the war, the big war, Inocencio—may he rest in peace—lived for a while up above Harper's Park."

"I remember."

"He built a little house. When we were younger, we would sometimes drive up there on a weekend. But never on Sunday, Padre; we never missed Mass."

"I know," the priest said.

"When Inocencio went to his reward, may he rest in peace, the lawyer told me that the property, the little house and the land, not much land, ten acres, I think, now belonged to me. But what would I do with it without Inocencio? And so I have done nothing. I have not even seen it for three, four years. And now Juan Cisneros wants to buy it, but all I can think is that it was Inocencio's, the land he worked on, the house he built, and I do not know what to do."

Father Rodriguez was silent, thoughtful.

"Two thousand dollars," Angelita said, "is a great deal of money. We are poor people. With two thousand dollars—" She raised eyebrows, shoulders, and hands all at once in a gesture of awe at the enormity of the sum. "Maybe a new cookstove. Boots like the vaqueros wear for Felipe. Luis wants a—skateboard, María-Victoria new pants that are almost indecent. What should I do, Padre?"

"There is no need for haste," the priest said. "You have waited this long, another day or two—"

"Juan Cisneros says that when he decides to do something, he wants to do it quickly. Or not at all."

That was Juan Cisneros all right, the priest thought. "Give me a little time, Angelita. I will think about it and let you know." Dismissal.

The priest watched Angelita waddle down the aisle of the church, pause, turn, and genuflect and then walk out into the sunlight. Father Rodriguez turned his thoughts on Juan Cisneros.

Like the mayor, Juan Cisneros (HONEST JOHNNY'S—TV—RADIO —APPLIANCES) was a product of the *barrio*. To Father Rodriguez, Johnny was also an enigma.

Father Rodriguez had watched Juan Cisneros grow up, hustling, always hustling, a businessman by the time he was eight, working the Plaza, the *turistas*, as guide, purchasing agent, pimp, knowing the places where one could get a drink on dry Sundays, or a joint of Mary Jane for those whose tastes ran that way, knowing available women, bargains in silver-and-turquoise jewelry (neither silver nor turquoise), genuine Indian rugs (from machine looms in Mexico), always on his toes, always running.

Boys like Juan Cisneros sorely strained the good father's faith in humanity, and yet HONEST JOHNNY's warehouse on the riverbank and the retail store up near the Plaza, right on the fringe of the high-rent district, were proof that such boys did not always turn out as lost as one would expect.

The father was not a betting man, but his long life in the *barrio* had acquainted him with betting practices, and watching Juan Cisneros grow up he would have given six, three, and even that Johnny's eventual niche, if not an early grave, would be at the heart and core of whatever rackets were most profitable among the inmates of the state penitentiary. Instead, behold the respectable businessman. And yet in the back of the father's mind was the conviction that beneath the legitimate Johnny Cisneros, there still lurked the boy Juan who never took his eye off the ball, and never did things without reason, inevitably profitable.

Angelita Leyba's dilemma wanted careful thought, the priest decided. And what if in the end his advice was wrong? He was no businessman. Nor, he told himself sternly, was he in a position to shirk his responsibilities. He had been asked for help. He would give the best help it was in his power to give.

.   .   .

Father Rodriguez walked from the *barrio* church to the Plaza, and on, into the alien territory of the better shops and high-rise buildings where HONEST JOHNNY's retail outlet was located. He stood for a little time outside the store, admiring the shining window display.

There were television sets of great magnificence with screens larger than any the priest had seen, housed in obviously expensive cabinets. There were allegedly high-fidelity tuners, amplifiers, and receivers combining both, each with myriad dials and knobs, the uses of which the priest did not even attempt to guess. There were loudspeakers, and one, a cutaway, showed not one actual speaker inside, but eight, evenly spaced; they seemed to stare arrogantly at the small man in the rusty black suit and the black beret as if the genie within the monster understood full well the awe in the good father's mind.

The priest roused himself at last and walked inside the store. A salesman intercepted him with a skeptical smile. "Something I can do for you, Father?"

"I would like to speak with Juan Cisneros."

"Johnny? Sure. He's back in his office." And then, with a broad smile: "Has he been sinning?"

I would not be at all surprised, the priest thought, but merely smiled indulgently and followed the salesman's pointing gesture through the floor displays to the rear of the building.

Cisneros was at his desk, the telephone to his ear. He saw the priest and waved him to a chair. "What I mean," he said into the phone, "if you want the business, then you perform. I can deal with Dallas or Denver just as easy as I can deal with you. You said you'd ship today. Now you say maybe next week. I don't do business that way, you understand what I mean? I tell a customer he'll get his TV tomorrow morning first thing, then he better be home because his doorbell will ring at eight o'clock sharp. That's the way I perform. I expect my suppliers to perform the same way. Okay? Now let's cut this shit about next week. I want those sets on the truck today rolling in this direction." He hung up and swung his chair to face the priest.

"You're lucky you're in your business, Padre. Here it's nothing but hassle. What can I do for you?"

Away from his church and the majesty it represented, Father Rodriguez thought, he was at a disadvantage. Here he was dealing with the secular world which he did not understand, where the ground rules were different and values were those which man, not God, had set. And Juan Cisneros, like a jungle cat in his native habitat, was a creature who combined craftiness, strength, and a total lack of scruples. For a moment the priest regretted his decision to come, and told himself that the weakness was both craven and unworthy.

"You have offered to buy the property of Angelita Leyba, Juan." Unconsciously, as always in times of stress, he spoke in Spanish.

Nothing changed in Johnny's face, or even in his eyes; he remained the picture of a man without guile. "Sure." He spoke English, totally unaccented. "Like I told her, Padre, I want a place where I can relax. You know, a little fishing, maybe a few pals up from here for drinks and some food and a friendly poker game. That kind of thing." He winked, and smiled suddenly. "Maybe privacy too, Padre, but we won't go into that."

The priest was aware of the man's reputation for womanizing, and while of course he disapproved, there were, he had long ago decided, worse sins than those of the flesh. "Those are your only reasons, Juan?"

Johnny's smile was open and friendly. "What else?"

The trouble was, the priest thought, he could think of no answer to that question although he had been trying ever since Angelita's visit to find the ulterior motive he was convinced was there.

Johnny watched the priest's face, and let his friendly smile disappear. "Hell, Padre—excuse the expression—but if the old girl wants to make such a big deal out of it, probably using you to try to shake me down for more money, why, let's forget the whole thing. I just thought I'd do myself a favor, and her too, but not if it's going to get into a hassle. I got enough hassles right here. I sure don't need any more."

Juan's motives sounded plausible, Father Rodriguez thought, especially the hint about privacy in which to indulge his carnal desires. And all he, Father Rodriguez, had to set against Juan's stated motives was unfounded suspicion, which was an attitude both uncharitable and unchristian. And the last thing he wanted was to spoil a legitimate, and for Angelita profitable, transaction. "I will tell Angelita what you have said."

Johnny's expression now turned doubtful. "I don't know, Padre. I just don't know. I don't want the old girl bitching that I pulled a fast one on her. Maybe I better just stay clear of the whole thing."

There was here a false note, the priest thought, and he pounced upon it. "I do not recall that anything anyone ever had to say about you weighed very heavily upon your conscience, Juan."

Johnny smiled easily. A shrewd little old bastard, he thought, who saw things a lot more clearly than you would expect, but he had his own ready answer. "I'm a businessman now, Padre, and I got a reputation to worry about. You get people talking, and, you know—or maybe you don't know, Padre, but it's true—people start saying bad things and business starts to fall off. That's why I don't want the Leyba woman unhappy. But if you say it's okay, then I'll go along. Tell her the offer holds. But I want to wrap it up, you know what I mean? I hate having things dragging along. She can have the money this afternoon, soon as she signs the papers my lawyer will bring her. Okay?"

He was over his depth, Father Rodriguez told himself, floundering around in this alien environment. It was small consolation that he thought he had done his best because he had a feeling that somehow he had failed. But there it was. "I will tell her, Juan," he said.

Johnny watched in the angled wall mirror which showed the entire store until the priest was out on the sidewalk. Then he picked up the phone and called his attorney. "All systems are go on that land purchase I told you about, Manny. First thing this afternoon get the fat bitch's signature on the bill of sale and give her the money. Two thousand. I want the whole thing recorded and wrapped up today."

"What's the hurry, you're so anxious to start fishing? You don't even like fish."

"Manny, I told you what I want. Do I have to give you reasons?"

"Okay. Okay. Don't get in an uproar. I'll handle it."

"And call me soon as you have it locked up." Johnny started to hang up, and then changed his mind. "And, Manny? That bill of sale. I want it to read 'For one dollar and other valuable considerations,' you know what I mean? No actual sale price."

"I know exactly what you mean," Manny's knowing voice said. "Okay."

One more call to make, this one to State Senator Walt Duggan at his insurance brokerage business. "Okay, Walt. We'll have the Leyba property this afternoon. You're sure about that dam enlargement approval?"

"I told you, Johnny. It's just a formality, but it has to go through my committee, so I have the word direct. And I don't want my name in the deal at all."

"It won't be. Just your money. By the way, there's one thing. The fat Leyba bitch sent the priest up here. He just left."

"Why did she send him?"

"Why do you think? You're a *barrio* Chicana like she is, and you got questions, you go to the church. The church fixes everything. Including the price of land."

"Now, wait a minute, Johnny."

"Four hundred bucks an acre. Four thousand dollars. You want in, or not?"

"Damnit, Johnny, we agreed on two!"

"That was before the church got into the act. Now the price is four big ones. I'm going to take it. If you want in—"

"Goddamnit, Johnny, it was my idea! My information!"

"So do you want in, or not?"

There was heavy silence on the phone. Walt Duggan said at last, "Okay. Fifty-fifty, as we agreed."

"I'll expect your check for two thousand."

Duggan's voice was both resigned and resentful. "You'll get it soon as I see the bill of sale."

"Fair enough, Walt."

Johnny hung up again and sat quiet for a time, thinking that the goddamned smug Anglos were just as vulnerable as anybody else. No matter how you looked at it, Honest Johnny Cisneros was going to come out of the deal with half the Leyba property, which was going to be worth a bundle, which was not bad, not bad at all.

On the strength of his triumph he made yet a third telephone call. It was a female voice that answered.

"Dinner tonight, baby," Johnny said. "How about the Hilton?"

"Well, well!"

"Okay?"

"Okay."

"I want you in a real good mood. I got things in mind for after dinner."

The girl's laugh was soft, pleased, bringing to Johnny's mind memory of those splendid breasts and soft, silky-smooth thighs. "Don't you always?" the girl said. "I'll be ready."

Johnny hung up. All in all, he thought, a good morning's work.

•   •   •

The sky was the incredible blue it frequently was when you saw it from high elevations through thin atmosphere; against it the jagged mountains stood out sharp and clear. Only the raucous sound of the outboard motor disturbed the scene, Jay thought, and when he switched it off and let the little boat drift, the silence was a welcome relief.

Slowly the ripples died away. The surface of the lake became flat and again transparent. "There it is," he said, pointing downward. "A dead museum. There's the church, minus its bell. There's the mill, the smithy, houses, barns—" He looked at Kate's face and tried to probe her thoughts.

"You resent it, don't you?" Kate's voice was quiet, expressionless.

"It has nothing to do with me. Not really. I just wanted to see it." That was the original idea, true, but it was a little more than that now.

First there was Pancho's offhand mention of the tremor and the seiche; then Bill Williams's confident talk of the dam enlargement; and finally telephone calls to three widely spaced seismographs where he, Jay, had geophysicist friends. And now what both impelled him and troubled him was more than mere curiosity and the simple desire that each year sent all those tourists to Europe and the U.K. to have a look at the tombs of their ancestors—if they could find them.

Kate watched him pull on his fins, struggle into his air tank harness, and fasten his weighted belt. There was about him this morning, she thought, a kind of intensity that had not been discernible last night, a certain purposefulness in his movements as if each motion was of more than ordinary importance. "Is something wrong?"

Jay glanced at her briefly and shook his head. "Nothing wrong."

"I hadn't thought of it before, but don't scuba divers usually dive in pairs? I read that somewhere."

"The buddy system." Jay nodded. "Sometimes. But there's nothing to worry about here. I'm not going into any of those buildings where I might need help if I got stuck."

Nothing to worry about, he thought, unless another tremor hit. Three-point-nine on the Richter Scale, the seismograph records had showed. No big deal like a major quake, but enough, ample to set the lake water in strong motion, which would fling him about like a chip in a river rapid. Okay, that part of it he had to put up with if he was going to dive at all.

He dipped his faceplate into the water, emptied it, spat in it,

rubbed the front, and put it on. He started his watch to time
his air supply. "Thirty minutes," he said in a hollow, nose-
blocked voice, "no more, maybe less." He slipped his mouthpiece securely into place, put his hand over his faceplate to
hold it tight, and, with the underwater light in the other hand,
made little splash as he slipped over the side. Kate watched
him begin his descent into the cold, clear water.

She could remember before the dam was built when the
village had been occupied, but her memories were vague.
Harper's Park then had been merely a place you went through
on your way into the high country for picnics or camping trips,
and if it had any particular flavor it was not apparent to a girl
engaged in the difficult business of growing up.

Now, looking down through the water, watching Jay glide
effortlessly like a large aquatic beast among the buildings and
into the graveyard, she found herself wishing that she had
taken the time and effort to know the village and the people
who lived in it before it was covered by the waters of the lake.

She knew of old Jed Harper, of course, as who in the area
did not? He was the local legend, the real-life mountain man,
no doubt blown up to larger than lifesize by tales that had long
since lost their fine accuracy, but even free of embellishment a
figure at whom one could gaze in awe when you thought of his
lonely challenge to all this mountain vastness.

She supposed that she was being ridiculously romantic to at-
tribute on such short acquaintance some of old Jed's bold
qualities to his three-times great-grandson, but the temptation
was there, arising from several sources.

First and most important, probably, was her father's reaction. From the beginning last night, Kate had felt in her father
a sense of respect for Jay, something he accorded few men and
then usually only after long acquaintance. "Honey," her father
had said once, "you work with a man, or maybe you fish with
him or hunt with him or play poker with him, and finally you

get to know him. And most men don't stack up. Those that do —well, you count yourself lucky when you find one."

But last night her father's reaction to Jay had been immediate, and unhesitating. Maybe some kind of male chemistry had been at work. And Jay, she thought, had felt it too. Despite the age disparity, the two of them had hit it off—there was no other way to say it.

Sam, on the other hand, had resented Jay, probably precisely because of her father's reaction to him. Why? Jay posed no threat; he was here today and would be gone tomorrow, merely passing through. Why then waste energy on resentment? It was, she told herself, a woman's question and probably without meaning for men.

She concentrated again on the village buildings she could see so clearly on the lake bottom. Few people had still lived there, she remembered, when the dam was planned. There had been opposition, of course, to loss of homes and property; and she remembered sympathizing privately when she thought how awful it would be if her own home were to be purposely destroyed.

Now, submerged, she thought, the village took on an importance in her mind it had not had before. Studying through the cold, clear water the empty streets, the buildings themselves, the church, the smithy, the houses, all of them known to her from long ago, she could almost feel what Jay had said last night, that you would not be surprised to find wash hanging on a line because a sense of *living* still remained.

But against the needs of the city, the feelings of this tiny hamlet simply had to be unimportant, or so it had been decided when the dam site was chosen and approved, and of course she had accepted the decision as she accepted most grownup decisions, decrees from on high. It occurred to her now that she was no longer sure that the greatest good to the greatest number ought always to be the basic criterion. But wasn't that precisely what the environmentalists maintained, thereby frequently raising her father's blood pressure?

"Goddamnit, if they had their way," Williams had been known to say, "we'd still be living in caves and hunting with bows and arrows for enough food to keep us alive. Of course you have to upset some things when you start a project of any size. Why, hell's bells, just dig a well or a foundation for a house and you foul up some kind of 'ecology'—and you end with some extra dirt you have to get rid of too. The point is, is the benefit worth it? And when you're talking about more electricity and an assured water supply for a city of half a million people, then, goddamnit, the answer has to be yes."

Again looking down and watching Jay, who was nearing the limit of the graveyard, the light flashing intermittently as he went from headstone to headstone, Kate thought: I don't think he would agree with Daddy's assessment, and yet his life seems to be devoted to finding oil and gas in unlikely places, and doesn't that frequently involve basic changes too? One interesting question among many in her mind concerning Jay Harper.

.   .   .

Jay flashed the underwater light on the next gravestone and, with a little shock of recognition, stopped swimming to read carefully. The crudely chiseled and weathered letters read merely: "Jedediah Harper 1801–1888."

No epitaph, Jay thought; probably, from what he had learned about him, because old Jed had wanted it so. He had come into this country without fanfare, making his own way, asking help from no source. He would leave it in the same fashion, and unquestionably he had given orders to that effect.

No doubt it was being now in the actual presence of the grave that started a train of memories, and the exact words old

Jed had spoken, and Julia had recorded in her journal, now popped unbidden and with stunning force into Jay's mind:

"I've had a good life doing just what I wanted to do," the old man had said not long before his death. "Not many can say the same. Why, by God!, some folks spend their lives being afraid of living, and then they're afraid of dying! Will you tell me what sense that makes? I've gone whichever way my stick floated, enjoyed damn near every minute of it, and I have no regrets. You can't ask for more than that."

No, Jay thought, you couldn't. In capsule form those words summed up a lifetime, and when Jay had first read the journals he had thought long and hard about the words until he was sure he understood them.

"Whichever way my stick floated" was the key, and the old man's creed. It was whichever way curiosity and desire and courage and conscience led. Or impelled. Big words; big thoughts. Something for a boy to remember. Something to remember now. The thoughts were enough, more than enough. With his free hand, Jay made a gesture of farewell to the gravestone and swam on.

Julia's gravestone was newer, less weathered, chiseled by a more skilled hand. It read: "Julia Hopkins Harper, 1855–1930, Beloved Wife and Mother. R.I.P." She too, Jay thought, had gone where her stick floated, out of the settled East to this mountain valley, and here she had stayed. No epitaph needed for her, either; her journals spoke for themselves.

He realized that he was tense again, as he had been yesterday, one part of his mind and all his senses tuned to, even waiting for, the first movement of the water. He had no idea whether the time had passed quickly, or at a creeping pace, and he put the light on his watch to see. Twelve minutes of air left. Decision time, he told himself.

The choice was quite simple: whether to take the first step toward what might become involvement, or ignore what was actually none of his business and head at once for the boat. He had seen as much of the village as he had intended to see. He had found and paid his respects to Jed's grave and Julia's. As the military said, mission accomplished, no? No. Not yet.

Because, in Jed's phrase, his stick was floating now in a different direction, through no fault of his own, true, but he had damn well better follow it anyway, as Jed had followed his, or risk spending the rest of his life regretting that he had not.

He turned and swam purposefully toward the right-hand shore where the dam met the side of the gorge.

From the boat, Kate watched him disappear, and wondered where he had gone, and why. In only a few minutes she caught sight of him again, a figure and a shadow on the bottom, swimming back across the dam's face toward the far left-hand shore, and once more he disappeared.

She did not see him again until he surfaced suddenly only a few feet from the boat, raised his faceplate, took out his mouthpiece, and, treading water, handed the light over the gunwale. He followed it himself with a dexterous heave, and in only moments had the outboard motor started and the boat headed for the dock. Only then did he feel himself start to relax. Two dives and no trouble, he thought, no sudden water movements throwing him around helplessly. He was lucky. He would not crowd his luck again.

"Your teeth are chattering." Kate had to raise her voice above the engine's sound. "I felt the water. It's almost freezing." But there was something else, she thought, something troubling him deeply. "What is wrong? It is more than the cold."

He could smile then, but without conviction, a dissembling smile. "You should feel the North Sea." Jay shook his head. "The divers there, working on the bottom, setting up the drill-rig cables and anchors. They earn their pay." And then, as if in sudden decision, "Can you stick around? I'll buy you a cup of coffee. Twenty minutes in Pancho's greasy spoon."

"Of course. Will you tell me then what's wrong?"

He could still walk away, he told himself, and avoid any possible entanglement. But where, really, could be the harm in merely reporting what he now almost certainly knew? "I'll tell you part of it," he said. "But I have some work to do before I go into the whole thing."

7

On this day George Harrison took State Senator Walt Duggan to lunch at the Hilton. George did not much like Duggan, finding him deficient in education, gluttonous in his appetites, and coarse in his humor.

On the other hand, a state senator of Duggan's seniority was frequently useful in this far from perfect world, and George had seen to it that the balance of obligation between Duggan and himself was always weighted in his own direction.

As an apéritif George ordered a Beefeater martini, straight up, with a twist of lemon. Duggan took Bourbon, straight, with a ginger-ale chaser—a combination George considered an abomination—and compounded the offense by extending his pinkie and smacking his lips when he drank. George ignored the display as best he could.

"Full speed ahead on the Harper's Park dam enlargement, I understand," George said for openers.

Duggan shook his head admiringly. "You do get around, George. I just got the word myself."

"I have friends. I had the word yesterday from Washington."

"And now," Duggan said, "you're sitting pretty with that quarter section which will be lakefront property when the new water level is reached. Pretty smart, George."

"That," George said, "was what I wanted to talk to you about." It was difficult to keep annoyance, even anger out of his voice. Through the first drink, the second, and the main course—chef's salad for George; T-bone steak and baked potato for Duggan—George explained his predicament and his conviction that Bill Williams had bilked him.

Duggan thought about Johnny Cisneros, the Leyba property, and his own profit expectations and said at last, "I don't hardly see what I can do for you, George. Much as I'd like to oblige."

"I realize," George said, "that all of the formalities have been observed, studies made, environmental impact considered, all of that kind of thing."

"Right down to a gnat's eyebrow."

"But have you considered that an investigation may result, anyway, Walt?"

Duggan put down his knife and fork as if he had suddenly lost his appetite. "Why? I mean, what makes you say something like that?"

"It smacks of collusion, don't you think? Bill Williams is being blatant. But you and I know that there are others, insiders, who will turn out to have profited greatly. And federal funds are involved, which means that the General Accounting Office will be interested in those profits and in those who make them."

Duggan took a deep breath. "Jesus, George," he said, "just because somebody is lucky enough to buy land at the right time—"

"Lucky enough, or merely unscrupulous, Walt. These matters have a way of surfacing these days."

Duggan chewed a large mouthful of steak thoughtfully. "Just what do you want me to do, George? You want to spit in Bill Williams's eye. I see that. But what do you think I can do?"

"At least see that Williams does not get the contract for the work on the dam enlargement. For him to profit from his lack of scruples *and* from the construction contract as well would be just too much. Don't you think?"

"Oh, brother!"

"What does that mean?"

Duggan set down his knife and fork again. As he spoke he

emphasized his words by slapping his open hand lightly on the table. "In the first place, going up against Bill Williams is like picking a fight with a buzz saw. A man can get skinned up real good. In the second place, Bill's is the only construction outfit in the state big enough to do the job, and if we brought in somebody from outside there would simply be hell to pay and no pitch hot. And in the third place, that Harry Wilson dude up in the Governor's Mansion and Bill Williams are buddies from way back, and if you don't think Harry can get mean as a rattlesnake when he thinks somebody's trying to cross him, why, you just haven't tried butting heads with him, and I have." Duggan shook his head and slapped the table lightly once more. "No, George. I'd like to oblige you, I purely would. But this is a hassle I'm going to stay out of." And protect my own profits in the process, Duggan thought, but left that part unspoken.

All in all, George thought as he walked back to his office from the Hilton, it was pretty much a wasted luncheon. But he was not without influence in other directions, and this first rebuff had merely stiffened his resolve to see that Bill Williams failed to get at least some of his expected profits.

．　．　．

Again Jack Marble sat in Tom Gentry's office in the bank, this time feeling uncomfortable. "Uh, twenty-two thousand five," he said, "unsecured? I mean, you know how the Comptroller's people have been clamping down on that kind of loan, sir. Ever since the Lance business—" He stopped. He had been about to repeat himself, and those cold, gray eyes unnerved him. "Uh, how long would this loan be for? I mean, sometimes we know when the examiners are coming, of course, but sometimes we don't, too. I mean, either."

"I am buying some property, Jack," Tom Gentry said. "The property will secure the loan."

"Oh." In the single word there was vast relief. "Uh, may I ask where it is, sir? I mean, hadn't we better have a plat and a bill of sale, that kind of thing?"

"Fifty acres, Jack," Tom Gentry said. "Up near the Harper's Park lake. Four hundred fifty dollars an acre."

"Brooks Thompson's land?" Jack regretted the question as soon as it was asked.

"Do you have objections, Jack?"

"No, sir. I mean, no, not at all."

"Good."

Jack stood up. "You'll be wanting the money, won't you? I mean, a check?"

"Yes, Jack."

"Then I guess I'd better get right on the paper work." Those damned cold eyes, Jack thought; you could really imagine for a fact how they would look at you across the room, waiting for your first move toward your gun. Your first move, and almost certainly your last as well. "I'll get right on it."

"That will be fine."

.   .   .

His Honor Mayor José-María Lopez y Baca sat in his office without his jacket, shirt sleeves rolled up, necktie loosened. It was hot, and there was no air conditioning in the old city offices.

The mayor could remember vividly how sweltering it had been in late summer down in the *barrio*, where tin roofs in bright sunlight turned shacks into bake ovens; and even when it cooled off outside after the sun went down, the houses did not. You sweated all night, wished for morning, and, as a kid, assumed that this was man's normal lot. So now he paid little attention to the heat, and concentrated on the matter at hand.

"What we've got here," he said in his accentless English, "is one of those damned things everybody thinks somebody else ought to be responsible for, and nobody is. Carlito here"—he nodded at Carlos García, the schoolteacher—"brought it to my attention." He looked from the city chief of police to the city fire chief. "What happens if we get a disaster of some kind? Have we got any kind of plans?"

The chief of police was named Bud Henderson. He was large and beefy, a southwestern-born-and-bred Anglo who resented having a Chicano as his official boss, but that was the way the cards fell, there was nothing he could do about it, so he endured with what patience he could muster. But he could snipe a little. He said, "What kind of disaster?"

The mayor shook his head. "I don't know. A big fire. The kind of floods they've been getting in Texas. Maybe a tornado." He spread his hands. "The sort of thing you can't predict but would take evacuation of at least some part of the city. How would we cope?"

The fire chief, Rudy Smith, was also Anglo, but a quieter, more thoughtful man than Henderson, and lacking in racial resentment. He said, "Some time ago we had civil-defense plans. To tell the truth, I don't know what happened to them. They're probably in a file somewhere. But you're right, Mr. Mayor, we ought to have contingency plans at least for the *barrio*. It's a firetrap, and a rabbit warren." He glanced at Carlos García. "Sorry, but that's the plain truth."

"Hell," García said, "I know it better than you do, Rudy. The *barrio* goes right down to the river and that's what started me thinking when I read about those floods in Texas. It's a deathtrap too."

"There's the National Guard," the mayor said. "We could get them in. But we damn well better do some thinking in advance. You agree, Rudy?"

"I agree."

"Bud?"

"I'll go along with the crowd. One thing, though." The chief took his time. "You're talking about evacuating the *barrio*.

That's fine. Then you get looting." He too nodded at Carlos García. "He knows. Some of those smart-ass Chicano punks he tries to teach will steal anything that isn't chained down, and if they can find a pair of bolt cutters they'll steal that too."

The mayor opened his mouth and closed it again carefully. He looked at Carlos García and waited. García said slowly, carefully, his Spanish lilt quite plain, "Unfortunately, for reasons you would not understand, Chief, what you say is only too true."

"Okay," the mayor said then, closing the door on further possible provocation, "we just take looting into consideration as one of the factors involved." His voice had hardened a trifle. "What I want from you, Rudy, and from you, Bud, are disaster plans. Concentrate on the *barrio*, but don't forget the rest of the city, either. Let's meet here again next week. I want to see something on paper then."

And when the two chiefs had left: "They're hard to get along with sometimes, aren't they, Carlito?" the mayor said.

"We have our own who are just as bad," García said. "Maybe sometimes a little worse."

"Like Honest Johnny Cisneros?"

"He's a good example."

. . .

As before, the two German shepherds appeared as Jay got out of his car in the Williams courtyard. It was evening, and in the high-country twilight the dogs studied him gravely. "Do you want to frisk me for weapons too?" Jay said.

It had been a long, busy day and he was tired, but tonight he felt looser, easier in his mind than he had last night. Maybe it was because this was a business call, dealing with matters he understood, rather than a purely social engagement at which he was quite aware that he was never at his best. Only a few more minutes, and he could be on his way, conscience clear, having, like old Jed, followed where his stick floated without deviation.

Kate opened the door, unsmiling. She spoke to the dogs and they turned away. "Daddy's waiting," she said, and led the way across the entrance hall to a carved door Jay had not seen before. "I didn't really know what to tell him. You didn't tell me much."

"You'll hear it now, if you're interested."

She turned to study him as if in indecision. Slowly she nodded, knocked on the door, and opened it. "I am interested," she said, and walked into the study. Jay followed. To her father she said, "I am invited to stay. I'll be quiet, I promise."

Jay sat in a comfortable leather club chair facing Williams behind the desk. Kate sat on the leather sofa, legs curled beneath her.

"This is your show," Williams said to Jay. He was not today the affable host of last night. The change was subtle, but plain: he viewed this visit as business.

"Okay," Jay said. "I won't try to improvise a presentation. I don't have any charts or computer printouts. As a matter of fact, I have little data, but they seem to me conclusive. I had a close look at the sides of the dam this morning, on the bottom, and a little above it. The rock sides of the gorge which support the dam show signs of fracturing. You had an earthquake—"

"It was a damn little one," Williams said. "We hardly felt it."

Jay nodded. "Down here. Up there, according to local accounts, the water in the lake sloshed the way coffee does in a cup when you carry it on a saucer. That's called a seiche and it means there was more than a little bit of earth movement nearby. There was. I did some telephoning to some people I know. The Richter Scale reading on the seismographs was three-point-nine, and the epicenter was right in the area, which is why you didn't feel the tremor as much down here."

"Hardly noticed it."

Again Jay nodded. "Have you noticed the others?"

"What others? There haven't been any."

"I did some more phoning after I dove this morning," Jay said. His smile was wry. "I probably used up whatever Brownie points I had accumulated, but I got some people to check back on seismograph readings for the last five years. During that time in the area we're talking about, Harper's Park Valley, there have been twenty-three measurable tremors, of which this last, at a Richter reading of three-nine, was the strongest." Jay spread his hands. "I thought you ought to know." Again that wry smile. "For free."

Williams's face showed nothing. "And your conclusion?"

The wry smile was gone. Jay said slowly, "That enlargement of the dam doesn't seem like a very good idea. That it may not even be safe as it is.

"The Corps of Engineers keeps routine track of all dams of any size, and they'll have this one on their lists as 'highly hazardous.' That doesn't mean they think it's unsafe: Obviously they don't, or after their investigation they wouldn't have given you an okay for enlargement.

"What 'highly hazardous' means to them is that the dam is above a large population center, and if anything were to happen, maybe wartime and a missile strike, bombing, anything at all, why, the dam could kill an awful lot of people if it broke. And with 'highly hazardous dams,' that is dams above large population centers, I don't think you can take *any* chances. Or shouldn't."

Williams took his time. "A lot of people talked about danger when we built it. But it's still there. Even with all those earthquakes you say have happened."

Jay said nothing. Williams's reaction was neither more nor less than he had expected. Unpleasant news is rarely palatable and resistance here was almost inevitable. He was conscious that Kate was watching him, but he kept his eyes on Williams while he waited.

Williams said obliquely, commencing a fresh line of resistance, "If you'd been here ten years ago—"

"I'd have been against building a dam," Jay said, "flooding a village and ruining a lovely valley. But I'd just have been clicking my teeth, and I'd have known it. I'm talking about something else now."

"Suppose," Williams said, "that you thought the dam was perfectly safe. How would you feel then about enlarging it?"

And this question too, Jay thought, was merely a continuation of the resistance. "To get more electricity to run more hair blowers and can openers?" he said. "And more water to sweep grass cuttings off green lawns that have no business in this part of the world in the first place?" He shook his head. "I'd be against it." He smiled wearily. "But I'd still just be clicking my teeth and I'd know it. The great god 'progress' is both demanding and insatiable."

Williams watched in silence, his face expressionless.

"So," Jay said, "if you're implying, as you are, that my testimony is biased, then I can only say that I'm giving you my best professional advice, not personal preference. On the data that I have, which is admittedly incomplete, in my judgment that dam you have up there, as it stands, let alone with any enlargement, is a potential hazard that had better be looked into very carefully."

The room was still. Williams said at last, "The lawyers like to use a word, 'arguendo,' meaning let's suppose. Okay, 'arguendo' your worry is correct. What could happen? And why hasn't it happened already?"

Jay nodded. This was something tangible to explain. He settled down to make it clear. "A few facts. The lake is close to twenty feet below normal now. Let's say, very conservatively, that the lake is ten square miles in area. It's more than that, but no matter. Ten square miles is six thousand four hundred acres. One acre-foot of water is just what it says: the amount of water it would take to cover one acre to a depth of one foot. You're with me so far?"

Nothing changed in Williams's face. "I can follow the arithmetic."

"Now, one acre-foot of water," Jay said, "weighs a little under three million pounds. I thought the question might come up, so I worked it out. Multiply the weight of that single acre-foot of water by the number of surface acres, and multiply that by the twenty-foot depth of water that isn't there now, and you come up with just under one hundred and seventy-five million *tons*, not pounds, of additional weight of water that dam will have to hold back when it is filled to normal again. That may be why nothing has happened already: because of the drought, that additional weight, pressure against the dam, hasn't been there."

Kate closed her eyes. Unreal, she thought; and yet it was not, not if the man knew what he was talking about. She opened her eyes to watch him again.

"Now," Jay said, "when the drought breaks, it may break gradually, and then again it may not. Last night's thunderstorm dumped a lot of rain somewhere in a very short time."

Williams said, "How do you know that?"

"Because the stream coming into the lake was carrying silt this morning, which meant that it had been cutting, eroding, instead of flowing in its normal clear harmless way."

Williams's nod was almost imperceptible, grudgingly accepting the point.

"But suppose the drought breaks," Jay said, "not gradually, with a succession of gentle rains, but all at once with four, five, six inches of rain in the mountains, the kind of drought break they've had in Texas. Then instead of a slow rise of the lake level, what you get is a gully-washer banging down from those high canyons. You grew up here. You know what flash floods can do."

Again that barely perceptible nod, mere reluctant acknowledgment, no more than that.

"For all practical purposes," Jay said, "water, any liquid, is
noncompressible. That's what makes hydraulic systems work."

Williams shook his head. "I don't see the connection."

"You have a container full of water," Jay said, "and you hit
it on the side with a hammer. It doesn't give like a sofa cushion, compressing and absorbing the shock. Instead what it does
is transmit the force of that hammer blow in every direction
without losing any of its force. If you have a weak place in the
container, maybe a pane of glass clear on the other side, it will
probably break."

Slowly Williams nodded. "I think I see it now."

"So," Jay said, "a flash flood of, say, a few million tons of
water banging down into the head of that lake would be exactly the same as if it slammed against the dam itself because
the lake water, being noncompressible, would transmit the entire impact just like the hammer blow."

Kate made a restless, stirring movement on the sofa, but said
nothing. Her eyes were fixed almost hypnotically on Jay's face.

"And if there is weakness in the supporting rock structure,"
Jay said, "if the signs of fracturing I saw this morning are indicative of what I think they are, and the tremors on the seismograph records have damaged or distorted the existing rock
formations, then your dam might be unable to stand the shock
of that flash flood."

Williams said tonelessly, "Go ahead. Finish the story."

"If the dam gives way in only one place," Jay said, "then the
whole thing goes as well because its strength is its unity. The
term 'highly hazardous' wouldn't be just a designation on a
piece of paper any longer. Think of Johnstown in 1889, only
this would be worse, much worse, with the whole city downstream."

Kate sat motionless, her eyes turned now on her father. He
had not moved in his chair and his expression had not

changed. Not even his strong hands, she thought, had made any of the small telltale motions that betray emotion. At that moment he was a stranger, almost a nonhuman unaffected by the possibility of disaster.

Williams said at last, "As we agreed, 'arguendo.' *If* this, and *if* that—you paint quite a picture. But as you said last night, you try not to be wrong any oftener than you can help it."

"I could be wrong," Jay said. "I hope I am."

"But—" This was Kate, unable any longer to keep her silence. "But you don't think you are."

Jay's face too was expressionless, and his tone betrayed nothing. "But I don't think I am." He stood up. "That's all I came to say. That, and thanks again for the dinner last night."

Williams still did not move. "What now?"

"There's that job waiting in Alberta." Jay smiled gently at Kate. "I can find my way out, and the guard troops will see me to the car."

"I haven't thanked you for this morning, the village, the—"

"*De nada.* It was a pleasure." He was gone.

They heard the front door close gently, and somehow Kate and her father were very much alone in an empty room.

"You—" Kate began, and there she stopped and shook her head, her eyes on her father's face, but no words in her mind.

"Still giving me the benefit of the doubt, honey?" Williams said. His smile was crooked, painful. "Let's not jump too fast." He raised one hand as Kate started to rise. "No, stick around, while I try to see where we are." He took an address book from the desk drawer, consulted it, pulled the phone close, and dialed a ten-digit number.

While he waited for the connection to be made, he sat quiet, as before, staring at the window, the great mountains, deliberately closing his mind to the implications of the possibility Jay had suggested.

There were always the doom chanters, the viewers-with-alarm, the damn fools who assured you that the world was going to end next Tuesday at exactly half past ten. There were those big brains too who figured out that the universe was either collapsing or exploding, and it didn't make much difference which because there wouldn't be anything left when it was all over—in two, three hundred billion years. And there were—

To the quiet voice speaking suddenly in his ear he said, "J.G.? Bill Williams here. How the hell are you?"

Kate sat quiet, legs tucked beneath her, watching her father's face, listening to his voice, which suddenly seemed no longer a part of him, but rather the voice of an actor speaking another's lines, filled with false camaraderie, or maybe it was real, but which had no place here and now.

Preliminary greetings over, Williams said at last, "A young fellow here, a geophysicist, does oil work. I wondered if you'd ever heard of him. Harper is his name, Jay Harper. He—" He stopped, and was silent, listening.

Kate watched her father's face and all at once his eyes met hers, held them, still the expressionless eyes of a stranger. She wanted to look away, and could not.

It seemed an interminable time before Williams said at last, "Thanks, J.G. I don't know whether I like it or not, but that's what I wanted to know. No, it doesn't have a goddamned thing to do with oil or gas. I wish to hell it did. Fly on up one of these days and I'll give you some fishing. See you." He hung up and leaned back in his chair.

Kate said, "He knows him? Jay?"

"He's done work for them." Williams produced a smile that was not convincing. "J.G. says he's one of the best, one of the new breed I don't know much about, computers and seismographs and gravity measurements and God knows what all, *and* the kind of mathematics you can't even read, let alone understand, symbols instead of numbers—" He stopped suddenly. "I'm babbling."

It was an admission totally unlike her father, and Kate felt a sudden pang of pity. "What are you going to do?" she said.

Williams seemed to gather himself. He produced a fresh smile, almost natural and convincing this time. "The point is, honey, you put him at an oil field with all the equipment he needs and a computer to work things out, and he's a ring-tailed whiz. But down on the bottom of a lake, just looking at rock, he's probably no better than the next guy. So I'm not going to go off half cocked and start hollering 'Fire!' Not yet. Not by a long shot."

"You won't do—anything?"

"Of course I will, honey." His voice gathered confidence as he spoke. "I'll talk with Sam Martin, and we'll plug in the Corps of Engineers, and all around we'll just make sure that everything's all right. Maybe we'll have to patch up a little here, and a little there, Sam can work on that, but the important thing—"

"You won't—stop the project until you're sure, call in other experts, geologists, people who know?"

Williams put his hands flat on the desk. "Honey," he said, "it's taken almost two years to get the enlargement plan where it is now. You stop a project at that point, and you've killed it. Dead. Believe me, I know." He shook his head. "We'll go ahead. We'll use some caution, but we'll go ahead. It can't be as bad as Harper thinks. It stands to reason it isn't." The smile appeared for yet a third time, full-blown now. "How about the benefit of the doubt, huh? You'll see. Your old man knows what he's doing."

He watched Kate uncurl her long legs and stand up slowly, her eyes avoiding his. She said nothing as she walked to the door and went out of the room, closing the door gently behind her.

She did not believe his assurances, Williams told himself. And the goddamned trouble was that he didn't believe them himself.

8

The pikas were out, squirrel-sized, industrious high-elevation rabbit cousins, sunning themselves in the rocks on this fine afternoon while they watched over their carefully gathered grasses spread out to dry for winter fodder.

A vulture soared past on dihedral wings, rocking gently in the variant updrafts, but the pikas paid no heed. No danger there; vultures were interested only in dead meat. An eagle, now, or a large hawk—

Somewhere on the slope a marmot whistled, the sound as shrill as that from a man with two fingers thrust into his mouth. Instantly the steep slope was alert. The vulture watched without much interest.

There was a trail of sorts, faint, in places broken away, rising in sharp switchbacks on the mountain face; and a man came up it at the slow, deliberate pace of the experienced mountain walker.

He wore shorts and climbing boots over heavy rolled socks, a khaki shirt with the sleeves rolled up, and a shapeless brimmed hat with a single vivid blue feather from the tail of a Steller's jay stuck jauntily in the band. He carried a bulging day pack and a staff, and he wore a 35mm camera and a pair of lightweight binoculars, their carrying straps crossed on his chest.

His name was Pete Otero. At a distance, standing alone and with no measuring standards nearby, he might appear to be a muscular, well-built middleweight. He was in fact six inches over six feet in his socks and still held his playing weight of two hundred and sixty-five pounds. There was an eight-inch surgical scar on his right knee, and there were times when he wondered if the scar was in his mind as well.

He was in no hurry this fine afternoon. The Mount Union fire lookout would put him up for the night, snug and warm, very warm. Strictly speaking, this kind of hospitality was probably against Forest Service regulations, but Bernie was an understanding girl, and she and Pete had long had this kind of occasional thing that worked well for both of them, something more than casual, but far less than demanding, and whose business was it but theirs, anyway?

The marmot whistled his warning again. Pete grinned at the sound, waited until the echoes had died across the high valley, and then with two fingers in his mouth blew a precisely tuned answering whistle which sent nearby pikas skittering to their tiny cave entrances to wait upon further events.

"I'm harmless, fellows," Pete said aloud as he walked on. "Honest."

The trail was steep, and here at something over twelve thousand feet the air contained little oxygen, but Pete's pace was steady, if deliberate, and his breathing deep, but still easy. There was nothing wrong with his wind, and the knee was as good as ever, almost. There were even times when he was tempted to give it another try, just turn up at training camp one early fall as a free agent and see what happened—and he knew perfectly well that stupid as he might be sometimes, he wasn't that stupid, because the best orthopod around had made it plain that one more injury of the wrong kind and Pete Otero would walk with a fused knee and a stiff leg for the rest of his life.

And so, he had to tell himself from time to time, you can't even dream any more. It's too dangerous. That was the part that hurt worst of all.

That was why sometimes his need for Bernie Adams was much more than just physical. The best way he could explain it even in his own mind was that between himself and Bernie there was a kind of like-to-like attraction.

During summers Bernie deliberately chose the lonely life on top of a fourteen-thousand-foot mountain when most guys and girls her age, and his, were frolicking in weekend groups. Well, he, Pete Otero, maybe because of his size, had felt that same kind of need for withdrawal all his life too.

It was deep stuff, that; the kind of jive shrinks handed out. And Pete saw no real need to take motives or feelings apart. It was like pulling the petals off a flower to see what held it together.

What it all amounted to was that he was comfortable with Bernie just the way he was comfortable with these big mountains, the warm sun on his back, the sky that stretched from here to yonder and beyond. Yes, and even that buzzard swinging in his wide circles on those invisible updrafts. So why try to break it into pieces and maybe spoil it?

It was an hour now since his last stop; time to take five. He sat on a flat-topped, sun-warmed rock, slipped off his pack, and got out the small plastic box of gorp—mixed peanuts, raisins, and chocolate M&M's; quick and lasting nutrition. Unconsciously while he munched, he unslung the binoculars and had a look around.

From Bernie's lookout on top of Mount Union, the view was unobstructed, but even here, with high peaks all around, he was looking at God only knew how many tens of thousands of square miles of country, some of it forested, some naked rock, here and there the sparkle of water, running or still, there the sprawl of the city's outskirts and the painted plains stretching endlessly beyond.

Closer, he caught movement in the glasses and quickly brought into focus three mountain goats moving on a treacherous, almost nonexistent ledge as easily as if it were flat meadow. He watched them for a few moments, admiring their balance and easy agility, smiling as he thought what a running back that big fellow would make, all horns and hooves and shifting pivots to fake a tackler right out of his socks.

It had often amused Pete to think how puffed up humans tended to be about their physical accomplishments when all you had to do was look at animal speed, strength, or agility to realize how puny man really is.

He started to put the binoculars down when something else caught his attention; the sparkle of standing water where he remembered none quite so high. He studied it for a time seeking the cause.

The torrents of rain that had fallen during last night's thunderstorm, he decided, had loosened rock from the steep mountain face, and this had plunged down and across a natural bowl, what Pete believed they called a hanging valley, to come to rest at the bottom and form a kind of dam behind which a small lake had formed fed by constant seepage from rock fractures above.

There were times, he had often thought, when it almost seemed that the mountains arranged things to suit themselves, sometimes malevolently, as when they loosened rock slides or avalanches to trap or crush unwary humans; sometimes selfishly, as with Denali, the Great One, which some called Mount McKinley, generating their own cloud cover to hide themselves from view; sometimes, as here, setting about reconstructing the landscape in whatever form and shape they chose. He supposed it was a childish concept, but there it was. When you got to know the mountains, they were *alive*.

He hung the binoculars around his neck again, put away the plastic container of gorp, and heaved the pack to his shoulders. When he stood up from the flat rock, there was stiffness in his right knee, but it no longer caused him even annoyance.

Maybe, he thought as he started on up the trail again, just maybe he was beginning to learn to live with the realization that Pete Otero was not the superman he had once privately thought himself to be.

Mountains, even young, jagged mountains rarely rise to sharp, witch's-hat peaks. Mount Union, 14,026 feet, dominated the local area, but its top, tilted only slightly, resembled a huge, irregular table with ample space for a helicopter to land periodically with supplies for Bernie Adams in her solitary lookout post.

Pete Otero came over the rim of the table in his steady, unhurried pace, waved at Bernie in her glassed-in eyrie, and paused as he always did for a brief look back. So, he had often thought, must the gods have looked down from Olympus.

He could see now the entire course of the stream and its tributaries that flowed into Harper's Park, the lake behind the dam, the curving gorge the river had cut below the dam with its occasional wide, green meadows dotted with houses, the further course of the silvery water where it curved around The Bend and entered the crowded area of the city proper.

The east-west rails gleamed now in the setting sun, and light reflecting from a thousand windows winked up at him. On the horizon, clearly etched against the sunset, the symmetrical peak of Teta, one hundred and fifty miles away, dominated the western plain.

Northwest to southeast, a full one hundred and eighty degrees, the lesser peaks of this mountain mass marched off into infinity, their lower slopes already in shadow.

To the west above the setting sun heavy clouds suspended tendrils of virga, precipitation evaporating before it reached the ground, threat, but not yet actuality. To the north the sky had darkened, gray cloud masses streaked here and there with reflected sunset glow which, when it colored snowcapped mountains, the Spanish had named Sangre de Cristo, Blood of Christ.

Bernie had come out on the walk-around porch of the lookout. She wore, as usual when she was dressed at all, faded jeans, wool socks, leather moccasins, and a flannel shirt. A large Malamute dog had appeared beside her. He stood quiet, watching. Bernie was smiling. "Did you just walk up to admire the view?"

Pete nodded solemnly. "More or less."

"Then have your look and walk right back down again."

"It's getting dark, lady."

"Tough."

"Where am I going to cook this steak I brought?"

"Oh."

"And drink the wine?"

"No martinis?"

"Gin and vermouth. I figured to put them together. Carefully. I even brought a lemon."

"Under those circumstances," Bernie said, "I guess we'll have to put up with you." She snapped her fingers at the dog. "Go down and bring him up, Sam."

Inside the lookout it was warm despite the growing outside chill. "Wonderful stuff, solar heat," Bernie said. "Some days I have to open up to get rid of it. Sun coming through all this double-pane glass—" She stopped, suddenly shy, aware that Pete for all his strength and bulk felt it too. For a few moments there was silence between them. "Well," Bernie said, "aren't you going to take that thing off your back?"

Pete slipped off the bulging day pack and handed it to her. With both hands it was an effort for her to carry it to the sink shelf. She was smiling again. "A burro wouldn't carry this up that trail. Neither would a mule."

"I'm not as smart as either one."

"Cut that out. You hear?" She shook her head in sudden anger with herself. "Sorry." The smile reappeared, not quite convincing. "How's the knee?"

"Fine."

Bernie watched him steadily.

"As good as it's ever going to be," Pete said, "which is good enough for anything I'll need it for."

Bernie said slowly, carefully, "I read you were in Hollywood."

"That's me." He wore now a crooked smile. "Old football players never die; they just go to tinsel town. You see a lot of old friends, Jimmy Brown, Karras, O.J., Dandy, Woody Strode I watched when I was a kid." Pete shook his head.

"But you came back."

He nodded then. "There was somebody I wanted to see." It was a statement, no question, but his mind was still while he waited for the response.

Bernie's fingers were not quite steady as she undid the day pack. She said at last, "I'm glad. Very glad, Pete." And then, quickly: "Will you mix the martinis, or shall I?"

They sat companionably close, not yet touching, on the sofa bed with their drinks while they watched the last of the flaming sunset fade quickly and disappear.

"I could turn on the radio," Bernie said. She spoke a little too fast. "One thing about being up here, I can get every FM station and every TV channel line-of-sight without any kind of outside antenna. Would you like some music?"

"Not now." Pete was watching the girl carefully, and trying not to be too obvious about it. There were overtones, harmonics he did not understand. "What's the matter, Bernie?"

"What do you mean?" She was smiling, a tolerant smile.

Pete hesitated. "Maybe I'm just being stupid—"

"You're not! I don't want you to say that! Not ever!"

"—but," Pete said as if she had not spoken, "something's wrong. What's bugging you?"

"Nothing." Bernie shook her head emphatically, too emphatically. "There's—" She was silent, motionless, and then all at once she shivered. "I'm scared," she said in a voice from which all bravado had disappeared. "That's all it is. Have you ever been scared, Pete?"

"Hell, yes."

"I've never been scared before," Bernie said. "Up here, I mean. I've been through winds, and blizzards and thunderstorms—but not like last night, never like that. Hailstones"—she made a circle with her thumb and forefinger—"that big. Thunder that wasn't thunder, it was explosions. Lightning I could almost see it strike. I, we were right in the middle of it, Sam and I. He crawled into bed with me, and we pulled the covers up over my head and just held each other and it went on and on—"

"Easy," Pete said. He laid one large hand on hers, squeezed with gentle strength. "Easy. It's all over now."

Bernie shook her head. "And then I dreamed," she said. "Nightmare, really. All summer we've had fires. I've lost count. There were times when it sounded like I was boxing the compass just calling off smoke vectors. No rain. And then last night, that storm and the dream." She looked up at Pete's face. "I never thought I was a hysterical female, Pete."

"You aren't."

"I am now. Last night was just a—warning. I know it. This drought and all those fires. Sooner or later droughts end, Pete. Always. And when this one ends—" She shook her head and was silent.

"Go on," Pete said. "Finish it. You're worried about what will happen up here?"

"No." She was watching him steadily now. "Nothing will happen up here. Even another storm like last night—" She lifted her shoulders and let them fall, even smiled faintly. "I'll pull the covers up again. The building is anchored. We're grounded for lightning. Hail can't break these windows. Nothing like that, Pete. I'm safe here. We're safe. That wasn't the dream at all."

Pete was silent, waiting.

"That view you admired," Bernie said. "I admire it too. Every day. I look down on the real world and it's—beautiful. I like seeing it from a distance. But what do you think Noah must have felt when he looked down from the top of that mountain after the rains had stopped and the water had— receded? That's what the dream was, looking down from here after it was all over and seeing—nothing!"

9

Kate Williams drove at less than her usual high speed up the Harper's Park road which followed the river's course. It was almost dark now, and the headlights of her little sports car seemed to carve a tunnel in the gloom.

Dinner with her father had been a quiet affair, filled with long, awkward conversational pauses in which the gentle sounds of silverware on china seemed overloud.

Mother would have known how to handle this situation which had arisen, Kate told herself; and found it a lack in herself that she did not.

Daddy could be balky as an overloaded burro; she had long known this. But, then, with both Daddy's and Mother's genes in her makeup, so could she.

"I think you should tell the governor, Daddy," she had said at one point, not even bothering to identify the subject as the dam since Jay's recent discourse was very much on both their minds.

"There's nothing to tell him yet, so let's forget it, honey."

"Do you think it's fair to keep it quiet? Your friend J.G. says Jay is an expert."

"I told you we'd look into it."

"Sam Martin." She was astonished to hear the depth of the scorn in her voice.

"You used to think Sam was quite a fellow."

Reluctantly but truthfully: "I did."

"He hasn't changed."

"No," Kate said, "I have."

Silence.

"It was your mother's idea to send you East," Bill Williams said. His voice contained a defensive note.

"I know. We talked about it. I wanted to go. But it wasn't just the East that changed me. It was Mother's dying."

"That changed pretty much of everything."

"You wouldn't let me come home."

"There wasn't anything you could do, honey. There was no need to put you through all the—bad part."

There was another long, awkward silence.

Kate said at last, "That was when I changed, Daddy. When I realized I was useless."

"Damnit, you aren't useless!"

"I was."

And maybe I still am, she thought now, remembering the conversation as she drove through the gathering darkness up the winding mountain road. But at least I can do what I think is right.

• • •

Jay's rubber wet suit was thoroughly dry. He dusted it carefully with powder and folded it into its storage bag. Heaven only knew when he'd want it again; at least, he thought thankfully, it would not be here with the threat of another tremor hanging over him while he was submerged in the lake.

Had he known about those twenty-three earlier tremors, he told himself, he would not, repeat, not even have made his second dive. And yet neither would he then have seen the actual signs of fracturing in the rock sides which supported the dam, and mere suspicions would have carried no weight at all. On the other hand, what he had told Williams hadn't seemed to make much impression anyway, so it was probably all effort wasted.

But he had tried, his conscience was clear, and he even felt a measure of relief that he had not become further involved.

Like Jed Harper, he had gone where his stick floated—and reached a backwater. Now his stick floated toward Alberta.

He looked around the motel room. All drawers and the single closet were open out of long habit to make sure he had missed nothing in his packing. He walked into the tiny bathroom, looked again behind the door and into the medicine cabinet. Like a mother cat moving her kittens, he thought; always making one extra check.

Back out to the telephone then, to sit on the bed and ask the man at the front desk to put through a call to the Alberta number.

Cooley's voice filled the room almost immediately as if Cooley had been sitting waiting for the call. "You clear now, boy? Then make it the Palliser Hotel in Calgary. I'll have word for you there. Anything you need we can collect up here. Did you find whatever the hell you were looking for?"

Jay smiled at the wall. Jed's gravestone and Julia's, and signs of danger no one heeded—a mixed bag, he thought. "Yes and no," he said, "but I had a couple of nice swims."

"There are times," Cooley said judiciously, "when I don't think you play with a full deck of cards. You—"

"Hold it," Jay said at the sound of a knock at the door. He raised his voice. "Come in!"

The door opened. Kate Williams stood quiet in the doorway, unsmiling. "I'm interrupting. I'm sorry." Her face was troubled. "Please. It's important."

Jay hesitated only a moment. Into the phone: "I'll call you back," he said.

"Look, boy!"

"Not long," Jay said, and hung up. He stood up from the bed to face the girl. "Come in. Leave the door open if you want."

She came slowly into the room and shut the door behind her. "I am not *that* concerned about my reputation."

No, she wouldn't be, Jay thought. She had her father's assurance, perhaps his stubbornness as well. Maybe 'arrogance' was the word, the proper name for the quality usually masked behind her smile. "It wasn't a girl on the phone," he said. "You're not smashing a romance. Sit down. Tell me what you want."

She sat in the single chair and looked around the room. "You've packed. Are you leaving now?"

"There's a plane at ten o'clock."

"Alberta," Kate said.

"My own work."

"Will it make you rich, this work of yours?" Strange, tangential question.

Jay shrugged. "I've never thought much about it. They pay me. And I don't come cheap."

"No. You wouldn't." She had already had her father's assessment. Now she had a new one. "After you left," she said, "Daddy telephoned Houston. A friend of his. J. G. Harkness. Do you know him?"

"Everybody in oil knows J.G."

"He told Daddy you were one of the best."

"I've done work for him." Jay shrugged again. "I don't think he'd complain. But I still don't know why you're here."

"To ask you to stay."

"Just like that?"

Kate was silent and motionless. Her eyes did not leave his face.

"Did your father send you?"

"He doesn't even know I'm here."

"Then I don't get it. I've told you all I know."

"I heard. And I believed you."

"Your father didn't."

"But I did. Do you fly?"

"Sometimes on jobs. I'm not a pilot."

"I am."

Yes, Jay thought, you would be. You probably have a number of other expensive hobbies too. "So?"

"I know how the river rises. I've seen the hundreds of tiny streams—tributaries?" She watched Jay nod. "The flash flood you described—it could happen."

So that was it. "In this part of the world flash floods can always happen," Jay said. "That's how all those dry arroyos are made." Perversity was suddenly a contagion in his mind, forcing him to challenge her thesis based on his own words.

Kate sat quiet for long moments as if she understood. And then at last: "You know I am not talking about just another flash flood. I am talking about the kind of—I hate to use the word 'catastrophe'—that you described. If you saw it all from the air—"

"I've seen the topographical maps."

Kate's nod was acceptance. "Then it is perfectly clear to you. All these mountains drain right down into Harper's Park, just the way you said."

His shrug was eloquent. "And there's nothing I can do to change it. So?"

Kate said slowly, "I am trying to like you, or at least not to dislike you, not that it makes any difference to you. But you resent me—"

"What is it you want me to do?"

"Stay over just tonight."

"Why?"

"And fly with me tomorrow morning."

"Why again? I've seen the maps."

Kate sat very straight, and still. "I am not used to begging—"

"No, you wouldn't have to be." That contagion of perversity was still in his mind, and its nagging pressure suddenly angered him. "I'm not usually this kind of bastard," he said. "Sorry."

"Will you stay?"

"Tell me why."

"All right," Kate said. "It's because I have—faith in you. Don't ask me why. I have faith in you that I don't have in the others, Sam Martin, yes, even Daddy. They've gone too far to admit they're wrong, and they'll convince others, they have convinced others that everything is all right, fine, ginger-peachy." Her tone was bitter.

"And all you want me to do is change everybody's mind, lead them out of the wilderness." Jay shook his head angrily. "Jesus Christ, call me Moses! Look." He spread his hands. "In my business I do my work, my computations. I make my reports and I make my recommendations. I've done that here. Once-over-very-lightly, true, but I wasn't even asked in the first place, so I think I've done more than my share."

"What you are saying," Kate said slowly, "is that you have satisfied your conscience, is that it?"

Damn the woman anyway, Jay thought. She saw too deep. "Put it that way if you want."

Kate said, "Do you remember what you said to Daddy and me: 'Think of Johnstown in 1889, only this would be worse, much worse, with the whole city downstream.'"

"You're a real Bible-banger when you get started, aren't you?"

"Will you stay? And fly with me in the morning?"

"What the hell for?"

"I don't know. All I can hope is that you might see something that isn't on the maps, something no one else has seen, or noticed, something that might mean something to you because you are what you are. Another piece of evidence to convince Daddy. That's all I can say."

"Oh, brother!" Jay was looking at the telephone. He could just hear Cooley's voice when he heard about this. He looked again at Kate. "You're going to be awfully disappointed."

"Then you will stay?" Her smile appeared quickly, shaky around the edges.

"Okay." In the simple word there was resignation. "I'll stay. I'll buy your goddamned violets if only to show you there's nothing I can do."

"Thank you. Thank you very much." There was no mockery in her voice, and her eyes were somehow open, no longer unfathomable. She made no move to rise from the chair.

"Just tell me where and when to meet you in the morning," Jay said, angry with her, and with himself.

He stood in the doorway of the motel room and watched Kate walk to her car. For the first time, he thought, they were on even terms, and he could look at her now, not as a kind of symbol or as the daughter of Bill Williams, local big wheel, but purely as a woman, a very attractive woman who in that fleeting moment after his acceptance just might in her gratitude have been offering a little something more than friendliness, and maybe it would have been fun to find out.

He went back inside, closed the door, and walked to the telephone to call Cooley again. He had a fleeting feeling that he was losing control of the situation, that events were gaining the upper hand, which was, of course, nonsense.

And yet something of that feeling must have communicated itself to Cooley too, because his only reaction to the sudden change of plan was a question: "Are you sure you know what you're doing, boy?"

Jay hung up with the question unanswered in his own mind.

. . . . .

Mary Thompson, bathed, scrubbed, and wearing a dress instead of the jeans she usually wore, was waiting in the living room–dining room with pass-through kitchen in the tiny house they rented on the fringe of the *barrio* when Brooks came home that evening.

She had set the table with her grandmother's silver and Lenox plates, and two of the fine Baccarat wineglasses stood next to the Waterford decanter filled with the least expensive domestic red wine she had been able to find at the *barrio* store.

She had thought about gin and vermouth for martinis, and

decided that they would be too extravagant. The steak had already taken what was left of the week's food budget.

She sat, now expressionless, on the sofa, the evening newspaper folded on the coffee table in front of her. "How did it go?"

"Well, I'll say one thing," Brooks said. "Gentry does what he says he'll do. The papers were all ready, all in order, plat, bill of sale, the whole thing. And a certified check waiting. Jack Early came in as a witness." His eye caught the set table. "Hey, why the display of opulence?"

Mary said slowly, "I thought we—deserved a celebration. I mean, maybe a toast to the future with some—capital to help us."

"Okay. I'll go along." Brooks sat down beside her on the sofa and put his arm around her shoulders. "Back in New York twenty-two thousand five hundred dollars didn't seem like riches. But here, after these last two years, I have a little different viewpoint, sort of a worm's-eye angle. I think now we can make it go."

Mary's head nodded.

"And we'll find some more property—when we can afford it."

Another nod.

"In the meantime, there's that small tractor. I think with a power takeoff to handle an auger as well as a blade for setting in young trees. And maybe—"

Mary's shoulders were shaking, although she was making no sound.

Brooks caught her chin with his hand and raised her head. "What's the matter? Did I say something?"

The tears were still soundless, running down the sides of her nose, dripping unheeded into her lap. She pointed at the coffee table and the folded newspaper. "I—" She stopped and tried again. "I—tried to call you. But the bank switchboard—was—closed!"

Brooks released her and reached for the paper. He unfolded

it slowly, and stared for long, silent moments at the eight-column banner head: DAM ENLARGEMENT APPROVED.

He refolded the paper then and set it down gently. "So the property he just paid twenty-two thousand five hundred for," he said quietly, "is going to be worth ten times that when the lake is enlarged. At least ten times." He put his arm around Mary again. "I was right the first time, wasn't I? He is what Wall Street calls a gunslinger. I can think of other names for him too, the son of a bitch."

Mary's voice was unsteady, but the words were clear. "My fault. I—pushed you."

Brooks shook his head and squeezed her shoulders. "No fault. Like the kind of insurance lawyers fight. No fault, no blame. Just damage done. To us."

. . .

It was well after dinner, and they had driven in Honest Johnny Cisneros' big shiny car back to the girl's apartment. The girl's name was Linda, but, as Johnny had said once, "You got a Chicana name, but you sure as hell aren't Chicana. You're Anglo from the word go."

Her Anglo identity was probably her greatest attraction for Johnny. God knew, it was not her brain. But she had the kind of body that Chicana chicks only had, if at all, when they first entered pubescence, and even then there was a difference.

The young *barrio* chicks Johnny had played around with when he was their age had been slim, some of them at least, and gently rounded, sure, but they had rapidly put on weight, turned fat and sloppy, and only then developed the big tits he liked, but they always tended to sag. Besides, Johnny knew better than to play around now with the young ones.

Anglo Linda, on the other hand, was still slim in her twenties, and her big tits, marvels to admire and play with, did not sag a bit; they stuck out clean and clear as that mountain Teta, which in Spanish meant breast, way over on the horizon. Linda was something to contemplate.

Once inside the apartment, Johnny plumped himself down on the sofa and kicked off his loafers. "You still got some of that fancy French brandy I brought you last time?"

"Sure." Linda was gone only a few moments. She returned with the bottle of Courvoisier and two balloon glasses. She poured the cognac carefully and handed him one. "What do you say? *Salud?*"

"It means 'health.' *Salud, amor y pesetas, y tiempo para gustarlas.* Health, love and money, and time to enjoy them." Johnny raised his own glass. "You know what we're drinking to?" He was a little drunk, he thought, but what the hell.

"I thought we were drinking to us."

"That too."

Linda's brow wrinkled in the effort of thought. "But what else?"

"Not what. Who. Take off that dress and I'll tell you, okay?"

"You like to look at me?" Linda's tone was coquettish.

"You know it. Go ahead."

Linda put down her glass. She reached back over her shoulders and started the zipper down, then bending slightly forward, reached back and up and opened the zipper all the way. She straightened, drew the dress down from her shoulders, and stepped out of it. She wore now only shoes and bikini panties. She shook her shoulders gently and smiled at Johnny as she picked up her glass again. "Now who are we drinking to?"

"An old bag."

Again the brow furrowed in thought. "Your mother?"

"No." Johnny was still smiling. "She was an old bag too, but we're drinking to another one. We completed a business deal today."

"You and the old bag?" Linda's brow was still furrowed. "What kind of a deal?"

"A very profitable deal, baby. That's the best kind, isn't it?"

The brow was smooth again, and Linda's smile was happy. "Lots of money?"

"That's it, baby. That's it." Johnny drank his cognac at a gulp. "Now let's forget about her and concentrate on you and I, okay?"

The girl started toward him slowly, smiling still. "Sure, Johnny. Whatever you say. I like it all, you know what I mean?"

Those splendid tits, those soft, silky thighs, and those long Anglo legs. Johnny took his time savoring it all. "Right on," he said at last. "Right on."

10

Bill Williams sat behind his desk, and Sam Martin, summoned, sat in one of the leather visitor's chairs pulled up close. Sam had rolls of drawings on the table, and so far Williams had refused to look at them.

"I'm not interested in pictures, Sam. I trust your engineering and so do the Army people. But what about the geology, the rock fracturing Harper says he saw?" It had been a long, restless night for Williams. Two Valium tablets had helped, and there had been none of that arrhythmia nonsense to complicate matters even further, but his mind, like a runaway engine with a stuck throttle, had refused to turn itself off or even slow down. "What it gets right down to," he said in sudden exasperation, "is how strong is that fucking dam, anyway?"

Sam was less than comfortable. Williams in this kind of mood was unpredictable. "We designed it properly," Sam said, "and we built it well—what else can I say, Bill? And we aren't talking about something like an airplane where weight has to be considered and you design right up to the loads you expect to encounter. We've got a built-in safety factor—"

"We did have. Since then we've had not one earthquake, but according to Harper twenty-goddamn-three of them, and how do we know what they might have done?" Williams was aware that he was repeating Jay's theories, and he was hoping that somehow Sam would squash them flat.

"The dam doesn't show any signs of weakness," Sam said. "I've been down below it and there's nothing there to show any problems."

Good point. From the downstream side the entire dam structure was exposed, unlike the lake side, where you would have to dive through all that water to have a look. Still. "The lake is twenty feet below normal now," Williams said, and plucked Jay's figures out of memory. "Say the lake is ten square miles, and that's conservative—do you know how much one acre-foot of water weighs, Sam?"

"I never worked it out, but it's simple enough—43,560 square feet times about 62—"

"Almost three million pounds," Williams said. "That's a lot of weight, Sam, and you multiply that out and— Oh, hell, I'm just talking and not proving anything." He pushed back his chair, got up, walked to the windows, and stood looking out at the mountains, his broad back to the office. "We've put a lot of work into this enlargement idea, Sam," he said without turning. His voice was quiet, thoughtful.

"And money, Bill. And you stand to make it all back, and then some, if we go ahead as planned."

Williams turned to study Sam's face. "What does that mean?"

There was something in Williams's manner that made Sam even more uncomfortable. "Is it a secret, Bill? The Harrison property you bought? I mean, hell, if I'm not supposed to know about it, okay, it's forgotten. No business of mine."

Williams walked back to his desk, lowered himself into his chair, and put his hands flat on the desk top, his movements deliberate, controlled. His eyes had not left Sam's face. "It's no secret, Sam," he said in a new, quiet voice, "but I'm just wondering where you happened to hear about it."

Sam shrugged. He hoped he seemed unconcerned. "Just around, I guess."

Williams shook his head gently. "Not good enough, Sam. Who have you been talking to? More to the point, who's been talking to you?" Of course, he thought, of course. "George Harrison?"

"He bought me a drink yesterday."

"Nothing wrong with that, Sam."

"At the Territorial Club. I'd never been there before."

Williams's smile was wry. "That puts you one up on me. I've never been there. Go on, Sam, what did George have on his mind? The dam enlargement?"

"He wanted to know how it was going. I didn't see any harm in talking about it, Bill. I mean, was there?"

"No harm at all. And then he happened to mention the property he sold me?"

"Well, yes, I guess he did."

"What did he want you to do, Sam?"

Sam shook his head with emphasis. "It wasn't anything like that. He didn't ask me to do anything. We just—talked. I mean, he asked me what I thought of the whole idea of making the dam bigger, was it necessary, was it safe, that kind of thing."

Williams's smile was turned inward again, mocking himself. "Right back where we started, aren't we? Is it safe? And what did you tell him, Sam?"

"The same thing I've been telling you." Sam's hand went automatically to the rolled drawings as if to draw strength from the precise lines and dimensions they contained. "Just because some character we don't even know goes diving with scuba gear, Bill," he said, "we suddenly begin to sweat about all the calculations we've done, all the engineering and the planning—now does that make sense?"

Williams sat for a long time in silence, his eyes fixed on the far wall as if somehow the answer was written there. He said at last, "Maybe not, Sam. Maybe not. Let's think about it." He raised one hand in a gesture of caution. "And let's not talk about it while we're thinking. Not to anybody. Is that clear?"

"I won't talk." It was dismissal. Sam gathered the rolls of drawings and stood up. As he walked to the door he had the feeling that he had somehow made a lucky escape, but from what, he could not even guess. "See you, Bill," he said, and walked out with a feeling of relief strong, almost overpowering in his mind.

· · ·

From the Mount Union lookout that early morning, the world consisted of islands in a white sea that stretched to infinity. Above, the sky was clear, blue, directly overhead almost purple, and although the air was chill, the direct sun was already beginning to warm the day.

"Sometimes on mornings like this," Bernie said, "I pretend that I'm the last person on earth. But not for long. And"—she smiled with sudden brilliance—"I like it better like this, with one other inhabitant, preferably large and male." The smile disappeared. "I won't let it become habit-forming," she said. "That's a promise." And then, quickly, as if embarrassed: "How about some breakfast? A man your size needs nourishment."

"Look," Pete began, "about last night—"

"No." Bernie's tone was emphatic. "Eve provided the apple, but I'll bet it was Adam who worried after he'd eaten it, and tried to make amends. Let's keep it just the way it is."

The radio loudspeaker came to life without warning, a male voice speaking what sounded to Pete like gibberish, and Bernie smiled at the expression on his face. "That's Charlie Hunt," she said, "over in the Rainy. He takes a little getting used to." She listened for a few moments. "Low-pressure system—you don't care about the millibars, but it's a real low—moving 115 degrees, that's our direction from him, carrying a full bucket, which is Charlie's way of saying we've got some kind of precipitation coming."

The voice stopped with a laconic "We down," and Bernie smiled again. "Charlie's using CB talk this morning. You sit on top of a mountain alone"—her smile now was sheepish—"and sometimes it gets to you. The way it did to me last night when you came up over the rim."

"You recovered well," Pete said.

"The treatment was just what I needed. I'm whole again. Now about that breakfast."

They sat out on the encircling porch with their second cups of coffee and watched the white mist burn off and the valleys and canyons begin to appear beneath them. "I never get tired of it," Bernie said. "It's always a surprise like the packages under the tree Christmas morning. The air warms up, the water vapor evaporates, and there's the world again, just the way you left it last night." She glanced at Pete, smiling again. "Well, not quite the way I left it last night. This morning it looks a lot better."

"It does for me too." Pete's long legs were stretched out. His eyes went to the surgical scar on his knee, and then quickly away. He was aware that Bernie watched him, but she said nothing. "Smoke over there," Pete said, pointing, attempting distraction. "Aren't you supposed to report it?"

"That's a sawmill. Sooner or later they'll get it cleaned up. They hope." Bernie looked at her watch. "Time for the full weather report." She got out of her chair. "Why don't you sit here in the sun and enjoy it." She walked inside and voice sounds began almost immediately on the muted speaker.

Bernie had her life act pretty well together, Pete thought, which was more than he could say for himself, a lot more. And although he hadn't really thought about it before, it was probably vague guilt feelings about his lack of direction, along with a perfectly understandable sex drive, which had brought him up that long trail yesterday to sit here now, look out at the world, and try to do some thinking.

He glanced again at the scar. Eventually, of course, he would have had to face the question of what next? Not even a George Blanda went on forever. But *eventually* had seemed a long time off, and decision time was suddenly now, long before he had expected it.

Some ex-jocks went into coaching, some into broadcasting, some tried their hands at acting or selling cars or insurance or playing front men at restaurants; the list was endless. And some tried to live the rest of their lives on their reputations and ended up as just plain bums.

Some, of course, had known right from the beginning where they were going and they had never taken their eyes off the goal. Bobby Brown of the baseball Yankees now a doctor, Eddie LeBaron a lawyer, why, hell, Whizzer White sitting on the Supreme Court and Mo Udall in Congress.

But nothing like that was going to happen to Pete Otero. In fact, nothing was going to *happen* to him, period; no fairy god-mother was going to wave a wand and set him up as a resident millionaire anywhere. It was going to be just the way it had al-ways been: anything Pete Otero got was going to be as the re-sult of his getting off his ass and going after it.

So all right, already, as Tim Bernstein from Flatbush, the best defensive end Pete had ever played with, used to say when he got himself down, dug in, and defied anybody, any-body at all to try to go through, around, or over him. My thought for the day, Pete told himself, and felt suddenly, unac-countably better.

He sat quiet, even relaxed in the sun then and looked down at the city. He watched a small, sleek red airplane taxi to the head of the municipal airport runway and then make its run, lifting off gracefully, tucking its wheels into its belly and reaching for the sky. He wondered idly who was in it and where they were going.

"We've got weather coming," Bernie said at his shoulder. "Of course, that's a maybe. These last months a lot of storms have looked as if they were coming right at us and then changed their minds and swung away. But this one, coming down from the north, looks serious, and if it and Charlie's little

number with the full bucket collide, we could catch it for fair."
Her voice was solemn.

"Go on," Pete said. He looked up at her face. "You're saying
something, aren't you?"

"I guess what I'm saying," Bernie said, "is that you'd better
split now, or figure that you might have to stay awhile. You
don't want to be caught on that mountainside in a big one."
Her hand touched his shoulder with tentative affection. "And I
don't want you to go. Not yet."

"Carnal, aren't you?" Pete was grinning.

"That's me. I told you I liked the treatment."

"Why, then," Pete said, and covered her hand with his, "it's
settled, isn't it?" His own problems could wait a little. He
looked again at the red airplane now in a wide climbing turn.
"Pretty, isn't it?"

Bernie's smile was wistful. "I'd like to fly like that, wouldn't
you?"

"Lady, I like it right here on our mountaintop."

.   .   .

Kate flew the sleek red plane with almost professional com-
petence, Jay thought, as he was sure she did many things. She
was, he had decided, that kind of person; it was easy to picture
her riding a horse, swimming, driving a car, playing tennis or
golf with effortless, almost scornful grace.

He had not been sure how long it would take him to drive to
the municipal airport, and so he had arrived ten minutes ahead
of the appointed time. Kate was not yet there, but the red
plane was already wheeled out of the hangar and waiting.
Kate arrived precisely on time, and although normally Jay ap-
preciated punctuality, that feeling of perversity Kate seemed
to generate in him made him wish that she had been some
minutes late, thereby demonstrating at least a hint of weakness.

Now, the city beneath them: "I told Daddy I was flying you over the dam this morning," Kate said suddenly. She turned her head to smile at him. "I told him it was my idea, not yours."

"Did you also tell him I thought it was a waste of time?"

"I told him that too."

That feeling of events gaining the upper hand was still with him, but he pushed it aside. He was here, and he had no excuse for further foot dragging. He settled down to study the terrain below.

He remembered reading once that Napoleon had asked one of his officers what the island called Haiti—the Mountainous Land—was like, and the officer had crumpled a piece of paper and dropped it on Napoleon's desk, saying, "It is like that, sire." The land beneath them now could have been illustrated the same way.

Jay had seen the topographical maps, as he had told Kate, and had one open on his lap now, but the reality, particularly of light and shadow, provided a different dimension. Contour lines crowded close on a map indicated steep slopes or even sheer cliffs; but rock faces dropping into darkness, bottomless canyons into which the sun would penetrate only for short hours or even minutes a day—these were the features of another world.

In north-facing crevices and hollows, last year's snow still held. Here a steep talus slope testified to exfoliation, the relentless erosion of alternating heat and cold, expansion and contraction, water seepage expanding into ice during the night hours. There a solitary conifer, half its branches dead, roots exposed in a writhing struggle for existence, still clung tenaciously to a rocky slope too steep for a man to stand on.

"Oxygen," Kate said, and handed him a light mask. She already wore her own, and her voice was muffled. "We'll be up above fifteen thousand, and it can sneak up on you."

Jay put on the mask without a word, his eyes still fixed on the terrain below, sharply sidelighted by the early sun.

From this height, the dam and the lake behind it were small indeed, mere toy representations of the real thing; a child's playbox came to mind. There was the stream that fed the lake, and as Kate had said and as Jay remembered from the maps but now actually *saw*, there were the countless tributaries of the stream, some gleaming faintly with running water, some now dry but easy enough to pick out from the way they extended upwards from the main stream course like branches of a tree.

On the flat top of the highest peak he saw the fire lookout building. Someone waved, and he succumbed to the impulse to wave back although he doubted if his motion inside the plane could be seen. Kate's eyes above her mask seemed amused.

He had warned her to expect nothing, Jay reminded himself, and yet his professional pride rebelled at the thought of returning to the ground entirely empty-handed.

Where they were now, a thousand feet above the highest mountains, the view was spectacular, awesome; more mountains, some snow-covered, stretched northwest as far as visibility went. It was through this unknown, tangled mass, Jay thought, that old Jed Harper and others like him had found their lonely way. Whatever else they might have been, and some of them were probably unsavory types, they were men.

But that had no bearing on the present, and all those mountains in view were no part of the local scene. Kate seemed to be waiting for some kind of signal, some sort of response, and that too was annoying. Because I have nothing to give her, Jay thought, nothing at all. But that sense of professional pride made him swing his hand in a circular motion, and he spoke with difficulty around the edge of the mask. "Maintain this altitude, but swing back over the lake and dam again." He watched her nod, her eyes no longer amused, and at once the horizon shifted as they began their wide swinging turn.

The ground moved slowly beneath them, illusion of course, but helpful for observation. Jay caught the gleam of standing water near the top of a high canyon, the same new lake Pete Otero had noticed yesterday during his climb, trapped behind the natural dam the thunderstorm had created.

Jay oriented the map on his lap by the fire lookout station on flat-topped Mount Union and the lake behind the dam, and searched in vain on the map for a small lake where the standing water was. Strange. He marked the spot, and resumed his ground study.

They were coming over the dam and its lake now, and although he had no idea what he might be looking for, he searched carefully every slope, every canyon, every steep drop-off and peak—and saw nothing that held meaning.

The dam was behind them, and ahead the curve of The Bend, and then the city sprawled in the morning sun. Kate was watching his face, and Jay wished she would not. It was sheer exasperation that made him repeat the circling motion of his hand, indicating that they should go back to the dam area. Instantly Kate obeyed, the wing dropped and they began their return swing.

The early low sun came in slantwise, creating elongated shadows and strange, almost surrealist effects. The curving dam structure seemed to continue beyond the edge of the gorge as if Sam Martin in his engineering had forgotten to stop; a trick of the light, no more. And on the opposite side of the gorge there was a corresponding line, another optical illusion.

Or was it?

Kate's eyes were on his face, and her voice, muffled by the mask, said, "What do you see?"

Jay shook his head in silence. He studied the map. There was nothing there to support the illusion, to explain the shadow that was almost a straight line. He looked at his watch and checked the time: 8:22, their altitude: 15,000 feet, and marked the data on the map beside the dam.

Kate's questioning eyes had not left his face. "Damnit," Jay said, "I don't know." It was no time to throw out half-baked theories. "I want to think about it." They were over the dam now. "Let's make one more pass from the downstream side."

It took seven minutes by Jay's watch to turn, fly back downstream, and make another approach upstream to the dam. The shadow illusion was gone. "Okay," Jay said, "that's it. We can pack it in now. I've seen all I'm going to see." If I've seen anything at all, he thought with growing annoyance.

They landed at the municipal airport and taxied to the hangar where the red airplane was stored. In silence they got out, Jay with his map. At least, he thought, she hadn't kept pestering him with questions. But it wouldn't last.

Kate fooled him. "When you make up your mind," she said, "or whatever it is you are trying to do, perhaps you will let me know what your conclusions are. Thank you for staying and having a look, anyway." She walked to her car, then, back straight, got in, started the engine with a snarl, and drove away.

Jay walked slowly to his own car. A prickly, unpredictable female, he thought, used to having her own way—and if that kind of thinking made him out to be a male chauvinist pig, why, so be it.

He had told her that nothing would come from this morning's flight, and possibly nothing had. He was strongly tempted to leave it right there and with no more delay get on the plane to the hotel in Calgary. But there was that matter of professional pride, and the puzzle of that disappearing illusion which bothered him because he was not sure whether he understood it or not.

Wrong, he told himself; he was splitting hairs like a professional moralist. Because he was pretty damn sure he did know what that disappearing illusion was. And again that feeling was strong that events were getting the upper hand. He had told himself that, in Jed's phrase, his stick floated toward Alberta. Now, damnit, he was not at all sure, and—

A car coming into the airport parking lot at speed swung in a tight curve, throwing gravel, and slid to a stop beside him. Sam Martin was out of the car before it even stopped moving. Sam was still uncomfortable from that scene with Bill Williams, and now his annoyance had a new focus. "I saw Kate's plane in the air," he said. "And I met her driving away just now. Were you flying with her?" A large, solid, now truculent man. "Well, were you?"

Jay tossed the topographical map into his car. Over his shoulder he said, "Why don't you ask her?" He opened the car door.

"I'm asking you. Goddamnit, stand still and answer me!" Sam caught Jay's arm just above the elbow, and after that things happened a little too fast for immediate comprehension.

Jay spun like a dancer, threw off the hand, caught Sam's wrist in midair, and delivered a chop to Sam's forearm that paralyzed it from elbow to fingertips. Then, standing quietly balanced: "Don't ever lay a hand on me again," he said. Overreaction, he told himself, pure release of frustration. Okay, so there it was. He felt no urge to apologize. "Is that understood?"

Sam was holding the hurt arm with his good hand in angry bewilderment. No words came to mind.

"If you're chasing after the boss's daughter," Jay said, "that's your business, not mine, yours and hers. But what I do is my own business. Remember that." He got into his rented car then, closed the door, started the engine, and drove unhurriedly away. Sam, still holding his hurt arm, watched him go.

Back up the same road he had traveled this morning, past the curve of The Bend, with the fine houses which were almost estates; climbing steadily to Harper's Park Valley; and there

Jay pulled his car to the side of the road and sat studying the dam and the sides of the rock gorge.

He could see nothing to explain the optical illusion he had seen from the air. But I know what it is, regardless, he told himself, and all I need is corroboration.

Damn that episode with Sam Martin, anyway! It only served to show how off-balance he had let himself become.

Okay, so that was how it was. One more step, he thought as he put the car in gear and drove off, and then I'll walk away, back to my own world.

He drove on to the motel, and for the fourth time had the desk clerk put through a call to the Alberta number. Cooley was there, and after his initial, shouted greeting, he listened in silence for a time. Then: "Jesus H. Christ, boy, what's got into you? You taking up residence there?"

"I need help, Cooley, and you're the best rock man I know."

"Flattery isn't going to buy you a thing. We're sitting on a pool of oil up here, or I'm just as crazy as they come. I don't know anything about dams, and I don't want to know anything about dams. All I want—"

"Maybe you didn't hear me, Cooley. I need help."

There was a long silence. Cooley said at last, "Okay, I owe you a couple. But this is the goddamnedest time to collect. Come on up here first, and then—" The roaring voice stopped suddenly. "Okay, okay. I'll come down. You say they've got an airport there?"

"And a pretty girl to fly you in the morning for a look-see." Jay was suddenly smiling. "You can sit right next to her and everything."

"Jesus Christ, now you've fallen in love, is that it? Okay, I'll let you know when I'm there. Today sometime, I suppose."

One more telephone call, this one to the Williams house. Kate's voice was cool.

"Can we fly again tomorrow morning?" Jay said. "Three of us, same time."

"Am I allowed to know who, and why?"

"The best rock man I know. I want him to see what I saw this morning, if it's really there."

There was silence on the line. Kate's voice said at last, "The airport. Same time." She hung up.

11

In the large, air-conditioned, paneled office above Pine Street the sounds of New York traffic were muted almost to silence.

Only the occasional blare of a horn penetrated faintly as if from another world.

The intercom on the desk buzzed, and his secretary's modulated voice said, "Mrs. Brooks Thompson is calling, Mr. Willoughby."

"Thank you." Spencer Willoughby picked up the phone smiling. "Hello, dear. Are you making the desert to bloom like a rose?"

"We're trying, Daddy, but I'm afraid we're not setting the world on fire yet."

"And a good thing too. That particular figure of speech has menacing connotations these days. Is this a social call, or is there something I can do for you?"

Always he had been able to see right through her, Mary thought. Now even two thousand miles away he had caught immediately the overtones of pain and frustration. "What do you do, Daddy, when you've been—cheated?"

Willoughby looked at the paneled wall, and the Eric Sloane painting that he liked so much hanging upon it. There was directness in the painting, and honesty, as well as beauty. A man could lose himself in contemplation of it and emerge refreshed. "That's a hard one, dear," he said. "But then you have always asked hard ones."

"And you have always answered them."

Willoughby's smile was fond. Warm words, he thought. He

said, "I would say you have several choices. You can grin and bear it and walk away, hoping you have learned something. You can see if it is possible to turn the tables and recoup your losses. Or you can do the purely human thing, which is to strike back however you can. The last choice can bring you nothing but a kind of grim satisfaction. But sometimes that is worth it if only for peace of mind."

"It's Brooks I'm worried about, Daddy."

"I take it he is not there?"

"No. I'm home. He's at the nursery. I went all female this morning and pleaded a headache."

Willoughby was still looking at the picture. "Do you want to tell me the story?" He listened quietly, expressionless, and when Mary had finished: "Yes," he said. "I see why you and Brooks are upset."

"It is our fault. I can't deny that."

Good for you, Willoughby thought; the admission took courage.

"The trouble is," Mary said, "it is more my fault than Brooks's. I pushed him. But he is blaming himself. He's a babe in the woods, he says. He mistrusted Mr. Gentry's motives from the beginning, but he let me talk him out of it. We had bought the property, by the way, with your wedding present."

"Then you have already made a profit, dear. My check wasn't that large."

"Yes, we do have that consolation." There was even a hint of a smile in her voice. It disappeared. "I talked to Mr. Gentry just before I called you."

Willoughby said quietly, "And?"

"He was not very—pleasant. He said we should have stayed in the East. I guess I can't blame him."

But I can, Willoughby thought. "Does Brooks know?"

"No. And I'm not going to tell him. I'm afraid he might—do something rash."

"Good. I think you are behaving admirably. And I am sorry that I have no solution to suggest."

"I feel better just for having talked to you."

"That is very pleasant to hear. I will say one thing, dear. It won't help much, but maybe it will give you a little further consolation. It is simply this: W. C. Fields's dictum is not correct. You *can* cheat an honest man; it happens all the time, as in this instance. Far more experienced people than you and Brooks have been cheated. Badly."

"Thanks, Daddy."

"Damn little, dear. I am sorry."

Willoughby hung up and leaned back in his desk chair, his eyes still on the Sloane painting. Beautiful mountains, he thought, magnificent sky, the kind of country to which Mary and Brooks had gone and, secretly, he did not blame them. He was not unacquainted with the West, nor with its myths and its mores.

He did not know Gentry, but his single reported remark to Mary, that she and Brooks should have stayed in the East, told volumes. The effete East, Gentry was saying, as opposed to the West, where men were men, etc., etc.

Well, sometimes, Ivy League and all, we know how to play hardball too, Willoughby thought, and leaned forward to flip the intercom switch.

"Yes, Mr. Willoughby."

"I want to speak to Mr. Thomas Gentry, please. He is president of the First National Bank . . ."

The call went through quickly. "This is Mr. Gentry."

"This is Spencer Willoughby in New York, Mr. Gentry. I am just about to telephone an old friend of mine in Los Angeles. His name is Henry Warfield. Do you know him?"

"I've met him." There was uncharacteristic caution in Gentry's voice.

"He is president and major stockholder of the holding company which owns your bank, among numerous others. I say that just to refresh your memory."

"I know who he is. But—"

"I am going to tell Henry a sordid little tale about one of his bank presidents. It concerns dubious use of inside information, deliberate fleecing of one of the bank's customers, and I shouldn't be surprised if it also concerns hasty arrangement of the kind of 'insider loan' which the Comptroller of the Currency, who is also a friend of mine, is viewing with considerable displeasure these days in the National banks which he is charged with regulating. I just thought you might like to know. I can guess at Henry's reaction. Can you?"

"Who the hell are you?"

"I told you, Mr. Gentry. My name is Spencer Willoughby. My office is on Pine Street in New York City."

"I mean, what the hell business is this of yours?"

"Mrs. Brooks Thompson, Mr. Gentry, is my daughter. When you are looking for a new job and seeking character references, I would not suggest that you ask her or her husband, but you might remember them. Good day."

. . .

Gentry hung up angrily, made himself sit quiet for a few minutes trying to sort out his thinking, and found that his temper overrode all rational thought. The idea of some eastern son of a bitch threatening him, actually threatening him, was almost more than he could take. He—

His telephone buzzed and he picked it up with a jerk. "Yes?"

"Mr. George Harrison is here to see you, Mr. Gentry."

"Well, I can't see him now. He doesn't have an appointment, does he? Well, goddamnit, he can't just walk in— Wait a minute. Tell him, no, ask him to wait a few minutes, huh? I won't be long."

He hung up, thinking rationally at last. Somebody was running a bluff. That was what it was. A phone call from New York and some dude with a la-di-da Harvard accent saying he knew Henry Warfield and was going to talk to him didn't necessarily mean a goddamn thing. Gentry had sat around poker tables himself, lots of them. He was feeling better as he got out his personal telephone directory and looked up the direct number of his good friend at the holding company headquarters in Los Angeles. He dialed with a steady hand.

"Joe? Tom Gentry here. How are you?"

"No complaints. What's doing?"

"I just got a phone call from New York. Fellow calling himself Spencer Willoughby. You know the New York scene. Does the name mean anything to you?"

There was a short pause, and when Joe's voice spoke again, it was filled with something that sounded very much like awe. "Jesus, Tom!" Joe said. "You really are playing in the big leagues. Spencer Willoughby? I don't know him, but I sure as hell know *of* him."

"You're kidding."

"Okay, I'm kidding. You've heard of the Chase–City Bank, number two in the world and gaining ground? Well, Spencer Willoughby is their general counsel, among other things. He sits on their board and half a dozen other little boards like GM and AT&T and IBM, and he's a golfing buddy down at Augusta National with J. Paul Austin of Coca-Cola—that kind of petty stuff. Look him up in Who's Who if you don't believe me."

"You wouldn't be shitting me, would you, Joe?"

"I'm giving it to you straight, Tom. Why?"

"Never mind. Thanks." Gentry hung up.

For fifty goddamn mountain acres, he thought, and the profit he might make on twenty-two thousand five hundred lousy bucks, he had walked into this—mess. Jesus!

And George Harrison was waiting, probably with some goddamned inconsequential crap on his mind. On the other hand, he, Tom Gentry, was in no position to make any enemies. He just might be needing all the friends he could lay his hands on.

He picked up the phone and punched the intercom button. "Send George Harrison in," he said, and hoped when he stood up from his desk that he looked as if nothing at all had happened to disturb him.

. . .

When he thought back upon it later, plump, pink George Harrison found in his entire conversation with Tom Gentry that morning a strange sense of unreality. It was not quite as if he had entered the tiger's cage and found a purring pussycat instead, but there *was* a quality of make-believe.

George sat on the bank's board, a position he had inherited from his father, who had put up some of the original capital to form the bank. George's photograph was on the wall of Tom's office along with those of the other directors, and always before it had been a source of some pride, but now, strangely enough, George almost wished it was not there. He could not have explained why.

"The long and short of it," he said to Tom with some sense of pain, "is that Bill Williams out-sniggled me. My pride is hurt. I admit it. But I am also concerned on a matter of principle."

Gentry, whose mind was still very much on other matters, said, "I'm not sure I follow that, George." Jesus, he thought, I have to sit here and listen to moralistic drivel while that son of a bitch Willoughby is probably hammering nails into my coffin over the phone to Warfield in Los Angeles.

Gentry had only met Warfield briefly on a few occasions, but he knew his reputation. Why, hell, Warfield even dressed like Herbert Hoover, and was reputed to have the same old-fashioned sense of morality. He— "What was that, George?" he said. "I'm afraid my mind was wandering." He made himself smile, a poor effort, and added, "Sign of age, no doubt."

"Maybe you have been working too hard," George said. "What I said was that I am outraged when someone like Bill Williams turns what amounts to inside information to his own profit. Aren't you?"

Gentry's poker face showed nothing. "Why," he said, "as a matter of fact, yes, I guess I am."

"Williams will bid on the construction," George said, "and no doubt will be successful. His, I am told, is the only construction firm in the state capable of handling the job. And for reasons of policy and politics, the state authorities will not want to go outside."

"Probably true, George."

"In such matters a construction loan is customary, is it not?"

"It is."

"And the posting of a performance bond?"

"Right again."

"Will this bank be asked for financial—backing? The construction loan, perhaps?"

"I would assume so, George."

"What would it take to ensure our refusal?"

It was here, George thought, that Gentry's reaction surprised him. He had not expected from Gentry the kind of flat rejection of his implied suggestion he had received from Walt Duggan with his mouth filled with steak. But neither had he expected from Tom Gentry such a mild, almost favorable response.

Gentry's gray eyes widened a trifle, the first time George had ever seen that. And Gentry appeared to be thinking hard about something George could not even guess at, taking his time as if he were weighing carefully various factors involved. Strange.

Gentry said at last, "It would take only a majority vote of

the directors, George. You have some influence, maybe more than you realize. And if you are determined—"

"I am."

"Then it might turn out to be a horse race."

And if I could show Warfield even a close vote, Gentry thought, and somehow convince him that I was actually trying to help the Brooks Thompsons out of their financial dilemma by buying their land instead of conning them out of it for my benefit, it might yet turn out all right.

Of course, Gentry was also thinking, if the goddamned enlargement project somehow failed to go through because Bill Williams didn't get his construction loan, then he, Tom Gentry, would be left with fifty acres of property which he needed like a hole in the head, and a twenty-two-thousand-five-hundred-dollar loan to pay off. But even that would be better than being tossed out on his ass because the Thompson woman's father happened to be a big wheel in New York who didn't like his darling child being taken advantage of in the big, bad world.

"Loans," George said, "don't normally go to the board of directors for decision, Tom."

True enough, but Gentry had a ready explanation. "In a matter of this importance, George," he said, "where a great deal of money will be involved, it is at my discretion whether the loan application is handled in a routine manner, or what amounts to a policy decision is requested from the board."

"And you would bring it to the board's attention?"

"Under the circumstances, I think I might very well."

"I appreciate this, Tom," George said.

Gentry's smile was as much as his normally expressionless face could manage. "I am considering the best interests of us all," he said.

Strange.

. . .

Bill Williams came home for lunch, something he did rarely these days. In the years before Martha's death, except when his presence was urgently required on a construction project or a business engagement in the city demanded his time, it was his habit to come home at noon for a companionable pre-lunch drink with Martha and talk of the morning's activities; just one more example of how much he had relied on her and failed to realize it until she was gone. His need for companionship was urgent today, and he hoped Kate might be at the house. Kate was.

They sat on the *portal* facing the great mountains, drinks in hand, while the silent maid set a table for two. "I saw your plane in the air this morning, honey," Williams said. "Young Harper with you?"

"He was. He saw something, but I don't know what it was, and he says he isn't sure either. I don't know whether to believe him or not. We're going up again tomorrow taking along what he calls 'the best rock man I know,' whatever that means."

"Geologist." Williams thought about it. "I'd like to know what they think. Tell Harper that, will you?"

Kate studied her father's face. "You're worried."

"Not really." Williams's smile belonged at a poker table. "I've always been a man to wear both suspenders *and* a belt. You know that."

Kate knew nothing of the kind, in fact quite the contrary. Her father had frequently demonstrated his scorn for the overly cautious. No matter. From her mother Kate had learned that merely seeing through a man's pretense or stratagems was no excuse for accusing him of them. She was silent for a few moments, staring at the canyon where the river dropped out of the mountains. She shivered suddenly. "What would happen if that dam did break?" She turned to watch her father's reaction to the question.

His poker-table smile did not waver. "Now, honey, we're

not even thinking about that. What we are thinking about is whether to go ahead with the enlargement plans. If we do go ahead, and I think we will, we'll move slowly and carefully and make damn good and sure everything is all right. Don't you worry about that."

"When I left the airport," Kate said, "I went to the library and took out a book they had on the Johnstown flood, the 1889 one when the dam collapsed." She was looking again at the river canyon. "A wall of water thirty feet high, twenty-two hundred people killed—" She turned her head then to look again at her father. "Jay Harper said this would be worse, much worse, with the whole city downstream."

"Goddamnit, honey, he was making a point, that's all."

"Do you really believe that?"

"Do you think I'd even consider going ahead if I thought any different? And there's something else too, honey. The easiest thing in the world to start is a panic rumor. That's how you cause runs on banks and stock market crashes and people getting trampled to death in crowded theaters when there's a little smoke that may not amount to anything."

"I never thought of it before," Kate said, almost as if Williams had not spoken, "but with that flood-control wall we're safe here in The Bend—"

"Probably."

"But the people down in the city—"

"Honey, you're dreaming up a nightmare the way you did sometimes when you were a little girl, remember? God only knew why. Maybe all kids do."

Kate studied him curiously. There were times when she knew him well, and other times, as now, when she felt she hardly knew him at all. "Did you ever have nightmares, Daddy?"

Williams, looking out at the mountains, could smile now, remembering. "Only one," he said. "That I wouldn't be able to support your mother and you. That one kept turning up for a long time." He looked up as the maid approached in her silent way. "All set, Carmen? Okay. Let's eat, honey, and talk about more pleasant things, huh? Like," he said as they sat down, "I had a letter from Bud Wilks this morning. You remember Bud? He's living in Honolulu now, and he says why don't I come on over and spend a few weeks. Would you like to go?"

Kate went along willingly with the conversational change. "You and Mother," she said, "were always going to take a vacation trip. A big one. Two, three months in Europe, something like that, but you didn't really want to go and I'm not sure Mother did either."

Williams studied his loaded fork and then set it down, untouched. "I watched you the other night," he said, "when Harper was talking about places he's been—Norway, the Middle East, Indonesia—"

"I'm not underprivileged, Daddy."

"You're tied down here."

"This is home, and I'm only tied down by choice."

"Because of me."

"Some people," Kate said, "don't even have homes. Jay Harper doesn't. He as much as told me so when he came here for dinner. So you see"—her smile was brilliant—"I'm the lucky one, Daddy, staying right here where I want to be."

"You need a man."

"Male chauvinist propaganda."

"Sam Martin wants to marry you."

"I know."

"You could do worse."

"That's a poor criterion."

"Okay, goddamnit," Williams said, smiling again. "I never got anywhere arguing with your mother either. But at least we aren't talking about that—dam."

"But we're both thinking about it, aren't we? We can't get away from that."

Food, even his own cook's superlatively flavored Mexican

food, suddenly lost its savor. Williams had a sip of ice water. Ice water, for God's sake! Because of that goddamned Jim Stark he wasn't even supposed to have beer with his lunch; one drink before lunch, no more than that. There were these constant reminders that he was no longer the man he had been. He said, "What do you want me to do, honey, scrub the whole enlargement project? After all the time and work, yes, and money we've put into it?"

Kate watched him steadily, in silence.

"Sam had it right this morning," Williams said. "Just because a character turns up and goes swimming in scuba gear and *thinks* he may have seen something, suddenly we begin to doubt all the engineering work we did, every bit of it, and does that make sense? The answer is that it sure as hell doesn't."

"But you still want to know what Jay Harper and his geologist think after we fly tomorrow morning?"

Williams picked up the glass of ice water and set it down again in disgust. He nodded slowly. "I'd be a fool not to, honey," he said in a quieter voice. "I may be pretty well over the hill, but I don't think I'm that far into senility yet."

"You," Kate said, "over the hill?" She shook her head, smiling, hiding the pain she felt at the concept. "That will be the day. Eat your lunch. I'm sorry. We were going to talk about pleasanter things."

Williams ate obediently, slowly, and tastelessly for a time in thoughtful silence, but what was in his mind would not go away. He set his fork down once more, this time with decision and finality. Was this why he had wanted to come home for lunch today, why he had hoped that Kate would be here? The mind played funny tricks; there was no doubting that. He said slowly, "Things don't go away, honey, just because you try to ignore them. If I hadn't learned that for myself, I'd have learned it from your mother, and maybe she's the one who really made me see it at that. What are you going to do when I'm not here any more?"

"Daddy!"

"Don't try to brush it off," Williams said. "I won't last forever. And I'll see to it one way or another that I don't just—hang on too long like some I know. What I want you to think about is what'll you do then?"

"Miss you. Just the way I miss Mother. But let's not talk about this kind of thing now."

Williams shook his head. "Sooner or later, if we have any sense at all, we're going to have to talk about it whether we want to or not. I don't want to make a big thing out of it, because it isn't, but in at least one thing I have to agree with Jim Stark, that damned old woman. When your heart begins behaving in a way that you notice it, where you never even gave it a thought before—well, then you start getting the message that you aren't going to live forever, after all, and you start thinking about things you maybe put off attending to because there always seemed to be plenty of time. Do you see what I mean?"

Kate was suddenly close to tears. She could only nod in silence.

"Okay," Williams said, and for the third time picked up the glass of ice water, glared at it, and set it down with an angry thump. His voice remained fond and gentle. "You're the main thing, of course. I guess that ought to go without saying. I'd like to see you married." He held his hand up quickly. "Let me finish. I'd like to see you married, *and* happy about it. Otherwise, to hell with it. That's the first thing. Okay?"

Again Kate could only nod.

"Now, this house," Williams said. "You call it home. That's fine, that's great. But it was *our* home, your mother's and mine. We planned it and built it and changed it around until it was the way *we* wanted it, and I'd hate to think that you'd feel you'd have to stay saddled with it for the rest of your life if you'd rather live somewhere else. If you want to stay here, fine.

If you don't, get rid of it. If we're where we can know about it, we'll understand."

She had mastered the tears now and could trust her voice. "I'll remember. Promise."

"Good. Now, I don't know what the hell to do about the business. You'll own it, but who's going to run it? Not Sam. Sam's an engineer, and engineers think with their slide rules, or these days with their pocket calculators. You tell Sam what to do and he's fine, but somebody has to tell him first. Well, I'll try to think of something." Suddenly Williams looked uncomfortable. "Now there's one more thing, and maybe it's most important of all."

"Daddy, please. You make it sound as if—"

Williams shook his head again, stopping the protest. "I've given this a lot of thought, honey," he said, "and this is something I've been wanting to say, not just write down for you to read after I'm gone. I'm no good at writing down things I feel. I never could. Your mother knew that. We used to laugh together at the letters I wrote her when I had to go away on business trips. All I could think of to say was what the weather was like and what I had to eat Hear me out, okay?"

Those tears were close again. Kate managed the single word "okay," and then sat silent.

"You aren't going to be the richest girl in the West, honey," Williams said, his voice quiet and dead serious now, "but you're going to have quite a pile. I've been stashing away like a pack rat ever since my first paper route. And that's what I want to talk about. *Enjoy* it! That's the thing. Blow the bundle, if you want, although you'll have one hell of a time doing it— but *enjoy* it, don't just let it sit there multiplying like a cageful of mice doing nobody any good but the bankers. After your mother died, and it was too late, I realized what a damn fool I'd been because I was always more interested in adding to the pile than in enjoying what was already there. Like that vacation trip you talked about. I don't know if your mother really wanted to go or not. I never even tried to find out, and she wasn't about to tell me unless I asked. And now I'll never know. Don't you make that mistake. The man was dead right when he said he'd been rich and he'd been poor, and rich is better. But only if you get some pleasure out of it. Remember that. Okay?"

Kate nodded, swallowed, and managed a faint smile. Her voice was not quite steady. "Okay," she said.

. . .

Cooley Parks got off the plane carrying a worn canvas kit bag reinforced here and there with leather. In it, Jay would have been willing to bet, were a geologist's pick, a spare pair of pants, a pair of lightweight, worn boots, toilet gear, a clean shirt, a clean pair of socks, Cooley's passport, and a bottle of whiskey. With that bag, the clothes he stood in, the hat he wore, and the raincoat over his arm, Cooley was prepared to go around the world or any place in it.

"What kind of a goddamned goose chase is this, anyway, boy?" Cooley's voice echoed in the passenger terminal.

"I hope that's all it is. Then I'll apologize, and we'll head for Canada as fast as we can go."

Cooley's eyes were pale blue in a lined, tanned face. They looked long and carefully at Jay. "And if it isn't?" His voice now was quieter.

"I haven't thought that far ahead. Have you eaten?"

Cooley accepted the temporary evasion. "Since I was coming down here to good cattle country," he said, "I figured I'd wait." He held thumb and forefinger about two and a half inches apart. "A steak like so, nice and rare? Something to drink? And maybe some talk along with it?"

"You have a deal." They walked out to Jay's car. "By the way," Jay said. "Thanks for coming."

Cooley's voice regained full volume, covering the parking lot as if from a public-address system. "A little thing like that? Why, hell's bells, boy, it's only twelve, fifteen hundred miles, no big deal."

The steaks were large and rare and good. Cooley ate, listened, and drank quantities of Danish beer. He said at last, "I always wondered where you came from. This figures. Your three times great-granddaddy, huh?"

"California," Jay said, "that's where I come from. You know that."

"No. L.A. never figured. There had to be big mountains, like these, in your background. But let it go, boy, I'm into my swami act. Do you want to tell me what you thought you saw from the plane this morning?"

"I want you to see it without any preconceptions."

"You're no wet-assed kid with his first geologist's pick. You know damned well what you were looking at."

"Maybe, but I want your opinion."

"Anything on the topographical map?"

Jay shook his head. "Twenty-foot contour intervals. Anything smaller wouldn't show."

"I told you, I don't know a fucking thing about dams."

"They hold back water, lots of water."

"Yeah." Cooley finished his beer, held up a finger, and watched the waiter nod and scurry off. "And every now and again," Cooley said, "one of them comes apart at the seams. That's what's worrying you."

"Actually," Jay said, "when you come right down to it, it's none of my business."

Cooley's smile was amused. "No? In that case give me time to finish this fresh beer and we can go back to the airport and see about planes to Calgary."

"Damnit, that wasn't what I meant."

"I can see that. Your great-granddaddy's country's got hold of you. And maybe the girl too. Is she pretty?"

"Look—"

"Or maybe she's rich? Always pick one or the other. And bear in mind that most times money lasts longer than looks."

It was still light enough to see when they drove out of the city, around The Bend, and along the course of the river into the canyon that climbed to Harper's Park.

Cooley, sitting quiet and relaxed in the passenger seat, let his eyes swing automatically, almost metronomically from side to side, studying rock formations, the river's course, the high sloping walls, and the occasional green meadows dotted with houses. "Nice, young country," he said. "When these mountains were pushing up not all that long ago, I'll bet it would have seemed pretty busy if there'd been anybody here to watch."

Jay said nothing. Cooley was not one for totally idle talk.

"Igneous and metamorphic rock," Cooley said. "Nothing sedimentary right in here."

"I haven't been over enough of it to know," Jay said.

"I picked up a geologic map of the area. I was looking at it a bit on the plane."

Which meant, Jay thought, that a detailed picture was already plain and clear in Cooley's mind, and that he knew right now, and would know tomorrow in the plane, precisely what he was looking at, and even possibly for. Long before there were computers there were minds like Cooley's which could absorb, store, and at will retrieve incredible amounts of minute information to be fitted together into a geologic pattern.

I do it with instruments, machines, and mathematics, Jay thought; he does it intuitively, and if mine is the more precise way, his is the faster by far, and the broader. We complement one another.

They came around the final turn in the climbing road and there was the dam, blocking the gorge, rising high above the stream and the generating plant.

Cooley whistled softly. "All I can say, boy, is that if that thing decides to let go, I want to be above it, not below it. The water is how deep, you say?"

"About eighty feet, twenty feet below normal."

"And the gradient of that stream above the lake?"

"In places it's damn near vertical," Jay said. "In fact, there are a couple of waterfalls upstream, and some of those hanging valleys and high canyons that feed down have sheer drop-offs."

"Correction," Cooley said. "If this thing decides to let go, I don't want to be above it, I want to be fifteen hundred miles away in Canada."

"Wait till you see it tomorrow from the air."

12

Once again Bill Williams, a glass of Bourbon in hand, sat on the governor's *portal* with the moonlight making the nearby mountains seem ghostly, unreal. What Williams considered "highbrow" music played quietly and not unpleasantly in the background.

"It isn't like you to twist and squirm, Bill," the governor said. "You've always come right out and said what was on your mind. Now you're fancy-footing around like one of those political pipsqueaks I have to deal with every day. You've lost some of your enthusiasm for the dam enlargement? Why?"

"I didn't say that." But that core of honesty would not be ignored. "Not exactly."

The governor sighed. He had great respect for Bill Williams, and the added leverage of long friendship to deflect his impatience. "All right," he said, "let's agree that you didn't say that exactly, but why are you thinking it? Give me reasons."

"I don't have any reasons. Not real ones."

"Now, God save the mark, you begin to sound even more like a politician."

He shouldn't have come here, Williams told himself; it was a damned fool thing to do, probably just one more sign that he was losing his grip. He sipped his Bourbon in silence.

"Bill," the governor said, "I shouldn't have to tell you this, but I'd better make my position plain. Aside from the fact that I don't like to look silly or fatuous or fickle or stupid any more than the next man, I simply cannot afford to. We have pushed this project through Washington channels pleading urgent need. We have pounded on desks and twisted arms and made all the horse trades that were required. We have scratched backs and done favors and foreclosed on old debts. We have used the state's natural resources as bargaining chips and threatened to legislate our own energy policies and fight for them right to the Supreme Court if we didn't get federal cooperation on this enlarged hydroelectric project. Now before I make any change in my position, Bill, I am going to have to have some damned good reasons; otherwise I will be saying in effect that I didn't know what the hell I was talking about in the first place—and that is something a politician just cannot afford to do."

"The other night," Williams said, "you were the one asking if what we were trying to do was right."

"I was," the governor said. "I admit it. I was hoping, even trusting that you with your damn-the-torpedoes-full-speed-ahead attitude would pooh-pooh my doubts. Which you did. Now what I want to know is what has changed since then?"

Williams got out his pillbox. He popped a yellow Valium pill into his mouth and washed it down with Bourbon. He shouldn't have come, he told himself again, but since he had, there was no way out but explanation—and maybe that was for the best, anyway. "A character went swimming in scuba gear," he said. "He just wanted a good look at Harper's Park village because it was named after his three times great-granddaddy, and he'd heard about it all his life. I've never had any itch to go look where my folks lived in Kansas, probably because I might find out they were run out of town on a rail. But that's beside the point. He dove and he looked, and he found some things, he says, down at the bottom of the dam where it ties into the sides of the gorge . . ."

The governor listened quietly, from long practice expressionless, and when Williams finished talking, the governor sat without moving for a long time in silence. He said at last, "And what is your assessment, Bill?"

"I wish I knew."

"You're worried."

Kate had said the same at lunch, and he had denied it. Now: "I don't know, Harry, and that's the honest truth. But before we go ahead, we'd damn well better make sure."

"*If* we go ahead."

"Okay, *if.*" Williams had another sip of the governor's mellow Bourbon. It had almost lost its savor.

"Suppose we bring in a couple of geologists," the governor said, "publish their reports, and show that our hearts are pure and that we're taking no chances with public safety."

Williams shook his head. "You aren't that kind of a shit, Harry. You're a lawyer, you've heard expert testimony claiming black is white and the other side's experts swearing it's green. You can find experts to say just about whatever you want them to say, and that's a goddamned fact."

The governor's sudden smile was crooked, and unamused. "Your cynicism is showing, Bill."

"Okay, only I call it realism."

"But you seem to be putting a considerable amount of faith in Harper, whom you scarcely know."

"I called J. G. Harkness in Houston and checked him out. J.G. knows him and says he's one of the best, and that is good enough for me. But what's just about as important is that he hasn't any ax to grind that I know about. It's no skin off his nose what happens here. He's headed for Canada, and I have an idea he'd already be gone if Kate hadn't worked on him. So why shouldn't he give us his honest opinion?"

The governor was silent, thoughtful. He said at last, "That's what we're talking about, isn't it, Bill? Opinions, I mean. But what are the facts?"

Williams shook his head again. "I'm no geologist, but I've built a lot of things in a lot of places, and I'd say in something like this there aren't any goddamned facts, Harry. Opinions are all there are—until you see what actually happens. Out in California they've been waiting ever since I can remember for that big earthquake that's been predicted by all the experts, and it hasn't happened yet. Or ask J.G. how many dry holes he's drilled when the best opinions he could get said there was oil. Until you can actually see the results, all you have is guess-work."

The governor's mind was off in another direction. "We're sitting here talking, Bill, about something that could panic this city into an absolute madhouse. Do you realize that?"

He had told Kate almost the same thing. Williams merely nodded.

"The Big Thompson Canyon flood," the governor said, "that Teton dam breaking, this last flood in Johnstown bringing back memories of the big one—" He shook his head. "I want an honest answer, Bill. Let's put the enlargement idea aside for the moment. In your opinion is there danger *now?*"

He had thought about it and thought about it until he felt the way a squirrel probably felt running in the wheel in its cage and getting nowhere. He said, "I don't know, Harry, and that's simple truth. And that's exactly what's beginning to scare me." He finished his Bourbon at a gulp, set the glass down, and stood up. "I guess I'm glad I came, after all," he said. "At least I've got it off my back."

"And put it right on mine. Thanks." The governor stood up too. "Sit down, Bill. I'll get us a drink. You can't walk out on me now."

. . .

Sam Martin, flanked by the two German shepherd dogs, was standing at the front door when Kate opened it in answer to the echoes of the heavy knocker. She smiled. "A friend," she said to the dogs, who immediately lost interest and walked away. "Come in, Sam. You came to see Daddy? He isn't here, but he said he wouldn't be too late."

Sam came slowly into the entrance hall and waited for

Kate to close the heavy door. "I didn't come to see Bill," he said then. "I know where he is. I came to see you."

Kate's smile appeared again. "I'm flattered. You—"

"That's the hell of it," Sam said. "You aren't flattered. Not really. That's what I wanted to talk to you about." He had worked himself up to this confrontation, even tried to rehearse it, although he knew that it would not follow any script he could anticipate and he would have to improvise right from the word "go," which was a helpless kind of thing to contemplate, but there it was. And now, watching Kate's smile begin to lose its brilliance, he decided that right off the bat he wasn't doing very well.

"What's the matter with your hand?" Kate said in sudden concern. "You keep working the fingers. Did you hurt it?"

"It's all right. It's fine. I just—banged my arm against something." She had always had this trick of keeping you off balance, Sam thought; like a boxer with a good left hand, she never let you get set to throw your Sunday punch. And now, suddenly, he was in the position of supplicant rather than being, as he had hoped, in command of the scene. "Can we talk? I mean, you know, just sit and—talk?" He probably had to go back to junior high school and his first dance, he told himself, for memory of a situation in which he felt more awkward. "Damnit, Kate—"

"That's better." The smile had reappeared in all its brilliance. "Much better. We'll sit on the *portal*." She waited for no answer, turned, and led the way through the large living room. Sam followed, trying unsuccessfully to keep his eyes from the rhythmical movement of her rounded haunches as she walked.

Sitting on the *portal,* with those big mountains looking down on him, Sam decided that his prepared speech suddenly seemed ridiculous, out of place, unpolished, and unreal. But it was all he had and anything was probably better than a long, strained silence. He took a deep breath and began. "Once upon a time," he said, "we had a kind of—thing going. Didn't we?"

"We did, Sam." Kate was unsmiling now, but her expression was not unfriendly; it was even fond, or was the word "compassionate"? "A real boy-girl-type thing, the kind you read about, the kind that is supposed to happen and probably doesn't often enough."

"Maybe it—got out of hand."

"It didn't, Sam, believe me."

"I mean, that night—"

"Nothing happened that night that—spoiled anything. You can believe that." Her smile reappeared momentarily like sunlight bursting through cloud. "There are no scars on my psyche from that night, Sam, not even any unpleasant memories. As a matter of fact, some of them are very pleasant indeed." Again the smile. "And if that makes me—as they used to say—carnal and unmaidenly, why, so be it."

"I don't know you any more, Kate, that's for sure. Once upon a time I thought I knew all about you—"

"I wouldn't have been flattered to know that, Sam." Kate's voice now was light, teasing. "No girl would. We like to think we are—mysterious creatures. We aren't, of course, but we like to think we are."

His prepared speech was now in tatters, but he pressed doggedly on. "You went off to college. East, where I've never been. I don't know the ground rules there. I mean—"

"And something else happened too, Sam," Kate said, her voice no longer teasing. "Mother died, and I wasn't here, and Daddy wouldn't let me come home to what he called shadows and gloom. He said he was all right, fine, and he wasn't, he was —shattered, but it took me a little time to realize it. Then I saw that I was useless, a nothing, a nonperson. Maybe that's when I started to grow up. You see, Sam, I'm not hiding anything from you. When I came back finally, everything was changed."

"I wasn't."

"No. But I was."

There was a long silence. In the moonlight the great mountains looked down, untouched, unchanged, Sam thought, a western version of that goddamned Old Man River in the song, who just keeps rolling along. He took his eyes from the mountains with effort. "What do you want, Kate? What are you waiting for?"

"I am not consciously waiting for anything. Maybe I am even trying to avoid thinking about what will be. At lunch Daddy gave me a talk on what to do after he dies. Ever since, I've been trying to forget that, and I can't. What do you want, Sam?"

"That's easy. You."

"How? A roll in the hay? I am willing, if that's what you want. Does that shock you? I'm sorry. I wasn't trying to. But you don't want all of me, Sam. You may not know that, but I do. I would make life a hell for you."

"Because I'm not a gold-plated genius?"

"Sam, stop hurting yourself."

"Because I've never done all kinds of wonders on an oil rig anchored in the North Sea, or in Indonesia or the Middle East? Because I'm just a plain ordinary engineer and not something fancy like a geophysicist with probably a Ph.D. after my name? Because—" The words suddenly ran down. Sam sat silent, vaguely shamed by his outburst.

Kate's eyes had not left his face, and her expression, fond, gentle, was somehow the worst hurt of all.

"Jay Harper means nothing to me," Kate said. True? False? Place a check mark in the correct box, Kate told herself; and allowed no indecision to show. "He flew with me over the dam this morning—"

"I know." Sam flexed the fingers of his still partially numb hand. "That's how I got this. Superman didn't like being touched. It was my fault. I lost my temper, and got put in my place. I'm not in his league, Kate. I watched you make that plain that night here at dinner. I listened to Bill making it plain this morning. I'm just me, and, like you said, you've changed, grown up, and there's the trouble, you're ready for bigger things than I'll ever accomplish, so maybe you're right and I'd better play in my own ball park."

Kate's eyes closed momentarily. When they opened again they glistened with tears. "I'm sorry, Sam."

"It's okay." Sam stood up. "Now we have it all straight, don't we? You know, it's been quite a day. First Bill, then Harper, now this. The only thing lacking for me is getting a good licking and being sent to bed without any supper. Good night, Kate."

. . .

George Harrison sat alone in his beloved library on this evening, his well-read 1951 first edition of C. L. Sonnichsen's splendid *I'll Die Before I'll Run* closed on his lap while he thought again of his talk with Tom Gentry. Here in his own familiar surroundings, the books lining the wall, the piñon fire burning fragrantly in the corner fireplace, the balloon glass of Hine cognac on the table at his elbow, he still could not shake the sense of unreality Tom Gentry's reaction had produced.

And here came one of the maids with another surprise. "Mr. Sam Martin is here, señor."

George was unused to visitors, but he hoped he did not seem off balance. "Show him in, by all means."

Sam was both ill at ease and a little astonished to find himself here. He had driven away from the Williams house after his painful confrontation with Kate, seen George's gateposts, and on impulse turned in. Then, despite a change of heart, in the long drive finding no convenient place to turn around until he reached the garages and the parking area, and fearing then that he might already have been seen, he let his temper have its way, shut off lights and engine, got out, and marched up to the front door. Bill Williams probably wouldn't like his being here even a little bit, but Sam had had a bellyful of Williamses on this day, and to hell with what Bill might think.

George was all cordiality. "I am delighted that you stopped by," he said, and dispatched the maid for drinks, Bourbon and branch water for Sam and a refill of the balloon glass of Hine cognac for himself.

They sat in deep leather club chairs flanking the corner fireplace. "Did you hurt your arm?" George, watching Sam's finger flexing, was politely solicitous.

If impetus had been needed, the question, reminding Sam of that painful airport scene, supplied it. "It's fine," Sam said, took a deep breath, and launched into the only possible subject that could justify his presence here. "Uh," he began, "you know about the approval of the dam enlargement project. We talked about it."

George nodded in silence and sipped his cognac. He wondered what had Sam all upset, and decided that even if he asked he was probably not going to find out.

"Well," Sam said, "there's maybe a hitch."

George set his balloon glass down very carefully. "Will you explain that, please, Sam?"

"There's this Superman in town," Sam said, "and he's got Bill Williams more uptight than I've ever seen him. He's afraid of shadows."

"Indeed?" Bold Bill Williams, George thought, afraid of anything at all? It seemed unlikely. "What?" he said. "And why?"

Sam went through it all, and in the process drained his drink. "Maybe I shouldn't be telling you this," he said, "but—"

"Nonsense," George said, and pushed the bell beside his chair. The maid appeared immediately and George gestured at Sam's empty glass. "It concerns us all, doesn't it? What we are talking about, Sam, is a question of public safety, and that is not something that ought to be kept secret."

That drink he had just tossed down had helped, and the

temper that had brought him here in the first place was still almost intact, but suddenly Sam did not like the direction this talk was going. Bill Williams had been emphatic about keeping the matter under wraps while they considered it, and here George Harrison was saying it ought to be brought out into the open. The maid returned with Sam's refill, and he took it eagerly. "It isn't settled yet," he said. "I mean, it's just in the first talking stage." He had a long pull at the fresh drink.

"I understand," George said. "And I appreciate your bringing it to my attention."

"Look, Mr. Harrison—"

"My friends call me George."

"Okay. George. I—ah—work for Bill Williams." The temper was oozing away fast and the alcohol was not taking its place. "And if he knew I'd come here with all this, I'd end up with my ass in a sling. Bill Williams can be mean as a Gila monster when he thinks he's been crossed and he told me to keep my mouth shut." It was an ignominious admission, but under the circumstances, Sam thought, it was only prudent.

The piñon fire in the corner fireplace crackled faintly. It was the only sound. George held his balloon glass of cognac between his palms now, warming it automatically, but not bothering to sniff its fragrance while he thought about the matter. "I see your dilemma," he said at last.

It was not so much a dilemma as a predicament, Sam thought, and told himself to shut up, he'd already said too much.

"Nothing has been decided yet," George said, "is that right?"

Sam felt a little better. "Exactly. Bill is still talking to himself the way he does before he makes up his mind."

As if the decision were entirely Bill's to make, George thought, and felt anger stirring in his mind. Arrogant Bill Williams. Maybe this time he had managed to get his feet tangled, something George would dearly love to watch. "And Harper? What about him?"

Sam shook his head. "I don't know. He flew over the dam with Kate Williams this morning. Far as I know, he's still around, but he may not be."

"One thing puzzles me," George said. "Why does Bill place credence in what Harper tells him?"

"Bill checked him out in Houston." Give the devil his due, Sam thought. "J. G. Harkness says he knows his business."

Better and better, George thought. It was, then, a tale to be believed. J. G. Harkness was a man who paid top dollar and hired only the best. The fact was known throughout the Southwest. George had a sip of the cognac. It had rarely tasted as good. "If and when a decision is made," he said, "you'll be notified, won't you, Sam?"

"I'd better be. If we go ahead, I'll be the engineer in charge. If we don't, I'm going to have a lot of explaining to do to the Corps of Engineers people I've been selling on the project the last eighteen months."

George nodded. "Good."

Somehow, Sam didn't like the sound of that single word. He kept quiet, and waited.

"So you can keep me informed," George said, "can't you, Sam?"

"I don't know about that," Sam said. "I mean, what Bill tells me—"

"But you came here tonight," George said. "It was a matter of conscience, I'm sure, and it took courage."

And, Sam told himself silently, it had been a plain god-damned stupid thing to do, because now he was no longer his own man, or even just Bill Williams's man; he served two masters, and that was the hell of a position to be in.

Play ball with George, he told himself, tell him whatever he wanted to know about what was going on, and George wouldn't bother to mention this talk tonight. But refuse to keep George up to date, and it would only take a phone call to Bill, letting him know that Sam Martin had disobeyed his orders for silence, and Sam didn't even like to think about what would happen then. He had not been exaggerating when he had said that Bill Williams could be mean as a Gila monster when he had been crossed.

Well, that was the way it was, and Sam supposed he'd better start getting used to it. He had another deep taste of his Bourbon. Might just as well get a little drunk; he wasn't going to feel very good tomorrow anyway.

Sam Martin's somewhat laborious process of ratiocination, George thought, had been as easy to follow on Sam's face as it would have been in print. He understood and was satisfied with Sam's conclusions, and he raised his bubble glass in acknowledgment. "As I said, Sam, I am delighted that you dropped by. Another drink, perhaps?"

13

During the night, above the eight-thousand-foot level, scattered snow showers fell. Long after the city down on the plain was in near-darkness, Bernie and Pete from their fourteen-thousand-foot perch, still in sunlight, had watched the changing weather approach.

"Cirrus clouds first," Bernie had pointed out. "See them? Streamers. I think of them, like I read somewhere, as the outriders of the main storm body, carrying their warning flags." She was suddenly shy. "Silly, I guess. They're just clouds."

"I like it," Pete said. "Maybe there are bands up there too, and trumpets blowing. What does the main army look like?"

Bernie began to smile, her shyness suddenly gone. "Over there. See? Those are the troops, infantry, armor, artillery, the works. Those big dark masses are carrying the muscle, all the moisture and all the winds. And if they want to, maybe if they think a big show of force is necessary, they can break out the lightning and turn it loose"—she paused, unsmiling now, shaking her head gently in awe—"with more power," she said, "than you can believe possible, more energy released. They showed us time-lapse photographs of a big thunderstorm pod. You know, one frame taken every so many seconds, then when they run the film through a projector at normal speed you see the action actually taking place."

Pete nodded. "I dig."

"Well, those big black clouds aren't static. Inside they boil and churn and you get some impression of the enormous forces at work, updrafts, downdrafts, sudden cooling, sudden warming, electricity enough to light that whole city a dozen times over, maybe a hundred times, being generated and breaking out in lightning bolts."

Pete listened quietly, his eyes on the distant clouds.

"Little specks of dust," Bernie said, "on which moisture inside the clouds condenses, and as it goes up in an updraft it turns to ice. Then maybe it comes down, accumulates more moisture, and goes up again, forming more ice. Up and down, growing all the time. That's how you get hailstones the size of eggs." Bernie paused. "And all that cooling and freezing means that enormous amounts of heat are being given off, and heat is energy."

Pete was smiling. "You've studied all this."

"I'm a fire watcher," Bernie said. "That's my main job, but I turn in weather reports too, temperatures, humidity, barometer readings, wind direction and velocity—and, well, I like to know what part it all plays, and I like to watch the weather and have some idea how it works—" Again that shyness appeared. "I don't really know all that much. But Sam and I like to watch it." She rubbed the Malamute's ears.

"So do I," Pete said. "From right here."

They watched until the sun was down at last, the night closed in, and the air turned colder. Stars appeared and were blotted out as the clouds continued their advance. Bernie and Pete went inside, other matters on their minds.

Some of the night's snow showers were mere dustings which nevertheless held on the chilled ground and rocky ledges. In other places the passing storm dropped as much as three or four inches of dry snow which here and there accumulated in miniature drifts. Tiny alpine plants were buried. Talus slopes lost their harshness beneath the smooth white cover. There was created an illusion of uniformity which was far from reality.

Pete Otero, looking down this morning on the altered world, feeling the new chill that had come unheralded along with the snow, said, "Still want me to stick around for a while? I could make it down now okay. No sweat."

Her greatest fear, Bernie had long ago decided, was that she would try to cling to him after she was no longer wanted, and in the end despise herself for having spoiled what had been good. "Do you want to stay, Pete?"

"You're not supposed to take in boarders, are you?"

"Let me worry about that. Do you want to stay? It could be for some days if the weather really closes in. And the reports say it may."

"Hell," Pete said, "I'm enjoying myself, good food, lazy days, energetic nights." He was watching her face, and what he saw there stopped the words and turned him suddenly, uncharacteristically solemn. "I want to stay, baby. I haven't had near enough of you yet, and I'm beginning to think I never will."

"Pete. You don't have to say things like that."

"You underestimate yourself."

Bernie started to turn away to end the conversation before it got out of hand. "Let's have breakfast."

The strength in Pete's hand was almost unbelievable as he caught her arm and turned her effortlessly but with careful gentleness to face him again. His voice was quiet, still solemn. "I know what I am, Bernie, a big lunk, once upon a time real good at knocking people down on a football field. Now I'm going to have to find out what else I can do, and I think I can use some help. I didn't come up here with that in mind. Or maybe I did. I don't know. But—"

"Please, Pete. Don't say it. Let's—just—leave—it—the—way—it—is!" She turned again, pulled her arm free from his grasp, and almost ran into the building.

Pete looked after her, wondering if he should follow, and decided not. He turned away to give her a measure of privacy. It was beyond him why women cried.

The low sun lighted the mountaintops, turning their new snow to clear pink, accentuating the shadows of the canyons and valleys beneath. Down at the city airport, on the plain already in full sunlight, Pete saw, as yesterday morning, the red airplane begin its run, lift off, and reach for the clear sky. He watched it while he thought about Bernie—and himself.

. . .

Cooley Parks sat in the right-hand front seat of the plane; Jay behind him. Kate, going through the motions of flying with automatic ease, herself and the aircraft a cohesive unit, was trying to sort out her impressions of this "expert" Jay Harper had summoned, from where, Kate had no idea. She could not have said what she had expected, but Cooley did not fit the picture. He seemed entirely too casual.

Remembering Jay yesterday, Kate had said as they approached the plane, "No map, Mr. Parks?"

"It's Cooley, ma'am, and, no, I've already looked at a map. Nice country. It kind of stands on end, doesn't it? Like the Alps, only there's more of it." Cooley was consciously and politely keeping his voice well below its normal roar.

Airborne, over her shoulder now to Jay, Kate said, "Straight to the dam?"

Jay looked at his watch. "We've got a few minutes yet. What about a big circle to give Cooley a general look? Then let's follow the course of the river upstream."

Down on the plain, the city in sunlight, buildings rose like a child's toy blocks, and traffic of miniature automobiles was already heavy on the bridges and main thoroughfares. Cooley looked at it all in silence, thinking his own thoughts.

They completed their large circle and Jay looked again at his watch. "I think we start upstream now."

It was not a direct order, Kate thought, and yet Jay's voice carried a note of command and the man obviously expected immediate obedience. She put the aircraft into a swinging turn with more than necessary abruptness. Neither man seemed to notice.

They approached and then followed the river's curve at The Bend. "Quite a little swing there," Cooley said, looking down with interest now.

Jay was leaning forward, his head almost between the two front seats. "I was thinking the same yesterday."

They seemed to read each other's minds, Kate thought, and they spoke in a kind of shorthand which both impressed and annoyed her. In a way it was like hearing doctors speak together, surgeons in particular, at the hospital where three days a week she worked as a volunteer. As a layman she could not follow all of the implications of the laconic conversation, but from its very lack of emphasis she was aware that the matters they were discussing were far from trivial.

"In normal years," Cooley said, "that wall at the river bend comes in handy, yes?"

"There used to be occasional flooding," Kate said. "That's why—" She stopped and suddenly found herself looking at The Bend curve of the river with wholly new eyes. She had known objectively, of course, that the concrete wall at the curve had been built to protect The Bend area from those annoying spring floods, but all at once she was thinking now of what she had read of the Johnstown flood, a wall of water thirty feet high roaring down the river gorge approaching that turn—

"Water," Cooley said almost offhandedly, "tends to flow downhill in a straight line unless something makes it change course. Shouldn't wonder if there's an igneous intrusion in there that caused the bend in the first place." He glanced over his shoulder at Jay. "You agree?"

"Likely," Jay said, and glanced again at his watch. "We're just about on schedule I hope. I allowed a change of one minute from yesterday. That ought to be close enough."

Again that kind of verbal shorthand, Kate thought, and saw Cooley glance at her and smile faintly as if he understood, as apparently he did, because he said, "He's allowing for the change of sun angle in twenty-four hours. Shouldn't wonder if we're looking for shadows."

"There it is," Jay said. Suddenly the dam stood clear and plain ahead and beneath them. The waters of the lake glistened in sunlight beyond. As yesterday, the top of the dam seemed to extend beyond its boundaries in both directions. Jay said, "See anything?"

"Yeah." Cooley's voice was expressionless. "I sort of figured that was what you might have in mind. You're thinking horst?"

"Could be. What do you think?"

"Take some looking. You poked around?"

"That's why I wanted you."

"Slickensides?"

"I didn't find any evidence. Again, that's why I wanted you."

Kate said suddenly, almost explosively, "Horst! Slicken-what-ever-you-said! What on earth are you talking about?" She tried and could not control the impatience and excitement in her voice. "Or is it entirely too complicated for me to understand?"

Cooley said with gentle patience, "You know about faulting, ma'am, movements of the earth's crust?"

"Of course." She made an angry gesture chiding herself. "I'm sorry. There is no need for me to shout at you."

"I've been shouted at by a lot of people in a lot of places," Cooley said. "Doesn't bother me much any more. To answer one of your questions, a horst is an uplifted area bounded by two or more faults. That's the textbook definition. Sometimes it's almost a straight line of higher ground. That could be what's casting those straight shadows at each end of the dam. Could be."

"Oh." Kate's voice was subdued. "And the other, slicken-what-ever-you-said?"

"Slickensides." Again it was Cooley with the explanation. "When there's faulting, rocks rub together, sometimes, usually, under enormous pressure, and the rock faces become almost polished as if you'd ground them with a polishing wheel. Okay?"

Kate was silent. She looked down at the jagged mountains, the shining lake, the dam which from their height seemed tiny, a child's toy. She shivered faintly. "And what does it mean?"

"Maybe nothing." This was Jay. He spoke to Cooley. "You agree?"

"Why, hell, yes, boy, I agree. On the other hand—" Cooley left the sentence unfinished.

"On the other hand, what?" Kate said. She waited, but there was silence. "Well? You're going to tell Daddy, aren't you? Then why not tell me?"

"We don't know anything yet," Jay said. "We're just looking at possibilities."

"You thought enough of the possibilities," Kate said, "to bring Mr. Parks—"

"Cooley, ma'am."

"—from I don't know where."

"Calgary. Nice little plane trip. Good steak dinner last night. Fine scenery."

"On the other hand, what?" Kate said. Her voice was quiet now. She glanced over her shoulder at Jay. "You are the one who talked about the city downstream, all those people. On the other hand, what? What could it all mean?"

"Well," Cooley said at last, "it wouldn't be the first time a dam was built right smack on a fault, where it has no business being. But if I were you, ma'am, I'd keep that possibility to myself until we know better what we're talking about."

"I think we'd better go back now," Jay said. "We've seen all we can see."

"About time," Cooley said, "for me to get down to work."

·   ·   ·

His Honor Mayor José-María Lopez y Baca considered this matter too important for the telephone, so he appeared in person at the governor's office, and was shown in at once. He sat straight and angry in one of the leather visitor's chairs. "When we talked about the dam enlargement and water rates," he said without preamble, "I was almost beginning to think you were human, after all, Harry. Now I'm not so sure. Every time I start trusting an Anglo, what I get is a kick in the teeth."

"Sooner or later," the governor said, "I expect you will let me know what you are talking about, Joe. Then maybe we can discuss it."

"You know perfectly well what I'm talking about. The dam. It's unsafe as it is, and you know it."

"Oh?" Automatic reaction, a moment's respite while he gathered his thoughts. It was only last night that he and Bill Williams had discussed the dam's safety. How, then—?

"If that mother breaks, Harry," the mayor said in a different, quieter, but even more intense voice, "you know who's going to get it. It won't be the rich bastards in The Bend and it won't be you in the Governor's Mansion up on the ridge or all those Anglos with their hundred- hundred-and-fifty-thousand-dollar houses on the hillsides. It'll be the poor goddamned Chicanos down along the river and in Old Town, in apartment houses and trailers and rooming houses and shacks and hotels, they'll be the ones flooded out, drowned like rats in a cellar. That's what I'm talking about."

"Now, see here, Joe—"

"This isn't a political debate, Harry. You can snow the legislature all you want. There's nobody better at it, I'll admit. But this is just you and me. I've never liked you much. You know that. But I never thought you were the kind of shit who'd keep something like this bottled up and maybe get a lot of people killed just to save your goddamned reputation."

The large office was still. The governor said at last, "Is your temper tantrum over, Joe? Are you prepared to listen instead of foaming at the mouth? Then suppose I tell you that the first word I had that the dam might be questionable—*might be*—was last night. What would you say then?"

The mayor opened his hands, studied them in silence, obviously struggling for control, and closed them again, almost, but not quite, into hard brown fists. He looked up at the governor's face. "I'd be tempted to say, 'Bullshit!'" His voice was quiet now. "But what I will say is that I hope to hell you're telling the truth. Are you?"

"It is the truth, Joe. Bill Williams came to see me and told me."

"Bill is one Anglo I'll believe. How long has he known?"

"Night before last a man, a stranger told him what he thought—no, what he *suspected*, that the dam may have been weakened when we had that earthquake."

"That earthquake couldn't have done anything. It didn't even knock the pictures crooked in my house."

"Down here, yes," the governor said. "Apparently up at the dam it was harder."

Again there was silence. The mayor's brown eyes searched the governor's face. "Are you leveling with me, Harry? That's the way it is? And you heard first last night and Bill first heard the night before?"

"That's it. Now what I want to know is, where did you hear about it, and from whom?"

The mayor spread his hands. "What difference? They were talking about it over coffee this morning over at the Hilton. Somebody asked me what I thought, and I said it was bullshit, and then I came straight over here. I figured you'd have to know. So what about it? What are you going to do?"

The governor leaned back in his chair and looked out the window. The mountains were there, always the mountains, immutable, unaffected, in a sense impregnable. It was trite, but it was true: in their presence you felt small and insignificant, but that didn't decrease by one iota the weight of your problems.

"I wish I knew, Joe," he said at last. "We're waiting for more information, but if and when it comes, it isn't going to be definitive, I'm afraid, and in the end we're just going to have to make a judgment call." He sat up straight. "Before that happens," he said, "I'll let you know. That's a promise. That's the best I can do."

The mayor stood up. "I don't like the idea," he said, "of trusting you any farther than I could throw you. But I guess now I'm going to have to."

The governor stood too. His smile was humorless. "That's the way it is, Joe." His voice was solemn. "We don't want this to go any farther than we can help, newspaper, radio, TV—you have influence I don't have in some directions." He left it there, implications plain.

The mayor nodded. "If I have to," he said, "I'll scare the lights out of some people to keep them quiet. And if I ever find the bastard who started the talk—"

"As a lawyer I'll defend you for murder," the governor said. "For free. And if we lose, as governor I'll pardon you. And that's a promise too."

. . .

On the ground at the airport, the sound of the red plane's engine no longer beating at them, Kate said, "Now what?"

Cooley sighed. "I start poking. Someday I'm going to try to add up all the time I've spent on my knees, or worse, digging like a one-pawed badger to see what's under the surface. It's an undignified trade I picked."

Jay looked at Kate. "Are you free? Can you drive him up to the dam?"

Cooley said, "Where you going, boy?" Then comprehension dawned quickly. "Downstream, huh? Have a look-see there?" He nodded. "Good thinking. How about it, ma'am, can you give me a lift up the mountain?"

They were talking in their shorthand again, Kate thought, and again the analogy of surgeons discussing critical surgery came to mind. "Of course. My car is over here."

Driving out of the city, heading for The Bend turn, Kate said, "You and he—?" She left the question unfinished, hanging.

"We've known each other quite a spell, ma'am."

"I wish you would stop that 'ma'am' business. You know my name."

"Touchy Kate, the one in that Shakespeare play. In some ways you're like her, or try to be. Now don't rear back and spit in my eye. I'm an old man, probably older than your daddy, and age has its rights and privileges, or used to. To answer your question, I've known Jay since he broke into the oil business as a young pup, advanced college degrees after his name and all, bright-eyed and bushy-tailed and raring to go, and those of us who'd been around a long time just waited for him to make a horse's ass of himself—excuse the language, but there isn't any other that says it."

Despite herself, Kate was smiling. "And did he?"

"Nope. He made horse's asses of the rest of us, kept us from more or less rushing in the way we always had, drilling holes without enough planning and maybe lousing up a good field, and leaving oil and gas down in the ground damned near beyond reach forever. That was out in Indonesia."

Kate's smile had disappeared. She concentrated on her driving.

"Don't get me wrong," Cooley said. "He isn't sixteen feet tall with wings on his feet and he sometimes makes mistakes just like the rest of us. But he makes damned few of them, damned few. There may be better men than he is, but I've done a lot of work in a lot of places, and I've never seen one."

"You're loyal." Kate glanced curiously at the tanned, lined face. "He just called you, and you dropped everything and came down here?"

"I pay my debts, and I owed him a couple." Cooley smiled without amusement. "There was a night in Aberdeen I'd just as soon forget. You come in after three weeks on an oil rig in the North Sea and you maybe play a little too hard, and so does everybody else. One thing leads to another." He shrugged.

A man's world, Kate thought. Her father, with a life spent around construction jobs, would know about it. She did not. She changed the subject. "Why is he going downstream for what you called a look-see?"

"Oh, that." Cooley's voice was explanatory again, a teacher lecturing. "Just to get an idea of what we might be up against. This river has spent a long time cutting its channel. Look at some of these gorges. Stands to reason that in a few million years there have been big floods. I mean really big. Shouldn't wonder if out on the plain there aren't some rocks, maybe house size, carried down from the mountains by water. They'd be probably worn rounded by now, and maybe partly buried by alluvium, lesser material washed down in the river's normal cutting. But if they're there, and they probably are, there's only one place they could have come from, and that's upstream, torn loose and pushed down by water in flood." Cooley glanced at Kate. "And that's what we're all thinking about, isn't it?"

Kate shivered. "I read a little about the big Johnstown flood. It seemed—incredible."

"Lady, what water can do *is* incredible. Out in California during the Gold Rush they had what they called placer mining until they finally outlawed it. They had things like cannons that shot streams of water, and they washed down whole mountainsides just to get at the gold that was buried. Stand on the edge of the Grand Canyon sometime and have a look at what the Colorado River has done and you'll get some idea of what water can do."

"And that dam that we've just taken for granted—?" Kate said. Again she left the question unfinished and hanging.

"Yeah," Cooley said, and was silent.

"What can you tell?" Kate said. "And if you can tell anything, what can you do?"

"I'm a geologist, a rock man."

"But you know about these things."

"No." Cooley's voice was definite. "Nobody knows about them—until they happen. And then it's usually too late. We try to look ahead, and we think we are, but we're really looking backward because that's where our knowledge is. All the rest is just a matter of judgment. And luck. Mostly luck."

14

State Senator Walt Duggan hung up the phone and leaned back in his chair to stare hard at the ceiling. This was the third call he had had within the hour, each concerned with the same thing: the Harper's Park dam. Was it safe for enlargement? Was it even safe as it was?

The senator's business was insurance, but that, he knew, was not the reason for these calls. These callers wanted, not financial protection, but assurance from someone in authority, an elected official, that all was well, and that *government* (which frequently they scorned and berated as a useless burden) was in this time of possible danger on top of the situation and prepared to act if necessary.

And, of course, the senator had a personal stake in the matter as well, his share of those ten acres he and Johnny Cisneros had bought only yesterday from Angelita Leyba, land which would be a mere burden if the dam enlargement project was canceled. It occurred to the senator that if he knew the answer to the questions he was being asked *before Johnny Cisneros did*, it was just possible that he might persuade Johnny to buy out his share. Maybe even at a profit.

The senator sat up and punched the button on his intercom. "Get me Bill Williams, honey," he told his secretary. "If he isn't in his office, track him down, okay?"

Bill Williams was in his office. "You too, Walt?" he said when he heard the first question.

"What the hell is going on, Bill?"

"I wish I knew. I'd twist a few necks. This kind of talk is goddamned dangerous."

The senator could not agree more, but what he really wanted was an answer. "But is there anything to it? Is that dam safe?"

"Jesus, Walt, all I can tell you is what I've told everybody else. We built a good solid dam. It's been there almost ten years. The lake is way below normal level, so what danger could there be?" Not direct lies; merely evasive half-truths. The alternative was to add to the obviously growing concern, when the only sensible thing to do was put a stop to it. If possible. "Where did you hear this—this goddamned rumor? It's like Chicken Little and the-sky-is-falling-down."

The senator was a shrewd man, through wide experience in politics finely attuned to subtleties and nuances. Bill Williams was an honest man, but there had been times when the senator was sure that Bill, like any sensible man, had raked in pots when he held no more than two lousy pairs or maybe a busted flush. The senator had an idea that Bill was running a bluff right now, but if he was, he wasn't going to admit it. "Okay, Bill," the senator said. "Thanks. What you say makes sense. How's everything? How's that pretty daughter of yours?"

"You old goat," Bill said. There was relief in his voice, faint, but to an attentive ear discernible.

"See you," the senator said, and hung up. His expression was troubled. To the intercom he said, "Get me the governor, honey. Tell Clara it's important."

When the governor was on the line: "I'm wearing two hats, Harry," the senator said. "I'm asking as a Senate committee chairman, *and* as an insurance man with a lot at stake." He wore three hats, actually, he thought, but there was no point in mentioning his personal stake. "What's the straight story on the Harper's Park dam?"

The governor was no stranger to poker tactics either. His voice was filled with surprise. "Why, what have you been hearing, Walt? Is there supposed to be something wrong?"

But here the senator had leverage. "Harry, I'm not Joe Citizen. If I really put my heart into it, I can cut you and your administration right off at the pass as far as appropriations are concerned, and you know it. And if something does happen and I get up in the Senate *after* the event and say that I asked you for information and you withheld it, there'll be hell to pay and no pitch hot, and that's for sure too. I want a straight answer."

There was a short silence. The governor said, "I think you'd better come over here, Walt. I have a couple of appointments, but they can wait."

"That's me you see walking in the door."

•   •   •

Sam Martin, again summoned to Bill Williams's office, sat, faintly hungover and clearly uncomfortable, in one of the leather visitor's chairs drawn up to the conference table. Once more he had come prepared with drawings as well as piles of engineering data, and once more the material was doing him no good at all.

"We've got a geologist up there looking things over right now," Williams said, "and Harper's out on the plain looking around, God only knows for what." Kate had telephoned him from Harper's Park with a brief report. "You know what they're thinking is a possibility? Just a possibility, mind, but God help us if it turns out to be real. They're thinking that maybe we built that dam right on a fault line."

"We couldn't have."

"Tell me why. It's been done before."

"Damnit, Bill, the Army Corps of Engineers—"

"Yeah. They've been wrong before too."

Another argument had worked once, Sam thought, and maybe it would work again, at least as a diversion: "Look, Bill," he said as convincingly as he could, "it doesn't make sense that we get all uptight just because first one character and now another turn up out of nowhere and begin shaking their heads as if the world is coming to an end tomorrow morning. Who the hell are they, anyway, to turn into instant experts on local conditions?"

"I told you I checked Harper out with J.G. in Houston. And I just finished checking out this Parks geologist with J.G. too. They're top hands, both of them."

"Okay, if they're so good, then why are they here? No pay, no reason that I can see for them to take any interest at all." Except maybe Kate, Sam thought; and could not allow himself to say it aloud.

"Sam," Williams said, "the point isn't who they are or where they came from or why they're here. None of that matters a damn at the moment. What does matter is the problem they've raised and what we're going to do about it *if* it turns out to be real. Can we empty that lake?"

"Sure. In three, four weeks, maybe longer. The water level is already below the overflow spillway now and the only outlets are through the power station and they're designed to turn turbines, not drain a lake." He snapped his fingers. "Wait a minute. There's the old diversion tunnel. The way the water level is now, we'd have to blast a channel to it, but—"

"And if there's a fault, what would more blasting do?"

"I don't believe there is a fault."

"I'm not sure I do either," Williams said. "Yet. But if we get some kind of evidence that there is, then we'd better be ready with some answers that don't take three or four weeks to work. There's already talk. You've heard it?"

"No."

Something in the unequivocal tone and the instant decisiveness of the answer caught Williams's ear. He studied Sam carefully. "You said that a little fast, Sam. You haven't been getting any calls? I have. All morning. So has the governor." Williams pushed back his chair suddenly, stood, and walked to the windows to stand there in silence for a time with his back to the big office. Over his shoulder, his voice slow and distinct, "I'd hate to think you're a liar, Sam." He turned then, and stood legs widespread, head lowered and shoulders faintly hunched in the old truculent posture. "You wouldn't have any idea where this talk you haven't been hearing got started?"

"No."

"You wouldn't have been talking to George Harrison again either, would you, Sam?"

"I had a drink with him."

"The one at the Territorial Club, or another one?"

"I—had a drink at his house. Last night." A number of drinks, to be precise.

"And today the rumors start." Williams nodded, mere sad acceptance, no more than that, and some of the fighting-bull stiffness went out of his shoulders. "You're an engineer, Sam, trained to put two and two together. In my place, what would you think?"

"Look, Bill—"

"I asked you a question, Sam. I want an answer."

Defiance flared briefly. "Damnit—" Defiance faded and died. I am thirty years younger than he is, Sam thought, three inches taller, and twenty pounds heavier—and I can't face him down; I never could. Ignominious admission, but unavoidable. "Okay," he said, admission, apology, and appeal all at once, "I told Harrison what Harper had said, that we'd be crazy to think of enlarging the dam and maybe it wasn't even safe as it is. But I told him it was only one man's opinion and mostly guesswork at that, and how was I to know—?"

"That's enough, Sam." Williams's voice was suddenly weary, and although not loud it brought silence into the office. "You can take your toys, your pictures, and your papers and beat it now."

As if on cue, the telephone on his desk buzzed quietly. Williams reached for it, his eyes never leaving Sam's face. "You heard me," he said, sat down, lifted the receiver to his ear, and swung his chair to face the mountains again. He listened briefly. "Okay," he said into the phone. "Send him in. We're all through here." There was finality in the words.

Sam began to gather his papers and drawings from the conference table, trying without success to think of something to say. Williams did not even turn his chair to watch.

The door opened and Jay Harper walked in.

Sam picked up his material, walked out in silence, and closed the door behind him.

Williams swung his chair around to face his desk. His face was expressionless as he indicated the chair Sam had left and waited until Jay was seated. "Kate called me," Williams said. "She told me what you and Parks think."

"A possibility. Cooley's looking into it. If there's evidence, he'll find it."

"And you've been doing what?" The question was blunt, demanding.

Jay wondered what had been going on between Williams and Sam Martin that had produced this brusqueness in Williams's manner, and decided it was none of his business. "Poking around. Did you ever notice those big rocks behind your house? The gray ones, partially sunk in the ground? Twenty or so feet across, fifteen, twenty feet high, some of them?"

"I used to play in them when I was a kid." Williams closed his eyes briefly. Goddamn Sam Martin, anyway. What amounted to Sam's disloyalty affected him more than he would have thought possible. Twenty years ago, Williams thought, he would have taken instant, brutal action and then dismissed the matter. Now he just tried to keep himself under control. But Harper's mention of those huge rocks, bringing back childhood memories, had somehow plucked another, similar nostalgic chord. "I decided then," he said, "while I was still a kid that one day I'd build a house with the kind of view you get from those rocks."

Jay nodded. "I don't blame you."

"What about those rocks?"

"Did you ever wonder where they came from?"

"That's a funny question. Kids don't wonder about things like that. Why?"

"They came down out of the mountains," Jay said. "There's nothing like them in the basic rock structure anywhere around. The river brought them down. In one hell of a big flood."

Williams took his time. He said at last, "You're the expert, or supposed to be. But have you any idea what some of those rocks weigh? I've moved a lot of rock in my day."

Jay smiled without amusement. "I can make a very good guess. And they weighed more when they were carried down by the water because they've been there quite a while, and they've been eroded, weathered, some of them even split by vegetation, and that doesn't happen overnight."

The large office was still. "You come up with the goddamnedest things," Williams said. "Go on, what are you getting at?"

"The normal course of those old floods," Jay said, "the big ones, I mean. Maybe you know the engineers talk about hundred-year floods, and sometimes even thousand-year floods, meaning you can expect one of them maybe every hundred years or thousand years. I'm talking about more than that—ten thousand, maybe a hundred thousand years. But at least one happened. The evidence is right there in those big rocks and in the alluvial fan of the same kind of rocks below them. And when it happened, that's where it went, right where those big houses of yours are now."

In the silence: "Go on," Williams said. "What's the rest of it?"

"There wasn't a big concrete dam up there then," Jay said, "holding back all that lake water that could come down the canyon at once, so maybe now we're talking about something even bigger. That's the first thing."

"And the second?"

"There wasn't a concrete retaining wall at that curve, either. A big flood right now, or at least a part of it, might be contained by that wall and carried right around that curve. That's what I was looking at."

Williams's large hands were flat on the desk top. He kept them motionless with effort as he said slowly, "Right down into the city? Old Town? The low land, those trailer parks and river shacks? That kind of thing? That's where a flood strong enough to move those big rocks might go if we have one? That's what you're saying?" He wanted no misunderstanding.

"That's it."

Williams closed his eyes again, thinking of implications, stark, unrelieved catastrophe. He felt suddenly dizzy, as if the floor beneath his feet were rocking. Automatically, his eyes still closed, he got out the pillbox, fumbled for a Valium pill, popped it into his mouth and swallowed it dry with effort. He supposed that the mere act of taking the pill had some immediate psychological effect, because all at once the dizziness disappeared and the floor was again steady under his feet. He opened his eyes. Jay was watching him. "Nothing serious," Williams said as he tucked the pillbox away.

"I'm not so sure."

Williams was frowning now. "What do you mean by that?"

"Didn't you feel it?"

The frown deepened. "I felt dizzy, like the floor was moving. But how did you know?"

"The floor *was* moving," Jay said. "We just had another tremor, earthquake, if you like. And maybe, probably, like the others, the epicenter was up closer to Harper's Park and they felt it more." He got out of his chair. "I think we'd better go up and find out."

. . .

Again the mayor, jacket off, shirt sleeves rolled up and tie loosened, sat behind his desk. Bud Henderson the police chief,

Rudy Smith the fire chief, and Carlos García the schoolteacher all sat facing him. "Okay," the mayor said, "last time we met it was theoretical. Now at least we know what the problem may be. Either of you heard the rumor yet? Not you, Carlito; I know you have. Bud? Rudy?"

"I don't even know what you're talking about," Bud Henderson said. It was his private opinion that Chicanos rarely knew themselves what they were talking about, but he didn't quite dare say that here. The mayor was not somebody you went too far with. He could, and would, strike back.

"Okay," the mayor said, "I'll give it to you straight. There is a chance, a *chance,* mind you, that the Harper's Park dam isn't safe any longer. How does that grab you?"

Rudy Smith said softly, "Jesus Christ!" and was silent.

Bud Henderson said bluntly, "Are you kidding? That big, goddamn concrete structure, and the level of the lake twenty feet below normal?" He shook his head. "No way." He paused then and swallowed as the full implications struck him. "You are kidding, aren't you? I mean, you want us to pretend that's what we're up against and make our evacuation plans accordingly? Is that it?"

The door opened and the mayor's secretary appeared. "I am sorry to break in," she said in Spanish, "but the governor is returning your call."

"*Bueno.*" The mayor pushed back his chair. "Excuse me a minute." In the doorway he paused and turned. "You explain that I am not kidding, Carlito." He went out, closed the door, and sat down at the telephone on his secretary's desk. He kept his voice low. "I know where the dam story began, Harry. George Harrison. At the Hilton over coffee this morning. Nobody pays any attention to a Chicano busboy, and one of my wife's *primos,* cousins, heard the whole thing. There were five, six at the table." He gave names and could not resist adding, "All Anglos, of course."

"Thank you for the information." The governor's voice was stiffly formal, deep anger under control.

"The damage is done," the mayor said. "If the story isn't all over town yet, it will be soon, and people are going to want to know whether to believe it or not. Somebody's going to have to tell them something. Harrison's more your type than mine, so I thought I'd leave him to you. But if you want to string him up by his *cojones,* I'll be happy to provide the rope."

"Thanks, Joe." The governor's voice was free of irony. "What are you going to do?"

"Try to figure out how to evacuate Old Town and the *barrio,* and wait for final word from you." If politics produced strange bedfellows, as the aphorism had it, the mayor was thinking, then crises produced even greater anomalies. "This time," he said, "you and I are going to have to forget our differences, Harry, okay?"

"The same thought was in my mind, Joe."

The mayor hung up and walked back into his own office. Rudy Smith's long face was solemn, thoughtful. Bud Henderson looked scared. Carlos García said, "You want me to stay?"

"Yes." The mayor dropped into his chair. "You know the *barrio,* and the *barrio* people know you." He sat up straight and tugged at his tie to loosen it further. "Now we go to work."

It was then that the old building rocked gently in the new tremor Williams and Jay had also felt. The mayor could not resist a bitter half smile and an upward glance. "Okay, Lord," he said, "we've got the message."

. . .

Tom Gentry had been one of those sitting over coffee at the Hilton with George Harrison that morning, and he had listened to George's report in careful silence. When the coffee group broke up, it was Tom who walked out into the sunlight with George.

"I'm going to have to ask this, George," he said as they walked together. "As you know, the bank will probably be involved if the dam enlargement project goes forward." And I sure as hell will be involved either way, he thought, but kept that part to himself. "My question is this: What you told us wouldn't just be wishful thinking, would it? Just hoping that Bill Williams has finally fallen on his face, I mean?"

"*In vino veritas,*" George said. "In wine there is truth. Sam Martin was drinking Bourbon, not wine, but he got a little loaded—and, yes, I am convinced that he was telling the truth. They are not only concerned about enlargement, they are worried about the dam as it is."

"That," Tom Gentry said, "opens up all kinds of possibilities that have to be considered."

George looked at him sharply.

"Concerning the bank, of course," Tom Gentry said.

Now, in the privacy of his bank office, Gentry tried to figure out precisely where he stood. He kept his eyes closed while he thought. Every time he opened them he had the illusion that all the board members in the photographs around the walls were watching him as if he were a prisoner in the dock, and it made him uncomfortable.

If George was right, and Gentry had to assume that he was, and what Sam Martin had said was also right, and again there was no reason to believe otherwise, then the dam enlargement was just about out of the question. That was the only possible conclusion, little as Gentry liked to draw it.

So he was stuck with fifty acres of land he didn't want and probably couldn't sell, and a loan of twenty-two thousand five hundred dollars he was going to have to pay back. That too was inescapable.

What if he offered the land back to Brooks Thompson for exactly the purchase price? Before Thompson heard about the dam problem, of course.

What sales pitch would he use? Change of heart? Could he say that he had been thinking since Mary Thompson's phone call, and he felt that he did not want to leave the Thompsons with the impression that he had deliberately diddled them? Would that wash?

Probably not.

It was obvious to Gentry that Mary Thompson was her father's darling, and what would be more natural than for Spencer Willoughby to say, the next time he talked with his daughter, "By the way, honey, I lowered the boom on Gentry. It won't get your land back for you, but you can have the satisfaction of knowing that Gentry isn't going to enjoy very much whatever he may get out of his caper." So the simple change-of-heart approach just wouldn't hold water.

Well, what about confessing to Willoughby's phone call, admitting that he, Tom Gentry, realized that he was in bad trouble and, in a sense, throw himself on the mercy of the court and try to make amends by selling the property back? Would that work? Doubtful, but possible.

The hitch, of course, was that Brooks Thompson, who was really no fool, would find it out of character. It followed then that, once burned and twice shy, Thompson would almost certainly take his time to think about it. And it would not be long before he too got the word that the dam enlargement project was off and that those fifty acres of land were not going to be worth any more than he had sold them for, if as much.

Damnit, Gentry thought, and opened his eyes to defy the stares of the photographs on the wall, there had to be some way to get himself off the hook. He was a bank president and allegedly a smart fellow, and he could just imagine the smirks there would be around town when word got out, as it inevitably would, that he had been blown up by his own powder charge. He—

He felt the floor rock gently, and two or three of the photographs around the walls went askew, giving the portraits they contained the appearance of men with their heads cocked in question.

Gentry swore silently. That was just the kind of thing they were apparently worried about, he thought. Even the gods were against him. They—

This time the interruption was not another tremor, but the buzzing of the phone on his desk. He snatched it up angrily. "Yes?"

It was the bank switchboard operator speaking in a hushed voice as if she were in church. "There is a person-to-person long-distance call for you, Mr. Gentry."

"Well, where's it from and who is it?"

"It's from Los Angeles."

Gentry swallowed and waited.

"Mr. Henry Warfield," the switchboard operator said. "Isn't that—?"

"The man who owns us all, yes," Gentry said. He took a deep breath. "Okay. Put the call through."

15

Jay and Williams had driven up from the city, and they stood now looking out over the lake to the dam. Beside them, Kate stood quiet, waiting, listening, while Cooley Parks, in work boots, sweating, his sleeves rolled up on his brawny forearms and the knees of his trousers dusty, said of this last tremor, "Yeah, we felt it." He gestured with the fist that held his geologist's pick. "So did the water of the lake. I watched it—"

"A seiche?" Jay said. "Oscillations?"

"Just like the textbooks say. Against the face of the dam the water sloshed up maybe ten feet. Out in the middle of the lake at the node, there was hardly any movement at all."

"You were where?" Jay said.

"Out on the right-hand shoulder." Cooley pointed with his closed left hand.

Jay nodded. "The Coriolis effect. There'd be more scouring on the right bank when the stream was still cutting through that gorge. Find anything?"

Cooley brought his left hand in front of him and opened the fingers for them to see. In his palm lay one larger and half a dozen smaller pieces of grayish rock the faces of which glinted mirror-like in the sun.

Kate moved closer for a better look. "Is that what you call slicken—whatever it was?"

Jay merely nodded. His face was expressionless.

"Slickensides," Cooley said. "Yeah."

"Somebody bring me into the picture," Williams said. "That's supposed to be proof of what?" He listened to Cooley's explanation.

"Okay," Williams said then, "I'll take your word for it. There was faulting. When? Recent? A million years ago? What are we talking about, anyway?"

Cooley shrugged. "We might work it out within limits if we wanted to take the time and the trouble, but—"

"How would you work it out?" Williams's tone was not truculent, but it demanded explanation.

"All rock isn't the same age, and doesn't have the same structure." This was Jay, quietly authoritative, delivering a basic lecture. "Some of it is still more or less the way it was when it cooled from what we call the original molten magma, which is a thick soup of all minerals and solid elements. That's called igneous rock, and it's basic.

"Rock that's been formed by deposit, usually precipitation of small matter underwater compressed into something solid—sandstone, for example—we call sedimentary rock.

"And either igneous or sedimentary rock that's been altered by enormous heat and pressure after being buried again within the earth is called metamorphic rock—marble is an example.

"Now, if we wanted to try to work out when this faulting took place, we'd first find out what kinds of rocks are involved, igneous, maybe some sedimentary, metamorphic. By their positions and the established age of other samples identical to them we'd determine what age relationship they bear to one another, that is, which rock was already in place and was perhaps invaded by one or more of the others—do you begin to see what some of the complications are? A puzzle, but it could be worked out."

Williams nodded in silence.

"But it isn't important anyway," Jay said. "If there is a zone of fracture, an established fault, and those little pieces in Cooley's hand are pretty good proof that there is, then you've got an area of weakness—the San Andreas fault in California is an example everybody has heard about—and if there is movement of the earth's crust in the area, it's more likely to take place in that area of weakness than somewhere else. It's as simple as that. And now aside from all the earlier ones, we've had two recent movements of the earth's crust right in this area, tremors, earthquakes, whatever name you want. So you can see your problem, because the dam is right on that more or less unstable area."

Kate watched her father. He stood strong and solid, clearly accepting what he had been told, unflinching in the face of the implications. "Okay," he said. "Now what do we do about it?"

"That," Cooley said, "is something else again. I'm here. I can poke around some more, but I don't see much point in it. On what I already know, I couldn't draw you a detailed geologic map of the dam area, but you don't need it, because I can tell you that it has structural weaknesses and enough of those I can demonstrate. I might as well take the next plane back to Calgary."

Williams looked at Jay. "We're right back where we started, aren't we? You came here just to look at something and found something else. You told us about it, and now you've proved it, and by that much we're in your debt." As an afterthought he added, "And I pay my debts."

Cooley Parks, Kate thought, had said the same. Strange.

"Send me a bill," Williams said. "I'll see that it's paid."

"There is one more thing I can do," Jay said. And maybe it would do no good at all, he thought, but at least then he would have done his best, followed every lead, and he would be able to walk away with no feeling that he had slighted the job he hadn't even asked for in the first place. "I'll take one more dive and see if I can find any changes because of this last tremor."

"Don't be a goddamned fool, boy!" This was Cooley. "You don't know what that tremor did, how deeply it affected the rock structure. I told you about that water against the dam face. There was a lot of hydraulic force behind it. For all you know that dam is getting ready to go right now, and if you're down there when it does—"

"Or it could last for years," Jay said. "So I'll see if I can cast any light on its condition."

Cooley let out his breath in an explosive sigh. "I've dealt with mules," he said, "and I've dealt with camels and once or twice with elephants, but you are something else again."

"Besides," Jay said, "I'd like one more look at the village. If and when the dam goes, the village will go too and I'll never have another chance to see it. Maybe that's silly—" He shrugged, turned away, and started for the motel.

Kate watched him go. No, she told herself, it was not silly at all; if none of the others understood, she thought that she did.

. . .

On the Mount Union fire lookout tower they had felt the tremor too. "Sometimes," Bernie said, "gusty winds shake the tower. Oh, not really shake it, but make it vibrate, you know? But this is the second one of these I've felt in only the last week that was different, right down in the mountain, in the rock itself. It's kind of scary, isn't it?"

"Do you report it?" Pete said.

"Not really. When anything like this happens, what we do is, we usually get on the air and talk it around, and somebody makes a phone call to somebody he knows over at the university seismograph and then they pass the word around. If we see anything, like, say a rock fall—"

"Or an avalanche?"

"Well, sure, we'd report that. The Forest Service would want to know. We're supposed to report not just fires but anything that might affect the, you know, land or environment. Along with the weather, I mean. Pete, how can I make sense when you're doing that?"

"Want me to stop?"

Bernie's smile was slow, pleasurable. "No. I'll just stop trying to make sense."

It was difficult to get used to, Pete thought, being in a glass house on top of a mountain in plain view of the whole wide world, and yet just as private as if they'd been inside a cave with the entrance blocked. Unless, of course, an aircraft flew by, but that didn't happen all that often, and it was easy enough to step into a corner where you couldn't be seen when one did show.

Another thing Pete found strange. Here they were at 14,000 feet, and the shaded thermometer read somewhere around 50° F., but out of the wind and in the sun they were comfortably warm even if, as now, they were both naked as jaybirds, as they seemed to be most of the time. Pete was already beginning to match Bernie's rich, all-over golden tan which was marred by none of those pallid spots or stripes even the briefest of bikinis left.

It was a dream-world life, Pete kept telling himself, and high time he came down off his cloud and got back to reality, but something, and he could not have said what, kept getting in the way of that final moment of decision.

"My grandmother was a *bruja*," he had told Bernie once, grinning at the concept, "a witch, and some of it either rubbed off on me when I was a kid, or was already there in the genes, because while I can't tell the future the way she sometimes could, or seemed to, I do get feelings, and when I ignore them, I usually end up regretting it." Like that goddamned knee, for example, because he had awakened the morning that happened with a feeling of coming trouble and, sure enough, it had come—and how it had come!

"Pete!" Bernie's voice was breathless now. "You've got to stop! It's time for the weather reports!" She struggled out of his arms, laughing. "But I'll be back. Promise."

"You can tell me how all the little high and low pressures are," Pete said, "and whatever happened to that rain and snow we were supposed to get."

He lay back, arms behind his head, and grinned up at the incredibly blue sky. He decided that he knew what was keeping him here, and it wasn't any of his *bruja* grandmother's prescience, either. It was purely and simply a real live girl he was beginning to care more about than he would have thought possible. Picture Pete Otero really in love, all two hundred and sixty-five pounds of him. Incredible.

He was still lying motionless and relaxed, grinning up at the sky, when the radio sounds inside the lookout building stopped and Bernie came back out, unsmiling now, the seriousness of her expression contrasting strangely with her naked loveliness. "It's coming, Pete, and I think now maybe you'd better go while you can."

"You know," Pete said, "I never dug the vine-covered cottage bit, but I'm beginning to think there might be something to it, after all. There's a guy in Santa Monica—"

"Pete, be serious."

"I am, and he was, or at least he said he was. He's got this chain of sporting-goods stores—"

"Pete, you aren't even listening to me."

"—and the gimmick is that they're slanted toward male monsters. Like me. I mean, big guys, tall guys who can't find boots or golf shoes or sweaters—"

Bernie had dropped to her knees beside him. "Please, Pete."

"That is one marvelous pair of knockers you've got, baby. I never get tired of looking at them, and—"

Bernie caught his reaching hands in her own. "You aren't going to listen? This time it's coming for sure. Two fronts, converging on us."

Pete's hands had continued their reaching movements as if Bernie had not even tried to stop him. He touched her breasts and began to move them with that gentleness that was so unexpected from a man of his enormous strength. "I don't need to listen," Pete said, "because I'm not going anywhere. Not without you. Not ever again. I just decided. The only question is when do we leave here—together?"

Bernie took a deep, unsteady breath. "Pete—" And there the words stopped.

"I will be damned," Pete said. "Now what did I say to make you cry?"

.   .   .

It was, of course, inevitable, the senator thought, that Johnny Cisneros would hear the rumor and immediately call to ask about it. Johnny always had his ear to the ground as well as a sharp eye on the main chance. So any thought of selling his half of the Leyba property to Johnny, the senator told himself, had already gone down the drain. Now he faced another dilemma.

"What I want to know," Johnny said, "is, is it true? That goddamn dam is maybe going to break?"

From some long-forgotten English course the quote kept running through the senator's mind: "Uneasy lies the head that wears the crown." All very well, he thought, but what about the head that wears two hats? There is where you really have problems.

"Are you listening, Walt?" Johnny said. "You know where my warehouse is, down in the *barrio*, right by the goddamn river. And I got a whole truckload of TV's coming in. This year's models, some of them with price tags you wouldn't believe. Now, we unload them and put them in my warehouse, and you know what? Right away they belong to me, not to the distributor any longer. And anything happens to that dam and we get a flood, right away they belong to you, you know what I mean?"

The senator knew precisely what Johnny meant. He had been thinking of little else but this matter and others like it ever since he had seen the governor. He had written the insurance on Honest Johnny's warehouse *and* contents himself, as well as more similar policies than he liked to think about. "I get the message, Johnny."

"*Bueno*. Now what do I do? I try to stop that truckload delivery, what do I say, hmmm? And what happens to my semi-annual sale people count on? I don't like to let my customers down, Walt. I spend fifteen years building a reputation and something like this could blow it. All to hell, Walt. So I guess the thing to do is, I let the TV's come in and put them in the warehouse and if the dam does go and there's that flood everybody's talking about, then everybody knows Honest Johnny lived up to his word and tried to have his semiannual sale, but Dios had other ideas, so it's not Johnny's fault. And you pay me for what the flood ruins and all I lose is some time, and of course some sales too, no?"

"No," the senator said. "That's not the way to do it, Johnny. Get that truckload stopped." And empty that warehouse too, he thought; but would not go so far as to say it openly.

"How do I know these rumors mean a thing? Tell me that. I'd look like a fine horse's ass stopping a shipment, ruining a sale, and nothing happens, you know what I mean?"

"Johnny," the senator said, no longer sure which hat he wore at the moment, "Johnny, believe me, it's best if you stop that shipment."

There was a short silence. The senator had a shrewd idea that everything Johnny had said had led up to this moment, and the coming question. And here it came. "Just what do you know, Walt? You're a state senator, you hear things us plain citizens don't. You don't want those TV's in my warehouse, you got to give me reasons."

In his place the senator knew what the governor would do. The governor would sidestep the question with neatness and grace, probably saying something that sounded good and meant nothing at all. But the governor was not also an insurance broker with a large financial stake in Johnny Cisneros' decision.

"Come on, Walt," Cisneros said. "Either you know something or you're just guessing. If you're just guessing, playing it safe, then no dice. I take delivery and fill my warehouse with those TV's. If you know something, then you better tell me about it."

The head that wears the crown should have decisions like this to make, the senator thought. "Look, Johnny," he said, "I don't want this to go any farther, okay?"

"Sure. Sure. Just you and me. Now what do you know, Walt?"

"I don't *know* any more than you do, Johnny. But there is a chance that that dam isn't safe."

"I hear it here and there," Johnny said. "Maybe it's so, maybe it isn't, *quién sabe?* But you're not talking about what you hear in the street, Walt. You hear it and now you believe it. So where did you hear it?"

"Look, Johnny, won't you take my word for it?"

"You're a businessman, Walt. So am I. Maybe once they did business on a word and a handshake like I hear. But not now. You got to tell me more or I don't buy it."

Damned if I do, the senator thought, and damned if I don't. My promise of silence to Harry against a truckload of TV's. But he supposed that he had known from the beginning what the result would be. Money almost always came out on top. He sighed. "I talked with the governor, Johnny," he said. "Now that's strictly between us, you and I, okay? We don't want the word out that he's worried. You can see that. People start hearing that right at the top of state government they're concerned and—"

"Sure, sure." There was a subtle change now in Johnny's voice. "I dig you, Walt. Just between you and I. Okay. I'll try to stop that shipment. I'm not sure I can, but I'll sure as hell try."

"Thanks, Johnny." The senator hung up. Funny, he felt

worse now than he had while he was agonizing about whether to make the call himself.

.   .   .

The snow began in the mountains in almost tentative fashion, large, lazy flakes drifting down at first, touching the ground and melting instantly.

In only a matter of minutes the fall became heavier and the ground began to whiten. From within the fire lookout building the effect was magical, a swirling, shifting pattern of light, now obscuring, now revealing nearby mountain peaks, the almost bottomless gorges and canyons, the river, the lake, the dam, and the city far below.

"Quite a show," Pete said. "You arrange this kind of thing often?"

"Late in the season." Bernie was smiling. "We'll close down soon. One more year come and gone." But this year had brought a miracle she still did not fully believe and was afraid to examine too closely lest it vanish like smoke. How would it be between them down in the real world? There was the question, and the worry.

"Hey, Bright Eyes!" The voice from the radio speaker. "Come in, Bright Eyes! Over."

In bare feet Bernie padded to the radio table and picked up the hand mike. "Bernie here. I read you, Charlie. Over."

"Snow reached you yet?"

"Affirmative. Just beginning."

"Batten down the hatches and haul in the main brace, or whatever you do with it. We're going to catch it for good and for sure, and the word is there's a warming trend behind it. If that makes any sense to you, it sure doesn't to me, but there it is. First snow, then maybe rain, even at your elevation. Over."

"Thanks, Charlie. We'll hang on."

"You been feeling tremors?"

"Affirmative."

"Small stuff, under three on the Richter Scale, the seismograph types say, with the epicenters over in your area. Window rattlers, is all, in case you were worried."

"Thanks, Charlie. I'm fine."

"Someday I'm going to get to meet you, see what you look like."

Bernie glanced down at her tanned nakedness. She looked at Pete, and smiled. "I'm not much, Charlie. You can do a lot better. Over and out." She switched off the hand mike and set it down.

"The poor guy," Pete said. "He hasn't any idea what he's missing."

16

Cooley sat in the stern, hand on the tiller, the outboard motor throttled down, swinging the boat in slow, patient circles around the spot where Jay had gone over the side.

"I am sure as hell not going to shut this mother off," he had told Jay. "If we need to make a run for shore, we're going to need it already fired up and ready. Look, one more time, will you give up this goddamned nonsense?"

"See you," Jay said, adjusted his faceplate, popped in his mouthpiece, and with light and camera went over the side and swam rapidly down through the clear, cold water.

Williams and Kate stood on the shore watching. Kate said, "What are you going to do, Daddy?" She did not turn to look at him, because she knew what she would see and it was painful to accept. Williams had aged almost before her eyes. He still held himself straight, facing facts as he had faced facts all his life, but the confidence he had always exuded was no longer there, and for Kate it was as if a beacon light she had always had to guide her had suddenly been snuffed out.

"I don't know, honey."

"Maybe he'll find that—everything is all right."

Williams's smile was a wry grimace. "You know better. We're past even that wild hope."

"They could be wrong. You asked Jay if he made mistakes, remember?" Could it really be that the night of that dinner was only two days ago? Or was it three? Time had suddenly blended, and the days had lost their individuality. "He said that he just tried not to make too many of them. But this could be one."

"Stop patting me on the head, honey." As Martha would have too, Williams thought suddenly, and a wave of loneliness washed through his mind.

"You are blaming yourself," Kate said, "and it isn't your fault."

"Wrong." For a moment the strength returned, and the confidence. "The guy at the top is responsible. Always. He may try like hell to wiggle and weasel and pretend he didn't know or he didn't mean to or he was let down by people he trusted. You've seen that, we've all seen it, and a goddamned sick sight it is, because all it adds up to is a crock of shit." He was not speaking to his daughter; he was speaking his mind to and about all those before and after him who found the temptation of evasion irresistible. "That's my dam. I built it. And if it's in the wrong place, then it's my fault, period. Not Sam's, not the Army Corps of Engineers, not anybody's fault but mine."

Kate tucked her arm through her father's, and stood silent. She had no more words. There was only the lake and the spreading ripples from the circling boat, and the time of waiting that seemed to have no end.

She stared at the dam structure rising high, too high above the level of the lake, and with effort restrained a shudder. The dam had always seemed to her a massive structure built to withstand the ages. Now, like her father, it had suddenly become vulnerable, its term of life finite, its weaknesses perhaps hidden, but nonetheless there, and known. Around it the mountains, by comparison, stood as they had always stood, but all at once their steep, towering slopes, deep fissures, hanging valleys, and sheer cliff faces had become more menacing than beautiful.

And the stream she had always loved with its clear water, its rapids, its trout pools and picnic spots, and, higher up, its waterfalls and secret caves, even, she remembered from a pack trip years ago, a beaver pond in a meadow and the beavers themselves scuttling into the water—all of this now seemed part of a harsh environment, no longer friendly.

She tried to picture Jay as she had watched him from the boat only the other day, gliding among the gravestones in the sunken cemetery, flashing his light like an aquatic glowworm. There had been no hint then of menace.

Now, watching the slowly circling boat and Cooley's attention fixed, everything was changed. Cooley was not a fearful man; she had already seen enough of him to know that. He was not a man to seek out things to worry about. But he was worried now about what might happen while Jay was in the lake, and that somehow brought the entire desperate matter into sharp focus in Kate's mind, and all she could do was stand tense, holding her father's arm, and watch, and wait.

It was Williams who broke the silence between them, and it was evident that their thoughts had been running in the same general direction. "That's a good man down there," Williams said, "the hell of a good man. They both are. You can't just go out and buy men like that. There isn't money enough. They'll do what they think needs to be done, and pay has nothing to do with it."

Was he talking merely to fill in this time of waiting? Kate wondered. No matter. What he was saying was true; and from some source she drew further sure knowledge too. "You are that kind of man, Daddy."

"Maybe. I always tried to be."

Kate squeezed his arm. "You were. You are." And again they stood in silence, watching, waiting.

In the boat Cooley looked at his watch. Come on, he thought; *come on!* He stared at the dam as if it were an enemy. "Are you about to give way, damn you?" He said it aloud, but softly in the voice of a man accustomed to solitude and his own personal monologues. "They tied you into quicksand, or near enough, into rock that's already been tested beyond its strength. What the hell did they expect, miracles?" And then, looking at his watch once more: "Goddamnit, boy, will you haul your ass up out of there and let us get safe ashore?"

Eighty feet down, it was colder than Jay remembered it; and he told himself it was only his imagination. Or fear. Face it, he thought, you don't like this any better than Cooley does, and you'd be a damned fool if you weren't scared. He found small consolation in the logic.

He was already beyond the end of the village and almost touching the base of the dam itself. The one last look at the village could wait. Now he swam along the dam face, playing his light constantly on the weed-covered structure.

He expected to find no obvious flaw. Not yet. If he did, he thought, he would head for the surface just as fast as he could go, because even the smallest crack would mean that the dam was already crumbling.

It was at the sides, where the dam tied into the walls of the gorge, that he might find indications of possible imminent trouble, further fracturing of the supporting rock structure, however minor, which, viewed against the broad pattern of Cooley's analysis, could lead to only one conclusion: that the dam was already unsafe and probably beyond repair.

He wished he had taken pictures of the minor fracturing he had first seen two days ago. Then, by comparison with the pictures he would take now, an accurate and dispassionate judgment of any deterioration could be made. But he had not taken pictures, and that was that. He would have to rely on his memory for comparisons.

He swam up and well above the outlet which ran down to the power station, even then feeling the drag of the flowing water, and thinking how easy it could be to allow himself to be pinned against the outlet screening, unable to fight loose, if he were foolish enough to get too close. Funny, he hadn't even given it much thought two days ago. Now his mind, as if of its own volition, took off in a different and yet logically extended direction.

He was up here, fully expecting to find that the dam was of at least questionable safety. Immediately below the dam, turbines in the power station were turning as if nothing was amiss, generating electricity for the city as they had for ten years—in a sense, business as usual. He hoped the power station was fully automated with no one even on standby duty, because if the dam were to go, the power station would be the first downstream structure to disintegrate and disappear.

Jay had never seen a rampaging flood, or even the immediate aftermath, but after seeing those house-sized rocks behind Williams's home, and knowing how they had come to be there, he needed very little of his scientific training to imagine something of the full force and fury of which this watercourse was capable even without the added factor of the man-made lake, which alone, if the dam did collapse, would suddenly fill the lower river channel from bank to bank with a wall of water sweeping into oblivion everything in its path. Everything, and everyone.

It was not his field, he told himself, not his responsibility, and not even any of his damn business, and someone else would have to explain, if he could, why Jay Harper was down at the bottom of this lake right now. Maybe a shrink would be able to explain, Jay thought bitterly, and continued his sweep of the dam wall, concentrating on the weed-covered concrete revealed in the light; and finding no flaws.

And here was the side of the gorge, the rock structure rising almost sheer, apparently solid and strong—but only at first quick look.

There was—yes, he was sure of it—a freshly exposed face of rock, not large, perhaps a square meter in area. But his memory protested that it had not been there two days ago, and that was the important thing.

He swam quickly to the bottom, searched for and found some of the pieces of rock which must have come from that freshly exposed face. In the light he examined them.

No question; this side of this piece had been exposed to the water of the lake for a long time, and this side had been protected, hidden, a part of the rock structure itself—until it had been shaken loose.

By today's tremor? What else? There was no current in the lake to speak of, and the changes in water temperature would be minimal, far too little to produce contraction and expansion and subsequent exfoliation.

But one swallow did not make a summer, he told himself, and one fractured bit of rock face did not make for deep deterioration.

In this instance, the hell it didn't; he had all the indication he needed. Holding light and camera carefully, he took four pictures: of the fresh face and of the pieces lying on the bottom.

Okay, he thought, now we get the hell out of here. Free at last.

He started for the surface, and after only a few feet hesitated, arguing with himself. A job half done; the phrase refused to leave his mind.

The shadow he and Cooley had seen from the air extended from *both* sides of the dam structure, and if it was, as they had almost but not quite proved, indeed indication of a fault line, then there might, and probably should, be some indication of damage from today's tremor on the other side of the gorge as well as this. And while that would not be proof positive, it would double the evidence he already had of what the legal types called clear and present danger. Wouldn't it? Well?

The question was rhetorical. He was already swimming back across the dam face like, he told himself, that stupid bear going over the mountain to see what he could see. Professional pride was a dreadful force, and the worst part of it was that it would not allow itself to be ignored.

. . .

On the shore, waiting still, while the tension grew and stretched and Cooley in the small boat circled endlessly, Williams said without warning, "Our talk the other day, honey."

Kate gave his arm a little squeeze. "Daddy, not now."

Williams understood her protest and its reasons, and he could even smile faintly. "No more instructions," he said. "Just something I want to say, and probably should have said then because it's been in my mind." He did not look at her, but kept his eyes fixed on the circling boat.

This was going to be embarrassing for us both, he thought. He was not a man for gushing compliments, never had been. But this was something he did not want to leave unsaid, and the feeling in his mind was strong that he might not have another chance to say it. Matters, of which that circling boat was the symbol, were coming rapidly to a head and when he would have another quiet time alone with Kate he could not even guess. He took a deep breath.

"I always thought they broke the mold after they made your mother," he said, and his voice sounded funny even to his own ears, almost angry; maybe "gruff" was the word, whatever that meant. He shook his head, partly in annoyance at himself, partly in negation of the statement he had just made. "They didn't," he said. "You came out of it too. I just wanted you to know." He was silent, still staring at the boat.

"Daddy." Kate's arm tightened on his, but she said no more.

"Okay," Williams said, still in that almost-angry voice, "for a long time I didn't think so. It's only since you came home that I've seen different." He hesitated. "It's been almost like having Martha in the house again. I wanted you to know that too."

Kate closed her eyes. Tears were close.

"I said no more instructions," Williams said. "Okay, so I'm going to cheat on my word. Find yourself a man, honey, the best man you can find. No matter how good he is, you'll make him better. I know. Without your mother I'd still be running constuction crews for somebody else and sometimes using a pick and shovel to give them a hand. You—" His voice stopped suddenly and the muscles of his arm tensed in reflexive protest. "Jesus!" he said. "Do you feel it? Do you see it? The water's moving like they said! And he's still down there!"

. . .

Jay had reached the far side of the gorge when he felt the water beginning to move, and almost simultaneously heard—or was it sheer imagination?—a deep rumbling sound as of rock in torment.

He played his light on the dam face. It seemed to be holding solid. Quickly he turned the light on the rock structure. Pieces of the rock face, as if in slow motion, detached themselves from the parent mass and dropped like falling autumn leaves to the lake bottom.

A crack appeared in the rock face. Around it more rock detached itself and drifted down through the water.

The sound was gone, if indeed it had actually been, but the water was still moving, oscillating with sluggish, but irresistible force.

Jay waited for no more. He drove himself up with desperate strokes of his fins, broke surface before he expected, and shot waist-high out of the water like a performing seal.

Cooley saw, and headed the boat toward him at speed. He slowed quickly and, reaching with one brawny arm, almost lifted Jay bodily over the gunwale. "Of all the stubborn, goddamned fools!" His voice was its customary roar. The little boat's bow lifted as he opened the throttle and they headed toward the slip.

Williams and Kate came toward them at a run.

Arms full, Jay scrambled from the boat to the slip. Behind him Cooley switched off the engine, clambered out, and dropped the boat's painter eye splice over a cleat. He and Jay hurried toward the shore, Jay with his face mask pushed up, mouthpiece hanging loose, both hands busy carrying light and camera, and his feet still encased in the suddenly absurd flippers which made slapping sounds as he ran.

They reached the shore, stopped, and turned to look. The dam stood apparently unscathed, and the sloshing of the lake water mixed with the boat's wake was beginning to die away.

Jay turned to face Williams. Breathing was difficult, and he controlled his voice with effort. "Okay, that's it. I can tell you what I saw and what I think—wrong, what I *know* now. Then it's all yours."

The reaction had set in; his knees were suddenly weak and there was an empty hollowness in his stomach. "The best I can do," he said.

"That," Cooley said, "I'll believe when I see it."

* * *

The governor sat behind his large desk, unsmiling. George Harrison, sitting next to his attorney, whose name was Lucius Cabot, faced the desk somewhat in the manner of a schoolboy summoned to the headmaster's office.

"I asked you to come here—" the governor began, and the attorney interrupted.

"We were not asked, Harry. We were told in as high-handed a display of outrageous authoritarianism as I have ever encountered."

"When you hear what I have to say, Lucius," the governor said, "I think you will understand." There was cold fury in his voice, and although usually he made a point of concealing his emotions, this time he did not care if it showed. "There are rumors in town," he said, "that the Harper Park dam is unsafe." He saw, and noted, the sudden look of surprise in Lucius Cabot's face, quickly hidden. "Do you know anything about them, George?" the governor asked.

"No. And I resent—"

"Among other things, George," the governor said in a tone which commanded silence, "you are a liar."

Lucius Cabot said, "Now, Harry—"

"At the Hilton this morning," the governor said as if Cabot had not spoken, "at coffee, seated with"—he named the names the mayor had given him—"you started the rumor, knowing perfectly well that it would spread and intending that it should. You were overheard."

Lucius Cabot stirred in his chair, and opened his mouth to protest.

"If you are going to mention the First Amendment guarantee of free speech, Lucius," the governor said, "I will point out Mr. Justice Holmes's celebrated comment that that right does not extend to shouting 'Fire!' in a crowded theater. And that is precisely what George has done."

"Surely you are not serious, Harry."

"I am dead serious. Mayor José-María Lopez is no favorite of mine, as you well know, but I have never known anyone to accuse him of cowardice and he is a frightened man right now, both frightened and angry. He told me on the phone only a little time ago that if we were planning on hanging your client up by his testes, he would be happy to supply the rope."

Cabot said in a conciliatory tone, "Let's be sensible, Harry. We are grown men—"

"Two of us may be. George is still the spoiled brat he has always been."

George's face was bright pink. He sat very straight. "Now, see here, Harry," he said. "Those are not rumors. They are true. And—"

"I suggest, George," Lucius said coldly, "that you keep your mouth shut. Tight." He looked at the governor. "What, if anything, do you intend to do?"

"I haven't decided yet. I am expecting a report from Bill Williams—"

"He's at the bottom of the whole thing," George said. "The great, bold Bill Williams—"

"I told you, George," Cabot said, "to keep your mouth shut. One more word from you and I will walk out of here and no longer represent you. And legal ethics be damned." He turned toward the desk again. "When will you have this report, Harry?"

"I am expecting it momentarily."

"Will it be definitive?"

"In a word," the governor said, "no. Indicative, but not definitive. It is my understanding that in matters such as this, there is no way to foretell with accuracy what is going to happen, or when." He turned his head to look at George for a long time in silence until George's eyes fell away. "Which means, of course," the governor said, speaking again to Cabot, "that there is also no way to refute the rumors George deliberately set in motion this morning."

There was silence in the office. The digital clock on the governor's desk suddenly turned a new minute. The click seemed overloud.

Cabot said slowly, with emphasis on the first word, "*Is* there a possibility of the dam collapsing, Harry?"

"Apparently there is the possibility, yes."

The intercom buzzed. The interruption brought a frown of annoyance to the governor's face, and he opened the switch with obvious impatience. "Yes?" His voice was unusually sharp.

"Mr. Bill Williams is on line one, Governor," Clara's voice said. "He said it was important."

"Very well." There was a sense of relief in the two words. The governor pushed the appropriate button. "Yes, Bill?"

"The word isn't good," Williams said. "You felt that new earthquake? Never mind. We did up here. I could tell you the whole story, but I want you to hear it from the horse's mouth, okay? We can be there in a half hour."

"Come along," the governor said. He thought for a moment. "Should I have anyone else here?"

There was a short silence. Williams said at last in a new, tired, almost defeated voice, "Harry, I just don't know what the hell to say. Or do. José-María's the only one I can think of who ought to be plugged in, but you hate his guts."

"I will have him here," the governor said, and hung up.

Cabot studied the governor's face. It showed uncharacteristic lines of strain and uncertainty, and he seemed wholly oblivious of the fact that he was not alone with his concerns.

It was at times like this, Cabot thought, that a sensible man might well wonder why anyone would be foolish enough to seek public office and the sometimes crushing burdens of responsibility it entailed. He had his own decisions to make, of course, and at times they were difficult, even agonizing, but they affected at most only a few clients and their usually selfish interests, whereas here, now, the governor was faced with a situation which could violently affect hundreds of thousands of lives and vast amounts of property, and he lacked even the opportunity to ask for a supporting poll of public opinion.

At least, thank God, Cabot thought, that fool George Harrison was keeping his silence. "Is there anything I can do, Harry?"

The governor's hand had not left the telephone. He shook his head as he lifted the handset again. "Just take your client away, Lucius. I don't want to look at him any longer." Into the phone: "I want to speak to the mayor, please, Clara. Wherever he is."

17

Because by unspoken agreement they had always proceeded during their relatively short married life on the theory that there would be no big secrets between them, Mary Thompson told Brooks of her telephone call to her father.

"It was a sneaky thing to do, I know, and now I'm sorry I did it."

They were sharing a thermos of hot coffee and the salami sandwiches Mary had brought from home, sitting on the bank of the river in front of their nursery and small greenhouse, enjoying the first respite of the day.

"I didn't mean to belittle you by calling him," Mary said. "Honest. That part didn't even enter my mind. It should have."

Brooks smiled at her. "I can stand it." The smile spread. "I'm just vindictive enough to enjoy thinking about Spencer's reaction."

"I don't know what he can do."

"Honey, I don't think you appreciate how much clout your father has, or what kind of a man he really is. He doesn't use his clout all that often because he likes to do things the unspectacular way, and he doesn't see any point in making enemies unnecessarily. But if he thinks the situation justifies it, somebody gets hurt. He didn't get where he is by being Mr. Nice Guy all the time."

Mary chewed her sandwich and thought about it. "Then I'm more than ever sorry I called him. I wouldn't have, but I was—furious. Mr. Gentry—" She looked at Brooks. "Yes, I called him first. I shouldn't have done that, either."

Brooks's smile had disappeared. "And what did Gentry say?"

"That we should have stayed in the East."

Brooks drank coffee and stared at the river. "Maybe he's right. We haven't done too well here, have we?"

"We're just beginning!"

"All morning I've been thinking," Brooks said. "We've got twenty-two thousand five hundred dollars in cash. We've got a loan on this place and I don't think we could sell it, even piecemeal, for more than the balance of the loan. So until it's paid off, we're more or less tied here, scratching and scrambling."

"We said we could use part of the money to pay the loan off."

"That's what I've been thinking about. I don't think we want to. I think we want to keep that money intact, work off the loan, and then—"

"Then what?"

Brooks shook his head. "I don't know. But I don't want to see you with cracked fingernails and grubby hands for the rest of your life. The pioneer spirit sounds great, and maybe for some people it is. But maybe for us Gentry was right."

"He wasn't! What you're saying is that because he can make his way here he's a better man than you are. And he isn't! And he isn't better than I am, either!"

Brooks poured the last of the coffee into their joint cup, slowly recorked the thermos, and stood up. He was smiling again. "Okay, tiger. Let's get back to work."

. . .

Angelita Leyba stood in the doorway of her little house shifting from one fat slippered foot to the other in acute discomfort. "You will not come in, Father?" she said. "The house is—not tidy. I was not expecting your call. But to stand here, in the street!" It was unseemly, she thought, but the words did not come easily to her tongue.

"I cannot stay," Father Rodriguez said in Spanish. "I must try to make amends. It is my fault—"

"No, Padre!" Angelita too had switched to Spanish, the *barrio* language of serious business. "It is not your fault. It is the fault of Juan Cisneros, who, as the world knows, is not to be trusted, and who always knows before anyone else when things like the enlargement of the dam are going to happen."

"He cheated you. I allowed him to cheat you. It is my fault. I will see now what I can do to remedy the situation." The priest turned away with finality.

Here in the city it was still bright sunshine, the kind of cloudless, benign day on which nothing bad could happen. Even the banks of the river, usually littered, the priest thought as he walked, seemed to have a fresh, just-cleaned look which defied explanation.

What surpassed the good father's understanding was why Dios, from whom all things came, could allow such creatures as Juan Cisneros to enjoy the benefits of such days too. From time to time the father found himself wondering guiltily if he might ever have the opportunity to ask that, and other similar questions, and have them answered.

He passed the schoolyard where children were at play. Some of them waved. One little girl curtsied gravely. The priest smiled at them all to hide his sense of guilt. What a sham he was, unworldly, gullible, unworthy, allowing Angelita Leyba, that good woman, mother and widow, to be cheated of what might have been riches. And now—

"Padre! Padre!" A young female voice behind him, filled with urgency.

The priest stopped and turned. "Teresa! *Qué pasa?*"

"You have heard?" The girl's voice hurried on, slurring her words. "It is said that the dam is not safe! That it may break! Do you know of this, Padre?"

"Heard?" the priest said slowly, wonderingly. "From whom did you hear this—this rumor, Teresa? Tell me."

From Juan, her brother, who heard it from Antonio, who drove a taxi, and Antonio had heard from a garage mechanic who had been told by one of the busboys who worked at the Hilton and overheard men at coffee talking. . . . "Is it true, Padre? That we will all be washed away?"

"No, Teresa, we will not be washed away. And you must tell this to no one. Do you understand?" Was it always girls-not-yet-women who received and passed along special news? the priest found himself wondering. As at Lourdes? As in Haiti, as he had heard, at a village with the unlikely name of Ville Bonheur? "Do you understand, Teresa? No one!"

The girl hesitated. She said at last with vague disappointment, "If you say so, Padre."

"Good girl." The priest turned away again and began to walk more purposefully this time, no longer with reluctant steps. He would find out the truth of this rumor from the man who always knew before anyone else what was happening.

Johnny Cisneros was supervising two crews of men loading trucks with television, radio, and record-player equipment from the warehouse on which the huge sign HONEST JOHNNY'S—TV—RADIO—APPLIANCES appeared. He saw Father Rodriguez approach, and he sighed. Well, sooner or later Angelita Leyba and her goddamned ten acres of land would have to be discussed, and it might just as well be now. "Hi, Padre," Johnny said. The priest surprised him.

"It's a little early for your fall sale, isn't it, Johnny?" The father's voice was not unfriendly, and he spoke in English.

"Yeah. Well, you know, Padre, you got to get ready."

"For what?" There was a little emphasis this time, but Father Rodriguez spoke still in English. "You don't believe in rumors, do you, Johnny? Not you."

"Rumors, Padre?" Johnny felt off balance because fat Angelita Leyba and her property had not been mentioned. He was tempted to tell the old fool to buzz off, but in the *barrio*, awe for the Church and by extension for those who represented it was absorbed along with mother's milk, and you could as easily get rid of the calcium in your bones from the one as the fear in your mind from the other. "I don't know any rumors," Johnny said.

"You were always a very skillful liar, Juan." The priest had switched to Spanish, a sure indication that what was in his mind was a serious matter. "As," he went on, "the other day when we spoke of Angelita's property. But now I refer to the talk about the dam at Harper's Park and the possibility that it is weak." He watched Johnny's workmen loading the trucks at a pace they would not usually maintain. "Could that be the reason for your haste?"

"Look, Padre, I'm real busy." Johnny stuck to English. "What I mean is, we've got a lot to do."

"*Claro*. My question is, why the haste?"

"These guys cost money, Padre. With minimum wages and all that, you got to get as much work as you can for each buck, you know what I mean?"

Father Rodriguez studied the matter. He said at last, in Spanish still, "I do not believe in threats, Juan. But I believe I can say with assurance that a very long time, if not eternity, in damnation awaits those who turn their backs on their fellow men and allow them to perish when they might be saved."

"Damnit, Padre, I'm not doing anything."

"Precisely." There was a change in Johnny's manner, the priest thought, subtle, but there. From countless hours spent listening in the confessional box, he recognized the signs. He was convinced now that he was on the right track. "What is it you know that is the cause of this desperate haste?"

"Look, I already told you, Padre, what you got to pay these guys—"

"Juan! This time I will not be trifled with!" He was a small man, Father Rodriguez, in shabby black suit, beret, and dusty shoes, but there was dignity in his manner, and force in his formal words. "I will ask you once again, Juan. What is it you know?"

He didn't believe a bit of it, Johnny told himself, and yet, goddamnit, he couldn't shake the feeling that there just might be something to it after all, who the hell knew? And maybe the line of strength, yes, and authority as well, actually did stretch like they said all the way from this little bastard right across the country and across the ocean to Rome and right from there to both heaven and hell. Resistance collapsed, as it had so many times in the confessional. "Oh, shit, Padre," he said. "The dam is going to go. Even the governor knows it. He just isn't talking yet. Now are you satisfied?"

Father Rodriguez did not answer. He turned away and hurried toward the church. So Teresa had been right, and now there was much to be done.

 .   .   .

The governor sat behind his desk in the position of command. The mayor, Bill Williams, Cooley Parks, and Jay were in chairs drawn up in a rough semicircle facing him.

"Go ahead, young man. Start at the beginning," the governor said to Jay, and sat quiet and intent, waiting, listening, evaluating.

"Two days ago when I was diving," Jay said, "just on a hunch I had a look at the sides of the dam where it ties into the rock structure. I found signs of fracturing. I told Williams that night."

Williams nodded. "First I'd heard of it, and I wish to hell—" He shook his head wearily. "Never mind. Go on, Harper."

"Yesterday morning I flew with Kate Williams over the dam," Jay said. "It was her idea. I didn't expect to see anything, but I did. I was pretty sure I knew what it was, but I wanted expert corroboration, so I called Cooley. We flew again this morning, and he saw it too. Then he went up to have a close look around." He looked at Cooley. "Tell them," he said.

They all looked at Cooley. He was, the governor thought, a man you would believe; they both were. When you were dealing with real experts it had a way of coming through to you that you were hearing facts, not guesses, not half-truths or evasions, not distortions; facts. "The long and the short of it," Cooley said, "is that the dam sits right on a fault line." No hedging, no elaboration, mere flat statement; take it, or leave it.

Jay said, "I dove again after today's first tremor. I saw further signs of fracturing. And while I was still on the bottom today's second tremor hit, and that time"—he smiled grimly—"although I didn't stay around too long to watch, I did see more actual fracturing taking place."

The mayor said, "You're talking about the bottom of the lake? That's where you were?" He shook his head in what amounted to awe, and subsided into further silence.

The governor said, "All right, what does it add up to?" He looked at Jay. "What do you think?"

Jay spread his hands. "Anybody's guess. We can tell you that the supporting rock structure is weak, that it has been affected by the tremors there've already been and that it will probably be affected by any more that may happen. I can also tell you that as far as I know, no concrete dam has ever failed just because of an earthquake."

"But," Cooley said, "there's a first time for everything."

Jay nodded in agreement. "Beyond that—" His shrug was expressive.

"It is snowing in the mountains," the governor said. "The Weather Service is predicting up to a foot of snow, turning to rain, a reversal of the usual progression, something to do with the tropical storm from the Gulf that has broken up over land. I assume that is one more factor to be brought into the equation?"

"There isn't any equation," Cooley said. "That's the hell of it. On the data we have, not even Jay and all his computers could give you a firm fix."

"We get a flash flood," Williams said, "it'll be worse than one of these little earthquakes, right?" He looked from Jay to Cooley, and waited.

"I can't even give you a definitive answer on that," Jay said, "but my guess is that it would. I'm talking about a real gully-washer now."

The governor looked at the mayor. "Joe?"

The mayor spread his hands. "All I can say is that we're already working on plans to evacuate the *barrio* and Old Town and other low spots in the city, just in case. But we're flying blind. At best it will be the hell of a job, and for how long? What about looting, with shacks and trailers, whole apartment buildings and stores vacant? And how much warning would we have if that dam does start to go?"

Jay said, as if he had been waiting for the question, "I clocked it driving down just now. The road follows the river, it took us twenty-one minutes and we were driving pretty fast, maybe faster than the water could flow. I'd say you'd have that much time at least."

"You think of the goddamnedest things," Cooley said. "Me, I was just thinking about getting down before anything happened. I'm getting nervous about this whole thing. I admit it."

The governor was silent for long moments, his face set in its expressionless mask. In the office there was a waiting silence. The governor said at last, the words coming slowly, with reluctance which added emphasis, "I will be frank. What we have here is the unsupported word of one man." He raised his hand to forestall interruptions. "I am stating facts, not my opinions, which are quite different. Only one man has actually seen indications of rock failure, is that not correct?"

"That is correct," Jay said. His smile was grim. "I'll lend my scuba gear to anybody who cares to have a look for himself."

The governor's answering smile was fleeting. "I am sure

there will be no takers." He looked at Cooley. "We have your opinion, the opinion, I am told and believe, of an expert, that the dam is actually resting on a fault line. That, too, is correct?"

"An *active* fault line, Governor," Cooley said. "I usually label my reports as considered opinion, but I'll stake my reputation on this one. What you *can* do is bring in a couple more rock men. I'll show them what I've found and let them make up their own minds. Then—"

"Have we time for that—leisurely approach?" The governor looked at Jay and then back again to Cooley. He waited.

"I'd say no," Cooley said. "But Jay's been down there and seen what's happening, and he ought to have a better idea than I do."

"I say no, too," Jay said. "There are probably other considerations. There usually are—money or politics or higher approval, things that are out of my field. But on the basis of my technical knowledge, I'd say you'd better start doing what you can yesterday afternoon. Or the day before that."

Nothing changed in the governor's face. "And just what steps do you suggest?"

Not my field, Jay told himself, and none of my damn business anyway; merely repeating the thoughts he had had at the bottom of the lake. And with the same lack of result. He was *here;* he was somehow *involved;* and that was an end to it. Swift thoughts, passing swiftly through his mind and disappearing.

He set himself to answer the demand. "You'd better start draining that lake as fast as you can to relieve pressure on the dam structure. Divert what upstream water you can into other channels. Set up a careful weather watch on that rain situation. Keep the seismograph monitored so you'll know about any further tremors in that area. Above all, set an around-the-clock watch on the dam structure and decide what to do about anyone in those summer cottages below the dam because they won't have nearly as much warning as the city itself."

The governor was making quick notes on a legal pad, nodding as he wrote. He was much impressed by what he was hearing, by the calculator speed with which Jay's mind worked, its clarity, and above all its decisiveness. He had already had Bill Williams's assessment of the man, and now he could listen and judge for himself. "Go on," he said.

"You'll probably want a standby warning system," Jay said, "both TV and radio. And people too, standing by to direct that evacuation you"—he nodded at the mayor—"are already planning. And there is one thing more—"

The mayor said, interrupting, "What about sandbags on the riverbank? That has been suggested."

Jay had already considered the possibility and rejected it. He said now, "I don't think it would do much good. We're not talking about a river that rises to flood stage and above over a period of days. If, as the British say, the balloon does go up, we're talking about some millions of tons of water coming two thousand feet downhill all at once, slamming through some of those narrow gorges between here and the dam and being channeled into a solid wall of water thirty–forty feet high traveling at maybe forty miles an hour. The sandbag levee you could build in the next day or so would only be more loose debris to be tossed around."

There was silence while each man thought about the picture Jay painted.

Bill Williams said at last, "Yeah. Okay, what was that one thing more you started to tell us?" He turned as he saw the faint smile on Cooley's face. "You know what he's talking about?"

"I can guess. Go ahead, boy, give it to them."

Jay nodded. "That flood-control wall at the big bend of the river," he began.

"What about it?" This was Williams again.

"That flood-control wall ought to be mined," Jay said. "And if the worst happens, it ought to be blown. When the river is normal, its natural course is around the curve and on down to the *barrio* and the city. But as you found out when you built out in The Bend, even little spring floods would sometimes refuse to make the curve and slop up over The Bend property. That's why you put up that concrete flood-control wall, isn't it?"

Slowly, reluctantly, Williams nodded. He said nothing.

"As I told you," Jay said, "the evidence shows that at least a good part of the big, ancient floods also refused to make the curve and went straight on, right over where that flood-control wall is now. What we're talking about is a flood of a different order of magnitude. Destroy that wall and let *some* of the water go straight instead of around the curve, and you've at least helped the *barrio* and the city. And every bit of help is important."

Jay looked now at the governor. "As I said, there are probably other considerations. There always are. I'm a technical man, and I just give technical recommendations. But, as Cooley said, the hell of it is—" He stopped and shook his head.

The governor looked up from his pad. "Go ahead." His voice was sharp with command.

"Okay. Nothing may happen," Jay said, "and none of this may be necessary at all, and then you've frightened a lot of people and caused a lot of work and confusion and expense— for nothing."

"You've spudded in," Cooley said, "and drilled your hole— and it's dry as a bone, no gas, no oil, nothing but a lot of wasted time and effort and money. We can't give it to you any plainer than that. What I mean is, even if you do believe us, we can't tell you what to do."

The governor put down his pencil and sat up straight in his leather chair. His face showed the strain and fatigue, but his voice was strong, steady. "It doesn't happen often," he said, "but every now and again an elected public official, like Joe, like me, comes to a situation where it's up to him to earn his pay and everything else that goes with his office. This is one of those times. You've given us your best advice. Now it's up to us to make the political decisions." He looked at the mayor. "You agree?"

The mayor nodded. All animosity between them had disappeared. "Like you said, that's what they pay us for."

"And so," the governor said, "if you gentlemen will wait outside"—his smile was wry—"we will try to live up to our responsibilities."

In the governor's outer office Cooley picked up a magazine from the center table, put it down again, walked to an aerial photograph hanging on the wall, glared at it briefly, rattled the loose change in his trouser pocket, and then spun around suddenly and looked at Jay, who was watching him and smiling.

"Go ahead," Jay said, "say it."

"I don't recall signing on for the duration," Cooley said, "and I never figured to settle down here and grow up with the country. Maybe you did."

Jay's smile was gone. He shook his head. "No. Just passing through."

"I haven't seen any sign of it. Goddamnit, boy, there's a whole new oil field waiting for you. And me. The kind of thing we know something about."

"Yeah."

"But what?"

Williams, leaning against the wall, said, "I always liked to finish what I started, and most times I have. Maybe he feels the same way." He too had been much impressed by Jay's lucid presentation. Even if he didn't like all he had heard, he wished Kate had heard the man too.

"He didn't start this," Cooley said. "Neither did I. Whoever built that dam is the one who began it all."

Williams nodded. His face showed nothing. "That's why I'm

not going anywhere until the whole thing is settled. However it comes out, I'll be right here."

"That's your business," Cooley said. "Mine is petroleum geology. And his—"

"Simmer down," Jay said. "Nobody's made any decisions yet. We've told them all we know, and what we think, and there isn't anything more we can do."

"In many ways," Cooley said slowly, "you're a real smart fellow, probably the smartest I know. But in some other ways you ought to be kept on a lead. You—"

The door to the inner office opened and the governor, standing with his hand on the doorknob, looked at them all. "Will you come in, please, gentlemen?" Again that wry smile. "For once the municipal and state governments are in accord."

As before, the governor sat in the position of command behind his desk, and the others faced him. He was smiling no longer. "I am not going to declare an emergency," he said. "Not yet. The mayor agrees that under the circumstances such a declaration would be premature." He looked at the mayor for corroboration.

"It would scare the hell out of too many people," the mayor said, "maybe for nothing. Maybe."

"But," the governor said, looking at Jay now, "we are thinking of following your suggestions, to start draining the lake, diverting upstream water, establishing an around-the-clock dam watch, and so on. There are already rumors concerning the dam, so there is no way we can disguise what we will be doing, but we will attract as little attention to it as possible. You agree with the necessity for all of this?"

"Probably," Jay said. And then, remembering the sight of rock breaking from the parent structure under the force of that last tremor, he amended his answer. "Yes," he said. Because what he had witnessed was only a minor by-product, a tiny indication of what had to be happening deep within the earth's crust.

Somewhere, at what the seismologists would call the epicenter, enormous forces were at work, producing pressures that would have to be calculated in millions of tons, rock against rock, slipping, grinding, crushing, even through the generated heat of that vast pressure polishing solid mineral matter into the minute evidences of slickensides Cooley had held in the palm of his hand.

When the earth itself stirred, something, everything had to give, and the pieces of rock he had watched drifting down through the water like autumn leaves had been merely visible proof of the existence of those hidden forces which could at any time tear the dam itself apart, or crumble its supporting rock structure and leave it to collapse of its own weight.

Whether or not he and Cooley could say with certainty that the dam was in imminent danger, the problem was there, undeniable, and logic and just plain common sense dictated that it be dealt with at once. "Definitely," he said. "You have no choice."

"I am glad you see it our way," the governor said.

"Oh, Jesus," Cooley said, "here it comes."

Jay turned to frown at him.

"You still don't get it, do you, boy?" Cooley said. "We should have gotten the hell out of here yesterday. Or this morning at the latest. Go on, Governor, say it. You might as well."

"We want you to oversee the entire operation," the governor said to Jay. "You are the one on the scene most familiar with the situation, and we feel that, as you said yourself, there is not time to bring in someone else who would have to acquaint himself with all of the facts."

Jay opened his mouth, and closed it again in silence.

"I am putting the resources of the state at your disposal," the governor said. "If manpower is needed, I can and will call out units of the National Guard. The State Engineer and his people will be under your direction on this matter. We will try to get you whatever you think you need to prevent—disaster.'"

"That goes for the city too," the mayor said. "What we want is one man in charge, not a whole goddamned committee."

"I'm a geophysicist," Jay said in protest. "This isn't my field. And it's none of my business either. I came here only to have a look at a village on the bottom of a lake, and—"

"Why don't you stop clicking your teeth?" Cooley said suddenly, in disgust. "Sometimes I think our Saudi friends have it right: *It is written*. Right from the beginning this was where we were going to end up." He pushed back his chair and stood. "Let's get at it. The sooner we do, the sooner it'll be over. One way or the other."

18

His first reaction, Jay realized, was resentment, anger, and resistance. There had always been those who deliberately sought the responsibilities of command. And he had always viewed them with what amounted to amused tolerance, by far preferring his own freedom of action and choice, and the privacy that went with them.

I am not an administrator, he thought angrily. Give me a job and let me do it, fine, but let others do the planning and take the broad overall view. The question here was: what others?

He looked from face to face. They all watched him, probably not even beginning to comprehend what he felt, right? Wrong.

The governor wore a faint, weary smile. He said in that precise, cultivated way of his, "Like Mark Twain's character, tarred and feathered and being ridden out of town on a rail, if it weren't for the honor of the occasion you would rather walk, is that what you are thinking, young man?"

Okay, so at least one of them understood.

The governor nodded then, emphasizing his comprehension. "We fancy that we are in control of our own destinies," he said. The nod became a shake of the head. "At times like this we see the fallacy of that belief. Like it or not, young man, you have volunteered. As your friend says, *It is written.*" The tension in the room was suddenly gone.

"My office," Bill Williams said. "You don't want orders coming directly from here, Harry." He looked then at Jay. "Don't worry, I'm taking orders, not giving them. You're the boss man. What's first?"

Again every face watched him and again the resentment rose. This time it was Cooley who broke the silence. "Just as if you knew what you were doing, boy," Cooley said. "Man can't do better than that."

Okay. That much, anyway, was obvious, Jay thought, and took the first step into the morass. "Around-the-clock watch on the dam." He spoke to the governor. "National Guard. They've got the equipment and manpower—"

"By the time you get to Bill's office," the governor said, "there will be an officer reporting to you. You give him his orders. Have Bill phone me for anything else you need." Dismissal.

In Bill Williams's car: "Your engineer," Jay said, "Sam Martin, we'll want him, with his drawings and specs." In for a penny, in for a pound, he thought. There was no drawing back now.

Williams, driving, said, "I don't even want to lay eyes on the son of a bitch. He's the one turned all the rumors loose. I told him not to talk, but his big mouth—"

"I don't care what he's done," Jay said. "He was chief engineer on the dam, wasn't he?"

Williams was silent. Slowly he nodded, an almost imperceptible head movement, chin set.

"Then we need him, period."

Williams drove two more blocks in silence. "Okay," he said at last, "you'll get him."

From the rear seat: "You're used to giving orders, is all," Cooley said, smiling. "So am I, as far as that goes. Taking them again just takes a little getting used to."

There was a full colonel of the National Guard waiting in Williams's office. "Colonel Watkins. I was told to report to you, sir," he said.

Williams shook his head. He pointed with his thumb at Jay. "To him."

The colonel's lips tightened and the muscles in his jaws

worked as he studied Jay's jeans, sneakers, and heavy sweater, but he said nothing. Jay seemed not to notice. "A twenty-four-hour watch on the Harper's Park dam, Colonel," he said. "Floodlights at night, and constant radio communication to this building. Any indication that the dam is showing signs of weakness, any cracks, any leakage—"

"Any rock fracturing at the sides," Cooley said.

Jay nodded. "Exactly."

"Sir," the colonel said, "the Army Corps of Engineers—"

"You do your job, Colonel," Jay said. "We'll take care of the consultations." He turned to Williams.

"Yeah," Williams said, and reached for the telephone. "Sam Martin coming up." His eyes went to the colonel, who stood uncertain. "If I were you, Colonel," Williams said, "I'd start moving my ass in a hurry. You've got your orders." Into the phone: "Sam Martin, honey. Find him and get him here with all his papers."

Cooley watched the colonel's stiff back disappearing. The door closed with a small bang. Cooley grinned. "Bird colonels don't like taking orders, either. Especially from civilians." The grin disappeared. "Suppose," he said to Jay, "I rustle around and find out who runs the seismograph, wherever it is. By now they'll have had a fix on today's two tremors and we can see where the epicenters were. Okay?"

"Keep in touch," Jay said. He looked again at Williams. "Now the Weather Service."

"Tell me what you want and we'll get it."

"Forecasts and reports kept up to date on everything this side of the watershed." Jay rested his hip on the corner of the big desk. His mind was already off in another direction, his resentment for the moment forgotten. "You're a construction man. How are you fixed for dynamite?"

"We use it. We've got it. What's on your mind?"

"Upstream diversions, for one. For another, the most important one, some way to drain that lake. And mine the flood-control wall. And we may even think of getting ready to blow one of those big bridges and drop it across the stream. It wouldn't stop a flood, but it would slow it and disperse it a little."

Williams whistled soundlessly. "When you get started, you're a real high roller, aren't you?"

"We're playing for lives," Jay said. "And they're the biggest stake I know." Williams's reaction was probably typical, he told himself, and tucked the knowledge away.

. . .

Carlos García was on the telephone in the mayor's outer office when the mayor returned from the State Building. The secretary was standing off to one side, pretending not to listen to the conversation, which was in Spanish.

Carlos looked up as the mayor walked in. "*Bueno*," he said into the phone. "He is here. I will tell him." He listened briefly. "I understand the urgency." He hung up.

"*Qué pasa*, Carlito?" Unconsciously the mayor spoke in Spanish too.

"Ramón Sanchez, the druggist." Carlos watched the mayor nod, acknowledgment of the name, the man. "Father Rodriguez called a meeting at the church. Ramón and others. Ramón thought you might like to know. The padre has ideas about warning the *barrio*."

The secretary said to the mayor, "The padre wanted you, too. But you had already gone."

"About the dam? The padre has heard the rumor?" Of course, he told himself; in the *barrio* all word reached the church. It had always been so. "Okay." He switched to English. "I'll go down and see him." He walked to the closed door of his inner office and held it open. The police and fire chiefs looked up from the conference table. "I have to go out again," the mayor said. "Carlos will sit in as my deputy. I want some kind of plans when I get back."

Driving down through the streets of the *barrio*, still familiar after all these years, catching now and again glimpses of the placid river, feeling, as the priest had felt, the calm beauty of the day, it was hard for the mayor to believe what he had heard in the governor's office.

He had been born here and had lived here all his life, and except for the annual spring flooding before the dam was built, there had never been any indication of real danger to life or property from natural causes.

But Bill Williams was one Anglo to be believed, and he was convinced of the danger. And those two strangers were both men who obviously knew their business. And for all his dislike of the governor, the mayor had to admit that Harry Wilson was not a man to panic.

So there it was, something that had to be faced, which meant keeping everybody in line, including Father Rodriguez, who just might be a problem.

Inside the church, the mayor was uncomfortable, in effect bearding the priest in his own den. They stood just outside the low doorway which led to the Santuario where the worn hole in the brick floor was filled with mud believed to be holy. The walls of the Santuario were hung with discarded braces and crutches, the sight of which always sent shivers up and down the mayor's back. He could not help thinking of them now.

"Padre," he said in Spanish, "we cannot allow this rumor to be spread further." Thank God for Ramón's report, the mayor thought; at least he had a chance now to prevent whatever the priest had in mind.

The priest watched him in silence.

"These are your people," the mayor said, "your flock. They are mine too. They elected me to do what was best for them."

"And you think it is not best for them to save themselves while they can?"

"What I am concerned about, Padre, is panic. We know nothing yet—"

"I have been told that the governor himself—"

"I have just come from the governor. He and I have conferred—"

"It is well known that you and he are less than friendly."

"True." The mayor was silent for a few moments, choosing his words. "There is a problem, Padre. I admit it. The governor admits it. We do not yet know the extent of the problem, but because it exists and because it may be grave we have put our differences behind us. You must believe that. When anything definite is known, he will tell me. I can rely on that."

The priest studied the mayor's face for a time in further silence. He said at last, "I have taken counsel with some I trust. I would have included you, but you were not to be found. We have decided to ring the church bells, summon as many people of the *barrio* as we can and warn them."

"I heard. That is why I am here. To prevent it."

"And if you are wrong, José-María?"

The mayor raised his hands and let them fall in a gesture of helplessness. "I have no answer, Padre. Panic, looting, these are real dangers, and they are what your warning will produce. The other danger is still uncertain. That is my best judgment."

There was a long silence. "I will pray for guidance," the priest said.

The mayor nodded. At least he had won delay. "You do that, Padre. I hope you get it."

. . .

In the fire lookout building on the mountaintop they were alone now, the rest of the world obliterated by the swirling snow which no longer melted as it touched the ground. From time to time the radio speaker crackled. Bernie gave it her full attention, and after a moment or two relaxed again.

Pete said, "I can't make out a damn thing. Are you actually hearing something?"

"Enough. You get used to it. Sometimes the static is so bad you can't make out anything, but it isn't like that yet. The Weather Service people are calling each lookout. They'll come to us."

There was another crackling sound from the speaker, and this time Pete could make out a voice, but no understandable words. The voice ceased abruptly. He watched Bernie pick up the hand mike and speak into it. "Roger. Mount Union here. Over."

Through the static the voice returned and went on at some length. Pete, watching Bernie, still comprehending no words, nevertheless understood that this was no mere routine. Bernie's eyes were closed, and her face tight with emotion as she listened.

The voice ceased. Bernie said into her mike, and her own voice was not quite steady, "Roger. We will keep you posted. Heavy snow now. Visibility zero. So far we have had an estimated three inches. It is holding. Over, and out." She put down the hand mike as if it were hot.

"What's doing, baby?"

"Oh, God, Pete!"

"That's no answer."

Bernie shook her head as if to clear it. "That dream," she said. "You remember that crazy, far-out dream I told you about, looking down from here and no world left?"

"Make sense. Come on, baby, straighten out." He was smiling as he caught her shoulders in his big hands and shook her gently, with great care.

Bernie took a deep, unsteady breath. "The dam. The Harper's Park dam."

"What about it? The water's low, is all."

"It may go. That's what they're afraid of. That's why the Weather Service wants everything we can give them. Like if that warm front does come through, and this turns to rain instead of snow—have you ever seen what a flash flood can do, Pete? Have you?"

"You're looking for trouble, baby."

Bernie shook her head in firm negation. "The Weather Service doesn't usually get excited, Pete. They have their satellite photos and their instrumentation and computers and reports and charts and graphs, things like that to play with, and they seem to live in their own world. Sometimes, honest, sometimes they don't even seem to look out the window to see what's really happening."

"But this time is different?"

"They're uptight, Pete. I've never heard them like this."

Pete nodded and gave Bernie's shoulders another gentle shake. "Okay. So we give them information just as fast as anything changes, right? There isn't anything else we can do, is there?"

"That's right. Not a thing."

"So what we do," Peter said, "we sit on the sidelines, on the bench, and we watch and we hope and we wait. And that's the hardest part, waiting, but that's the way it goes sometimes."

. . .

Sam Martin came into Williams's office as if he were entering a courtroom for sentencing. His arms were filled with rolled drawings and papers, and once he had pushed the door shut with his hip he just stood, waiting to be told what to do next.

"All right, goddamnit, put them down on the table," Williams said. "You have the dam drawings and specs there? Okay. Harper here is in charge. You got that? He says 'frog,' you start hopping. And this time you keep your goddamned mouth shut about what happens in this office, is that clear?" He walked around the big desk and plumped himself down in his chair. Automatically his hand brought out the small silver pillbox, took out and popped into his mouth a dry Valium pill. He swallowed with effort.

Jay was already bending over the conference table and the piles of papers. "You have a topographical map here? Good. Let's spread it out. While you were pouring the dam, where did you set your upstream diversions? Here? Here?" His pointing finger moved swiftly, without hesitation. "Maybe here?"

None of Sam Martin's resentment of Jay had disappeared or even begun to fade, but now listening to and answering the man's quick, probing questions; witnessing the almost bewildering speed with which Jay's mind recognized, grasped, and fully understood problems which he, Sam Martin, graduate engineer, had spent weeks and sometimes even months grappling with; seeing fresh ideas appear and take workable shape as if by some kind of magic; he found himself running hard just to keep up in his own area of expertise, which had little or nothing to do with Jay's own field of the geophysics of the petroleum industry. It was a chastening experience.

Sam was unaware that the office door had opened and Kate had come in silently. She leaned against her father's desk now, watching, listening, her hand resting lightly on Williams's broad shoulder.

"The outflow through the turbines in the power plant," Jay was saying. "Have you a way of controlling that flow?"

"We had to have a way to shut down if we needed to work on a turbine," Sam said. A defensive note had crept into his voice.

"Of course. Can you also increase the flow?"

"Well, sure. We had to be able to adjust it. But the turbines can only take so much. What I mean is—" He stopped, suddenly in the presence of another fresh idea coming out of nowhere. "Oh," he said.

"Yeah," Jay said. "If there's no other way, we'll open that outflow wide and to hell with the turbines. How much increased flow would that give us? Never mind exact figures. Would it be appreciable?"

"Maybe ten percent."

Jay nodded. "Every bit will help. The variables are the weather and—"

The office door opened again, and Cooley came through. He closed the door with audible force. "About two-point-eight and two-point-nine on the Richter Scale," he said. "Settling tremors, is all. That's the more or less good news." He had a sheet of paper in his hand, but he had no need to consult it. "The bad news is that we may get more little settling tremors, which we don't need. And the epicenters—guess where?"

"As close as they can fix them," Jay said, "they're probably right where we don't want them—under the dam area."

"Bingo," Cooley said. "And so was the one six days ago. We checked it out. It was three-point-nine on the Richter Scale. Not big, but bigger than today's. That is probably the slippage that is still settling."

Williams said, "What does that mean?"

It was Jay, now firmly in charge, who explained. "Pressure builds in the rock structure," he said. "No need to go into the why. There can be a variety of reasons. But when the pressure reaches the point where the rock structure can't stand it, something gives and you get diastrophism, a movement of the earth's crust, producing what you call an earthquake. The movement is rarely exactly enough just to relieve the pressure. Usually the movement goes too far and creates pressure in what you might call the opposite direction. Then it shifts back a little, and maybe goes too far again, and you keep getting those smaller shifts until at last the rock structure reaches equilibrium. That's the settling Cooley is talking about. And it's been going on for some time."

"And with the epicenters, the centers of movement, probably right in that fault line under the dam," Cooley said, "every one of those settling tremors is having its effect on the dam structure and its anchorage in the rock. Reinforced concrete isn't completely rigid, almost nothing is, but it doesn't give very much without fracturing." He grinned suddenly. "If you want it in big words, reinforced concrete doesn't have a very high modulus of elasticity."

Sam Martin took a deep breath. "You're sure about that fault?"

Cooley nodded. "We're sure."

"There was no indication. None. Damnit, the Army Corps of Engineers—"

"Look," Jay said in a tone that commanded silence. "We're not trying to fix blame. Somebody else can do that if they want to. What we're trying to do is figure out what to do now."

"And?" This was Williams, chin set, shoulders squared. "What do we do?"

Jay nodded, acknowledging the question. Right up to you, he told himself; never mind how you got in this position, you're here, and that's all that counts. "First," he said, "those upstream diversions. They'll take time which maybe we have and maybe we don't, but we'll have to try anyway to shut off the flow of water into the lake." He looked at Sam. "You did it once when you were building the dam. You can do it again, but on a crash basis this time, and never mind if you can't stop all the flow, just do whatever you can to stop as much of it as possible."

Sam looked at Williams.

"Don't ask questions," Williams said. "Just do it." He looked at Jay again. "What else?"

"The power station," Jay said. He spoke to Sam. "Is there a by-pass? Good. We'll open it too." He turned to Williams again. "Let the power company decide how, but we want all the water flow we can get and if it means losing the turbines, then that's what we have to do. We've got to drain that lake."

Williams looked at Sam. "That diversion tunnel. How about it? You said you'd have to blast a channel to it, no?"

Jay said to Sam, "Diversion tunnel? Near the dam?" And then with instant comprehension, "Used to divert the stream during dam construction?" He watched Sam nod. "Okay," Jay said, "you're the engineer. Take our word that the dam sits on a fault that is active. Take my word that there has already been more rock fracturing at the sides of the dam today. I was down there on the bottom and watched it. Would you do any blasting in the area?"

They all watched him, and Sam wished they wouldn't. He felt on-stage in the pitiless glare of a spotlight, naked and exposed. "If what you say is so—"

"Goddamnit," Williams said, "stop weaseling. Take the man's word for it and give us an answer. Can we blast a channel?"

"I'd—hate to."

"That's no answer!"

Cooley said, "I'll go up with him and have a look. I've crimped a cap and set off a charge or two in my day."

"Okay," Jay said. "Call us."

Cooley caught Sam's upper arm in a hand that was as hard as the rocks Cooley handled. "Come along, sonny, and show me where that tunnel is. I didn't see it when I was poking around up there."

"In the meantime," Jay said to Williams, "the outflow to the generator plant is our first move. That, and getting the military started mining that flood-control wall."

It was the first Kate had heard of it. "At The Bend? Oh, no! Our house! All those lovely houses!"

Cooley, at the door, looked at Kate, and then looked at Jay. There was approval in his expression as he urged Sam out, and followed.

Williams said, "I'll talk to the Public Service people and see about blasting equipment." His voice was expressionless, and his shoulders were squared as he too walked out.

Kate and Jay were alone. Three days ago, Kate thought, she

had not even known that this man existed. Now he threatened what amounted to destruction of her world. "Are you enjoying this?" she said.

Jay straightened from the map and turned to look at her. What was in his face changed her mind. "Wrong question, wasn't it?" Kate said. "I am sorry. I'll change it. Why are you doing it?"

"Ask your father. Ask the governor."

"I am asking you."

He took his time, his eyes steady on hers. He said at last, "There is no one else," and turned to the map again.

19

There was a column of military vehicles winding slowly up the Harper's Park road, and Sam Martin, driving, fell obediently in behind them. Cooley was patient for a few minutes in the passenger seat, but he said at last, "I think you'd better get this thing moving, friend. They may not be in a hurry, but we are."

"You really think something may happen." It was a statement, no question, but it demanded an answer anyway.

"Swing out and get going," Cooley said, "and I'll tell you what I think."

He sat relaxed, apparently unconcerned, as Sam bore down on the throttle, swung into the left-hand lane, and began to pass the trucks loaded with soldiers, towing generators, searchlights, and portable radio equipment.

Sam swung in quickly behind the lead jeep when an oncoming car appeared around a blind curve, then swung out again after the car was by, passed the jeep, and hurried on up the winding road.

"You get hunches," Cooley said, "and maybe, like some of the headshrinkers say, they're the result of subconscious thought process, or maybe they come out of nowhere, I don't pretend to know. But I make it a point to follow my hunches, and more often than not I'm glad I did."

They came suddenly around the final turn that exposed the entire dam structure and the generator station at its base. Cooley studied it in silence for a moment. "What I've got now," he said, "is more than a hunch. It's a feeling that I want to look in all directions at once because something is likely to fall on me if I'm not damn good and careful."

Despite himself, Sam was beginning to feel the same way, but he said nothing.

"I think," Cooley said, "that you designed and built yourself a fine dam, sonny. I just think you put it in the wrong place. And if that's true, and if those big black clouds up yonder in the mountains mean what I'm afraid they mean, then we've maybe got big trouble brewing. Now let's park well above the dam and see about that diversion tunnel."

Sam led the way, on foot, off the road and into brush and rocks, while the military column ground noisily up the last few hundred yards of the road and began to park in neat formation. Soldiers jumped out of the trucks and scattered in a scene of organized confusion.

"We cleared all this out," Sam said, indicating the loose rock around them, "and then we diverted the stream down this way to the tunnel, which is just over there."

Cooley followed the pointing hand. "Maybe you've got better eyes than I have, but I don't see it. We *are* talking about a hole in the rock, aren't we?"

"Damnit," Sam said. "It *was* there. Right there."

"You pushed this loose rock back in here. You didn't block the tunnel then?"

"Why would we?"

Cooley shook his head. "I'm not going to play with riddles. You say there's a tunnel. Let's find it. Until we do that we can't begin to know what we're talking about."

It was Cooley who finally solved the mystery. After minutes of fruitless searching, he stopped and pointed. "That's no natural talus slope. It's too steep an angle of repose. Those rocks were piled there. Carefully, and damned cleverly. It's good dry-wall construction."

"But who would go to all that trouble?"

"I told you: riddles aren't my thing. Facts are. Okay, so under those rocks there's a tunnel. What about the other end of it? Let's see that."

• • •

The mayor was back in his own chair again. Carlos García said, "There's a lot we don't know. That's one of the problems."

"There's the hell of a lot that nobody knows," the mayor said. "That's the major problem. So we just do the best we can with what we do have." He sounded, he thought, like a commander whose heart wasn't really in it, trying to rally troops for an assault that was bound to fail. Like back in Nam, memories still vivid.

Carlos said, "How much warning will we have?"

"That's one of the things we do know." But only because that bright Anglo Harper had been smart enough to time their car trip down the winding road which followed the river. When you had somebody like that in charge, the mayor thought, somebody who noticed things that could turn out to be damned important, then you had the feeling that whatever you were told to do made some kind of sense. "Call it twenty minutes," he said. "They're setting up radio communication with the dam and they'll know the moment anything starts to happen."

"*If* anything starts to happen," Bud Henderson, the police chief, said. He had regained some of his usual confidence by almost convincing himself that the whole thing was simply a large case of the jitters. It was just like a Chicano to push the panic button, he thought. "That dam's been there for ten years and nothing has happened. And the lake level now is twenty feet below normal, so I don't see—"

"Bud," the mayor said, "if you want to sit this one out, you go right ahead. But you'll be sitting out permanently, is that clear? It takes a vote of the City Council to fire you. I'm aware of that. Do you want to try it and see if they'll think my way after this is all over?"

The office was still. The mayor watched Henderson steadily.

The others looked away. At last Henderson shrugged, and his eyes fell away.

"Okay," the mayor said, "let's get on with it. Figure twenty minutes' warning, like I said. You have some ideas, Carlito?"

"We can't clear the *barrio* in twenty minutes." Carlos's voice held a strong Spanish lilt. He would far rather have spoken in Spanish, but Henderson and Smith had to be considered. Always Anglos had to be considered. It was an Anglo world. "Old people," he said, "sick people, handicapped people—they have to be moved well ahead of time."

"*Claro,*" the mayor said. Then, in English again: "Okay. And we need places to put them. School buildings, the hospital, the convention center—"

"I've got room in the firehouses," Rudy Smith said. "It won't hurt the equipment to stand outside a night or two. Inside, we'll need cots, and bedding—"

"The National Guard," Carlos said, "will they—?"

"They'll give us what we need," the mayor said. He made a note, and added, grinning wickedly, "The governor and I have signed a nonaggression pact for the duration. How about that?"

"Food," Carlos said. "We can use the school kitchens, and volunteer help."

"The Red Cross," Rudy Smith said. "If it turns out to be real bad, they can get us national help, donations, clothes, that kind of thing. Medicines."

The mayor was making rapid notes. "Okay. The old people, the sick, the handicapped—we get them out at the first sign of trouble, at least to high ground, okay?"

Carlos said, "But what is the first sign of trouble, Joe?"

"Yeah. Good question." The mayor put down his pencil and leaned back in his chair to think. He said at last, "I'll tell you what they're scared to death of." He raised his hand, fingers spread. "Two things. Either another earthquake like those two today." He folded down his forefinger. "Or heavy snow turning to rain back in the mountains." He folded down the middle finger. "Either of those is the first sign of trouble, and we start to move." He sat up straight again. "Now let's get down to details. What about transport?"

. . .

Colonel Watkins was back in the office. "We're setting up at the dam," he said, "and starting work at the flood-control wall, and in a few minutes we'll have communication here. I've arranged for a direct phone line to the Weather Service, and they'll try to keep us up to date."

Williams was back too. "Just try?" he said. "What's the matter? Do they knock off work and go home at five, that kind of thing?"

"A matter of contact," the colonel said. "Communication with that Mount Union fire lookout is bad and getting worse, and that's their best source of information on local mountain conditions. It is snowing up there, or was an hour ago."

"As long as it stays snow," Jay said, "we're maybe all right. You don't get flash floods from snow. But if it turns to rain, as they say it may—" He spread his hands. "You'd better send a man with a walkie-talkie well upstream from the lake, Colonel. He can keep an eye on the water level, and the color of the water too, particularly the color. If we start getting silt, it may be working up to something serious, and he can give warning."

Kate sat quiet, watching, listening. Jay Harper dominated the scene; there was no other way to express it. It was not that her father had shrunk by comparison, but, rather, that he had deliberately taken a back seat, confident that the situation was in capable hands.

And it was, Kate thought, hands that were perhaps more capable than any she had ever seen before. She was not sure that her admiration was free of resentment. Why?

Well, for one thing, Jay was so—damned sure of himself. He

took it for granted that he was right, and somehow he made being right seem easy, which was almost unfair. He thought of things that others did not, grasped immediately what was essential and what was superfluous, explained when he had to, but did not labor points the way most men, and women, did.

All these were admirable qualities, she thought, but when you put them together in one package, they were just a little too much. And there was also that almost offhand mention of mining the flood-control wall which protected their house. Despite the brief glimpse she had had of his feelings, she thought, she wondered if he was really a man to care.

And yet her father and Cooley, both superior men, apparently found no grounds for resentment. Sam Martin had, but Sam was very conscious that he was viewing from afar, and Kate could not blame him for being unhappy about it. Poor Sam.

Jay turned suddenly from the topographical map to look again at the colonel. "Is there an Air Force base nearby?"

Colonel Watkins opened his mouth and closed it again. He nodded in silence.

"What do they have?"

The colonel was a foot soldier, Kate thought, and only part-time at that. She said, "Fighter-bombers. Usually a big-bellied transport or two. There's been a squadron of choppers around recently, and I assume they're based there too."

Good for her, Jay thought. He had forgotten that she was a pilot, and obviously knowledgeable as well about other kinds of aircraft than what she flew.

Kate said now, "The choppers would be best for rescue operations."

Jay shook his head. "Rescue operations are for *after*, if there's anything left to rescue. What we're concerned with now is *before*. It's the fighter-bombers I'm interested in. Do you know the commanding officer at the base, Colonel?"

Colonel Watkins nodded again. "I know him. But what do you think his fighter-bombers could do?"

"Just what they are designed to do," Jay said. "We can maybe use some upstream bombing. Have a look at this map."

The colonel approached slowly. His expression was skeptical, even incredulous.

"Here," Jay said, pointing with his forefinger, "here and here. Steep, narrow river gorges. That's where runoff will concentrate if and when we get it. That's how flash floods are generated. Suppose we bomb those gorges, fill them with as much loose rock as we can break down. Then instead of water concentrating, flowing, gathering speed and force unimpeded, it will have to seep through—the difference between water coming through a sieve and blasting out of a fire-hose nozzle. Do you see it now?"

Colonel Watkins opened his mouth and closed it again carefully. He stared at the map as if he had never seen it before. "I will call Colonel Simpson," he said at last. "He will need clearance from higher authority, of course."

"He has until morning," Jay said. "It's getting late and he can't fly bombing runs in the dark."

.   .   .

Again it was Cooley, determined and indefatigable, who crawled around in the brush and loose rock until he found the lower end of the tunnel. He summoned Sam and, sitting on his heels, pointed.

"Okay," he said, "there's your explanation. Ten will get you twenty that it's kids. A ready-made hidey-hole. All they had to do was block the ends, which was the hell of a job, but so were the Pyramids, and they were built by hand too."

It was a small entrance, surrounded by tons of carefully placed rocks, hidden by transplanted brush, and blocked by a stout wooden door with a cheap combination padlock.

Sam watched, shaking his head in wonder at the amount of work that had gone into the project, while Cooley picked up a large rock and hammered on the padlock until it came apart.

He removed the padlock from its hasp, and with great care began to open the door. "I wouldn't put it past them to booby-trap it," he said over his shoulder. "Obviously they don't want strangers breaking in."

He had the door partway open now. "There we are," he said, and, reaching in, unhooked a bent wire which passed through a heavy staple driven into the inside of the door. Then he opened the door wide. The air that emerged was dank, musty.

"A lantern and matches, right handy," Cooley said. "Nice of them. Let's have a look. Don't step on that wire. It probably leads to a deadfall right over the entrance."

It did. By the light of the lantern they examined the simple, but possibly lethal booby-trap, a shelf of heavy rocks above the entrance, supported by two slanting wooden braces. Attached to the braces was a rope which led through an eye bolt and then back to the end of the wire which had been hooked to the door.

"Open the door without unhooking the wire," Cooley said, "and you jerk loose the supports and down comes the rock, blocking the entrance, maybe with you partway inside. Nice kids."

Sam shook his head again. "How did you know it would be here?"

"I'm a suspicious fellow. Let's have a look at the other end. It's the one that's important. If we can get water to it and through it with the kind of force the weight of that lake will give us, we won't have to worry about this end. The water will blast those rocks loose without even slowing."

He was the engineer, Sam thought, and yet as with Jay, he was now lagging far behind in recognizing what were essentially engineering possibilities. Bill Williams was good, better than Sam at seeing the whole picture, no doubt about that. But these two were something else again, something beyond Sam's ken.

He remembered what one of his college professors in engineering had said. "You go where the big money is, and you'll find yourself up against people who are used to the fast track, world class people, and there aren't very many who can keep up with them." Sam hadn't paid much attention then, but now in retrospect and with present experience, he recognized the professor's words for what they had been: a warning, maybe out of the professor's own bitter experience, not to step out of his own class.

He followed Cooley and the dim light of the lantern the length of the tunnel through the dank, cave-like atmosphere, past improvised furniture, discarded mattresses, candle sconces festooned with wax; the floor, ceiling and walls carved out of solid rock; and always the humming, whirring sound of the power station generators nearby sending their vibrations through the rock to add an inescapable feeling of menace. A running monologue drifted back over Cooley's solid shoulder:

"Air vents there." Cooley pointed upward. "They hid them outside. This is not the kind of thing for little kids who dig small caves or build rickety tree houses. Ten will get you twenty— Hell, *five* will get you twenty these were big kids, interested in alcohol, pot, maybe occasional hard drugs, and almost certainly girls."

It was, Sam thought, like something out of a movie, but, then, this entire script was unreal.

In a far-fetched way, he told himself, it was like one of those Westerns where the stranger rides into town, Clint Eastwood, say, and immediately everything is turned upside down and the town's entire contents are shaken out on the ground and relentlessly exposed to the light. The town's leaders shrink to smaller than life-size, local heroes turn into cowardly bums, established love affairs and marriages come apart at the seams, and avarice, selfishness, dishonesty and downright rottenness turn up everywhere like a black contagion.

It was a script he had never really believed, and yet in a way, here it was happening. Who would have thought that Bill Williams would ever be dominated by anybody as he was right now by Harper? Or that anything on earth could bring the governor and the mayor out of their long feud to work together, or at least to try? And haughty Kate, of whom even in intimacy Sam had always stood in awe, now being treated just like any ordinary chick, and standing for it? Incredible was the word, Sam thought, and suddenly found himself almost eager to see what would happen next.

They reached the tunnel's upper end and Cooley held the lantern high to examine the careful rock work which had blocked the opening. "I don't know who the kids are," Cooley said, "but I'll bet you couldn't hire them to do all this work. But when it's their idea, they'll go at it like beavers. For free. There's a moral there somewhere, but I don't know what it is. Let's get down to cases. How do we get water here from the lake?"

Sam said doubtfully, "We blocked off the channel because we didn't think we'd ever need it again."

"Okay, now we do, so we unblock it. Obviously the water level of the lake is much higher than we are, because you were just diverting the stream which is now at the bottom of the lake, no?"

"Well, yes."

"We've got a lot of rock to move, including all this. And once it's moved, a lot of water is going to start coming through this tunnel. You've got a pocket calculator?"

Sam had. He handed it to Cooley, wondering what he intended.

"A ten-foot tunnel," Cooley said, "water coming through at —let's take Jay's forty-mile-an-hour figure." He punched buttons, viewed results, multiplied further. "I make it about

276,000 cubic feet a minute coming out of that lake. That will relieve a lot of dam pressure. That sounds worthwhile."

"We reinforced that rock we replaced with concrete."

"We'll blow it too."

"That's going to take a lot of blasting. Do we have the time?"

"No. At least that's the assumption we're working on."

"Then," Sam said, "I don't see—"

"We'll just blow it all at once," Cooley said. "And we'll hope that the dam stands it, and that we've got our dynamite in the right places, and that the good Lord's on our side."

"You can't do that!" Sam said. "I mean, that isn't the way—"

"Sonny," Cooley said, "some people don't like to hear profanity, and others get all riled up when they hear what they call blasphemy." He shook his head. "There's only one word that upsets me. Do you know what it is?"

Sam shook his head in bewilderment.

"It's 'can't,'" Cooley said. "It makes me lay back my ears. We'll blast a channel for water down to this tunnel because there isn't a thing else we can do that amounts to a good goddamn. Now let's find a phone and call Jay."

.   .   .

Kate answered the phone in the office and handed it to Jay. Cooley's voice almost filled the room. "Okay, boy, we've got the tunnel and a few little problems. But if things work out, we can start taking eighty-five hundred tons of pressure a minute away from that dam, and the way I see it, that's worth a few risks. How do you feel?"

"You know the stakes."

"I sort of hoped you'd say that. Okay, I need compressors, drills, men, and dynamite. Will Williams get in on it? He's a construction man."

Jay glanced at Williams, who nodded. "He's in," Jay said.

"Okay, I'm coming down. We can estimate from the drawings."

Cooley had not mentioned Sam Martin, Jay thought, and decided that he understood why. But there was a place for Sam, anyway. "Drop Sam Martin off at the flood-control wall," he said. "Have him make sure the military are mining it so if we do have to blow it, there won't be any question about its going. We'll be waiting for you here." He hung up and returned to the spread map.

Williams heaved himself out of his chair. "It'll take him a little time to get here," he said. "I'm going to stretch my legs." He looked at Kate. "Want to come, honey?"

Jay glanced up from the map as father and daughter walked together out of the office. He could guess what they were going to talk about, he thought, and he couldn't blame them a damn bit. Nor, he told himself, was there anything he could do about it. What had to be done, had to be done. He bent over the map again.

In the hallway, walking slowly: "The flood-control wall," Williams said. "That's what you're thinking about, isn't it, honey?"

Kate tried to keep it light. "Am I that transparent? I was trying to keep a stiff upper lip." Not funny, she thought; he feels it just as much as I do. "What are you going to do about it? It's all to save that horrible *barrio*, isn't it?"

"Maybe not even save it," Williams said. "Maybe just lessen the damage to it."

"You said I was like Mother," Kate said slowly. "I'm not. I'm selfish. She would have thought of all those people crowded in the *barrio* maybe losing what they have, even if it isn't much. I don't. I think of us and others like us and all we have to lose even if I didn't have anything to do with getting it in the first place."

"You're honest, anyway. I think about the same things."

"Sam is in charge of it."

"Sam's a good explosives man. And he built that wall. He'll know how to tear it down."

"You could talk to him."

Williams glanced at her. "Yeah, I could, honey, but I won't."

Kate felt herself blush at the implied rebuke. "You could talk with the governor and a few of the people who live in The Bend, and maybe stop it."

"Maybe."

"You don't think I'm behaving very well, do you?" Kate said.

"Just understandably, honey. But maybe we're talking about something that isn't going to happen, anyway. Parks thinks he can open up that tunnel, start taking pressure from the lake and the dam."

"I heard him too, Daddy. He said, 'if things work out' and 'it's worth a few risks,' and that didn't sound very hopeful to me. It sounds like they're gambling. Jay even used the word 'stakes,' didn't he?"

Williams stopped walking and turned to face the girl. "What it means, honey, is that they're two men who are willing to risk the bundle and go for broke, because it's either that or walk away and not look back, and they're not that kind of men. Harry Wilson gave young Harper a job he didn't want, but he took it with no *ifs, ands,* or *buts,* and he'll give it everything he's got."

"No matter what gets destroyed or who gets hurt?"

"That's right."

"And if in the end they fail anyway?"

"Then they've done their best, and it wasn't good enough because your old man built a dam in the wrong place." There was finality in his tone, closing the subject.

But it was not closed in his mind, because there was more, something haunting him he had thought long since laid to rest almost in the old ghost-story manner, buried at the crossroads with a stake driven through its heart—that Harper's Park village down at the bottom of the lake *his* dam had created.

That part of planning and building the dam had always bothered him, although he had never admitted it even to Martha. Those stone buildings had been lived in, and by that much in a strange kind of way, they had been *alive* themselves, and now were dead, drowned by his hand.

He had experienced a kind of shock when Jay Harper had said that first night before dinner that the underwater village was not like a movie set, false, lifeless, but that, funny as it sounded, he had almost expected to find wash hanging on lines as he swam past the houses.

And it was the village, nothing else, which had brought Harper here in the first place, so maybe strange forces were at work, because if Harper had not come and had not made those scuba dives, they would not have had any warning at all of the danger which he, Bill Williams, now accepted as fact. An old man's maundering thoughts? Maybe, but Williams didn't think so. And goddamnit, he wasn't that old, either!

"Time to go back, honey," he said. Maybe work, activity was just what he needed.

20

George Harrison dined early, alone, and well that evening at the Territorial Club. The encounter with the governor had been painful, but the mere fact that the governor had seen fit to deliver what amounted to a tongue-lashing was proof positive that he took the problems of the Harper's Park dam very seriously indeed. And that knowledge far outweighed any discomfort George had suffered.

Because at the very least it meant that the dam enlargement was now out of the question; that what George saw as Bill Williams's chicanery was thwarted; and that in the end it was George, not Bill, who profited from the sale of that quarter section of now almost worthless mountain land. All very satisfactory. George savored his victory over a snifter of the special Hine cognac and a Club cigar.

The sun was just sinking below the distant horizon, throwing the mountain Teta into sharp, breast-like silhouette, when George walked out to his car. There was a traffic ticket for overparking beneath the windshield wiper. He plucked it out and automatically tore it into four pieces, which he dropped into the gutter along with the half-smoked cigar. He felt comfortably full and relaxed as he slid in beneath the wheel, started the engine, and drove slowly away.

There were floodlights at The Bend where the river swung in its great curve. There were also mobile olive-drab compressors, alternating between subdued clatter and thunderous racket while air hammers drove star drills deep into the face of the concrete flood-control wall.

George stared, slowed and then braked the Mercedes to a

stop. He got out, saw Sam Martin among the military, and headed straight for him. "What in the world is going on, Sam?"

On the job Sam wore his hard hat, and in it he felt more his own man, competent, knowledgeable, at ease in surroundings and at this job which he understood. Besides, that nighttime visit to George Harrison's house was no longer secret, guilty knowledge; the damage was already done. "Pretty obvious, isn't it?" Sam said. "We're drilling holes—"

"I can see that! But why?"

George's burst of impatience gave Sam a feeling of intense satisfaction. The memory of George's veiled threat that night still rankled. "—in which," Sam went on smoothly, "we will place explosive charges. When we detonate them, they will blow this flood-control wall all to hell. Does that answer your question?"

Suddenly the euphoria of the evening was all gone. George considered the full implications of what Sam had said, and his voice turned quiet. "On whose authority?"

Sam shrugged. "I got my orders from Jay Harper." Through Cooley Parks, but that was unimportant.

"And just who is Jay Harper to be giving orders like these?"

"And from Bill Williams," Sam said. He turned away, studied the nearest soldier's air hammer and the depth of the star drill it was driving, and raised his voice above the clamor. "That's deep enough! Move on to the next hole!"

George, recognizing rebuff when he saw it, shut off the angry words that were in his mind and went back to his car. He turned the Mercedes around and headed it toward the city and the governor's residence on Mansion Ridge.

The governor was on his *portal*, a telephone at his elbow. He had just finished talking with Jay Harper at the improvised command post, and, like Bill Williams, he had read between the lines of the brief conversation, and understood the gamble Jay and Cooley were about to take.

"There's a diversion tunnel," Jay had said. "It's blocked now. It has to be blasted open, and a channel blasted to it. If we can do that successfully, we can take half a million tons of pressure away from the dam every hour. We're going to go ahead and try."

And perhaps destroy the dam in the process, the governor thought. That was the unspoken warning. But once they had agreed there was a crisis situation, what was the alternative? "Good luck," he said. "I will stand behind your decision."

Now came George Harrison, and the temptation to have George sent away, with escort if necessary, was almost overpowering. Instead, reluctantly, out of long acquaintance and habit: "Send him in," the governor said. And when George appeared: "What now?"

"They are mining the flood-control wall at The Bend."

"I am aware of it."

"Is the plan to destroy that wall if—?" George stopped. Only a short time ago he had contemplated the possible failure of the dam with complete equanimity. Now he could not even bring himself to speak the words.

"If the dam fails," the governor said, "that wall will be destroyed, yes, George."

"My house is there."

The governor said nothing.

"Bill Williams's house is there."

"That shouldn't disturb you." It was, the governor told himself, a cheap shot, but irresistible.

"You can't do this, Harry! The—important people have their houses in The Bend! And against them you have—what? The *barrio?* Shacks! Trailer homes! Cheap hotels and run-down apartments and little stores—"

"And people, George. Thousands of people. Against perhaps two hundred." The governor shook his head.

"We'd be better off without most of those people! You know that just as well as I do!"

"I will not argue genetics with you, George. In fact, I will not argue with you at all."

"You are committing political suicide." George's voice was quieter now. "There are more votes in the *barrio*. It would be fatuous to deny that. But cattle go where they are driven or led, and the drivers and leaders live in The Bend."

"Like yourself, George?" the governor said, and instantly regretted it. Another cheap shot, he told himself sternly, and one that should have been resisted.

"No." George's reaction was quiet, calm, even dignified. "My family's house was the first in the area, I was born in it and I would live nowhere else." Until this moment he had not realized the depth of his attachment to his roots. "But I have few illusions about myself, Harry. I am not one of the movers and shakers."

"And you want your home protected." The governor nodded. "Understandable."

George nodded. His expression was grim, determined. "I will do everything I can to see that it is. Do you want money, Harry? I have money."

Nothing changed in the governor's face but when he spoke his voice was almost inaudible, a hoarse whisper of emotion. "I think you'd better leave now, George." He paused for emphasis. "I won't say that again. I will have you put out instead." He reached out to place his finger on the bell button mounted in the wall.

George hesitated and then turned quickly and walked away.

He drove home by a circuitous route, the windows of the Mercedes up and the ventilating fan running to shut out as much outside noise as possible. But when he parked at his house, switched off the engine, and opened the door, the sounds of the air hammers down at the flood-control wall reached him clearly through the high, thin evening air, bringing a sour taste of anger into his throat.

He let himself in, and as if impelled by some kind of

tropism, went straight to his beloved library. There he closed the door and temporarily shut out the world.

There was a piñon fire laid in the corner fireplace, the logs standing on end in the Indian custom. George lighted it and watched the flames creep up the wood, sending their warmth and fragrance into the room. He sat down in his large reading chair and tried to relax.

On the table beside the chair was the book he had put down —was it only last night?—when Sam Martin was announced: C. L. Sonnichsen's splendid *I'll Die Before I'll Run*. George stared at the title, and thought of its origin, which is a piece of western verse running in part: ". . . and fetch me down my gun. / I ain't much hand for fighting / but I'll die before I'll run."

Heroic stuff, but in the present context not really too far-fetched. Just down the hall from George's library was a room filled with memories of the Harrison past—the Harrison arsenal contained in a locked, glass-fronted case, and on the wall the mounted trophy heads of bear, deer, elk, pronghorn, mountain goat, bighorn sheep, and a single snarling cougar, all taken on the plains or in the towering mountains of the area.

Not on view, but still green in Harrison memory, were other targets Harrison rifles had faced over the years since the first Harrison wagon had rolled into this country and stopped for good beside the river.

In the glass-fronted case was the old black-powder, muzzle-loading Dimick rifle, .40 caliber, octagonal barrel, weighing twelve pounds. It had faced Plains Indians and buffalo, among other, lesser creatures on the long trek West; as well as marauding Apaches and questionable Anglos on horseback here where the city now stood, the Anglos maybe just passing through, and maybe with something else like plunder and rap-ine in mind.

There was the lever-action Winchester 30-30 carbine, successor to the Dimick, its bluing worn through in places from countless miles, countless hours in a scabbard strapped to a Harrison saddle.

The 30-30 and a terrified horse had been George's grandfather's only companions when he met a grizzly unexpectedly on a mountain trail one day, and for a few seconds, as he was perfectly prepared to admit, he wondered if either he or the bear was going to live to tell about it. "I figured I could put enough lead in him to kill him," Grandfather had said, "but we were on the level and he would have gotten to me anyway, no 30-30 slugs were going to stop that, and then it would be Kitty, bar the door." But the bear was in a peaceable mood, and after a few moments of contemplation had turned away and ambled off down the mountainside. "Took me a good half hour," Grandfather said, "to get that horse calmed down, but that was all there was to it in the end."

The modern .350 Magnum in the case had killed the big grizzly whose head was mounted on the wall, but the shots had been downhill, from above the bear's level, and even then and against the massive striking power of that heavy weapon, the beast had managed to come a long way toward his enemy before he dropped.

None of these heroic tales had anything to do with George himself. But he had grown up with knowledge of them, and now, with the sounds of the air hammers at the flood-control wall reaching even into the quiet of the library, the sight of the book on the table beside him brought them strongly to mind.

He found himself unable to sit still, and at last he got up and walked out of the house, something he rarely did at night. Standing in the patio, he looked up at the stars in the black sky immediately overhead. Lightning flashing in the mountains caught his eye, but it was too far away and he could hear no following thunder.

But he could hear plainly the continuing chatter of the air hammers, and he felt a rage rising such as he had never known, an actual physical sensation of near-suffocation. He turned away and walked into the house again, closing the door firmly in a vain attempt to shut out the sounds.

. . .

Even at their elevation, the daylight was gone, blotted out by the clouds and the falling snow all around the Mount Union fire lookout building. The lightning flashes and the crashing thunder were closer now, but not yet surrounding them.

At a time like this when there was nothing to do but wait, Pete thought, talk was best. It passed the time. Besides, what was on his mind wanted to be said.

"You know, I meant it." His voice was casual, with occasional pauses for thunderclap interruption. "That guy I know in Santa Monica, I mean, the one with the string of sporting-goods stores for big guys, tall guys. Like I want a sweater and I walk into a regular store, and all they do is try not to laugh when I say I need a size 60, or maybe a 58 will do if they run big."

Bernie understood both that talk was good and that what he was saying was something he wanted her to know. "Would you be happy, Pete? I mean, doing just that, selling things?"

Pete took his time. "I had a defensive line coach once, baby. He taught me a lot, and one of the things that stuck in my mind, he said, 'Look, Pete, nobody can do everything. Nobody, not even Bronco Nagurski, although he came damn close. What you want to do is know your strengths and your weaknesses. Then you play to your strengths and make the other guys come there too. That goes for everything.'" Pete smiled at Bernie. "You see what I mean?"

"I'm—not sure."

"Okay. So I did what he said, and I took a lot of time figuring out what I could do and what I couldn't do so good on a football field. And it worked. And I've been doing it ever since, or trying to, like he said, in everything. Like, I'm not the brightest guy in the world and math is not my bag, so I'd make a lousy stockbroker. That's an example. But I do get along with people, and a lot of guys know who I am, and what I don't know about sporting goods I can learn because sports has always been my bag, so I think I could do a good job for the Santa Monica guy. And when you know you're doing a good job, it feels good, and so, yeah, I could be happy doing that, selling things. And besides I'd have you around close, not sitting up here on the top of a mountain."

Bernie felt near to bursting with joy. She controlled it with effort. "I could work too, Pete. I mean, you wouldn't mind that, would you? Lots of girls help their guys out that way."

"I always thought I'd do the work," Pete said. "If I ever got settled down, I mean. But, sure, if that's the way you want it. If—"

"Pete." Bernie's voice was quiet, but sharp. "Pete, listen! Don't you hear it?"

"What? What are you talking about?"

Bernie was on her feet. "Listen, Pete! That isn't snow any more! It's *raining!* That warm front they talked about—it's moved in!"

She trotted to the radio table and switched on the speakers. Static filled the room. She picked up the hand mike, pushed the button silencing the speakers, and spoke into it. "This is Mount Union calling the Weather Service. Come in, Weather Service! Over!"

Static again filled the room as she released the mike button. There was no faintest sound of an answering voice. Bernie advanced the gain and the static was louder as Bernie raised the hand mike once more. She spoke with urgency now. "This is Mount Union! We have rain, not snow! Repeat! We have rain, not snow! Acknowledge!"

Static again filled the room and through it Pete's voice said audibly, "Jesus! Did you see that? It—"

The sudden crack of thunder drowned the rest of his sentence, and all at once the lightning and the thunder were all around them, flashing, crashing, filling the tower with light that made the sheeting rain sparkle as it blinded the retina, and then with darkness that seemed to be filled with showers of sparks.

In one of the flashes Pete saw Bernie put down the mike and stumble toward him. She was sobbing as he gathered her in. "They can't read me, Pete! I can't get through!"

Pete held her tight and tried to think of something to say, or do.

"They have to know!" Bernie said. Her voice was a lament. "About the rain! And we can't tell them!"

. . .

A fresh column of olive-drab trucks wound up the road toward the dam, this one carrying mobile compressors and drilling equipment and men skilled in their use. Colonel Watkins rode in the off-side seat of the lead jeep; Cooley was in the rear.

"They know where they're going," Cooley said. "Let's take it on up ahead and I'll show you our little problem."

Minutes later, standing with the colonel and a captain of Engineers: "That's all we have to do," Cooley said. "There's going to be quite a bit of rock flying around unless your men are good and careful, but it can't be helped."

The Engineer captain said, "Jesus! All at once?"

"Stagger the blasts, if you want," Cooley said, "but what we don't have is time for one small charge and then a cleanup operation before the next one is set. This isn't a neat-and-pretty job. Let's say the Indians are coming over the rimrock, and you'd damn well better blast open the gorge and let the water through before they get to you, okay?"

The captain looked doubtfully at Colonel Watkins.

"Those are our orders," the colonel said. "You better get to it, Captain."

. . .

The lightning still flashed around them and simultaneous deafening thunder shook the lookout structure. Sam had crept to Bernie's feet and lay huddled against them, trembling.

"They're really laying it on us, aren't they?" Pete said. "Scared?"

In a flash of lightning Pete saw Bernie's head shake. "Not scared. Sick." She stood up. "I'll try again." Her voice sounded hopeless. She walked to the radio table, Sam following close, and again static filled the room, and no answering voice came through. Bernie walked slowly back to her chair and dropped into it. Sam took his place at her feet once more.

Pete said, "So what could they do if they did know it was raining up here?"

"I don't know. Yes, I do! If they're that worried they could start evacuating people, couldn't they? I mean, instead of waiting until the last minute when it might be too late?"

"Maybe you have it wrong," Pete said. "You weren't hearing them very good with all the static there was even then. Maybe they're not really all that uptight about the dam."

In silence Bernie reached down to pull Sam's ear gently.

After a moment: "Okay," Pete said, "so you did get it straight."

"I did, Pete."

"How about the other lookouts? Maybe they're getting through. That Charlie character, say?"

"We're the only important ones, Pete. What's happening in other places doesn't make any difference. It's what happens right here, at the head of the drainage system that feeds that lake, that's important, what we say that counts. And we can't say it. We can't give them warning."

For long moments Pete was silent. In the intervals between thunder crashes he could hear the rain drumming on the roof, beating against the tempered-glass walls. In a lightning flash he watched the rain falling, sheeting, wind-driven.

He had never been much for religion, but there were times, like now, he thought, when it did seem that things were *arranged*. Maybe there were little men somewhere who wrote in a big book and then knocked themselves out laughing when they watched humans behaving as if they thought they were in control of their own actions.

Or maybe it was only sheer chance that he was here on this mountaintop at this particular moment, in love with this girl and wanting above all else to make her happy. Who the hell knew? And what did it matter anyway? He already knew what he had to do, didn't he? Well?

He had a professional's disdain that amounted to contempt for heroics. You did what was there to do, and that was all there was to it. So, okay, put me in, Coach. I'm a defensive lineman, sure, but you need one yard for the first down you have to have, and I can get you that one yard, so tell your ball carrier to follow me and that'll be it. Simple as that.

He said, "You know, you asked me once did I know what flash floods could do. Yeah, I do know. I didn't spend my whole life on a football field. I've known the mountains since I was a kid. I was even a Boy Scout once, how about that?"

There was something new in his voice that frightened her, Bernie thought, something elemental and almost savage, indicating a side to him she had never seen before. Maybe this was what he had been like on a football field. "Pete—"

"Excelsior," Pete said, "and all that jazz. You know, like in that poetry you get in high school?" He stood up. "Where's the nearest phone?"

"Pete, no! What you're thinking—I won't let you!"

"Where's the phone?"

"It's—it's clear down at the dam! At Harper's Park! And you can't! Not in the dark! Not in this weather!"

"I learned a long time ago," Pete said, "that I'm not what they call water-soluble. I've been wet before and I didn't melt."

"No, Pete. That trail—"

"I'll borrow your big flashlight, and I'll leave my pack here. It'll be a lot faster going down. Two hours, maybe two hours and a half."

"Pete, please!" Bernie too was standing. At her feet Sam watched them both, trembling still.

Pete's big hands caught Bernie's shoulders. "Baby, it's fun up here on your mountaintop. But we're still part of the real world, part of people. You know that too. That's why that dream shook you up like it did. That's why you're sick that you can't get through on the radio."

Bernie closed her eyes. Tears stung her eyelids. "Pete, if something happens to you—"

"It's the guys keep worrying about getting hurt who always seem to get it. It happens, it happens; forget it, baby. It took the whole NFL twelve years trying to bust me up before they finally made it."

"Oh, God, Pete!"

"Funny thing. I've been carrying this poncho around in my pack for years, and I use it so seldom I have to figure out each time where my head goes through. There." His hands reached for her shoulders again and squeezed them with gentle strength. "You and Sam," he said. "You hold the fort up here. Keep trying the radio. If you can get through, fine, but if you can't, I'll tell them what's happening, okay?"

"It's not okay, Pete! It's—"

"See you, baby."

The sliding door opened and the entire room was suddenly filled with sound, wind, rain, and fury. The door slid shut again, and it was quiet, and lonely.

In a lightning flash Bernie saw Pete's enormous, ponchoed figure, bent into the storm, disappearing down the outside stairs.

21

On the theory that a sober man had a distinct advantage over a man who was even mildly under the influence, Tom Gentry was usually circumspect in his drinking. But on this night, for what he considered good and sufficient reasons, he had taken more than his usual amount of alcohol, and had now reached that stage where inhibitions no longer seemed important and issues appeared in stark black-and-white without distracting shades of gray to confuse clarity. To have an idea was to act upon it immediately.

He appeared at the Thompsons' small house without warning and, finding no doorbell, hammered on the door with his fist until Brooks Thompson appeared.

"Out here," Gentry said, "we kill our own snakes."

Brooks blinked in surprise. The last time he had seen Gentry was at the closing of the land sale in the bank, and the difference in the man now was startling. He had shucked off his air of calm as one shucks off an overcoat, and sheer fury was exposed. "I'm not sure what that picturesque statement means," Brooks said, "but I think you've had too much to drink, Mr. Gentry, and you'd better go home."

"What it means," Gentry said, "is if you've got a bone to pick with a man, you don't go behind his back and get somebody else to do the dirty on him."

So Spencer had reacted, Brooks thought, as he had rather imagined he would. "I take it you've heard from my father-in-law?"

"That is just what I'm talking about. The son of a bitch has got me fired."

Mary appeared beside Brooks. "I am sorry about that, Mr. Gentry."

"I'm afraid I'm not," Brooks said. "I know something about banking ethics, and you abused them rather severely. What Spencer probably did was bring your behavior to the attention of someone in a position to do something about it, and leave it to his discretion to decide what. You have the profit you're going to make from that land to console you."

"Why, goddamn you, I don't have anything, except a twenty-two-thousand-five-hundred-dollar debt, and fifty acres of land I don't want! There's not going to be any enlargement of the dam! All they're thinking about now is how long before the dam collapses!"

Mary said, "Oh, no!"

Brooks could not hide a smile. "So you are hoist with your own petard?" he said. "May I say that it couldn't happen to a nicer fellow?"

Gentry's voice changed. "I don't pick on women," he said. "Not physically, I mean. So I'm going to take it out of your hide. Do you understand that picturesque statement?"

Brooks nodded. "I understand it very well, Mr. Gentry." His smile was gone. "And you are going to do nothing of the sort. I don't want to hurt you, so you are going to get in your car and go away."

"Take off your glasses."

Brooks shook his head gently. "They're in no danger, but you are, Mr. Gentry, if you persist in this childishness."

Gentry threw his first punch. It was also his last.

Brooks caught the fist as an infielder catches a line drive, and with the same sound of impact. In a single movement and without apparent effort, using the captured hand and arm as his lever, he spun Gentry around to face the other direction, the arm now bent up behind his back in a painful hammerlock.

"I can dislocate your shoulder without any trouble, Mr. Gentry," Brooks said. His voice had not changed. "Any more foolishness, and I will. I can also kill you with my bare hands in a variety of ways. You might remember that."

He gave Gentry a sudden, hard shove as he released the arm. Gentry stumbled a few running steps, and almost fell. Slowly he turned, his eyes wide with surprise.

"Now walk out to your car, Mr. Gentry, get in it, and go away. In your vernacular, if I have to, I'll kill my own snakes. Meaning you. I don't need Spencer's help for that." He turned, gestured Mary back inside, and closed the door.

He and Mary stood in embarrassed silence in the tiny living room.

"I didn't want to do that," Brooks said.

"You don't have to apologize." Her smile was faint. "For a moment you were wearing your green beret again."

"Yes. Well, I'd just as soon not go back to that either." His tone changed. "So no dam enlargement. And maybe a dam collapses. We'd better keep the radio on."

"That awful music."

"If we're going to stay here, we'd better get used to it."

Mary's eyebrows rose in surprise. "Are we staying? You've changed your mind?"

"I wouldn't like anybody to think we'd been run out. Would you?"

. . .

On Mount Union, although the intense violence of the thunderstorms had diminished, the rain torrents still fell, and wind gusts shook the building. Wherever Bernie walked in the single large room, Sam followed as if tied to her by an invisible cord.

From time to time Bernie tried the radio, but the static was as bad as ever. Once or twice she thought she heard the voice of the Weather Service radio trying to reach her, but the words, if they were words and not illusion, were impossible to understand, and her responses obviously useless.

She imagined Pete on that trail, maybe hurt, maybe badly hurt, and once, for a few moments of near-hysteria, she even thought of going down the trail herself; but when she opened the sliding door and felt the force of the buffeting wind, she knew that she did not have the strength to cope with it. And so all she could do was wait, and hope. She knelt, put her arms around Sam, buried her face in his warm fur, and wept.

. . .

On the mountain trail Pete Otero used the big flashlight sparingly, relying mostly on lightning flashes to show him the precarious way. In his playing days more than one sportswriter had likened him to a big cat for his sense of balance and his ability to shift his weight with almost unbelievable speed and accuracy to adjust to changing forces. To opposing linemen it had been axiomatic that just when you thought you had the big guy blocked helplessly out of the play, here he was already past you gathering in a massive armful of runner and football and taking them down with a crash that seemed to shake the turf.

Here, nothing but the elements came at him, but they were quite enough, even more than he had expected. Among these high mountain peaks the storm winds buffeted and swirled in all directions, now blasting at him head on, now attacking from the flank or even the rear, threatening not merely to block him out of a play, but to throw him entirely off the narrow trail and down the mountainside, and it took every bit of his agility and strength to maintain his balance and forward momentum.

Rocks turned unexpectedly beneath his feet. An advancing foot found support not where it had been anticipated but inches higher or lower, and adjustment had to be instantaneous to prevent a stumble or a fall.

The rain was a torrent, the heavy drops wind-driven with the force of hail; and Pete's poncho, far from protection, was instead a menace, catching wind gusts and filling, he thought, like one of those colored spinnakers you'd see on San Francisco Bay on a Sunday afternoon when all the sailboats were out. It threatened to set him sailing right off the edge. It was an effort to get the poncho off, and then, lacking his pack, he had no place to put it, so he merely let it go sailing off by itself into the storm and the flashing darkness.

Without the poncho, he was cold, but he had been colder. When you went up to play those polar bears who called themselves the Packers or Bud Grant's Vikings on their home turf late in the season you had to close your mind to things like snow and ice and frozen fields; physical punishment was a way of life, and what mattered then, as now, was getting the job done.

You settled into what you were doing, which right now was merely getting down this trail in one piece, with a stubborn singleness of purpose, knowing that there was no easy way and that the one thing you had to believe and keep on believing was that if anybody gave up it wasn't going to be you.

The buffeting wind and the driving rain played rough; he would give them that. And if the lightning and the crashing thunder were on anybody's side, it wasn't his. So all right, already, as Tim Bernstein used to mutter, there was a trail, wasn't there? And it was downhill, and all he had to do was stay on it, keep putting one foot in front of the other, keep himself more or less upright in the process, and eventually the punishment would cease.

My thought for the day, he told himself, or for the night. Come on, you bastards, he shouted silently at the storm, you haven't shown me anything yet I couldn't handle!

His first fall was not too bad. A rock slipped beneath his

foot, he felt himself going down with nothing to stop him and he deliberately shoulder-rolled on the trail toward the mountainside, away from the drop-off. It was bare loose rock he rolled on, not even artificial turf, which would have been bad enough, and he had no pads to cushion him.

So, okay, he thought as he picked himself up, I've got a few scratches and some bruises. Small damage.

The second fall was different, and not of his doing. There was no warning; in the crashing darkness he probably would not have been able to hear if there had been. A sudden shower of wet dirt and rocks loosened from the mountainside above the trail hammered him to his knees, almost covered him, and left him blinded, bloody, bruised, and choking on mud that had somehow filled his eyes and mouth.

He struggled free from the small avalanche, by the light of the flash found a solid rock face to lean against, and raised his face skyward to let the rain wash off some of the debris.

How long he leaned there, he did not know, but at last, as if at the sound of an inaudible whistle, he pushed himself away and started off into the storm once more.

It was the third fall that almost finished it. It was unexpected, unavoidable, as sudden as a crack-back blind-side block, and as vicious.

He felt himself fall, away from the mountainside this time. as part of the trail gave way without warning, and not all of his twisting agility or balance could keep him from going over the edge backwards.

He felt his head hit rock, and then his shoulder and ribs, so he must have cartwheeled. His head hit again, and his flailing, reaching hands found only loose talus as his bad knee slammed with agonizing force against something unyielding, loose rock, solid rock, what difference?

He heard himself shout, "Jesus!" in a great roaring voice, the word immediately torn away by the wind. His head hit again, face down this time. And then, at last, he stopped.

For a few stunned moments he lay motionless. Then, pure reflex action, he gingerly moved his neck, his hands, and his feet. Everything worked. At least no broken back, no paralyzing spinal damage. He got his right hand up and rubbed his face, feeling blood and mud and rain, funny mixture—how the hell did that happen? And where was he, anyway?

He was lying on a steep slant, head downhill. He took a moment to make sure which way was up. Then, clumsily, he maneuvered himself around until he faced uphill, got his good knee beneath him, and began a clawing crawl up the talus slope toward the trail, dragging the bad leg.

He came at last over the edge to more or less level ground again, moving entirely by feel now because the flashlight was lost somewhere down the mountainside. He stopped for a little rest before he struggled to his feet and stood motionless, almost afraid to try the bad knee. But miraculously, although painfully, when he put weight on it the knee held and would even flex a little without collapsing.

It hurt to breathe, so a couple of ribs were probably cracked. Despite the driving rain he tasted blood running down his face from his torn scalp. And his right shoulder felt as if it needed attention, but it was going to have to wait too. The important thing was that he still functioned.

The wind still blew, howling and tearing at him down mountain slopes, around rocky gorges. And the rain had not subsided; the heavy wind-driven droplets felt like tiny clubs beating at him relentlessly.

He had no clear idea where on the trail he was. The lightning flashes produced kaleidoscopic, distorted pictures of the terrain, and if there were familiar landmarks, he could not identify them. No matter. There was only one trail and he was still on it, still going downhill, which was all that counted. He started forward again, limping badly now, favoring that damaged knee.

On the way up, he remembered, that marmot had whistled

his warning and the pikas had scuttled for shelter. Sensible small people. They would long since have fetched in their piles of hay, stashed them in the safe dryness of their holes, and were themselves inside too, snug and warm, well sheltered from the storm. And man, Pete thought, had the nerve to think that he was a superior creature, better able to cope with his environment. It was funny how your mind wandered sometimes under physical duress. Concentrate on what you're doing. Remember—if you can—what day of the week it is and in what city this game is being played. That's how you hang on to your sanity. Think—

A sudden lightning flash illuminated the entire scene and seemed to endure and endure almost like one of those magnesium flares that used to light up nighttime targets so pitilessly in Nam. And there—yes, by God, this he did recognize!—there was that small lake he had noticed on the way up, but, Jesus!, it was a big lake now, and getting bigger by the moment; water was spilling through the rocks that dammed it, but more water was pouring down the mountainside from above—

A crashing whipcrack of thunder suddenly filled the canyon, deafening, echoing and reverberating among the rocks, intensified by the sudden darkness after the blinding light—but the lake had been there, no illusion, and even in the brief moments during which he had seen it, he had understood that sooner or later the loose dam of rocks which contained it would give way, which was exactly the kind of thing Bernie said the Weather Service people were so uptight about, the start of a flash flood roaring down from the mountains with unchecked fury.

Okay, he told himself, all I can do is carry the message to them. And maybe Bernie will already have reached them by radio with a warning, or maybe she hasn't, but what I have to tell them won't do a bit of good anyway. Still, at least it's a try. Come on, knee, go ahead and hurt if you want to, but get me there, you son of a bitch, and I'll see that you get a brace or maybe even a crutch, how about that? A bargain? All right, goddamnit, let's keep going! He limped painfully on into the howling darkness.

* * *

The soldier stationed well upstream from the dam with walkie-talkie and large flash lantern felt shivers and goose bumps when he saw first mere movement, and then in the light of the lantern Pete's enormous, bloody shape limping toward him like something out of a horror movie.

"Turn that goddamn thing somewhere else," Pete said. "What're you trying to do, blind me?" He kept coming. To stop was to break the painful rhythm he had established, and perhaps not to be able to start again.

The soldier raised the walkie-talkie and spoke into it in a voice that was not quite steady. "Somebody coming down the trail. He looks like he's hurt. Bad. Over."

"Coming from where?" the disembodied voice on the walkie-talkie said. "Over."

"Mount Union lookout," Pete said. He was still moving forward, and the soldier was backing up to stay with him.

The soldier repeated what Pete had said, and added, "Down that trail? Jesus! Over."

"Can he make it here by himself? Over."

"Can you?" the soldier said.

"If you get the hell out of my way."

* * *

Pete heard the clattering roar of generators and compressors and the hammer of drills before he came into view of the Hollywood-like night scene, floodlighted and crowded with men in uniform, who, one by one, stopped to gape at him as he emerged from the shadows.

There was a bird colonel, Pete saw, and a captain and other assorted ranks, and a civilian with obvious authority who caught Pete's upper arm in a powerful supporting grip and helped him to a nearby rock.

"Put it here," Cooley said, and lowered Pete to a sitting position, his bad leg extended stiffly.

And it was the civilian who did the talking.

"What's it doing up there?"

"Raining like hell. Lightning. And I saw a lake . . ."

The civilian listened only briefly and then gestured to the colonel. "Get on the horn. Tell Jay we're coming down. We'll want to locate that lake on the map." And, to Pete again: "Can you make it? Can the hospital wait?"

Pete lifted his bloody head. "Screw the hospital. Give me a hand up, is all."

"Good man," Cooley said, and with that hard hand almost lifted Pete to his feet for all his bulk, and helped him to the colonel's jeep.

Two soldiers watched the jeep, the colonel driving, swing off down the road. One of them said, "All the way down that trail from Mount Union, at night, in rain and thunderstorms like he said! And look at him! Jesus!"

"That's Pete Otero," the other soldier said. "I seen him play lots of times on TV. Nothing stopped that guy, nothing! Twelve years, he never missed a game, hurt or not."

In the jeep: "We better make tracks," Pete said. "I only came out of the rain maybe a mile, two miles back. It's a flash flood you're afraid of, you got all the makings."

. . .

Kate, Jay, and the governor, summoned, were waiting in the office when Pete limped in, one hand resting heavily on Cooley's solid shoulder. The bad knee had stiffened, probably for good this time, Pete had decided, but there was nothing to be done about that. And the knee, his ribs, his entire shoulder, and now his torn scalp too all hurt like hell, now that the cold and the shock had worn off, but he and pain were old acquaintances, you might even say old friends, and at the moment that was unimportant too.

Kate gave him a little gasp as she looked at him, enormous, dirty, bruised and bloody; and Pete produced a crooked grin for her benefit. "The mountain plays rough," he said. "I'll give it that. Which one of you do I talk to?"

Jay said, "It's raining hard, right? Was there much runoff?"

A little guy, Pete thought, but he moved well and he asked questions as if he knew what he was about. "When I started out, the runoff was just normal for a rainstorm, a good heavy one. But I was in it maybe two hours, and streams that hadn't been there the other day were beginning to form, some of them good-sized. All I could see was in lightning flashes."

Jay was at the topographical map. "That lake you told Cooley about." He put his finger where he had seen water from the plane that first day flying with Kate. "About here?"

"Jesus," Pete said. "I know north from south by a compass, and I don't get lost very easy, but picking out a spot on one of those contour maps—" He shook his head.

To Cooley, the map and the contour lines were plain as printed words. He said, "Here's your trail." His finger traced its course. "You'd be seeing the water off to your left, across a canyon and fifty feet lower than you were. The drop-off below the trail where you were standing is about like this." He tilted his hand at a steep angle. "On your right side and above you the mountain is almost a sheer cliff. Mountain-goat and rock-climbing country. On either side of the spot where we think the lake may be, there's a ridge, and the whole thing comes out on a kind of shelf. Above the lake, about a quarter of a mile back, is more steep slope. Does that ring bells?"

Pete closed his eyes. Slowly he nodded. "Yeah. You may

have it. I was maybe a third of the way down." He opened his eyes again. "Does that figure?"

Cooley did not need to glance again at the map. "It figures."

Jay said, "And the bottom of the lake was a—natural dam? Rocks jammed together, maybe leaking, that kind of thing?"

"You've got it. When I first saw it, on the way up, it was maybe a quarter full. Now it's almost overflowing." Pete could close his eyes and see the picture the lightning flash had revealed, water pouring down the mountain slope into the lake, water in rivulets and tiny waterfalls leaking through the rocks at the lake's foot and falling, sparkling in the lightning's glare, into empty space.

Both Jay and Cooley were looking at the map now. "Oh, brother!" Cooley said. "Look at the drop when those rocks give way."

"I am looking," Jay said. He was counting contour lines so close as to be almost on top of one another. "Eight hundred, a thousand feet, and then a downhill run with the main stream."

Kate said, "Are you finished with the poor man now? If you are, I'll drive him to the hospital and see that he's taken care of." There was compassion, concern, and admiration all packed into her voice.

Pete showed his crooked grin again. Bernie wouldn't know it yet, he thought, but she could relax now because her message had been delivered, the job she was paid to do was done. Screw the pain, *and* the stiff knee. He felt good.

"You know, lady," he said, "that's almost the best offer I've had today."

22

Kate and Pete were gone. The governor, the colonel, Jay, and Cooley stood close, drawn inexorably to the table where the topographical map was spread.

It was as if the closely packed brown contour lines against the green and white of the paper merely emphasized the importance of the heavy blue line which represented the stream; and to the colonel, Jay, and Cooley, all skilled in map reading, the two-dimensional representation translated itself immediately into three-dimensional reality, and menace.

"All right," the governor said, "spell it out for me. What does it mean?"

"What it means," Cooley said slowly, without taking his eyes from the map, "is what we've been afraid of—probable, no, damn near certain flash flood." His forefinger tapped the map. "There's where the lake is. This blue line is the stream a thousand feet below. When that natural rock dam goes—"

"What makes you think it will? Apparently it hasn't yet."

"That's a hanging valley," Jay said, and he too stared only at the paper. "Once it carried water down to the main stream. But the main stream kept cutting downwards, and it's now a thousand feet below, as Cooley says. And from the looks of it the hanging valley has been glaciated, carved out into its present shape, which is more like a tilted bowl than a valley, so it will hold a lot of water. The rocks that are containing that water now were probably piled up in a rockslide caused by the thunderstorm and rain a few nights back."

"If that's it," Cooley said, "and, like he says, it probably is, then those rocks aren't anchored. They haven't had time to be filled in with dirt and scree and maybe some vegetation to hold it all together. They're a geological equivalent of a house of cards. When the water they're containing reaches a certain weight, the rocks will give way and down it all comes—a thousand feet down into the main stream."

The door opened and Bill Williams came in, and they all turned to look. He seemed younger, Jay thought, more as he had seemed that first night. Responsibility obviously agreed with him.

"Okay," Williams said, "dynamite, caps, wire, and detonators are on their way to both the dam and the flood-control wall. How's it going up—?" He stopped and looked from one to another. "Trouble?"

"Perhaps." The governor's voice was quiet, even calm. He looked at Jay, at Cooley. "I take it you cannot predict when this—break may occur?"

"No way." This was Cooley. "Even if we stood there watching, we couldn't say until it actually began to happen. And by the time we started to speak, it would be all over."

"Then," the governor said, "we still have a"—he smiled, mocking his choice of words—"fighting chance? If you can open that diversion tunnel, and start draining water through it before that rock dam collapses, might not the Harper's Park dam be able to withstand the shock of the flash flood when, and if, it comes?"

Cooley smiled grimly. "I never associated optimism with politicians until now, Governor," he said. "I thought all politicians did was view with alarm."

"We have our various facets." Strange, the governor thought, how much at ease he felt with both of these men even though they did live in different worlds. Kipling had said it, of course, that when strong men met, though they came from the ends of the earth, differences did not exist. Funny he should think of that now. "On the other hand," he said, "I think we had better take certain precautions. I will take the liberty of using your phone, Bill." He sat down at the desk and began to dial.

While he waited for the ringing to begin, he looked through the floor-to-ceiling windows at the city spread beneath, its lights like a multicolored carpet.

There were the bridges, and running beneath them the dark line of the river. In places he could even see the shine of the water; it looked harmless.

And there in that jumble of dimmer lighting was the *barrio* and Old Town, crowded with people, with poverty, with tensions, and now with danger.

Panic was the enemy, as the mayor understood as well as, if not better than, he. In any crowded place in time of crisis, panic always lurked, hidden, but ready at any moment to explode into the open. And we can precipitate that explosion, the governor thought, merely by acting too hastily; while on the other hand if we do not act in time, what we may produce could be even worse—catastrophe.

A Spanish-lilted female voice in his ear said, "The mayor's office."

"This is Governor Wilson. May I speak to Mr. Lopez, please?" Now, the governor thought, it all depended on the mayor's frame of mind and whether the spirit of cooperation between them still held. He could only hope that it did.

"Right here, Harry," the mayor's voice said.

"It is strictly what the referees term a judgment call, Joe," the governor said, and wondered if he was going about it in the right way. "But I think we have gone as far as we can without broad warning."

There was a brief pause. "Something's happened?"

"No one thing. A combination. I could list all the indicators for you—" He left the sentence hanging, implied question.

Again that brief pause. "No," the mayor said slowly, "I'll take your word for it. If you're scared—"

"I am. I admit it."

"Okay." The mayor's voice was suddenly brisk, decision made. "Then so am I. We'll start moving the old people and the sick and the handicapped out of the *barrio* to higher ground. We've got schools, churches, firehouses where they can go. I've alerted the TV and radio guys and they'll give me time on all channels and all frequencies. We'll need the National Guard troops to help us in the *barrio*—"

The governor could almost relax. "You shall have them."

"Then I guess that's about it. The best we can do. They'll blow that flood wall at the Bend if the dam does go?"

The governor thought of George Harrison and his remark about political suicide. Probably correct, he thought. So be it. Strangely, he felt no real regret. "They will," he said.

"Okay, Harry. Wish us luck."

"I do. And, Joe, if there is anything I can do to help—"

"I'll give a shout." The mayor's voice changed abruptly and took on a note of wonder. "And you know the funny damn thing about it? It's that I know you'll do whatever I ask. How about that?"

The governor hung up and sat for a few moments in silence, still staring down at the lights of the city. Unexpected fallout benefit, he thought. What was the old phrase, bury the hatchet? Was this how feuds finally ended, so suddenly? Incredible.

He roused himself and looked up at the others. "They will start evacuating the lame and the halt from the *barrio*," he said. He looked at Colonel Watkins. "The municipal authorities will require National Guard assistance, Colonel. Will you see to it, please?"

"Yes, sir."

"For the rest—" the governor said, and left the sentence unfinished as he looked at Jay.

"We push both projects," Jay said. "Cooley can ramrod the blasting at the dam." He looked at Bill Williams. "And if you will—"

"Make sure that we're ready to destroy my home," Williams said. His smile was bitter as he nodded. "Will do."

"I am sorry, Bill," the governor said.

"Yeah."

"If there were any other way."

"Let it go, Harry. There doesn't seem to be any other way, and that's it. It's only—"

"Only what?"

"Okay," Williams said. "How much good will it do?" Kate's question, which he directed now at Jay.

Jay shook his head. "I don't know the answer, and I'm sorry about that too."

As if he had expected it, and merely wanted open confirmation: "Yeah. See you," Williams said, and walked out of the office.

The governor said to no one in particular, "He will do it. What he says he will do, he does."

.   .   .

George Harrison was at the flood-control wall again, and once more speaking with Sam Martin, while the compressors roared, and the heavy chatter of the drills filled the air. Rock dust diffused the glare of the floodlights and made breathing uncomfortable.

"I have not met this Jay Harper person," George said. "I assume that you have?"

Dinner that night at Bill Williams's house, which has been the beginning of all this nonsense, Sam thought. Then that humiliating scene at the airport; after that, Harper coming into Bill's office as he, Sam, was leaving with his tail between his legs. And finally Harper again in Bill's office giving orders right and left. "I've met him, yes," Sam said. "Too many times."

"I take it you don't like him?"

Understatement, Sam thought, and wondered where George

was heading with this conversation. "You could say that." Harper cast a long shadow, he thought, too damned long. And why was George interested, anyway? He was taking very calmly what he certainly understood was going to be the destruction of his fine, big house. After that night at George's house, Sam was wary of George's devious mind.

"And the demolition of this wall is his idea?"

"That's right."

"What do you think of it?"

"Hell," Sam said, "I just follow orders."

George shook his head. "I think you underestimate yourself, Sam. A graduate engineer. Experienced. Already successful, and with a great future here in the Southwest. Unless—" George left the word dangling like bait.

"Unless what?"

"I wonder," George said, "if it is entirely accidental that you are the man in charge of this—preparation for destruction. Do you think it is, Sam?"

Sam shook his head, puzzled. "I don't get it." He turned to the nearest soldier with a drill, and raised his voice to a near shout. "That's enough! You'd better start setting the charges! Pass the word along, will you?"

"Do you think," George said, "that the people who live in The Bend are going to be happy about losing their homes, Sam? I am not, and I think the others will feel the same way."

"I can't blame them," Sam said. The compressor roar began to diminish as the drilling tapered off. "I can't blame them at all."

"But they can blame you," George said.

Sam opened his mouth and closed it again in silence. He said at last, "That's crazy! I'm just following orders!"

"That particular defense," George said, "hasn't been convincing for some time, Sam. There were the Nuremberg trials. And a number of Watergate people who were following orders went to jail."

"Now, look! The governor—!"

"And regardless, I don't think the residents of The Bend are going to care whether you were following orders or not. All they're going to care about is that you were the man who caused the destruction. That is what they will remember whenever your name comes up."

"Okay," Sam said, "so that's what they'll remember. I can't help it."

"There is a lot of money in The Bend, Sam."

"I know that."

"And influence."

"I know that too, damnit! But what do you want me to do, quit my job?"

"No. Not that." The compressors were silent now, and George lowered his voice accordingly. "You are an explosives expert, Sam. Suppose there failed to be an explosion? Or if the explosion did occur, it was not sufficient to destroy the wall? There have been honest mistakes in calculations before, especially when a job was hastily done."

Sam said simply, "It would be my ass."

"It would also be money in the bank. I am quite serious, Sam. And I will be very plain. If the Harper's Park dam does collapse, and this wall remains intact protecting The Bend, there will be twenty-five thousand dollars to your account wherever and however you choose to have it."

Sam swallowed hard.

"My reasons are quite simple," George said. "I want to protect my home. To me, it and what it contains are without price. I am a wealthy man, Sam, and I am prepared to pay for the protection of what I have. Twenty-five thousand dollars. You have my word."

•   •   •

Cooley braked the borrowed jeep to a skidding stop by the trucks parked above the dam, jumped out, and looked around. He was not a particularly fanciful man, he thought; that was more in Jay's line; but it did pass through his mind that this could be someone's video replay of a corner of hell.

In the glare of the floodlights men swarmed among the rocks, heaving their pneumatic drills from spot to spot, sending clouds of rock dust to hang shimmering in the air.

The bellowing of unmuffled internal-combustion engines made the night hideous with their noise, while octaves above them the whine of generators and the sporadic sudden roar of compressors challenged the constant clatter of the drills.

Above all, rising from the power station below the dam, came the almost painful scream of turbines spinning out of control.

The captain of Engineers came toward Cooley.

"The colonel has been in touch?" Cooley shouted.

"Yes, sir. I am to take my orders from you." There were overtones of protest, even resentment, but the captain said no more.

Cooley's grin was wicked. "I'm easy to get along with, Captain. Most times, that is. How we doing?"

It was obvious that the captain was undergoing an internal struggle. He was young, sandy-haired, with a friendly, open face now set in lines of concern. "Sir," he said, "I probably ought to keep my mouth shut."

"But what?"

"I know something about explosives," the captain said, "and if we set off what it's going to take to open a channel to that tunnel and open the tunnel itself all at once—"

"There's going to be the hell of a big bang," Cooley said. "Yes."

"Okay," the captain said, "I'll lay it on the line. If you're worried about the dam breaking anyway, then that kind of explosion may very well defeat your purpose by collapsing the dam all by itself. What we should do is set off part of the charges, then clean out the rock and see where we are before we blow anything more."

"You're absolutely right," Cooley said. His grin was gone. "But that isn't what we're going to do, and I'll tell you why. There's a hanging valley way upstream, and a lake that's going to come down on us all at once . . ."

The captain listened. He said at last, still unconvinced, "Okay, sir. You're calling the shots."

"Correct. Now how long before we can clear the area and blow it?"

"Maybe by daylight."

Cooley shook his head. "Not good enough. One hour. Two at the most. Yesterday would have been better."

.   .   .

Above timberline the rain continued to fall. Far at sea this storm had been born. It had grown almost to hurricane force as it gathered strength from the enormous heat machine that is the tropics. Then, spinning its way on an erratic course, drawing moisture from the limitless ocean as it moved, it had at last encountered the uneven contours of land and there begun to break up.

Still moving, still driven by pressure gradient and the earth's Coriolis effect, its separated parts swept inland, conquering lesser disturbances in their path.

This remnant of the main storm, heavy with moisture, challenged the high mountains. Rising in obedience to the terrain, it cooled and thereby lost its capacity to carry the water it had drawn from the sea.

What fell now, and had been falling for some hours, was a torrent that scoured rock clean, washed vegetation from its anchorage, loosened boulders embedded in the earth, and filled countless draws, ravines, dry washes, and canyons with silt-laden flood waters pouring down the watershed to join the main stream.

The natural lake Jay had seen from the air and Pete had seen in lightning flash from the trail was now approaching the ultimate limit of equilibrium.

23

Two soldiers sent downstream to warn anyone in the summer cottages turned in from the main road past five mailboxes. A single house showed light, and one of the soldiers went up to knock on the front door.

Instantly a dog inside began to bark, and after a few moments a voice shouted, "I'm coming, goddamnit, whoever you are!"

The porch light went on, the front door opened, a shotgun poked at the soldier's belly, and the dog stood his ground in the doorway, growling. A man in pajamas holding the shotgun said, "What in hell's going on?"

"Look, mister," the soldier said, "put away the artillery. I'm just here to give you a warning. The word is that the dam might begin to leak, and might give way altogether."

"This some kind of joke?" The shotgun remained steady.

"The governor doesn't think so."

"Screw the governor. In spades. That high and mighty son of a bitch never had a straight thought in his life."

"Okay, mister. You've had your warning." The soldier started to turn away.

"Wait a minute, goddamnit! You wake a man out of his sleep, tell him he's maybe going to get drowned, and then walk away. What kind of crap is that? Who says the dam may go bust? And when? What's the story?"

"Orders, that's all I know. We've got floodlights on the dam, and we're setting charges to open that old diversion tunnel, and they're mining that flood-control wall at The Bend to blow it if they have to—"

"Jesus H. Christ! You're serious? The Bend? Well, what am I supposed to do?"

"Mister, that's up to you. If it was me, I'd take a sleeping bag and climb that hill yonder and spend the rest of the night there. Just in case." The soldier indicated the other houses. "Anybody else here?"

The man lowered the shotgun slowly. To the growling dog he said, "Shut up," in an automatic sort of way. To the soldier again: "There wasn't anybody else here last night. I got tomorrow off and I came up to get some early-morning fishing, me and the old lady. Look, soldier, this is for real? Because if I thought it wasn't, just a joke of some kind, I think I'd blow your ass off."

"Mister," the soldier said, "I gave up trick-or-treating a long time ago. I'm telling you what they told me when they sent me out. They think the dam's unsafe and that's all I know." He turned then, walked back to the jeep, and got in. "He doesn't believe me any more than the rest of them. Nobody else here. Let's go."

"You know," the other soldier said, "I'm not sure I really believe it either. Maybe this is just one of those trial exercises, you know what I mean? Like they do on the radio sometimes to see if that emergency network they talk about still works?"

* * *

Kate Williams walked slowly down the hospital corridor with the staff surgeon, whose name was Warren Richards. "I'm not an orthopod," the doctor said, "but it looks to me as if Otero's knee will have to be fused. I don't think there's enough left there to work with."

Kate was silent, even vaguely shamed, feeling, as once before, totally useless, a mere bystander while others *lived,* and suffered.

"For the rest," Warren Richards said, "we're stitching him

up here and there, and strapping that shoulder—" He shook his head. "He's taken punishment before. Lots of it. He'll shake it off."

"He didn't have to do it," Kate said. "He could have stayed safe on the mountain with his girl."

"Sure." The doctor's tone was matter-of-fact. "Except in wartime there's usually some way to play it safe." He smiled briefly, without humor. "And even then there are always those who find a way to beat the system."

That, Kate thought suddenly, is what I have always done, beat the system. Because Daddy has always been an important man, and there has always been money and no need for me to —struggle, or even make hard decisions. But why should these thoughts rise up to plague her now?

"Rumors flying around," the doctor said. "I guess Otero's taking all that trouble to come down the mountain confirms them, doesn't it?" He glanced at Kate. "They're afraid of the dam?"

"Yes."

The doctor whistled softly. "Then we should be on alert." He glanced at Kate again. "Disaster is a big word," he said. "Flood, earthquake, hurricane—you can't predict which way any of them will spread. But there's one thing you do know: hospitals always get busy when that kind of thing happens."

• • •

It was fat Angelita Leyba's son Luis, his precious new skateboard under his arm, who brought the news home. "Hey! Guess what! You know that dam up to Harper's Park? Well, it's going to bust! How about that?"

Angelita's eyes grew large and round, and she shook her head in silent disbelief.

In the worn chair which he rarely left during the day, the

abuelo, the grandfather, Angelita's father-in-law, listened, expressionless.

"Everybody's talking about it!" Luis said. *"Todo el mundo!"* Luis was never sure whether the *abuelo* understood English, or even whether he understood much of anything. He never said much. Luis's father, dead now, had told him once that it was what they called the "death march" in a place called Bataan, or something like that, that had almost done the old man in and he had never been quite right since.

"Maybe there's something about it on the tube!" Luis said, and trotted across the small room to turn on the television set.

She had bought that set at Honest Johnny Cisneros' store, Angelita thought, and every time she looked at it now all she could think of was how he had cheated her in the matter of the land. But maybe, if what Luis said was true, Juan Cisneros had only cheated himself. Maybe her prayers, unworthy though they were because they asked for revenge, had nevertheless been answered.

The television screen came into focus and Luis turned up the sound. José-María Lopez, the mayor, with whom Angelita had gone to school, was speaking gravely. "We are merely taking precautions," he said, speaking slowly and repeating each sentence in Spanish for clarity. "We are asking all those in the *barrio* who are ill, or handicapped, unable to move quickly, to leave their homes now. There are soldiers in the streets who will tell them where to go and who will arrange transportation if that is necessary. There is no cause for panic. I repeat, this is merely a precaution."

"Hey!" Luis said. "How about that? *Qué cosa, no?* Now will you believe—?" He stopped, staring at the old man.

The *abuelo* was heaving himself out of his chair. His face was still expressionless, but his eyes showed a strange light, and he said nothing as he walked from the room.

"What's with him?" Luis said.

Angelita shook her head in silence.

On the television screen the mayor's face remained, and his words of solemn warning continued. Neither Angelita nor Luis heard.

The *abuelo* walked back into the room. He carried now the 30-30 rifle that had belonged to his son. In silence he sat down again in his chair, the rifle across his knees.

"Papa!" Angelita said. "Papa, what is it?"

In toneless Spanish: "They made me walk once," the *abuelo* said. "The soldiers. Little yellow men. I will not walk again."

Angelita closed her eyes. She took a deep breath before she opened her eyes and beckoned to Luis, who was still staring, open-mouthed now, at his grandfather. Angelita led the way to the kitchen.

"The good father," she whispered to the boy. "The padre. Tell him we need him. Quickly!"

"The old boy's flipped!" Luis said, and scurried out the back door.

. . .

José-María had kept his word, Father Rodriguez thought, which was as it should be. The warning was plain and clear. The father approved. He left the small television set on, its volume turned up against further, more urgent warnings, and went out to stand in the nave of the church where he would be available to those who would inevitably seek his advice.

Luis Leyba, young and active as a squirrel, was first through the open church door, pausing only briefly to make the faintest of genuflections and then cross himself on the run. Breathlessly he described the *abuelo* in his chair. "It's loaded, Padre! He always keeps it loaded!"

Behind Luis three more parishioners appeared, women all. They hurried up the aisle. And there would be others, the priest thought, many others, bewildered, frightened, wanting and needing his help.

There was no cause for panic, José-María had said on the television screen. Perhaps in logic that was so, but against ignorance and fear, logic had no force, as José-María himself had understood when he urged the priest not to ring the church bell and speak of danger.

"Padre!" Luis said. "I tell you, he's flipped his lid! He's got a funny look in his eyes!"

"I cannot leave here now," the priest said. "Tell your mother that I will come as quickly as I can." *If* I can, he thought helplessly, and once more found himself wanting, unworthy. "Go, Luis. Tell your mother. As soon as I can."

. . .

That really blew it, Johnny Cisneros thought as he watched the mayor's image and listened to his careful warning. Soldiers in the streets and old people milling around, leaving their homes unprotected, probably not even locked!

Knowing himself, Johnny was convinced that there was larceny in every man's heart, and only lack of opportunity or fear of being caught kept it under some kind of control. Look at New York when the lights went out. And this could be the start of something worse.

He had seen to it that his warehouse was emptied and those TV's and stereos hauled off to higher ground. Okay, so far. The building where they were now stored was safe from flooding, and wouldn't be broken into very easily.

The retail store was something else again. Johnny doubted if the store could be flooded, but given man's avarice—which who knew better than he?—there was always the possibility of looting, and what the hell could he do about that? Except hope?

So, okay, he was insured. Walt Duggan might have to take a bath, after all, but that was Walt's worry. Walt was already out the extra thousand dollars Johnny had gouged him for, but the

Leyba land idea was Walt's to begin with, so in a way he had asked for it, hadn't he?

So the store would have to take its chances. Except—wait a minute, goddamnit! Two thousand dollars in cash was sitting right there in the store! Just in case Walt had gotten suspicious and asked his pal Tom Gentry about it, Johnny had drawn the money from his own bank account so it would look like four thousand had changed hands, instead of the two thousand Angelita Leyba had actually received.

So the TV's and stereos in the store were insured, but there was no insurance on that two thousand dollars in cash, and that money, by God, Johnny was not just about to give up! Okay, there was nothing else for it but to go down and take the money out before there was any chance of some goddamned thief breaking in and finding it in the general confusion that was bound to occur.

Johnny rode the elevator down in his apartment house, debated briefly in the lobby and decided against taking his car. Better to walk, he told himself. Cars could be stolen too.

. . . .

Lacking a television set, which they had never found necessary, Brooks and Mary Thompson heard the mayor's warning on the radio as an interlude in a steady blare of country and western music.

When the mayor was finished, and the music began again, Brooks turned the volume down. "Silly thing," he said.

"What the mayor said?" Mary's voice was incredulous.

Brooks was smiling as he shook his head. "No. What he said makes a lot of sense. I was thinking of all the time and effort I put into studying French and German when Spanish is what we ought to have. Never mind. So it's going to happen, the dam's probably going just as Gentry said, and what do we do now? That's the important thing."

"We have the car. We can go where we want."

"Our precious nursery?"

"It's expendable. You said so yourself."

"Your grandmother's silver? The china? Your clothes?"

Mary drew a deep, unsteady breath. "We can lock the silver in the trunk of the car and park the car on high ground. The rest—" She shook her head.

"Go on, say it."

"Grandmother said it first," Mary said. "I've never forgotten it even though I think I never really understood it until now. 'Things aren't important, child,' she told me once. 'People are. Remember that.'" Mary was silent for a few moments. "I have Red Cross training," she said. "Maybe they can use me at the hospital." She studied Brooks's face. "That's what you were thinking, isn't it?" She smiled suddenly. "You see? I know you that well."

"Is that the way you want it?"

"It's the way we both want it."

Brooks nodded slowly. His smile was fond. "I'll see if I can make myself useful too. The mayor sounds like a sensible fellow. Maybe City Hall can find something for me to do."

. . .

The state's senior senator in Washington, oil rich and crusty, was on the line. "I'll take the call in the outer office," the governor told Jay, "and leave this phone open for you." As he walked out, he glanced at his watch. Three-thirty in the morning here, five-thirty in Washington. And the senator was not an early riser. So.

"What in hell's going on out there, Harry?" the senator said. "AP and UPI have both got me out of bed talking about a flood that will make Johnstown if not Noah's flood look like nothing. What's the story?"

The governor gave him the bare facts.

"Jesus H. Jumping Christ! What can I do?"

"If the dam is still intact by morning, we're hoping for up-stream bombing . . ." The governor explained, and the senator listened.

"Okay," the senator said. "I'll get the Air Force Chief of Staff out of bed in his four-star pajamas and twist his arm a lit-tle just in case. What else? You're sure you've got good men on this?"

Bill Williams, Cooley Parks, Colonel Watkins in the face of crisis achieving new stature, José-María putting their feud be-hind him, and above all Jay Harper planning, directing, carry-ing the pieces in his mind as accurately and as compre-hensively as one of the computers which were his usual tools. "The best," the governor said.

"Then who the hell's to blame?"

"At the moment that is unimportant."

"Christ, Harry! There are going to be questions asked—"

"Maybe later. Not now."

"By God, I must say you're taking it calmly enough. You used to have trouble making up your mind. Now you sound awful goddamned definite."

"Do I? Maybe I'm learning some things, Bert."

"Maybe you'll take my job one of these days. Or maybe the big one in the White House. This is the kind of thing that puts a man in the spotlight. Okay, I won't hold you any longer. If I can help from here, Harry—"

"I'll give a shout." It was, the governor thought, almost ex-actly the same dialogue he and the mayor had gone through on the telephone. "And I know you'll respond," he said, smiling as he echoed José-María's response.

"Good night, Harry. And good luck."

The governor hung up and got out of his chair as Jay came through the doorway and spoke to the soldier manning the radio equipment Colonel Watkins had had installed.

"See if you can raise the dam," Jay said, and stood waiting

beside the table. God, he was tired! But, then, so was everyone else, except maybe Cooley, who seemed to run on inexhaustible batteries. When Cooley's voice came on the speaker: "How we doing?" Jay said, and forced himself to concentrate, ignoring the weariness.

"We'll be ready to blow in about a half hour." Cooley's voice carried clearly. "We're going to have a fine big bang, boy. You'll hear it way down there."

Jay smiled briefly. "What does it look like? Any discoloration in the stream yet?"

"Wait a minute." There was silence. Then: "The soldier boy way upstream reports a little. Not much. We've still got a chance."

Jay nodded shortly. "Hang in there. Call me if there's any change." He hung up and looked at the governor. "How are you on prayer?"

"I am a heathen," the governor said, "so I doubt if anyone would listen. *Que será, será.*"

Again that curt nod. "My sentiments exactly," Jay said.

24

Bill Williams stood facing Sam in the white glare of the carbon lights at The Bend flood-control wall. Bill's legs were widespread, and his shoulders hunched. "You're dragging your feet, Sam. Why?"

"I want it to go right, is all."

There was something evasive in Sam's manner, Williams thought, something not quite right. Fear? That the flood might sweep down upon them unexpectedly? Perhaps. But Williams didn't like it anyway. "You have the powder, caps, wire, and detonator. Why aren't you ready to blow?"

"It means your house if we blow this wall, Bill."

"Don't you think I know that, goddamnit? Now get your ass moving and get those charges wired and ready!" Williams watched Sam turn away reluctantly, and added further impetus. "And make goddamn sure you do it right!"

He walked back to his car and got in, reached automatically for the silver pillbox and popped a Valium into his mouth. His pulse was erratic and overly strong; he could feel it pounding in his throat. Okay, so it was erratic! He was supposed to stay away from stress, Jim Stark had said. Well, just how in bloody blue hell was he going to stay away from stress under these conditions, having to apply pressure to ensure the destruction of his own home? So screw it. He picked up the car telephone and called the familiar number of his own office.

To Jay who answered: "I've got them moving here," Williams said. "It looks to me like maybe forty-five minutes and we'll be all set. I'll stay and keep an eye on things."

Funny, he thought, that he felt not the faintest reluctance in reporting as a subordinate to a superior. Earlier in the night he had. Now it only seemed natural. "Anything else?"

"A couple of things," Jay said. "Cooley says he'll be ready to blow within a half hour. If he gets that tunnel open, and he will, you'll have more water coming at you, quite a bit more. Don't mistake that for the real thing. There'll be radio warning if the whole dam goes, and you'll have plenty of time to set off your charges."

"Got it. What's the other thing?"

"Kate called. She's staying at the hospital." There was a subtle change in Jay's voice. A hint of approval? "She says she can be useful there. She wanted me to tell you."

"Thanks." Williams hung up and sat quiet, his hands resting on the smooth perimeter of the steering wheel. He thought about Kate, and about Martha, who was, really, never far from his thoughts.

The familiar fluttery feeling began without warning in his chest, and automatically he felt for and took his radial pulse. It was jumping in the insane pattern of mild arrhythmia. He took a second Valium and thought some more about his wife and daughter.

He was not a religious man, but he had the strange feeling now that one day, maybe one day soon, he might be seeing Martha again. He hoped that was the way it would be, and he even smiled thinking about such a possible reunion.

Seeing Martha meant leaving Kate, of course, and he would be sorry about that. But she had her own life to live, and he had long ago promised himself that he wouldn't stay around so long that he interfered with it, no matter what it took to get out of the way.

He had read somewhere that in some tribes they took old, useless people up into the mountains and left them there, and maybe there was something to that idea, after all. He had had his time and made his own way, he and Martha together. Now it was Kate's turn.

His eyes automatically watching the soldiers at work under Sam's direction, and his mind satisfied now with their efforts, he picked up the telephone again and called the hospital. Kate was known, and found. "Hi, honey. Just checking in. How's it going?"

"Daddy, these poor people! They're bringing them from the *barrio*. They've left everything they have! Everything! I could cry!"

"Real close up," Williams said, "it looks a little different, doesn't it?"

"Maybe I'm—just seeing things differently."

Better and better, Williams thought. Martha would be proud. Maybe he could tell her when he saw her. "I guess it's called something like humanity, honey," he said with uncharacteristic gentleness. "You've always had it, but it's just now coming out. Hang on to it."

"You don't sound very good," Kate said. "Are you all right?"

"I'm fine. I'm watching Sam do the work." Williams hesitated. No interference, he told himself; that was your thought, wasn't it? Well, the hell with it. Maybe, just maybe there wouldn't be another chance to say what had been growing in his mind. "I said it before," he said, "but I'll say it again: That's the hell of a good man sitting up there in my office making the decisions for all of us."

"Jay?"

"That's right, honey. You could go a long, long way and not do nearly as well. Just remember your old man said that. 'Bye now." He hung up quickly before Kate could answer.

• • •

Kate hung the phone up slowly. She was puzzled. The conversation had not been like her father, nor, indeed, had the call itself, having no apparent purpose, been the kind of thing he would ordinarily do. And that last bit, almost pushing her at

Jay Harper, whom she scarcely knew and was not even sure she liked, was totally out of character.

Kate's mother, really, had set the tone of the parent-child relationship. Wherever possible both she and Daddy had left it to Kate to make her own decisions, always with the tacit understanding that if she wanted help or advice it would be forthcoming, but only on request.

She had made mistakes, Kate told herself, and sometimes she was sure they could have been prevented by guidance she had neither asked for nor wanted. But none of the mistakes had been grave, and she was aware of no permanent scars on her psyche caused by them, so all in all she thought that the hands-off policy had worked pretty well. Certainly it had given her a chance to be friends with her parents, which was more than a number of her contemporaries could say.

And yet at this late date here was Daddy even trying his hand at matchmaking, which was the last thing she would have expected from him. Unless—sudden, dreadful thought—it actually *was* the last thing he intended to do, his last gift; unless out of the affection she had never doubted that he held for her he was throwing away all restraint. He—

"Another busload coming in," a voice behind her said. It was a new girl, a stranger who had merely walked into the hospital and started making herself useful, tall, composed, speaking with the private-school-and-private-college accent Kate had encountered at college in the East.

Mary Thompson, or something like it, was her name, and she wore a rueful smile now as Kate turned to face her. "I've spoken French ever since I can remember," Mary said, "but I don't really know a word of Spanish. So you are needed, not I."

Wrong, Kate thought. We are both needed, but I only because I do speak Spanish. Mary was the one to whom the old, ill, or handicapped people from the *barrio* turned instinctively for guidance, reassurance, a confident smile that everything was going to be all right. I have so much to learn, Kate thought, so very much. "Then let's go meet them," she said.

It was a yellow school bus, and its passengers came out slowly, hesitantly, strangers in a strange land. "There are sandwiches and soup and coffee inside," Kate said over and over again in Spanish. "You will be comfortable here, and safe." And, as she had told her father on the phone, she was close to tears as she saw the bewilderment, the fear of the unknown on almost every face.

Mary spoke to them too, in English, which some did not understand, but her tone and her smile conveyed the message of comfort clearly. But not all were reassured.

"They did not tell me it was the hospital we were going to," one man said in Spanish. He stopped at the bottom of the bus steps, rested both hands on the head of his cane, and looked at both young women defiantly. "Hospitals are for dying."

Kate shook her head. "This hospital is for living, señor. You must believe that."

The man studied her in silence. "Do I know you, señorita?"

"My name is Williams." There is no "W" in Spanish, so Kate pronounced her name with an initial "V." "My father—"

"Señor Bill?"

"*Eso es.*"

The man nodded gravely. "Then I will believe you, señorita." He straightened from the cane and walked slowly toward the doorway.

Mary said, "I understood enough of that. Your father is obviously well known."

"He is." And I want to go to him right now and find out what that telephone call meant, Kate thought, but I cannot leave here. In Spanish again: "Inside there are sandwiches and soup and coffee. Do not be afraid. You will be comfortable here, and safe." A litany of hope.

. . .

The mayor's office was busy. People hustled in and out and the talk was mostly in Spanish. Brooks Thompson stood against the wall sizing up the situation.

The mayor himself—Brooks recognized him from his picture in the paper—was at his desk in the inside office, taking telephone call after telephone call, speaking sometimes in English, sometimes in Spanish, but never with hesitation.

"The soldiers have their orders, Bud," Brooks heard the mayor say on the phone. "They've been issued live ammunition, and we'll just have to hope they have the discipline and the sense to use it wisely if at all. Your men know the city. I want them to work closely and well with the military. Is that clear?" The mayor hung up, and immediately picked up the phone again as it started to ring.

A man who appeared to be an assistant was here in the outer office, winnowing out visitors who came in from the hallway, allowing some to penetrate the inner office, keeping others out, dealing with some by himself. It was Carlos García, and there was resistance in his face when he looked up as Brooks approached. "A reporter?" García said.

Brooks shook his head.

"What do you want?"

"To make myself useful if I can, run errands, carry the water bucket, whatever."

"Do you speak Spanish?"

"Unfortunately, no."

"Then what—?" Carlos stopped. "There is a problem," he said. It had been bothering him for some time, and he would have attended to it himself, but his place was here, unofficial administrative assistant. And he knew no one else to send, because it would take a brave man of Spanish descent to challenge the good father's authority in his own church. But an Anglo, possibly even a heathen— "Do you know the *barrio*?"

"We live on the edge of it."

"You know the church?"

"That, yes."

"The priest?"

Brooks had seen him many times, small, frail, old, carrying himself with careful dignity. "Yes."

"He is in his church and he won't leave it. He ought to be in a safe place with the other older people." Carlos left it there.

The reasoning was plain, Brooks thought, and sensible as well. He wore a half smile as he nodded. "Consider it done."

.   .   .

Angelita Leyba was distraught. The priest could not come. She herself had exhorted the *abuelo* in both Spanish and English, which, as she knew, he understood very well, and he would not budge from his chair. Nor would he surrender the rifle.

Angelita had heard the tale of the Bataan experience from others who had been there, and she was aware that the *abuelo* had never been quite right since, so allowances could be made.

But the soldiers in the streets of the *barrio* were *not* Japanese, *not* the small yellow men the *abuelo* remembered, and they were only interested in getting him to a safe place, not a prison camp.

"I will go with you," she said. "Luis and the other children and I will all go with you." She was not at all sure that she and the children would be allowed on the bus to be transported, because the mayor had made it plain that only the ill, the elderly, and the handicapped were to be moved now. But the effort had to be made, anyway. "How about that, Papa?"

The old man's face was set, and the worn hands that gripped the rifle remained motionless. He stared straight ahead as if he had not heard.

"You heard the mayor," Angelita said, "José-María I went to school with. He is a good man, Papa. He is only trying to make you safe. Maybe there will be no flood and you can return here." Angelita was unaware that she had switched to Spanish again. "But maybe there will be a flood and this house is not high above the river and you could be washed away!"

It was, she thought, like talking to a statue, although the statue of the Virgin in the good father's church seemed to have more expression when Angelita prayed to her.

. . .

It was funny how few people there were in the streets, Johnny Cisneros thought as he hurried toward his store. Few people and almost no cars even here in the high-rent area of town, which was on high ground, probably well above flood level.

A yellow school bus loaded with passengers drove by, and Johnny studied it. Old people, at least some of them and probably all from the *barrio;* Johnny recognized a few faces by the light of the streetlamps. Obeying the mayor's orders, Johnny thought, and wondered how it would feel to be able to get on TV and radio and tell an entire city what to do.

A jeep with two soldiers passed him, driving slowly. The soldier in the off seat held an automatic weapon of some kind, its butt on his thigh. He looked at Johnny, and then spoke to the driver. The jeep stopped and the soldier with the automatic weapon got out and approached warily, his weapon at the ready. An Anglo, either uniform-happy or scared, consequently truculent. "You got business in this part of town, mac?" the soldier said.

When Johnny was a kid he had avoided authority like the plague, running and hiding when it appeared. But he wasn't a kid any longer, and he didn't have to take any more crap from punks in uniform he could now buy and sell in carload lots. "Get back in your kiddy car, soldier," he said. "I live here."

In the jeep the radio crackled suddenly, briefly, words at this distance unintelligible, but immediately the driver called, "Leave him, Gus! We got looting down at Sears!"

The soldier with the automatic weapon hesitated, and then turned away, trotted back to the jeep, and jumped in. The jeep roared off.

Looting, Johnny thought, just like he expected. And the sound of the jeep's radio had started another train of thought too. He should have brought along a transistor radio himself. Way it was now, how the hell was he going to know if and when the dam collapsed? A bad oversight, but one he could remedy. The store was full of radios, AM, FM, shortwave, you name it, take your pick. Okay, on the way back he'd be able to keep abreast of developments.

25

Cooley stood again with the captain of Engineers, and from his voice and his manner he could have been talking about the weather, which he was not, except in a peripheral sense.

With a jerk of his head Cooley indicated the nearby communications man surrounded by equipment. "The soldier upstream is reporting more discoloration," Cooley said. "That means more erosion. And it's raining on him now too, which means that the entire watershed is getting it. Your time has run out, Captain."

The captain said slowly, hesitantly, "I know I take orders from you, but—"

"Are you laying back your ears and digging in your heels?" Cooley's voice was unnaturally soft. "Because if you are, I'll take over right now and worry about the consequences later."

For a few long moments the captain tried to hold his ground. He had logic and standard practice on his side, and he clung to them. They were not enough. It was an unequal contest of wills bound to end only one way. The captain was a reasonable man. At the moment, Cooley was not, and it showed plainly.

"Clear the area," Cooley said. "There is going to be a lot of rock flying around. Then blow it. I'm not going to say it a second time."

The captain took a deep breath, opened his mouth, and then closed it again in silence as defiance collapsed. "Yes, sir."

"In a hurry," Cooley said, and, waiting for no reply, turned away and walked over to the communications center. "Get me the downtown building."

He stood quiet while he waited, at last turning to watch the orderly bustle as soldiers hauled their equipment out of the rocks and brush where the channel to the blocked tunnel and the end of the tunnel itself would be blown. His face was expressionless.

Every so often, he thought, there came a time when you shot the works—or walked away. Some men learned that young. Some never learned it at all and in time of crisis tried to compromise and lost everything. It was as simple as that.

"They're on the horn, sir," the communications man said, and handed Cooley the handset.

"Cooley Parks," Cooley said.

"Go ahead." Jay's voice.

"We're clearing the area and we're going to blow. Hold it a minute!" He turned to face the interruption. "Yes?"

The lieutenant in charge of the dam-watching detail said at Cooley's elbow, "You want us to pack up too?"

Cooley shook his head. "Definitely not. You take what cover you can, but keep your floodlights on that dam and your eyes wide open. If it shows any signs, any signs at all of weakening, we want to know it chop-chop. Got that?"

"We could move out and then move back in after the explosion."

"That," Cooley said, "is just what you can't do. You're our eyes. You stay put."

"Sir—"

"You heard me," Cooley said.

There was hesitation, but it was brief. "Yes, sir."

Cooley raised the handset again. "That's all I've got at the moment, boy. I'll stay on the line and keep you posted. I don't know whether you ought to wish us luck, or pretend it's opening night, as they do in the theater, and tell us to break a leg. I'll accept either one."

"You have them both."

. . .

Upstream it had suddenly happened. No man would ever know at what precise moment, but, like the house of cards Cooley had used as an analogy to the governor, all at once the natural dam containing the lake in the hanging valley was loaded beyond its strength, and it collapsed.

Given a few gentle rains, it is possible that randomly piled rocks might have been filled in with smaller material, and dirt, even after a time vegetation, and the whole gradually unified into a sturdy structure capable of supporting the weight of water the hanging valley could contain. In mountain country such dams are not unknown, and may endure at least for a time.

But this natural dam was too new, its interstices too generous, its rocky structure as yet too unsettled, and the inevitable leakage from torrents of water pouring down into the hanging valley from ledges and sheer faces above gnawed away at the dirt and scree supporting the major rocks until the moment of failure arrived.

Again as Cooley had predicted, the collapse took less time than it would have taken to describe it. The loosened rock at the lower end of the hanging valley simply toppled over the edge, and the hundreds if not thousands of tons of water it had restrained followed, dropping, as Jay had calculated from the map, eight hundred to a thousand feet into the gorge below, there to add its crashing energy to that of the already swollen and down-cutting stream fed by a thousand mountainside rivulets—and the flash flood was begun, from the moment of inception already a thundering monster.

It gathered more force and speed as it rushed downstream, now broadening and slowing momentarily as its head entered a wide place in the stream bed or a *ciénaga*, now narrowing and picking up more speed, and strength, as it entered the next gorge; all the while, like a ragged army gathering popular support as it moved toward its goal, gathering further strength and force from tributaries and normally dry channels down which water poured from the torrents of rain above.

The flood tore rocks from their beds, ripped all support from beneath trees, and rising six or eight feet above its normal height, it demolished a wooden footbridge in its path as if the sturdy timbers had been matchsticks.

It reached the soldier sent upstream to report the first discoloration. First he heard the approaching sound, a deep-throated roar. Then in his light he saw the ragged wall of dirty water sweep into view and past, and for a moment or two, stunned, he was unable to speak.

He raised his walkie-talkie at last. The immediate message he managed, heard distinctly down at the dam, was merely, "Jesus Christ! Here it comes! Watch out!"

 . . .

The captain of Engineers was standing near Cooley and heard that first hysterical message. He looked immediately to Cooley for decision, all thoughts of defiance now fled.

"We blow it," Cooley said. "There's no choice. Set the goddamned thing off!" And to the communications man: "Tell that upstream man to simmer down and give us some information!"

But the radio was already crackling, and the voice came clearly now. "It's a wall of dirty water! It's tossing heavy timbers like twigs, so it has to have taken out that footbridge, and the bridge is six, eight feet above the normal water level! Or was! I never saw such a thing!"

Cooley raised the handset. "We've got our flash flood, boy," he said into it. "And I've got to guess it's a good one." He told of the footbridge.

At Jay's shoulder Colonel Watkins, listening, said, "I know

295

that footbridge. There's only the one, and it's *ten* feet above normal water level, not six or eight!"

"Okay," Jay said. And into the handset: "You're going to blow it?"

"There she goes!" Only Cooley's roaring voice could have carried the message over the sound of the first great explosion.

To those who witnessed the series of explosions in the confines of that dammed valley, it was storm, war, apocalypse, deafening the ears and threatening the soul with its fury.

Rock and rock dust filled the air. The ground shook. In the glare of the floodlights the surface of the lake rippled and stirred, set in motion by deep earth shudders. Falling rock fragments splashed in the water like bullets from a strafing run.

Echoes of the explosion reverberated among the mountain peaks, a rolling thunder of sound to which each fresh explosion from the staggered charges added its force.

Explosion by explosion the channel grew, beginning at the lake's edge, gouging great scars into the earth and rock, moving inexorably toward the location of the blocked tunnel, a creeping barrage in the peaceful night.

"All I wanted to do," one soldier said later, "was dig me a hole, crawl into it, and pull the entrance in after me! Jesus, you never heard or saw such a thing!"

Cooley was crouching, his hands over his head for partial protection. His eyes had not left the exposed dam face rising above the water of the lake.

It was holding! No crack, no faintest blemish appeared!

And as he watched, water began to fill the channel the explosions had blasted free. Only a little water at first, too little and that sluggishly impeded by loose rock that still remained.

But, obeying gravity and the gradient, the quantity of water grew, a trickle, a stream, a small river, and then all at once a flood which began to toss aside rocks in its path, driven and speeded by the weight of lake water behind and above.

The final explosion opened the tunnel, threw rock high into the air, echoed and reverberated against the solid mountain flank, and where the boys' careful dry-wall construction had hidden it, the tunnel entrance suddenly appeared as a black hole, quickly filled by down-rushing water from the channel.

A voice on a walkie-talkie said, "There she goes! The tunnel's open all the way through! That water blew the rocks at the bottom end out like corks! Like something shot from a gun! How about that?"

Still the dam held, intact, and the captain of Engineers, his young face grimy from the dust of the explosions, shouted to Cooley in triumph, "You were right! You were right! Damnit, sir, you were right!"

Cooley was looking the other way now, his head cocked in a listening attitude. In the ringing silence that followed the last explosion they could all hear it now, even above the painful shriek of the spinning power-plant turbines, a full, deep-throated roar of the flash flood led by its ragged wall of dirty water and debris, slamming out of the last gorge upstream and approaching the waters of the lake.

"That's the one that counts," Cooley said, "and from the sound of it—" He shook his head. Into the handset he said quietly, "We'll know the whole story in just a couple of minutes, boy. Stay tuned for our next thrilling episode."

Jay said immediately to the colonel, "Get on to Williams at the flood-control wall. Tell him what's happened and tell him to stand by. If we give him the word, he'll have no more than twenty minutes to blast that wall apart." He watched the colonel hustle to a telephone.

The governor said, wearing a faint, deprecatory smile, "And my instructions, young man?" His voice was easy, but it contained no hint of sarcasm.

Jay nodded shortly. "Your friend the mayor. He'd better know too. He's the one to push the panic button."

My friend the mayor? the governor thought as he walked

into the inner office. Well, perhaps now that is the word; I would like to think so, our difference of background and culture set aside for good. He seated himself and dialed the city offices. What I told the senator is perhaps more accurate than I would have guessed: I *am* learning many things during this—crisis. Into the phone as between old friends: "Joe? Harry. This is the situation . . ."

. . .

Time, Cooley thought as he waited, handset hanging at his side, could stand still or move in quantum jumps, two facts no one seemed to have put together before. From the first explosion to the last had been a blur, a video tape with sound turned high, advancing at the whining Fast Forward speed of a tape recorder. Now, awaiting the appearance of the roaring monster they could plainly hear upstream, nothing moved, and the world held its breath.

And then here it came, all at once, and again the video tape shifted into overdrive.

Wall of water was not the proper description. The flash flood was led by an upstanding *face* of dirty water and foam, a miniature vertical cliff, a battering ram, unyielding as rock, slamming out of the upstream darkness and into the water of the lake.

Instantly there arose a wave such as one would expect to see only on an ocean shore in a great storm. Later accounts of its height varied from ten feet to thirty, but all agreed that it seemed to pause as if gathering strength and fury before it began its terrifying rush the length of the lake toward the exposed upstream face of the dam.

Of all who watched, probably only Cooley and the captain of Engineers gave thought to the unspectacular but far more dangerous underwater shock of the hydraulic ram pressure transmitted almost instantaneously against the dam through the unyielding body of lake water.

The surface wave slammed against the dam with a crash, some said, like that of a gigantic automobile collision. Others described it as the sound of ocean waves pounding on shore, but louder, much louder. Still others maintained that they could see the wall of the dam flinch with the impact and then somehow regain its shape, wounded, but still intact. Water and spray flew high into the dawn air.

Those manning the floodlights on the exposed downstream side of the dam—the lights themselves perched on high, safe ground—were unsure whether they saw shock effect on the concrete structure or not, but as if by magic a crack appeared in the concave face, every eye went to it instantly and the soldier manning the radio, in civilian life a welder, in a voice that was not quite steady, gave a report which, like that of the radio reporter at the Hindenburg disaster, has been preserved on tape, along with the immediate questions from the downtown command post and the conversation between Cooley and Jay:

"Jesus Christ! Yes! It is! There's a crack in the dam wall! It's maybe ten feet long!" (A calmer observer who was on the scene estimated the crack's length at about half that.) "It's twenty, thirty feet from the top and it runs diagonal-like from upper right to lower left! Over!"

"Roger. Is the crack enlarging? Over."

"Negative. At least it don't seem to be. What I mean is, I can't tell from here and I'm damn sure not going out there with a tape measure! Even if I could! Over."

"Is there any sign of leakage? Over."

"Not that I can see. Wait! There's a little water coming through! There's got to be! You know how a sidewalk turns dark in a rain? That's how it is! Over."

"Stand by. Over and out."

Cooley raised the handset. Time was running at its normal

pace once again, he thought, both too fast and too slow. "I heard, and I guess that's it, boy. I'm on the lake side and I can't see anything. But concrete doesn't heal itself. If that fracture has gone all the way through, and it has to if there's leakage, then it's all over. We swung and we missed."

"Right." Jay's voice was expressionless. "All whistles and sirens, everything we have." He was obviously speaking to someone other than Cooley.

The Engineer captain, again at Cooley's side, his eyes fixed on the dam, said softly, "It can't! It can't!"

Cooley turned to look at the boy. His shoulders drooped with fatigue. Rock dust and dirt covered his face and filled his hair. And as Cooley watched, two tears appeared and rolled unnoticed through the grime, down the sides of the captain's nose. "Damnit, it can't!" he said again.

Cooley's smile was gentle with understanding. "Hold that thought," he said, "but be ready to give it up too. We gave it our best shot. It just wasn't enough."

.   .   .

In the command-post office downtown, Jay stood alone with the soldier in charge of communications. The speaker tuned to the dam communication center was temporarily silent.

On the handset Cooley's voice said, "Remember Beirut? Even during the worst of the shelling, and the bombing, some wouldn't leave."

"I remember," Jay said. "The soldiers in the *barrio* have orders to get everybody out when the sirens and bells go. Can you hear them now?"

"Yeah."

"The soldiers have orders too to shoot looters on sight. Can you think of anything else?"

The speaker came suddenly alive, a hollow voice, high-pitched with excitement. "That crack's growing, and water's beginning to spurt through! It's like—like a hundred fire hoses all at once! You never saw such a damned thing!"

Into the handset: "You heard that?" Jay said.

"I heard it. Like I told the kid commanding the Engineers, we gave it our best shot, boy. It just wasn't our day for miracles."

The governor was back, standing beside Jay. The colonel came to join them.

"Oh, Jesus!" the speaker voice said. "It's beginning to go! The whole goddamned thing! It's like in the movies, like stop-action on TV!"

"I can see it," Cooley's voice said. "He's right. There's an illusion of slow motion. There's—"

The speaker voice drowned out all else. "There she goes, a-roarin' and a-snortin' till hell won't have it, she's just busted loose and filled that whole goddamned gorge from side to side and top to bottom with water, a wall of water—you know what I mean?—forty, fifty foot high, bangin' downstream like a runaway freight train! I never saw such a goddamned thing, and I hope I never do again! God help them down below!"

Cooley's steady voice on the handset said, "Luck, boy."

Jay looked at the governor and the colonel. His face was expressionless. "Twenty minutes," he said.

26

To the east the sky was beginning to lighten, and here in the sloping meadow where earlier the warning jeep had stopped and the soldier had roused the man with the shotgun, some details of terrain were already distinguishable and growing clearer.

The man, whose name was Carley, had laid aside his shotgun after the jeep had driven away, and wondered what the sensible thing was to do. He had no intention of following the soldier's advice to take a sleeping bag up the hillside to spend what was left of the night on hard, rocky ground. On the other hand, if what the soldier boy had said was even close to the truth, neither did Carley have any stomach for crawling back into the sack here in the house.

In the end he stomped back to the bedroom, where his wife, her hair wrapped in rollers and magenta toilet paper, was sitting up in bed wondering what all the fuss was about. Carley told her.

"Well," the wife said, "what do you think we ought to do?"

"How the hell do I know? But I'm going to put on some clothes anyway."

The wife looked at her watch. "Might as well call it a night," she said. "You'd be stumbling around in an hour or two anyway, the way you always do, getting ready to go down to the stream and fish. I suppose you want some breakfast?"

The fine odors of coffee and frying bacon filled the house when Carley came out on the front porch just to have a look, expecting to see nothing he had not seen before. Faintly, distantly, he heard the sounds of sirens, and then whistles, and what that meant he—

"Joe! Joe!" His wife's voice from the kitchen. "On the radio! Listen!" She came trotting out bouncing and breathless, the transistor radio waving wildly in her hand. "Listen, I tell you!"

"Shut up and let me!"

"The Harper's Park dam is collapsing!" the announcer's voice said. "This is not a test! I repeat, this is not a test! The dam at Harper's Park is collapsing, and all people are urged to—"

Joe switched the radio off. "Let's go! Come on!"

"But where?"

"Up that goddamned hill as fast as we can, that's where!" He whistled once, a shrill blast from curled tongue and pursed lips, and the dog pounded through the open door. "Come on, woman," Carley shouted, "move those fat legs!" He grabbed his wife's hand and pulled her down the porch steps. The dog preceding them, they began to run toward the hillside.

There was a trail of sorts, and Carley took it, panting himself and towing his panting wife, while the dog ran easily ahead.

Scrambling, stumbling, they reached a high rocky outcropping and there the wife stopped. "I can't go on!"

"Goddamnit, woman!" But Carley's own breath was exhausted too. He stood, chest heaving, estimating height above the stream. "Okay," he said at last, "maybe this is high enough! We're almost even with the top of that gorge up there, and—Jesus Christ, will you look at that!"

The gorge visible upstream was suddenly filled with water, dirty, churning water, and debris, trees, pieces of metal, raw earth, and tumbling rock; and the sound of the flood was a roar blotting out all else until it seemed as if the ground beneath them vibrated and shook.

The wife covered her face with her hands. Carley stared in fascination as the flood reached the meadow, spread, tore trees from the ground and boulders from their resting places, flung a single mailbox high into the air, and gouged great chunks of dirt and rock from the hillside beneath them.

Carley saw his station wagon plucked from its level parking spot and tossed like a toy tumbling on the dirty yellowish crest. Then his house, like the others in the small group, was lifted bodily from its foundations. For a few moments it retained its form and structure and then it simply dissolved into a mass of unconnected boards and doors, a panel of windows for the moment miraculously intact, a bobbing refrigerator, and there the stove, all carried along and finally disappearing into the irresistible turbulence.

Carley scrambled a few more feet up the hillside, and from there he could see the gorge below the meadow as the flood reached it and, suddenly confined once more, rose unbelievably to fill the narrow opening even to its upper limits, and beyond, spreading on the high rock plateau before it began its steeper plunge beyond the gorge, trailing its roaring, bellowing voice like an echo of doom.

"Joe!" His wife's voice was a scream. She had opened her eyes and was looking around. in frightened bewilderment. "Joe! Where are you?"

Carley rubbed his forehead with the back of his hand in a gesture of weary helplessness. "I'm watching the end of the world," he said. "Judgment Day."

. . .

Bill Williams walked from his car to the face of the flood-control wall, where Sam Martin stood. "You've got ten minutes," Bill said. "No more. Get finished up and get the men away. In ten minutes we're going to blow it."

"Look, Bill—"

"I'm not going to argue. I'm telling you. Hear those sirens?" His voice changed suddenly. "Goddamnit, Sam, do you think I like it any better than you do?"

He was tired, Williams realized, bone-tired, and he wanted nothing so much as to turn back to his car, drive away, and find some place to rest. Maybe forever. Strangely, the concept now even had appeal.

But only after he had first done here what he had to do. His voice returned to normal. "So get your ass moving!"

The telephone in his car rang. Williams hurried to it and leaned in to answer. "Williams."

"It's gone," the colonel's voice said, overly calm against rising excitement. "The dam just went. Harper says—"

"In nine minutes," Williams said, "we're blowing. Tell him that."

. . .

The priest was pulling on his bell rope and praying, his lips moving visibly, when Brooks walked into the church. From the church tower the sound the *barrio* had heeded for almost a hundred years added its voice to the newer, louder sounds of sirens and horns throughout the city.

"Time to go, Padre," Brooks said. "They sent me from the mayor's office to get you to safety."

A young Anglo, the priest thought. He had seen him on the street, but never in the church. "This is my church," he said, "my post."

"It's going to be under water. Just like that church up at Harper's Park. If it isn't washed away first."

"I cannot leave."

"Right," Brooks said, mere acknowledgment of the situation. From Carlos García's attitude he had anticipated resistance and already decided how to deal with it. "Sorry, Padre." He picked the priest up on his shoulder in a fireman's carry without visible effort, and held him fast as he headed at a trot for the door, the street, and high ground.

As he ran, it occurred to him irreverently that the priest could continue to pray just as well upside down as he could while pulling on a bell rope. Maybe even better.

. . . .

A young National Guardsman named Trujillo had a problem which he had promised to deal with. The promise had been the only way to get that fat woman and her brood on their way to high ground and safety.

"It is that the old one, the *abuelo*," the fat woman had almost screamed in Spanish, "will not leave the house!"

"I'll get him out, lady." Trujillo spoke in English. He understood more Spanish than he spoke. "You go on with the kids. I'll take care of Grampa."

"He has a rifle!"

"Okay. You go on, huh?"

"You are sure that you can persuade him to leave?"

"Sure. I'll take care of it. Soon as you're on your way to where it's safe."

So now he slowly, warily mounted the front porch of the little house and pushed open the unlocked front door with his foot. Sure enough, there was an old man sitting in a worn chair, a 30-30 across his knees.

A lot of the older ones in the *barrio* had no English at all, Trujillo thought, so he spoke in his halting Spanish. "Time to leave, *abuelo*," he said. "The water is coming."

In Bataan some of the little yellow soldiers had spoken Spanish too, the *abuelo* remembered, and they had spoken it badly, like this one. He raised the rifle slightly. "I will remain here," he said, and cocked the rifle with his thumb. The click made a loud sound in the quiet house.

Trujillo abandoned Spanish. "Look, dad, all I want is to get you where the water can't drown you, you know what I mean? You don't need to wave that thing at me. You can't stay here. It's on the radio and TV, and the sirens and horns are all saying the same thing: that dam has broken!"

The *abuelo*'s face was unchanging. "They made me walk once. I will not walk again."

So, Trujillo thought, just what the hell do I do now?

• • •

Johnny Cisneros was listening to the shiny new transistor radio he carried as he came out of the store and carefully closed the door behind him. In his concentration, he did not hear the jeep coming around the corner in his direction.

"This is not a test!" an announcer's voice was saying on the radio. "I repeat, this is not a test! The Harper's Park dam has collapsed. Everyone is urged to go to high ground—"

"Hey, you!" It was the same Anglo soldier's voice that had challenged Johnny before. "Stop where you are, goddamnit!"

The shiny radio in one hand, with the other Johnny quickly tucked away the envelope containing the two thousand dollars, instinctive reaction.

"What's that you just hid? Come on, what is it?" The soldier was already out of the jeep and advancing on foot, his automatic weapon at the ready.

"It is estimated that flood water will be at least forty feet above normal river level when it reaches Old Town!" the announcer's voice said.

Forty feet, Jesus! "Look," Johnny said, "we'd better get the hell out of here. You heard the man. I'm going home. I told you where I live, and this is my store."

"Sure," the soldier said. He was close now. "Sure it is." He held out his hand. "I want to see what's in that envelope you hid. And I want to know where you got that radio. You didn't have it when we saw you before."

Too much, just too goddamn much. "Screw you," Johnny said, turned away, and began to walk quickly up the sidewalk toward the high ground of his apartment house.

●   ●   ●

Brooks had gone the relatively short distance from City Hall to the *barrio* church on foot rather than bother with his car. Still carrying the slight burden of the priest over his shoulder, he retraced his route now.

Father Rodriguez's protestations had stopped. He hung over the broad shoulder like a sack of meal, scorning futile struggle, bearing his indignity with what fortitude he could muster since it was plain that this Anglo would do as he thought best regardless.

It was possibly José-María's idea that he should be plucked from his church, the priest thought, because José-María was a practical man with, really, small understanding of matters spiritual, and a strong belief that matters secular were of far greater importance. The ancient conflict between Church and State continued.

Here away from the *barrio* the streets were quiet, empty in this pre-dawn, but the sirens and whistles continued their cacophony. The sudden rattle of automatic-weapon fire seemed overloud and entirely incongruous, difficult to believe, but Brooks reacted instantly.

He stopped and lowered the priest to the sidewalk. "Stay here, Padre. I'll have a look-see, okay?"

"I do not understand—" the priest began.

"Neither do I, Padre. That's why I'd better find out in a hurry. You'll stay put?"

Already the church seemed far away in both time and place. The priest nodded slowly and stood motionless as he watched the young Anglo approach the corner.

Brooks moved, the good father thought, like some great hunting beast, poised, wary, ready to react instantly to any stimulus. And he went forward without hesitation. Shots meant danger, and danger had to be investigated—as in wartime. Somehow the priest understood this and wondered in what conflict Brooks had learned it. Brooks reached the corner of the building and looked around it, exposing no more than one eye and a part of his face for a single swift glance. He drew back immediately, and then stepped forward into the open. Over his shoulder: "Padre," he said, "you'd better come. I think you may be needed."

Johnny Cisneros lay face down where he had stumbled and fallen. The transistor radio lay a few feet away, still turned on but no longer finely tuned, and the announcer's voice was muffled.

The jeep was at the curb, its engine running, and the driver was now standing beside the soldier who had fired the shots, staring incredulously at the money from the envelope Johnny had hastily tucked away. Both soldiers turned quickly as Brooks and the priest hurried toward them.

"A looter," the first soldier said defensively, and held out the money. "Look at this! And the radio!" He pointed.

The priest had knelt. His hand was touching Johnny's cheek. Blood stained the sidewalk. The priest's voice droned quietly in Latin, and Johnny's watching eyes indicated comprehension.

It seemed only a short time before the priest's voice stopped and he made the sign of the cross in the air. The sirens and the whistles sounded on, but their noise seemed to have receded and here it was quiet.

Johnny's mouth opened. Blood ran down his chin as his lips moved. His words were scarcely audible. "Thanks, Padre," Johnny said as his eyes closed for the last time.

Slowly the priest got to his feet. He looked at the soldiers.

"A looter," the first soldier said again. He was aghast at what he had done. He held out the money. "See?"

. . .

George Harrison was in his library, a balloon glass of the special Hine cognac at his elbow, a piñon fire burning in the corner fireplace for comfort and hopeful reassurance.

He had not turned on either radio or television, and although he could hear the sirens, whistles, and horns and understood their message, he ignored them.

His offer to Sam Martin at the flood-control wall had been a considered act, and he was prepared to keep his promise. What he did not know, of course, was Sam's decision, and everything depended upon that.

Bill Williams had driven up to the wall as George walked away, out of the glare of the floodlights into the pre-dawn gloom, picking his way through and around clumps of prickly pear and cholla, scattered piñones and juniper to his own walled property.

Somehow, George thought now, he had expected Bill Williams to appear there at the wall. In these few short days, Bill had become the Nemesis in George's life, and it was inevitable that at this climax he would turn up almost on cue. The gods would have arranged it.

On the practical, logical side, Bill Williams would appear at the flood-control wall at this time of crisis precisely because he was Bill Williams, never a man to shirk his responsibility. Give the devil his due.

George picked up the balloon glass, held it cupped for a little time in the palm of his hand for warmth, sniffed the bouquet appreciatively, and took a sip to lie deliciously on his tongue.

In some ways, he thought as he set the glass down again, and by some criteria, Bill Williams was an admirable man. He was all of a piece, consistent as few men were consistent, courageous to a fault, totally without pretense, a man who had literally lifted himself by his own bootstraps out of the Avenue A milieu to his present position of wealth and importance by sheer imagination, intelligence, and hard work. He was the embodiment of the American dream. And George disliked him with passion, and always had. He would have liked to feel contempt as well, but he had never quite been able to manage that.

George knew his own limitations. They were many. But intelligence he did have, and taste, and it was galling that these were all he had to set against Bill's array of virtues, but George had spent his life trying to make the best of it.

He knew perfectly well what Bill's reaction would be if he learned of George's offer to Sam Martin to see to it that the flood wall was not destroyed. But George doubted that Sam would tell him, and Sam *was* the explosives expert and so in the end it all came down to what Sam decided.

George reached for the balloon glass again, and his eyes caught the bold title of Sonnichsen's book, which he had not replaced in his shelves. He read it, savoring its meaning: *I'll Die Before I'll Run*. That was it in a nutshell. Whatever Sam Martin decided, and regardless of Bill Williams, he, George Harrison, was not going to desert his home.

. . .

The *barrio* was alive now, aroused and swarming in what a young National Guard lieutenant found himself thinking was a macabre dance to the sounds of the sirens, whistles, and horns. He had been in discotheques that impressed him similarly.

The lieutenant's name was Simpson, and he was blessed if he could see what in the world his men could do to help except turn around those few confused souls who headed toward the river instead of away from it.

An unidentified voice said suddenly in Simpson's walkie-talkie, "The City Engineer says Avenue C and beyond will be safe ground. Acknowledge!"

"Ten-four," Simpson said. "Avenue C for Charlie." He beckoned a nearby soldier and gave him the information. "Pass the word. The captain has a bullhorn. Tell him." He caught a fat lady by the arm. "Not that way, lady. The other way!"

"It is that the *abuelo*—!" Angelita Leyba began, and stopped when she saw the noncomprehension in the lieutenant's face. In English: "The grandfather! He is still in the house! One of your soldiers said he would bring him out, but he hasn't!"

"Which house, lady?" Simpson listened to the rapid directions. "Okay. I'll get him. You go on. These your kids? Take them. Avenue C or beyond. Got that?" He hurried in the direction Angelita had indicated.

The front door of the little house was open. Simpson took the porch steps two at a time and almost knocked Trujillo down inside. "What gives, Trujillo?"

"Have a look for yourself, Lieutenant. He's not going."

Simpson studied the old man in the chair, the poised rifle. He said, "Does he speak English?"

"Not to me."

"Then tell him in Spanish—"

"I already told him."

"Tell him again! Tell him we have maybe fifteen minutes. No more. Avenue C and beyond will be safe, but not here. Tell him he can't stay here!"

Trujillo sighed. "Okay, Lieutenant, then what?"

"What do you mean?"

"So I tell him and he doesn't believe me any more than he already has, what do I do then? Shoot him?"

The rifle in the old man's hands lifted almost imperceptibly until it pointed straight at Trujillo's middle. Neither soldier noticed.

Simpson hesitated. He had no solution to the dilemma, but one thing appeared clear. "Get yourself out anyway," he said. "If you can't talk him into coming, make damn sure you get to Avenue C and high ground yourself. There's no sense two of you drowning here!" He turned away and hurried down the steps and back up the street to the post he had been assigned.

Trujillo looked at the threatening rifle. It made his stomach muscles tighten. "Put it down, dad, huh?" he said. "I'm not going to try to jump you." He reached into his breast pocket for cigarettes, held out the pack, and shook a single cigarette loose. "Here. You smoke? *Fuma?*"

Slowly the rifle muzzle was lowered. The *abuelo* looked for a long time at the offered cigarette, and then took it in one gnarled hand.

"Now," Trujillo said as he got out his lighter, "maybe we're getting somewhere, huh? We'll just go at it slow and easy. The hell of it is, we're going to run out of time if we aren't careful."

27

Two thousand feet the flood had to drop before it reached The Bend. Cooley, marooned at the dam site until the road was open again, stood quietly watching the water level of the lake diminish as if by magic, and hearing the trailing roar of the torrent as it poured through the gorge below. He was reminded again of the concept of watching a video replay of a corner of hell.

The floodlights still covered the scene, brighter by far than the early dawn, casting black shadows into what had been water and was now an expanding area of shiny mud.

Replacing the cacophony of compressor engines, hammering drills, and turbines shrieking in torment, there was now the bellowing thunder of the water as it tore through the gap where the dam had been and only a few remnants of concrete and reinforcing steel were left.

As more of the lake bottom emerged, Cooley's attention was fixed, not on what was, but on what was not. The stone buildings he had seen on the bottom of the lake while Jay was diving had disappeared, wiped away as if they had never been. Harper's Park was no longer merely submerged, it had ceased to exist. Cooley wondered what effect that would have on Jay.

"I guess it was like this after the Flood," the captain of Engineers said.

Cooley nodded. "Something like."

"And what's happening downstream—" The captain shook his head.

"This," Cooley said, "is just the preview of the coming attraction. Down below they'll be seeing the main feature in living color in damned few minutes." We tried, he thought, and we failed. Cooley disliked failure.

· · ·

The governor said, "Twenty minutes. That was your estimate."

Jay smiled wearily. "Call it little better than a guess. Given the weight of water, the average gradient, the cross-sectional area of the channel, some kind of factors for bottom drag and sidewall friction, and the values of one or two other variables, we could probably construct a computer model that would tell us a lot of things." He shrugged.

"What you are saying," the governor said, "is that in a very short time we are going to see what actually happens, so there is no point in trying to predict, is that it?" This was a strange, most unusual young man, the governor thought, both subtle and forthright, a rare combination. "Are you going to spend your life as a, forgive me, mere technician?" he said.

Jay turned to look at the governor. He said nothing.

"I have no doubt," the governor said, "that as Bill Williams was told on good authority, you are among the best in your field. Maybe you stand alone. I would not be surprised. But you have other talents as well, and perhaps they are even more important. You have that nebulous quality called leadership. Very few have it, and it is beyond price."

"You flatter me, Governor," Jay said in a tone that lacked interest. He looked at his watch. "Williams said nine minutes. He has two minutes left."

· · ·

The last of the National Guard trucks loaded with soldiers, and towing compressors, generators, and floodlights, pulled away from the flood-control wall. The sun was not yet visible, but there was ample light to see by as Bill Williams drove his car close and got out. "Okay, Sam," he said. "Time's up. You beat it. I'll blow it."

He spoke quietly and with determined calm, trying not to think too hard of the house that he and Martha together had planned, built, and revised until it was exactly what they wanted, and loved. If any hand was going to destroy that house, it was going to be his.

"It's a makeshift job, Bill," Sam said. There was that evasive quality in his voice again. "We had to hurry too much. And we didn't have as much wire as I'd like. Maybe the detonator's too close. Any explosion is tricky unless you have enough time to plan it. You know that as well as I do!"

Of course he knew it: that unplanned explosions were tricky went without saying. But what did require explanation was Sam's attitude. "You're dragging your goddamned feet again, Sam," Bill said. "Why?"

"Bill, it isn't going to do any good to blow it!" There, it was out! The twenty-five thousand dollars George had offered was a lot of money, Sam was thinking, and he had almost convinced himself that the destruction of the flood-control wall was a silly business anyway.

In the first place, it was of questionable efficacy. Sam doubted if much of the flood that was coming would be diverted from the city even if the wall was destroyed. And in the second place, even if, as Jay Harper had predicted, the destruction of the wall *would* lessen appreciably the damage to the city, it was too high a price to pay in the loss of all those lovely homes in The Bend merely to benefit the squalor of the *barrio*.

Bill controlled himself with effort. "Okay, Sam, that's how you think, and you're overruled."

"Look, Bill, I'm an engineer—"

"I'll give you that."

"And Lord God Almighty Jay Harper—"

"Has been right every step of the way," Williams said. "Now, beat it, Sam." His voice rose suddenly, filled with its old confidence and force. "Goddamnit, can't you see that this is something I have to do myself?"

"Why?" For the first time Sam thought he was beginning to see into Bill's mind, his thoughts, his motivations, and finding them more complicated than he had imagined. "Some kind of penance?"

"I don't know. Maybe that is the word. I'm not sure of a lot of things any more. But I am sure of this. Get out of my way, Sam."

I could stop him, Sam thought. I am young enough and big enough and strong enough. And no one would ever know except the two of us. And twenty-five thousand dollars was waiting wherever and however he wanted it—it was strange how confident he was that George's offer had been sincere—so why was he holding back?

Bill Williams watched him quietly, almost as if he could see the struggle in Sam's mind—and knew already how it would come out.

I am holding back, Sam thought, because I am just kidding myself that I could do otherwise. I'd have to kill him to stop him. That had always been the fact that you faced in Bill Williams, the fact of total commitment once the chips were down. There was the same quality in Harper, Sam thought suddenly, and in Cooley Parks as well. They didn't advertise it, any of them, but it was there, you could feel it, and unless you had it too, you were licked before you started. Painful, even devastating thought. His resistance collapsed all at once.

"Okay, Bill." There was a sense of shame underlying the words. Sam turned and walked quickly away to the military jeep that had been left for him. He did not look back, and he drove as fast as the jeep would go. He was a half mile away when he saw in the mirror, then heard and felt the explosion at the flood-control wall.

. . .

Inside the thick adobe walls of his house, George Harrison heard it and felt it too. He finished his cognac, put the balloon glass down carefully, and went outside.

The last stars were gone, and the sun was almost rising in a notch in the eastern mountains. In the direction of Harper's Park there were still clouds and probably rain, but down here the sky was clear. It was going to be a fine day.

George hesitated. He was determined not to desert his house. On the other hand, he wanted to know, he *had* to know what the effect of the explosion had been, whether Sam Martin had rigged it for futility, or the wall had indeed been destroyed. By George's watch there still remained a few minutes of the twenty predicted from the first sound of the sirens and the horns. He began to walk quickly, skirting cactus, piñones, and juniper.

He reached water where there should not have been water. And then he saw the debris of the wall, and for a moment the rage he had felt before rose in his chest and made breathing difficult. Damn Sam Martin! Damn Jay Harper! Above all, damn Bill Williams, who was inextricably woven into the entire affair! If it had not been for Bill Williams—!

It was then that he saw Bill's car. It was lying on its side, windows shattered, side panels dented as from massive hammer blows. And partially beneath it, pinned in the dirt now turning to mud, and the rock and the rubble, something moved like a squashed bug feebly waving its extremities.

George advanced slowly, his shoes making squishing sounds in the broken ground. He bent forward. It was—good God, it was Bill Williams, scarcely recognizable from the explosion!

George swallowed his nausea, put his hands against the heavy car, and pushed. Nothing happened except that his feet sank deeper into the dampening ground. He tried again.

"Cut it out, George." It seemed impossible that Bill could

speak, but his eyes were open, and his voice was audible enough. "Leave it. You can't move it. Beat it, man! It's coming. Can't you hear it?"

George *could* hear it, a distant sound that shook the earth as, he had read, the great buffalo herds had once shaken the earth of the Plains. He could almost picture the great flood pouring down upon them, tearing, destroying.

Another analogy popped unbidden into his mind, this one heard from his grandfather. "That coughing roar of a grizzly when he starts comin' at you—you hear that once, and you don't forget it! And you're damned lucky if you live to remember it."

"Beat it!" Bill's voice said. "Head for that high ground! You may still have time!"

Time? Perhaps. But time no longer had meaning, now that his mind was made up. "I've run all my life," George said slowly. "I've run and I've hidden." Unconsciously he quoted Sonnichsen's title: "This time I'll die before I'll run."

"That's just plain stupid!" Bill's eyes closed. The roaring flood was closer now, louder, and the earth *was* trembling. Bill opened his eyes again. "No," he said, "maybe it isn't at that. Sometimes a man has to make his choice." He closed his eyes again, for good this time, he thought. Martha seemed very close.

. . . .

The governor, the colonel, and Jay had watched the explosion at the flood-control wall from the windows of Bill Williams's high office, but the distance was too great and the sounds of the sirens and horns too loud for them to hear the actual blast.

Rocks and dirt blew high into the air, spreading a huge cloud of dust that began to settle slowly. Even at this distance, the enormous force of the explosion was plain.

Jay looked again at his watch. "Maybe ten minutes now," he said, "if our guess is anywhere near right." He glanced at the colonel, his face expressionless. "Are you ready?"

"Yes, sir." At a time like this, the colonel thought, maybe it was craven of him to make plain that he considered himself to be taking orders, but it did seem the prudent thing to do.

The governor looked from one man to the other. "And what does that mean?"

"If it's necessary," Jay said, "we have one more shot to fire."

There was something behind the words, and the office became still. "Am I to be told what it is?" the governor said.

Jay nodded slowly. "We've mined the railroad bridge."

The governor walked to the desk and dropped wearily into the big chair. "East-west rail traffic," he said, "serving not just this state but the whole Southwest. Have you any idea what cutting that will do in terms of the economy of this entire section of the country?"

"I'm not an economist, Governor, but I imagine it will cause quite a little stir."

"That," the governor said, "is a splendid understatement. Sacrificing the houses of The Bend is one thing. This is something else again."

The colonel watched and listened in discreet silence.

"Why was I not told?" The governor spoke only to Jay.

"I was sure you could be expected to react like this, and maybe issue countermanding orders."

"Then why do you bother to tell me now?"

"Because," Jay said, "without your approval the colonel here just might change his mind at the last moment."

The governor shook his head in a kind of wonder. Sheer audacity, he thought; there was no other word. "You take a lot upon yourself, young man."

"You gave me a lot."

"Maybe you took too much."

"Maybe." Jay leaned against the edge of the conference

table. "I tried this one on Bill Williams for size," he said. "I told him we might look into dropping one of those big bridges into the river, not that it would stop a flood, but it might help disperse it and slow it."

"And?"

"His reaction was the same as yours. He'd already accepted the fact that we'd have to blow that flood-control wall, which meant destroying his house. But when I mentioned blowing a bridge, he just whistled and called me a high-roller."

"He was right. It is my fault. I gave you too much authority."

"I told him," Jay said as if the governor had not spoken, "that we were playing for lives, and they're the highest stakes I know. How do you measure lives against the economy, Governor?"

The silence this time grew and stretched, and time seemed to stand still. It was the colonel, at the window, his back to the room, not wanting to witness this confrontation, who broke it at last. "Good God!" The words just popped out. "Will you look at that!"

Jay and the governor arrived at the window at the same time and all three men stared in silence, awed.

The flood had broken free from its final upstream confinement. Now, in the early-morning light, its dirty yellowish-white crest lifted high, it swept down upon The Bend, tossing aside as if they were pebbles great rocks and boulders in its path, gouging a fresh and wider channel, raging at the earth.

At this distance in seeming slow motion the cliff face of the torrent reached The Bend. A single dark object, Bill Williams's car, was picked up and thrown high, bounced for a few brief moments as a ball is bounced on a breaking ocean wave, and was then overwhelmed, disappearing.

Two far smaller objects were not even visible from the distant windows as they too were picked up, tossed, and then engulfed in the raging waters.

There at The Bend, where the flood-control wall had been, the torrent forked. One part swept toward and engulfed the houses the wall had protected.

The other part followed the river channel, rising high within its confines, too high, tearing at the earth and partially straightening the curve as, seemingly undiminished despite the division, it bore down upon the city and the spanning bridges.

Jay said with soft urgency, "Blow it, Colonel! Now!" He glanced at the governor, and waited.

The governor closed his eyes. He opened them again. Slowly he nodded.

The colonel hurried to the outer office and the radio.

．　．　．

They had worked all night, and the job was done at last. The lieutenant in charge of the detail which had mined the railroad bridge sat wearily on a bench high above the river smoking a cigarette. The detonator was on the ground beside him, and the men of the detail were scattered nearby.

Behind the bench the sergeant said, "You think they'll actually blow it, Lieutenant? Jesus, you know what those bridges cost!"

The lieutenant blew out smoke. "I wouldn't bet a nickel either way."

"You're an engineer, Lieutenant. If they do blow it, do you think it'll do any good?"

"I agree with the thinking, if that's what you mean. It's worth a try. Anything is worth a try if—" The lieutenant cocked his head suddenly, eyes squinted against the smoke of the cigarette in his mouth. "Good God! Hear that?"

It was, the way the lieutenant told it later, like the hollow, rushing sound of a subway train slamming into the confined space of a station, but amplified as in an echo chamber. It was the sound of heavy trucks pounding at speed over a bridge. It was thunder and the rumble of a deep underground explosion, a seismic shot out of control, an undercalculated underground atomic blast. It was all of these, and more, and it was growing louder as the as yet unseen torrent approached.

"You're wanted on the horn, Lieutenant!" The signalman's voice raised above the growing thunder.

The lieutenant jumped from the bench, and seized the mike. "Lieutenant Fisk!"

"Colonel Watkins!"

"Yes, sir!"

"Blow it, Lieutenant! Right now! Acknowledge!"

"Yes, sir! We're blowing it!" He waved one hand at the sergeant, who raised the plunger of the detonator and bore down hard upon it. "There she goes!" the lieutenant said. "Good, God, there she goes!"

The great railroad bridge shuddered, its truss superstructure shimmering as it vibrated in the sun's first light. The explosion was a roll of gigantic timpani as the sounds of the nearest charges reached them first and the farther sounds followed.

The bridge, intact, began slowly to lean, as planned, in an upstream direction. As it fell farther from the vertical its speed increased, its riveted steel structure still holding intact. Faster and faster, whatever sounds it made now drowned out by the thunder of the approaching torrent.

It fell at last into the river with a mighty splash, filling the channel from bank to bank, a barrier against the flood which now appeared, sweeping and tearing around a curve in the river channel.

"Hey, Lieutenant!" The sergeant had to shout against the clamor. "We done good, huh?" And then, when he saw the flood itself: "Jesus! Nothing can stop that! Nothing! Are we high enough here?"

Spray filled the air, and it was impossible to see. The bellowing roar of the monster flood drowned out all other sound. As the lieutenant told it later: "Like Baker [the sergeant] said, nothing could have stopped that flood, nothing! And—I'll god-damn well admit it—for a couple of moments I thought the end of the world had come! I think I shouted something, but I'm not sure, and I couldn't hear my own voice anyway! Man, you just can't know what it was like!"

The irresistible force of the water meeting the immovable object of the steel bridge jammed by its own weight between the banks of the river channel—the sturdy truss was twisted and bent by the impact, supporting members failed, the steel rails were contorted as if by a gigantic hydraulic press, and the entire structure was crumpled and compressed into an unrecognizable twisted mass.

But what remained of the bridge held, and the water in all of its raging power was forced to find ways through and over and around the obstruction while the torrent still poured down from the mountain gorge, adding its crushing pressure to the flood's drive for freedom.

Like an army regrouping its forces after surmounting a physical obstacle, the rampaging waters gathered themselves once more into a coherent force below the smashed bridge and bore down inexorably upon the *barrio*. Much of the flood's force, but not all, had been lost.

A mere shoulder of the flood caught the Thompson house, ripped it from its foundations, tore it to bits, and scattered the pieces and the house's contents along the route of its passage.

Bellowing like some wounded monster, the water demolished the church, scattered its pews, tore down its steeple, flung the pitiful collection of crutches and braces from the Santuario into mud-covered piles of debris to be found and wondered at later.

It smashed Angelita Leyba's house into kindling and lumps of adobe, and for a time bore a television set from Honest Johnny's store like an oversize eye on its yellowish crest before it too disappeared into the turbulence.

It caught the unwary, the unheeding, the careless, and

drowned them mercilessly. For days, even weeks, bodies of men, women, children, dogs, cats, pet birds, and omnipresent rats and mice would be found completely or partially buried in mud, rubble, and debris.

From the high ground beyond Avenue C, most, but not all, of the *barrio* residents watched the destruction, some crying aloud, some weeping quietly, some kneeling in prayer, some stunned and silent in their grief. It was as if Dios himself had decreed absolute devastation.

Automobiles and mobile homes, snatched up as units and smashed beyond repair or belief, were carried along on the flood until the waters reached the broad plains below the city where they could spread, dissipate their force and fury, drop the burdens they carried, and sink at last into the thirsty ground, leaving the area strewn like a wrecker's yard with sheet-metal carcasses.

How long the process of destruction lasted, no one watching would ever know for sure. To some it was quick as a tornado, to others the time was endless. Gradually the bellowing roar diminished. The water level dropped, exposing the devastation it had caused. At the twisted bridge the sound fell in volume until it became no more than a gurgle, the comparative quiet almost deafening.

Baker, the sergeant, said in a hushed voice, "Jesus, Lieutenant, did you ever see such a thing?"

The lieutenant shook his head in silence.

"Without we dropped that bridge," Baker said, "it would have been the hell of a lot worse, don't you think?"

"It sure as hell would. They ought to give the guy that thought of it a medal."

. . .

Now began the cleanup, the assessment of loss and damage, the fresh cries of anguish and of weeping grief. This day would be long remembered. And discussed.

• • •

On the telephone the governor said, "Keep me posted, please, Joe. I have a call in for Washington to see what help they can give us. Can you give me some assessment now?"

"It's bad," the mayor said. "God, it is bad! We did our best, and it wasn't enough! We got most of the *barrio* people out. *Most*, I said! How many we didn't get out, I don't know yet. Maybe one hundred. Maybe five times that."

The governor closed his eyes. What he felt, he thought, was almost physical pain, which would not have been so only a few days before. Strange.

"Upstream," the mayor said, "there is nothing left, nothing! I don't mean just The Bend. That's gone, and maybe it's good riddance, I don't know. But all those little houses up the valley, and the summer places, places with cows and chickens, the fish hatchery—all gone. Nothing left. Dead cows in treetops, that kind of thing." He was silent.

"I think," the governor said slowly, "that we need an overall look. I will arrange a Guard helicopter. Will you come with me?"

"Yeah," the mayor said. "Maybe between us we can figure out where things were—before. And how we go about starting over. We can't give up."

"No," the governor said. His smile was weary, but there was the beginning of warmth stirring in his mind. "That is the one sure thing: we can't give up."

28

When he looked back upon that day, Jay found mostly isolated and unconnected incidents and episodes in memory.

In the *barrio* there was the fat woman screaming in Spanish that her house was gone, and the *abuelo* with it, even though the soldiers had promised that the *abuelo* would be safe.

And, miraculously, a warm thing to remember, here came a soldier and an old man, both of them wet through, and muddy, but intact. And the old man did not relinquish his hold on an also wet and muddy 30-30 rifle even when the fat woman overwhelmed him, babbling and slobbering in her tears. . . .

There were minutes of frantic digging with his bare hands through rubble of a shattered house toward vague human sounds, thinking all the while of what Cooley had said about people refusing to flee from their homes even during the worst of the shelling and bombing in Beirut—how right Cooley was!

And presently there was someone working beside him, helping to lift timbers too heavy for one man, a tall, lean type, wearing glasses and cursing softly in a cultured eastern seaboard accent, when they reached the trapped man at last and made him lie still where he was.

There was unmistakable authority in the voice of the man in glasses when he shouted, "Medic! Here! On the double!" And there was gentle wry humor when he looked at Jay and said, "One down. How many more to go?" Somehow, even in that brief encounter, a man to remember. . . .

There was Cooley, solid and tireless as ever, saying, "Hi, boy. We didn't do so good, did we?" Nothing less than perfection would ever satisfy Cooley.

Well, he, Jay, felt the same way, although the disappointment was almost submerged. Almost. "How did you get down?" he asked. "The road has to be gone."

"It is. They sent a chopper. I hitched a ride." Cooley would always be where the action was. . . .

There was the priest, a little old fellow in a black beret, tirelessly comforting, advising, seeing to those who were hurt or bereft, bearing sadness for what was, and exuding hope for what would be.

Once Jay saw the priest and the tall, lean man in glasses passing one another. Their smiles seemed to have a special significance, and Jay wondered why, because he would have put the tall man down as pure Wasp. . . .

There were others, too many others to remember, working together, all differences put aside, forgotten. And he among them.

Strange. . . .

And then, without warning, and he could not later even remember from whom, he had the irrefutable word of Bill Williams's death, and all at once that brought into sharp focus what had been dispersed and confused.

Driven by a compulsion against which there was no defense, he left the *barrio*, and made his way past the Old Plaza to the hospital.

"Kate is very busy," a tall Anglo girl told him in an accent very similar to that of the tall man in glasses. "But if it is important—"

"It is. It concerns her father."

Kate knew, he thought, the moment she saw him. She seemed to falter, then gather herself and come on toward him.

Jay took her arm and urged her out into the sunshine, where they walked slowly, aimlessly in silence for a time. It was Kate who broke the silence. "How?" she said. There was only numbness in her mind.

"He blew the flood-control wall. I have that from Sam Martin. Then he didn't get away in time. We don't know why. I'm sorry."

"Why didn't Sam—blow it?"

"I think that he, your father—"

"Yes." Kate nodded gravely. "If the—house was going to go, he would do it. His home." At last tears were very close. "Thank you for coming to tell me."

There were strange thoughts in his mind. He had been unaware that they had been forming, but now that they had surfaced, he found them somehow inevitable, and even lacking the pain he would have expected. "I wanted to tell you something else too."

Kate watched him in silence.

"I—failed. I don't fail often, but I failed this time." Then the apology that had to be made. "I'm sorry, again."

"No. You didn't fail." Somehow this—reassurance to the living was at the moment more important than tears and grief for the dead. "You—succeeded." Kate could not have explained, but it was so. "Just as you will always succeed." It was strange that suddenly she was thinking of the stone buildings on the bottom of the lake. They were gone now, she had heard, all gone. "You came here—searching." And sure knowledge from some unknown source: "For home," she said.

"Maybe that was it. I never wanted a home," Jay said. "Before."

They had stopped, and now they merely stood facing one another in the sunlight. "And now," Kate said, "you are staying?"

"No," Jay said. "I—made a commitment."

"And you keep your commitments." As Daddy always had, Kate thought, and again found tears very close. Had Mother always—competed with commitments too? Or had she learned to live with them?

"I keep my commitments, yes. I'll keep this one." Jay hesitated, because what he was about to say was in fact another commitment, not to be made lightly. But it was a good commitment, and right, and it took no effort to make. "But I'll be back," he said.